PRAISE FOR A. L. SOWARDS

"There are some authors who consistently write novels of excellence. A. L. Sowards is one of them."

—Bev, DeseretBook.com review of *Codes of Courage*

"A. L. Sowards is such a phenomenal writer. Her books are full of history and offer the reader an in-depth knowledge of unsung heroes who deserve to have their stories told. She doesn't shy away from the realities of war but is able to write them with such class and respect for all readers. Her books always leave me wanting to do better, be better, and to really appreciate the things that matter most in life."

—Tasha, Goodreads review of *A Waltz with Traitors*

"It's always special when an author can take a part of history and transport their readers there. Sowards does this with all the detail and research that she puts into her stories."

—Jerrica, Goodreads review of *Codes of Courage*

PRAISE FOR *CODES OF COURAGE*

"*Codes of Courage* is a beautiful and poignant love story that brings to life the heartaches and the triumphs of those who helped break enemy codes during WWII."

—Marilee, DeseretBook.com review

"Wonderfully written, well researched, and masterfully executed! A. L. Sowards once again delivers an emotional journey of unexpected twists and turns alongside a beautiful love story."

—Tiffany, Goodreads review

"A. L. Sowards brilliantly weaves a compelling story of love, loss, death, war, and ultimately hope. WWII history comes alive in this fast-paced story that will have you reading late into the night. I loved learning more about the U-boats, codebreaking, and sea warfare."

—Melissa, Goodreads review

ROADS *of* RESISTANCE

OTHER BOOKS AND AUDIOBOOKS

BY A. L. SOWARDS

DUCHY OF ATHENS SERIES

Of Sword and Shadow

Of Daggers and Deception

FALCON POINT SERIES

Heirs of Falcon Point

Codes of Courage

Roads of Resistance

THE LEY BROTHERS SERIES

The Rules in Rome

Defiance

ESPIONAGE SERIES

Espionage

Sworn Enemy

Deadly Alliance

THE BALKAN LEGENDS

After the Crescent Strike (novella)

Beneath a Crecent Shadow

Beyond the Crescent Sky

Against a Crescent Storm
(coming November 2025)

STAND-ALONES

A Waltz with Traitors

Before the Fortress Falls

The Redgrave Murders

The Spider and the Sparrow

SHORT STORIES

The Perfect Gift

The line between enemy and ally can shift in a heartbeat.

ROADS *of* RESISTANCE

An Heirs of Falcon Point Historical Novel

A. L. SOWARDS

for Jessica, Andrew, Anna, Leah, Miranda, and Lucas

When my family moved to Alaska, we knew about as many people as Ingrid did when she tumbled into Arnhem. How blessed we were to move near a family as wonderful as yours. Thank you for your friendship.

Cover image: *Vintage Woman Pushing Bicycle* © Ildiko Neer / Trevillion Images; *Historical Airplanes* by Sundry Photography © Adobe Stock; *Parachute* by Mst. Shapla Begum © Vecteezy.com

Published by Covenant Communications, Inc.
American Fork, Utah

Library of Congress Cataloging-in-Publication Data

Name: A. L. Sowards
Title: Roads of Resistance / A. L. Sowards
Description: American Fork, UT : Covenant Communications, Inc. [2025]
Identifiers: Library of Congress Control Number 2024945042 | 978-1-52442-786-3
LC record available at https://lccn.loc.gov/2024945042

Printed in the United States of America
First Printing: July 2025

31 30 29 28 27 26 25 10 9 8 7 6 5 4 3 2 1

THE NETHERLANDS
THE NORTH SEA
WESTERBORK
HAARLEM
AMSTERDAM
IJSSEL
THE HAGUE
UTRECHT
OOSTERBEEK
ARNHEM
ROTTERDAM
LEK
NEDERRIJN
WAAL
WAAL
NIJMEGEN
MAAS
GRAVE
VEGHEL
RIJN
WILHELMINA CANAL
SON
EINDHOVEN
MAAS
SCHELDE
GERMANY
BELGIUM
ARNHEM AREA ENLARGMENT
VELP
ARNHEM
NEDERRIJN
IJSSEL
DRIEL
RIJN
50 MI

USEFUL TERMS

Abwehr: German intelligence service.

Dolle Dinsdag: Mad Tuesday. September 5, 1944, when the Dutch believed they were about to be liberated by the Allies. The Dutch celebrated while many Nazis and collaborators fled to Germany.

Engelandvaarders: Dutch refugees who escaped the Netherlands during WWII and reached England by sea or by land. Of the 1,700 who were successful, the majority joined the armed forces in the fight against the Nazis.

Fräulein: German courtesy title for an unmarried adult woman, similar to "Miss" in English.

Gelderland: One of the twelve provinces making up the Netherlands.

Green Police: German occupation police in the Netherlands and other Nazi-controlled countries. Officially the Order Police or Ordnungspolizei (Orpo for short), they were quickly nicknamed the Green Police after the color of their uniforms.

Guilder: The primary currency of the Netherlands at the time of this novel.

Hauptmann: Officer in the German Army, SS, or SD, similar to a captain in the U.S. Army.

Leutnant: Officer in the German Army, SS, or SD, similar to a second lieutenant in the U.S. Army.

Luitenant: Officer in the Dutch Army, similar to a lieutenant in the U.S. Army.

Mam: Dutch word for mom.

Mejuffrouw: Dutch courtesy title for an unmarried adult woman, similar to "Miss" in English.

Mevrouw: Dutch courtesy title for a married adult woman, similar to "Mrs." in English.

Moffen: Derogatory Dutch nickname for the Germans.

Moffrica: Derogatory Dutch nickname for Germany.

Mynheer: Dutch courtesy title for an adult male, similar to "Mr." in English.

NSB: Nationaal-Socialistische Beweging or National Socialist Movement. A Dutch political party aligned with the Nazis.

Oberleutnant: German Army officer, similar in rank to a first lieutenant in the U.S. Army.

Obersturmbannführer: An officer in the SS with a rank similar to a lieutenant colonel in the U.S. Army.

Onderduiker: Someone in hiding. The literal translation from Dutch is "under diver."

Onkel: German word for uncle.

Oom: Dutch word for uncle.

Opa: Dutch word for grandfather.

Pap: Dutch word for dad.

Razzia: A roundup. In this novel, it refers to roundups by the Nazis or their collaborators to find enemies, undesirables (such as Jews), or able-bodied people to be conscripted for involuntary labor.

Reichskommissar: A government title used by Nazi Germany, most often for the senior leader of an occupied nation. During the Nazi occupation of the Netherlands, the reichskommissar was Arthur Seyss-Inquart.

Reichsmark: The primary currency of Germany at the time of this novel.

Sicherheitsdienst (SD): German Security Service, an intelligence agency for the SS and Nazi party.

Soldat: An enlisted man of the lowest rank in the German Army.

Sturmbannführer: An officer in the SS, with a rank similar to a major in the U.S. Army.

Tante: Dutch word for aunt.

Unteroffizier: Junior noncommissioned officer in the German Army, similar to a corporal.

Utrechtseweg: One of Arnhem's major roads.

Westerbork: A camp in the Netherlands. Originally, the Dutch government established it as a refugee camp for Jews fleeing Germany. After the Nazi invasion, Westerbork gradually shifted to a transit camp where Jews stayed for varying amounts of time before being deported to Auschwitz-Birkenau, Sobibor, Theresienstadt, Bergen-Belsen, Ravensbrück, and Buchenwald. In addition to Jews, Dutch resisters and other people the Nazis deemed enemies were sent to Westerbork. Deportations to death camps ended in September 1944. Westerbork was liberated by Canadian troops in April 1945.

CHAPTER 1

February 1940

Ingrid Lang gasped for breath as she ran through the Vienna train station while the man who had murdered her father the day before chased her. A departing train moved along the tracks to her left, slowly gaining speed. She struggled to keep up with her brother, Karl. He had taken her knapsack from her, so he carried more weight, but he was two years older and had longer legs.

She glanced behind. Herr Sauermann, their father's one-time friend, wore the uniform of an SS sturmbannführer. He had longer legs than her, too, but she didn't think he could catch her and Karl before they reached the train. They were nearly there.

"Stop!" the man shouted.

Ingrid didn't obey. Nor did Karl. He grabbed her wrist and propelled her toward the caboose. She grabbed for the rail, caught it, and pulled as if her life depended on it, because she was fairly certain it did. The train moved faster now, but Karl held pace with it as he handed her both knapsacks, his and hers. Sauermann, with a drawn pistol, still ran after them, but he couldn't catch them now, not unless the train stopped, and he remained too distant for a clear shot.

Karl reached for the rail, but his fingers grazed the smooth metal, not gripping it. He stumbled, and the train pulled ever so slightly away from him.

"Come on, Karl!" Panic swirled in Ingrid's stomach and pounded through her limbs. He had to make it onto the train with her.

The red of his cheeks and his audible breaths revealed his strain as he forced his legs forward.

Please, she prayed. *Please let him make it.* Karl had always been faster and stronger than her, but the train was gaining more and more momentum.

A rail official ran toward her brother. Unlike Sauermann, this man wasn't trying to catch up from behind. He ran a perpendicular path, and he would reach her brother in seconds. She screamed.

Karl glanced to the side, saw the man, and added a frantic speed to his sprint.

Ingrid gripped the railing with one hand and reached for her brother with the other. "Karl!" She wasn't sure she could pull him to the caboose, but she had to try.

He aimed for the metal instead of her hand. He brushed the rail again, then the end of her fingers, then he stumbled as neither rail nor hand offered enough purchase to break his fall. The next moment, the railway official grabbed him, halting his progress. There would be no third chance for Karl to catch up to Ingrid and the train.

"No!" Her desperate cry merged with the whistle of another train somewhere in the station.

The last few days had been a succession of nightmares. First, Papa had been murdered because he wouldn't work for the Reich, then Ingrid and her siblings had fled their home while being chased by Nazis. She and Karl had been separated from their younger sister and their former nanny, and now this. Sauermann was quickly catching up to her brother and the railroad official. The official had pulled Karl from the tracks and now shoved him toward the platform. She wasn't going to leave her brother to face Herr Sauermann alone. She'd managed to help him before, when Sauermann had pursued them to the Linz train station. She'd think of something again here in Vienna, even if surrender, at the moment, seemed like her only option. She bent to grab the bags. The train moved quickly enough now that jumping would hurt, but what other choice did she have?

"No, Ingrid! Stay there." Karl's voice carried over the sounds of the station. "Find Anna, and I'll find you both!"

Obey her brother and escape Vienna so she could find her little sister? Or stay and help her brother face the man who had murdered their father? Tears blurred her vision, and she put a hand over her mouth to hold back a sob. Would Sauermann murder Karl the same way he'd murdered Papa?

She glanced at the rails, now blurry beneath her. She most certainly didn't want to jump, but it didn't look as if Karl would be able to escape Sauermann's grip at all, let alone find her and Anna. Getting off the train now, in full sight of Sauermann and the rail official, would be a mistake. But if she waited until the train disappeared from view, she could jump off and approach the station unseen.

She slipped her knapsack into Karl's. His was larger, and hers contained very little since most of its contents had been food from the family estate at Falcon Point, and they had already eaten all of it. One bag would be easier to deal with. She felt the added weight as she slipped it on her back, but it was only temporary.

The station, more distant, had already grown small. She saw neither Karl nor Sauermann, so they wouldn't be able to see her either. Another glance at the track just beyond the caboose made her head swim. The train was moving so fast. She focused on the track farther back, and the ties no longer seemed quite so blurry.

She inhaled deeply and prayed she wouldn't break a limb when she jumped. A noise behind her made her turn, and a gray-haired man in a conductor's uniform stood in the caboose's metal doorway.

"Whatever are you doing back here, young lady? Someone reported screams."

Should she deny the screams or use that to her advantage? "It was absolutely dreadful. Did you see?"

"See what?"

Ingrid pointed to a vague spot in the distance. "An automobile crashed into a horse cart. The poor horse." Normally, Ingrid wished she were older, but just then, she lingered on her final sentence, hoping she sounded younger than her fifteen years. The younger the conductor thought she was, the more lenient he would be when he discovered she had no ticket. She and Karl, nearly out of money, had planned to hide. She wasn't even sure where the train was going.

The man peered into the distance. She wished he would go back inside. She couldn't very well jump from the train while he watched, and the walk back to the station was getting longer with each passing second. He wrinkled his face in thought and turned to give her a careful study. She wore simple pearl earrings, a high-quality coat, with sturdy lace-up boots, wool stockings, and a fashionable dress, but the skirt visible beneath her coat was obviously wrinkled. She'd worn it yesterday, then slept in it. She hadn't had a chance to look in a mirror that morning, so she hadn't any idea what her blonde hair looked like. Was her face as red from exertion as her brother's had been?

Suspicion grew on the man's face. "Where's your ticket?"

Ingrid put her left hand into her left pocket, then her right hand into the right one. She unbuttoned her coat and pretended to search an inner pocket. For a moment, she considered searching through the knapsacks. Perhaps the man would grow bored and leave, and then she could jump. But time was not on her side. If she wanted to help Karl, she needed to finish with the conductor quickly. "I must have left it with my parents."

"And where are they?"

Ingrid swallowed. Mama lay in the graveyard of the church nestled in the valley below Falcon Point manor. And Papa . . . what had happened to his body after Sauermann had shot him? It had happened only yesterday. Perhaps he lay in a coffin now, probably unburied because whoever was in charge of the body would expect Papa's children to return for the funeral. The same pain that had almost suffocated her when Karl had told her what had happened returned. She couldn't manage words, but she pointed past the man to the rest of the train.

He huffed. "Well, we had best find them, hadn't we?"

Ingrid glanced behind her. The Westbahnhof Station had disappeared. Was Karl still alive? Or had Herr Sauermann taken her seventeen-year-old brother to an out-of-the-way part of the station and silenced him permanently?

"Come on." The conductor pulled open the door and motioned her to step ahead of him.

Ingrid looked from the man to the tracks behind her. Her sister, Anna, traveled with their former nanny, heading to Budapest, then Istanbul. She might be in Turkey by now, too far away for Ingrid to reach. But Karl . . . She rushed to the edge of the caboose's platform. Unless the conductor jumped down after her, she could still help Karl.

With one hand on the rail, she raised a foot. The ground below whirled past. She hesitated for only a moment, but that was all it took for the conductor to grab her by her knapsack and yank her away from the edge.

"What are you playing at?" His voice, never warm, now held alarm. "Do you want to end up dead?" He pushed her toward the door and kept her moving. "We'll want a word with your parents if you haven't a ticket, but it's not worth throwing yourself off the train over."

Ingrid didn't fight. The conductor was twice as big as she, and if he thought her parents were on the train, she had time to develop a story. He marched her through the baggage car and into a passenger car.

"Do you see your parents?"

"Not yet." How she wished Mama would appear. Always so elegant, with perfectly manicured nails, a classic taste in jewelry, vibrant blue eyes, and an unfailing faith. Mama always knew what to do. If Mama couldn't appear, she longed for Papa. Her wise papa always had plans and alternate plans and contingencies should those fail. What would Mama or Papa do now? Ingrid hadn't a clue.

They went through five passenger cars, and the conductor seemed to grow more and more irritated with each compartment or bench they passed. She caught sight of a lavatory and motioned toward it. "Sir, I need to stop here."

He groaned and nodded.

Inside, Ingrid glanced at her reflection. Her hair was untidy but not disastrous. She pulled a brush from her bag and fixed the loose strands, then dug through Karl's knapsack for anything useful. A knitted cap and wool mittens, a magazine, the keys to Papa's black Mercedes-Benz 230, a few coins, and two passports: Karl's real one and Papa's forged one. Not much else. She had the jewelry box Papa had given her that contained Mama's sapphire-and-diamond earrings. Plus a brush, a comb, several hairpins, a nail kit, an extra sweater, gloves, and a few crumbs from the sandwiches they had brought with them when they had left the family home. She counted the Reichsmark in her pocket. It might be enough to pay for a taxi back to the train station, but she doubted she'd have enough left after that to buy a train ticket. She felt the lining of her coat. Papa had asked one of the maids to sew jewelry inside. She would pull it out later. For now, it was safer where it was.

Someone banged on the door, then the conductor's voice called, "Come along, young lady. We need to find your parents."

She had hoped that if she took long enough, he would leave. It seemed less and less likely that she could jump from the train and find her way back to Karl. She would have to trust him to somehow make it to Istanbul with Frau Davies and Anna or make it to London on his own.

Ingrid inhaled, trying to plan her next steps. Depending on this train's destination, she could try to catch up to her sister or make her way to London and meet her siblings there. Karl had reminded her of the proper tube station to use, based on their trip to England four years before when they'd visited Frau Davies's sister. Neither of them remembered the sister's flat number, but she had worshipped at St. Michael's Church. That would be enough information to lead her to the right place. Anna would be there because she had Frau Davies to help her. And Karl . . . Ingrid squeezed her fists. If she weren't so worried about what might even then be happening to Karl, she would have imagined how glorious it would be to beat him to London.

The conductor knocked again, and this time, she didn't dare ignore him. She opened the door slowly to find two conductors waiting for her.

"Is something wrong?" The new conductor, a tall man with a salt-and-pepper mustache, spoke to his colleague rather than to Ingrid. "I hope you aren't harassing the passengers."

The first conductor bristled. "She can't find her parents, claims they have her ticket."

The mustached one smiled at her. "Don't worry, fräulein, we'll help you find them."

The other huffed. "I'm beginning to doubt she has a ticket or parents on this train."

Eyebrows that matched the mustache in color lifted slightly. "She's hardly dressed as a vagabond. I'll take it from here."

The first conductor rolled his eyes in exasperation but didn't protest. He went forward to another passenger car.

"Thank you for coming to my aid." Ingrid pasted a hesitant smile on her face. "He was . . . Well, he made me nervous."

"Franz?" The conductor winked. "Don't worry about him. He may be a grump, but he's harmless. I'll make sure you find your parents and make it safely to Berlin."

Berlin? The train was going to *Berlin*?

Dread made her throat tight, but the second conductor didn't seem to expect a response. He was more friendly, less suspicious, and easy to slip away from. When another passenger asked him a question, Ingrid turned around and walked from the third-class carriage while the conductor and passenger attempted to converse in a mix of German and Italian.

Ingrid had always been good at hide-and-seek, and she quickly found a suitable spot to conceal herself in the luggage car. It was unheated, so she pulled out her brother's knitted cap and tugged it on. What was Karl doing now? And what of Anna? They all should have been home still, enjoying new snow, warm hearths, and hearty food their cook had prepared. Only two days ago, they had all eaten dinner together: Papa, Karl, Anna, and Ingrid. She frowned at the memory because Herr Sauermann had been there too. He'd been trying to convince Papa to work for the Reich, but Papa had kept changing the subject, always turning it away from politics. Papa had asked about Sauermann's new brother-in-law, about his nephew, about a mutual acquaintance from their time in the Austro-Hungarian Army. The conversation had lacked warmth, perhaps, but it had been polite.

The next day, Sauermann had come back, and the two men had ensconced themselves in Papa's study. Ingrid had heard the raised voices, and Karl had heard the gunshot. Her brother had been with Papa as he'd died, had asked for and received confirmation that Sauermann had pulled the trigger. Ingrid shivered. An old family friend had become a murderer. He'd taken away her father, and his pursuit of the children had left them scattered. She expected to find Anna and Karl again, eventually, but she'd never had a chance to say goodbye to Papa.

The train stopped in Prague, but Berlin was closer to London, and she was confident she could remain hidden, so she stayed on the train, even though two conductors who knew her face might be looking for her. Most of the passengers seemed to be continuing to Berlin, because porters shifted only a small portion of the luggage.

When the train started again, she examined her coat. The stitches between the wool and the lining were different where the maid had resewn the seam. She took out her nail kit and used the small scissors to cut a few threads, then pulled out a triple strand of perfectly round pearls. They were longer than was currently fashionable, but she'd seen pictures of her mother wearing this necklace before. It wasn't something she would wish to part with, but she needed money if she was to make it to England. She would rather sell the pearl necklace than the earrings Mama had worn on her wedding day—sapphires with pear-shaped diamonds suspended below, surrounded by a halo of smaller stones. She would starve before selling those. She felt around the coat's lining until she found a brooch made of small gemstones: numerous emeralds formed a Christmas wreath, with diamonds and rubies for ribbon and berries. She didn't remember her mother wearing it, but she remembered her mother fastening it to Ingrid's coat for Midnight Mass the Christmas before Mama died.

Papa had been wise to have jewelry sewn into their clothing because his plans for a smooth escape from the Reich had fallen apart. Still, she wished he could have found items that didn't have so much sentimental value. She took out Karl's mittens and put the pearls in one and the brooch in the other so they wouldn't be scratched. Far more than she wished to keep the jewelry and the memories attached, she wanted to see Anna and Karl again, and she didn't think the earrings she currently wore, pearl studs, would be of sufficient worth to get her to London.

When the train slowed on its approach to Berlin, Ingrid moved from her hiding spot so as not to be found by the porters. She didn't wish to be seen by the conductors either. The cranky one might haul her to the nearest policeman, and the kinder one might haul her to the train offices to locate parents who wouldn't be found. She left her hat on, hoping it would hide her blonde hair, and stood with a group of passengers to disembark with them.

Berlin. City of her enemy. She may have escaped the Nazi officer chasing her and her family, but now she was in the Nazi capital, and she had another escape to plan.

CHAPTER 2

Rupert Altbauer hugged his mother goodbye in the front room of his stepfather's two-bedroom apartment, holding her until he'd hidden any emotion other than eagerness from his face. He didn't want her to suspect how nerves had turned his stomach to a churning mess. He was eighteen now, no longer a boy, and he'd lived away from home before—boarding school had been a welcome escape from his father—but Germany was at war, and that made joining his army unit far different from taking the train to school.

When he released her, she brushed her hand across his spotless tunic. "I still can't believe you're old enough to be in uniform."

Rupert smiled. Onkel Wilhelm Sauermann had written a long letter explaining Rupert's duty to join the fight, but Mama had resisted until Rupert's new stepfather had convinced her that for a man of eighteen, joining the war in some way or another was inevitable. He'd said *man*, not *boy*, and he treated Rupert with the same respect he gave other adults. He was the complete opposite of Rupert's father, and Rupert couldn't be more pleased. Nor, it seemed, could his mother. She smiled as her new husband put a hand on her elbow.

"You remembered to pack everything?" His mother finished dusting Rupert's uniform. "Warm socks? Extra underthings? Your address book?"

"Yes, Mama."

His stepfather chuckled. "He managed to pack for school every year, Hannelore. And I remember you saying you hadn't needed to ship anything to him during his most recent term. He's a man now. He'll do things right, or he'll learn. And the army has an efficient mail system if we do need to send something."

Mama ran a hand across Rupert's cheek. "Yes, I suppose you've been managing for a long while now. I forgot one thing." She turned back to the apartment's bedroom.

While she was gone, Rupert's stepfather shook his hand, pressing several bills into his palm. He winked. "Just in case you do need another pair of socks. Or a good meal."

"Thank you, sir. You'll take good care of my mother?"

"I will."

Rupert believed him. He remembered all the times his parents had shouted at each other, all the times his father had hit him and his mother. And he recalled the social stigma that had followed his mother as a divorcée. The only memory he couldn't call up was a time when his mother had been anywhere near as happy as she seemed now.

Mama returned and placed a pendant in Rupert's hand. "My father carried that to war. My grandma said it would bring him luck, and it must have, because he came home."

Rupert studied the metal image of St. George. Perhaps it would come in handy if he needed to slay any dragons. "Thank you, Mama."

"Are you sure we shouldn't take you to the station?" she asked.

"No. It's only a few blocks, and my bag is light." And if Rupert said goodbye here, in the apartment, he would have several minutes to compose himself before reaching the train station. He wouldn't want to become misty-eyed at the station and give his comrades reason to think him sentimental.

Mama gave him another hug. A tear spilled onto her skin. Rupert was most certainly too old for tears, so he kissed her cheek, pushed down any emotion, and escaped out the front door.

"I'll write to you tomorrow." He shifted his rucksack to his shoulder and waved goodbye.

He blinked rapidly as he walked down the hall and turned at the top of the stairwell. He would not cry. He'd left his mother plenty of times before, and this time, he was leaving her in good hands rather than in petty, abusive ones. As for Rupert, he was joining the greatest army the world had ever seen.

He left the apartment building and turned left, toward the train station. A block later, a young woman caught his eye. High-quality coat, blonde hair peeking from beneath a knitted cap, blue eyes scanning the names of businesses.

What was Ingrid Lang doing in Berlin? He hadn't seen her since that summer almost two years before, when he'd gone with Onkel Wilhelm to stay at Falcon Point for the last time. For five days, he and Karl had swum in the lake, hiked in the mountains, and challenged each other at chess. Then, with two days left of their stay, the Langs had thrown a formal supper party. Rupert had danced with Ingrid several times and afterward remarked how pretty she'd looked. Karl had avoided him the rest of the stay. What was more, Karl had kept Ingrid away too. Only later had a friend with several younger sisters explained Rupert's error. Older brothers did not want their friends thinking of their sisters as anything other than solidly unromantic young girls.

Ingrid had grown taller since their last meeting, and even without the evening gown, she was pretty. He glanced around, half-expecting Karl to appear and pound him for even thinking Ingrid was attractive.

Rupert checked his wristwatch. He'd left his stepfather's apartment with plenty of time to catch his train, so he wasn't in a rush. He could spare a few minutes to catch up with an old acquaintance.

Ingrid had wanted a jewelry store that reminded her of the ones Papa had shopped in. How else could she be sure of receiving a fair price for the jewelry she'd pulled from her coat lining? The candleholders, watches, rings, and silver tea service in the window of this store had drawn her inside, and she currently studied the earrings, necklaces, and other pieces beneath the glass in the store's interior. She doubted this store was the finest Berlin had to offer, but several beautiful pieces sparkled from their velvet backgrounds. The items, new and used, looked to be of good quality.

"Can I help you?" a man asked from behind the counter.

"Yes, I have an item I would like to sell." She pulled the pearl necklace from its glove and placed it on the counter.

The man lifted the triple strands. "A bit dated, but I suppose the pearls themselves can be restrung into something more fashionable." He turned his eyes on Ingrid. "Where did you get these?"

"They belonged to my mother."

He put a loupe to his eye and examined each pearl, then the gold fishhook clasp with the initials *L. L.* on it. "And your mother doesn't mind you selling them?"

"No. She hasn't worn them for years." Ingrid bit her lip. She hadn't lied, but nor had she told the entire truth.

"Perhaps not, but these are heirloom quality." He looked up from the necklace and studied her clothing. Perhaps she should have taken the hat off so she would look more impressive, but it was undoubtedly too late now. Removing it would leave her hair untidy, and the cap had already spoiled her first impression.

The man weighed the pearls in his hand, then handed them back to her. "Bring your mother or father with you, and I'll give you a good price."

Disappointment hit her like a deluge. She could sneak onboard another train, but hunger plagued her, and she didn't want to attempt stealing a meal. Moral implications aside, she wasn't sure she *could* steal something beyond train passage without getting caught. The bell on the door clanged, and a cool breeze wafted through the shop.

"I can't bring them in," she said. "We've been separated, but my father intended for me to sell these if needed to reach my destination."

The man glanced behind her. "I'll be with you in a moment." He turned his attention to Ingrid again and motioned to the necklace. "I've been in the business long enough to see plenty of thieves trying to pass off stolen jewelry as family heirlooms. I need to know I won't be facing an irate society lady trying to recover stolen jewelry."

"But I didn't steal these. They were my mother's!"

"I can't pay what they're worth without verification of ownership. If you're really that desperate, I can offer a portion of their value. Split the risk, if you will."

Ingrid fumed. Just because she was young, the shopkeeper seemed to think he could swindle her.

"What a blatantly transparent con," a voice behind her said. "Giving her half price just because her father isn't here?"

Ingrid turned to see a German soldier. She hadn't recognized the voice—it had changed over the last few years—but she knew the face. And with that recognition came fear: behind her stood Rupert Altbauer, nephew of the man who had killed Papa.

Rupert continued. "I can verify that Fräulein Lang's family purchases only the highest quality of jewelry. That necklace certainly wasn't stolen."

Ingrid focused on breathing despite the tightness in her chest. Rupert was not his uncle. He was trying to help her. Or maybe it was all a show, and he was trying to trap her.

The shop owner glanced between the two of them. "Ah, I see. I have also been in business long enough to see my share of young ladies trying to sell jewelry to fund an elopement. Is that what's going on? Rich young woman falling in love with an enlisted man and running off to get married without her family's permission?"

Rupert laughed. "Ingrid's only, what, sixteen?"

Ingrid nodded, even though Rupert had added a year. Fifteen or sixteen, it didn't matter. If Rupert was working with his uncle, she was once again in grave danger.

"She's not old enough to get married." Rupert placed a hand on the counter. "Nor am I, but I am old enough to recognize dishonesty when I see it. I expect you to give the young lady a good price."

"If you think you can come into my shop and accuse me of cheating someone . . ." The shopkeeper glared. "I'll report you to your commanding officer."

Rupert huffed. "Come on, Ingrid. Let's find a more reasonable man to do business with." He took her arm and guided her from the store.

She clutched her mother's necklace in one hand as she inhaled the cool air outside, anger and fear still warring in her chest—but fear of Rupert far outweighed her anger at the shopkeeper.

"Can you believe that man?" Rupert looked back at the shop with a frown. "Unless he's grossly incompetent, he knows the pearls are genuine, and for him to accuse us of conspiring so we can run away and elope." Rupert laughed again. "Goodness, we haven't even seen each other for nearly two years."

Ingrid walked away from the store, and Rupert followed her. "Yes, he was most disagreeable."

"I can imagine. But why are you selling your pearls?"

She didn't want to tell Rupert anything. She'd enjoyed his company those summers when he'd visited Falcon Point with Herr Sauermann, but so much had happened since his last stay. Back then, Papa and Rupert's uncle had still been friends, and though Mama had been ill, she'd still managed the duties of a hostess with grace and warmth. Ingrid answered with as little of the truth as she could. "We were separated while traveling. I know where to go; I just don't have cash for the train fare."

He glanced at her pearls. "So you're selling your mother's jewelry?"

She nodded.

"I'm headed to the train station. I'll walk you there. If I didn't have to report to my unit, I'd escort you back to your father, but as it is, I suppose this will have to do." He reached into his pocket, pulled out a billfold, and handed her several Reichsmark.

"Are you offering to buy my necklace?" The bills weren't enough to cover the full value, but she suspected it was enough to get her to London if she were careful, and she certainly didn't intend to revisit the jewelry store they'd just departed.

"No, I'm just helping you get back to your family." He shook his head as if surprised that she'd thought anything else. "Being a lowly enlisted man, I won't complain if your father wishes to pay me back, but you're a friend, and you seem to be in need. My stepfather was generous in helping me, so I would be most pleased to help you."

Emotion made her throat feel tight. She certainly hadn't expected to receive help from Herr Sauermann's nephew. "Thank you, Rupert. It's very kind. If I weren't so desperate, I'd refuse, but I would like to get back to my family." Or back to what remained of her family. Rupert had spoken of Papa as if he were still alive. Did that mean he hadn't yet learned of the murder? "Have you heard from your uncle lately?"

"Uncle Wilhelm? My mother remarried about a month ago, and I saw him then. He writes, of course. I heard from him last week."

Ingrid felt some of the fear dissipate. If Rupert hadn't heard from his uncle since the week before, he wouldn't know about Papa's death two days ago or how hard Sauermann had tried to get Papa to work for the Reich. "I'm pleased to hear about your mother. Do you like her new husband?"

Rupert smiled. He looked younger when he smiled, more like the boy who had come to visit Falcon Point several summers in a row. "I do. He's a vast improvement over my father. Drinks only for special occasions, doesn't lose his temper over a glass of spilled milk or a table imperfectly dusted. I've never seen my mother so happy."

"I'm glad." Ingrid hadn't actually met Rupert's mother, but she'd heard bits and pieces about the situation from Papa, Mama, and Herr Sauermann over the years. Herr Altbauer sounded like a vile man. And Herr Sauermann had proved to be pure evil. Rupert, on the other hand . . . If she weren't so worried that he would eventually lead his uncle right to her, she would be unspeakably grateful to him. "I gather she has earned some happiness."

Rupert nodded. "More than anyone I know."

"And you're in the army now?"

He straightened his shoulders. "Just finished my training. I had a bit of leave, and now I'm off to join the Sixth Army, guarding the Fatherland should the British or French try to attack."

"I wish you safety and success." Or maybe that wasn't entirely true. She had pleasant memories of Rupert, and she was grateful for his generosity in funding her flight from Germany, yet Papa had died because he'd hated the Nazis and wouldn't join them. That meant she could never truly wish a German soldier success.

The train station came into view. Rupert looked at his watch and swallowed. "I'm afraid I have to rush if I'm to catch my train."

Ingrid increased her stride so she could keep up. "Thank you for your help. I don't know what I would have done if you hadn't shown up."

"Glad I could assist. Say hello to your family for me." He smiled at her again. "I don't have time to pull out my address book, but I'll have my uncle send your address to me. I'd love to hear about your travels after you've returned to Falcon Point."

Ingrid forced a smile. She wouldn't be returning to Falcon Point while Herr Sauermann remained a threat. Rupert would write to his uncle, his uncle would spin a set of lies about how Papa had died, and then Rupert would know she'd been dishonest with him.

For a moment, she'd had a friend. It was a pity it wouldn't last.

Several routes could lead to London, but Ingrid didn't want to be in Berlin any longer than she had to, so she selected the first departure heading in the right direction. Rupert's assistance had been an unexpected and much appreciated surprise, but any further surprises were likely to be of the negative variety.

Berlin to Essen, Arnhem, Utrecht, then Amsterdam. From there, she hoped to find a ship that could take her to England. Soon, she would leave the Reich behind. The hope of freedom sent her soaring for a moment, until she remembered that she was also leaving her brother behind. If Sauermann had silenced Papa because he'd refused to join the Nazis, what might he do to someone who could prove the man guilty of murder? Had Karl escaped? Was he languishing in a Nazi prison? Or was he dead?

Worry for Anna wasn't as sharp as worry for Karl. Anna had Frau Davies to help. They'd likely arrive in London after Ingrid, but if Frau Davies's sister wasn't in her flat or couldn't help Ingrid, the pearl necklace would keep her from starving for some time, assuming she could find a buyer. Regardless, the first task she had to manage was getting out of Germany and into the Netherlands.

It had taken most of the day to travel from Vienna to Berlin, and the journey to Amsterdam would take most of the night, so Ingrid purchased a ticket for the sleeper car. Twilight enveloped the train soon after it left the station, and Ingrid quickly drifted to sleep in an upper berth. She woke near the border long enough to pass through customs, then returned to her bed, rearranged her things so she could more comfortably sleep, and pulled the curtain shut.

She yawned as the train began moving again. Soon she would be out of Germany, and she would feel much safer. The door opened and shut, but she didn't hear the voices of the family who had been sharing the car with her and had been behind her in the customs line. Instead, a deep, quiet voice said something she couldn't quite catch.

Another male voice answered, and the words were German. "One can't invade the Netherlands without taking the bridges."

"Yes, but if I'm caught . . ."

"Don't let anyone catch you."

A huff. "Anything else?"

The two voices discussed canals, bridges, roads, and train routes. Ingrid had been worried when the German customs officer had seized Reichsmark, liquor, and chocolate from the man in line in front of her. The officer had scrutinized her passport with a dour expression and searched her bag before sending her on. Thankfully, he hadn't felt her coat, where she'd widened the hole in the seam and placed all her valuables and unneeded documents, then pinned it together with her mother's broach. As unpleasant as customs had been, overhearing spies planning an invasion felt far worse.

The Netherlands was neutral. Hitler had taken over Austria and Czechoslovakia, but he'd justified both with the need for Germanic unity. When it had come time to attack Poland, there had been a somewhat questionable incident at a radio station on the border to blame, and in any case, Poland hadn't been neutral. How would Hitler rationalize an attack on a neutral country?

A week ago, Ingrid might have pulled the blankets over her head and prayed that the spies didn't find her. She'd heard little remarks from her father often enough to know he hadn't approved of the Nazis, and she'd trusted his convictions. But that trust had never given her sufficient motivation to act on those beliefs, nor had she had opportunity. Yet now her father, and maybe her brother, too, had given her a reason to want revenge. Uncovering a German spy before he gathered information in the Netherlands wouldn't bring Papa back or grant a quicker reunion with Karl, but it was *something*, and she wasn't sure she could do anything else.

The voices grew softer, and Ingrid scooted to the head of her berth, closer to the edge of the curtain that currently hid her. She knew what it was like to have one's country taken over by the Nazis, and she didn't wish that on the Dutch. Not that she knew anyone from the Netherlands other than Vermeer, Rembrandt, and van Gogh, and she hadn't actually met any of them, just their paintings.

Gently, she slipped a finger around the curtain and pulled it open a few centimeters. Both berths across from Ingrid's were now empty. Two men stood in the car's center, less than a meter from her. One wore a black homburg; the other wore a tan fedora. The man in the homburg had a bulbous nose and thick stubble across his cheeks. The other had his back to her. Ingrid focused on the man she could see, trying to remember details just like a detective from a novel would. She wasn't sure who she would report the man to, but she intended to have a thorough description, despite the car's dim lighting.

The men finished their conversation and glanced around the car. Ingrid drew her finger back and trusted the shadows to hide her, even if she could see out. The men moved into the corridor, and Ingrid felt a weight lift. She hadn't set out to tangle with German spies, but she was a Lang. Like Papa, she would do what she could to thwart the evil that had taken over Austria and threatened all its neighbors.

She prayed, then climbed from her berth. She pulled on her coat and deposited everything else into her knapsack, lamenting the lack of pajamas, which meant she'd had to sleep in her clothes two nights in a row. When she disembarked in Amsterdam, she would find a clothing shop and purchase something new. She couldn't very well show up in London with no spare underthings and a skirt and blouse both in need of a press.

First, she would go to the lavatory and wash as best she could, then she would find one of the conductors. If he were Dutch, she could report the spies to him. If he were German, she would wait. Or perhaps she would try to find the spies again so she could note where they disembarked and add a description of the man in the fedora.

She pulled on her knapsack and opened the door of the compartment. The windows in the corridor showed nothing but blackness, with an occasional spot of light in the distance. Still night. She yawned, tempted to return to her warm berth and forget about the spies until morning.

A creak sounded behind her, then a hand slapped across her mouth, pulling her against something hard. Ingrid struggled to break free. She pulled at the arm covering her mouth, kicked backward, and tried to wiggle away, but the person holding her was too strong.

"Easy," a voice whispered. One of the voices she'd heard in the sleeper car. "I thought the compartment was empty after those Jews were arrested at the border. Then I saw your finger disappearing around the curtain. Didn't your parents ever teach you not to eavesdrop?"

She would have liked to ask the man why his parents hadn't taught him not to manhandle young ladies, but his hand held her jaw shut. She hadn't seen anyone arrested at the border, but that explained why the family hadn't returned to their berths.

"Come on." He dragged her through the corridor and into the vestibule between cars. The man with the homburg waited there, so that meant the man with the fedora had her.

The man in the homburg glanced at her. "Younger than I thought."

She felt as much as heard the other man grunt. "Old enough to tell someone."

"Assuming she understands German."

"Too much is at stake to risk it. She's seen us together. That's dangerous enough."

The man in the homburg nodded. "This car is clear." He slipped through the vestibule into another corridor. He stopped near a door—the type of door that was supposed to remain closed until the train arrived at a station.

As the man in the homburg pried the door open, wind whipped into the train. Ingrid bucked and kicked as the other man pushed her toward the opening. The one with the homburg pulled a knife from his coat pocket, but he hesitated.

"Come on," the one holding her said. "Someone might come through any moment."

The other spy nodded. "I'm trying to pick out a river or a canal so discovery of the body will be delayed."

The body? They were speaking of her as if she were already dead. Did they intend to stab her, then dump her into the first canal the train passed? At this time of night, they'd have plenty of time to clean away any blood she left on the train. They were going to get away with murder, just like Sauermann.

Ingrid tried kicking the man holding her again. He only clutched her more firmly and squeezed her mouth hard enough to leave bruises. The one with the knife glanced at them, then returned to his vigil for a river or canal visible in the dark. She leaned against the man holding her, brought both legs up, and kicked as hard as she could at the man in the homburg.

She connected, he cursed, and he dropped his knife. The grip of the man in the fedora loosened just enough for her to break away, but both men blocked the way to safety.

Ingrid glanced at the dark landscape beyond the train as the icy wind pulled at her hair and coat. She could think of only two choices: wait for the men to push her from the train with a knife in her body, or jump.

She jumped.

CHAPTER 3

Gerrit Hendriks did his best to chase Tante Anita, but his aunt had the better bicycle, and no matter how hard he pedaled, he couldn't quite keep up. Most of the Netherlands was flat, perfect for cycling, but that was less true around Arnhem, where his opa lived. The hills weren't exactly the Alps, but they still made pedaling more difficult.

Anita glanced over her shoulder at him and grinned. A few wisps of her black hair fluttered in front of her bronzed face, and her dark eyes sparkled. Beside her, Anjing, Opa's Keeshond, ran to keep up. "Come on, slowpoke!"

Gerrit gritted his teeth and pedaled harder. His friends all had aunts who baked sweets and patted their cheeks and made up endearing nicknames for them. His aunt woke him up at the crack of dawn to go racing past the dormant tulip fields. At sixteen, Anita was only two years older than he, so perhaps it was fitting that she acted more like a cousin. Gerrit had older aunts, too, but none of them was even a quarter as much fun as Anita. She was the best part about visits to Opa.

Anita finally slowed on the top of a rise and allowed Gerrit to catch up. Below them stretched the Nederrijn, shimmering with sunlight as the sun peeked over the horizon. "I told you it was worth waking up for."

Gerrit grinned at the sight. "Agreed." Rotterdam probably had beautiful sunrises, too, but by himself, he wouldn't have been motivated enough to cycle away from the city for a view like this. They watched the sun for a while. Even Anjing stilled long enough to enjoy the view, or perhaps he simply welcomed the break from running.

"I wish you didn't have to go back today." Anita ran her knuckles across Gerrit's hair, likely sending his sand-colored strands into a state of disorder. "It will be so boring to ride my bicycle without a slowpoke nephew trying to keep up with me. Pap is always busy, and the girls at school . . ." Anita shook her head. "We'll have to plan something extraordinary over the summer when you come to visit again."

"Don't you have mates in school?"

Anita shrugged. "Not everyone is as accepting of Indonesians as Pap."

"Come to Rotterdam, then. It's never quiet at our apartment." His brother was ten, his sister was eight, and their two-bedroom apartment wasn't large enough to offer solitude.

"No, I don't suppose it is with Nellie and Johan about." Anita glanced across the fields again. "You don't know how lucky you are to have siblings."

"You have a sister and five brothers." Half-siblings, but surely that still counted.

"And most of them left home before I started school. They still treat me like a child. When Cas and Maude visited for Christmas, they gave me doll clothes. I haven't touched a doll in years, other than when I brought a pair down from the attic to keep their little girls happy."

"They treat me like a child too." Except when it came to doling out chores—Mam, Pap, Opa, and all his other relatives spread across the Netherlands, from Gelderland to South Holland, seemed to think him capable of a man's load when it came to housework or yard work. That was another reason Anita was his favorite—she woke him up to ride bicycles instead of to milk cows or refill coal scuttles.

"That's because you *are* a child." Gerrit ducked as Anita reached for his hair again. Maybe he didn't mind too much when she mussed it, even if most normal, boring aunts would smooth it instead of messing it up.

She giggled and reached again, and this time, he pushed off and cycled away from her, ahead in the race for the first time all morning, even if he'd only managed it by leaving while she was distracted.

"I'll still beat you home, Gerrit." Her voice carried laughter.

He didn't doubt that, but for the moment, he would enjoy being ahead. Not even Anjing had caught up to him yet.

Snow no longer covered the fields they rode past, and short bits of green broke up the otherwise brown stretches. A spot that didn't seem to fit caught his eye. Gray wasn't unusual, but that shape . . .

Gerrit slowed. Anita zipped past him, with Anjing running near her back wheel.

"Wait," he said.

"So you can pass me? That's not likely," she called back.

"No . . . I think that's a person." Why a person would be lying in the field by the train tracks was a mystery to him, but the closer he came, the more sure he was.

Anita stopped. "Where?"

He pointed. Anita left her bike on the road and ventured across the muddy field on foot. Anjing stayed with the bicycles, but Gerrit followed. Long blonde hair fluttered in the breeze, but nothing else moved. Was it a body? If so, he didn't want Anita to face that alone, so he ran to catch up to her.

They arrived at the same time. An adolescent girl lay on the ground, muddy and bruised. A torn knapsack lay a meter away. Gerrit looked from the girl to the train track and could pick out her likely path by following the broken brush.

"Do you suppose she's still alive?" Anita asked.

Gerrit couldn't tell. No obvious discoloration or decomposition, but it could have been a recent death, and the dirt and mud would cover that, at least partially. He bent to feel for a pulse the way he'd seen Opa do. The moment he took the girl's wrist, she pulled it away.

Gerrit let out a small cry of surprise. "Still alive."

The girl opened her eyes—a vibrant blue—and looked at them with panic.

"Do you need help?" Gerrit asked.

The girl turned toward him but didn't answer. She tried to sit but wouldn't accept his hand when he offered. She moved her legs as if to stand, then inhaled sharply and whimpered in pain. Ultimately, she stayed supine on the ground.

"Maybe you should lie still." Gerrit studied her legs, but between stockings, skirt, and mud, he couldn't see where she was injured. "Did you fall off the train?"

She didn't answer.

Anita crouched. "We'd like to help you."

The girl turned her gaze to Anita, but she didn't speak.

"Maybe she's foreign," he said to his aunt. If the girl couldn't understand them, that would explain why she didn't answer. "Do you speak Dutch?"

Anita repeated his question as if the girl might answer her instead of him. Then she tried it in Javanese.

Gerrit gave his aunt a frown. "She's not likely to speak Indonesian."

"It didn't hurt to try." Anita used French next. "*Parles-tu français*?"

The girl nodded. "*Oui.*"

"*Tu viens de la France*?"

"*Non. L'Autriche.*"

Anita sat back. "She says she's Austrian. You're learning German in school, aren't you?"

Gerrit felt his face heat. "A little." Not well enough to converse with a native speaker without feeling ridiculous.

"Well, go on, talk to her."

In his best German, which wasn't very good, he asked if she had fallen off a train. She bit her lip and didn't answer, but it looked as though she understood. He asked if she was hurt, and she nodded again and told him she thought her leg was broken.

When he translated for Anita, she glanced back toward the road leading to Opa's home. "Well, we know someone who can help with that. I'll go get Pap and his automobile, and you can stay to make sure she's all right."

"Me?" Gerrit didn't know the girl, and she'd already shown she didn't trust him enough to even say why she lay in the mud off to the side of the train tracks.

"Yes. You can talk to her in her own language. I can't."

"Barely. I'm not as good at schoolwork as you are."

"I can ride faster. She'll get help sooner that way."

Gerrit would rather Anita stay, but he could follow her reasoning, so he nodded. The girl wasn't threatening in any way. He just preferred to avoid the awkwardness that came from speaking a language he barely knew with a person who seemed reluctant to talk to him.

The girl's mouth opened with worry as Anita rushed back to the bicycles and the dog.

"She will fetch doctor," Gerrit said in broken German. "My grandfather."

She nodded.

"Which leg is broken?"

"Both, I think."

Both legs broken? He looked the girl over a little more carefully. The last time Gerrit had visited Opa, Oom Aart had been visiting from Haarlem. Aart had suggested Gerrit look through one of Opa's medical books, and a particularly gory case study about a fall from a bridge had piqued his curiosity. Could a fall from a train do the same thing—cause internal bleeding or a concussion? Gerrit tried to remember how Opa always did check-ups. Something about how the eyes focused might reveal a serious head injury.

"Watch finger." He held up his hand and moved his pointer finger to the left, then right, up, then down. The girl's expression informed him that she thought it was silly, but her eyes seemed to work properly as she tracked his finger. Yet her lips had a blue tint, and she looked extremely pale. Shock?

A gust of wind blew across the field, and she shivered. February wasn't terribly cold, not compared to January or December, but she was lying on the ground without the benefit of a vigorous bicycle ride to warm her.

Gerrit shrugged out of his coat and laid it over her, tucking it around her shoulders and torso. "My name is Gerrit."

She didn't smile, exactly, but her frown turned into something more neutral. "I'm Ingrid."

He stood and walked over to the knapsack. "Yours, Ingrid?"

"Yes."

He brought it closer. "Anything warm inside?"

She nodded, which he took as permission for him to search her bag. He pulled out a sweater to wrap around her legs below her skirt, then a knit hat that he snugged onto her head. A pair of gloves came next, and he put them on her hands. Then a pair of mittens with something heavy inside. From the first, he pulled a tangle of pearls. If they were real . . . Goodness, Mam had never had jewelry like that. He put the pearls carefully back inside the knapsack and used the mitten as a barrier between the back of Ingrid's neck and the cold ground. The last mitten had a brooch inside. That jewelry also went back into the bag, and he put the mitten around the front of her neck, under his coat. A scarf would have been better, but he didn't have one.

"*Danke.*"

"*Graag gedaan.*" That was Dutch. How did he say it in German? "*Gern geschehen.*"

How did a girl of her age come by such fancy jewelry? Maybe she'd stolen it from someone on the train, and her escape hadn't gone as planned, leaving her on a half-frozen field with a broken leg or two. Or maybe someone had tried to steal it from her, and she'd fled the train to get away from them. Human greed. That was undoubtedly the problem, just like Pap always said.

"Where are we?" Her worn voice trembled.

"Arnhem." If she didn't know where she was, Arnhem probably hadn't been her intended destination. "You go to where?"

She shook her head, either because his broken German was unclear or because she was hiding something. Her lips hadn't regained much color, so he looked through the bag again in search of anything that might help. He was feeling the biting cold himself now, but he resisted the temptation to take his coat back. He found four passports hidden behind a magazine. Four? Was she stealing passports as well as jewelry? Keeping them inside the knapsack where she couldn't see him snooping, he opened the first. Ingrid Lang. The second was also hers, but it listed Ingrid Eckerstorfer.

Two passports, two identities. Gerrit quickly reached the obvious explanation: the girl was a spy.

Ingrid couldn't ever remember being so cold or in so much pain. That fall . . . It still felt like a blur. Running from the men, leaping so she wouldn't be stabbed, falling into darkness, and then excruciating pain.

The Dutch boy with pale-blue eyes and sandy-brown hair sat beside her. He'd been gentle while finding layers to help her stay warm, but he seemed to have given up trying to converse with her. She wished he would try again—interpreting his rather poor German had given her something to think about besides the pain. She'd broken her arm when she was six. Maybe it had hurt this much, but if so, time had dimmed that memory, and this seemed much, much worse. But not as bad as a knife across her throat or into her heart.

Maybe it was just as well that the Dutch boy, Gerrit, had stopped talking because so many of his questions requested information she didn't dare share. She needed to tell someone about the men on the train, but she intended that someone to have more authority than a boy probably younger than she. A better grasp of the German language would also be helpful.

He'd said they were near Arnhem, so she ought to celebrate escaping the Reich. But the constant pain in her legs that flared whenever she moved buried any relief or satisfaction. So did worry that her siblings were still trapped.

The sounds of a car pulled her attention to the road, where a burgundy Opel eased to a stop. The young woman from before exited one side of the vehicle, and a tall, middle-aged man with graying hair exited the other. Soon, they had joined Ingrid and Gerrit in the mud.

The man bent next to her and gave her a reassuring smile. "Anita tells me you may have a broken bone. I can help." He spoke German. His accent was heavy, but he didn't have to pause on each word the way the boy did. "I'm Dr. van der Veen." He gestured to the young woman. "My daughter Anita." Then he gestured to the young man. "My grandson Gerrit."

The man's daughter and grandson looked nearly the same age, but the similarities ended there. Anita's eyes, hair, and skin gave her an Oriental appearance, whereas Gerrit's fair coloring, much like the doctor's, looked typically Dutch.

The boy spoke to his grandfather in Dutch, but Ingrid picked out her name.

"Ingrid?" Dr. van der Veen waited, as if verifying he'd been told the correct name.

Ingrid nodded.

"May I examine your legs?"

"You may."

Gerrit said something else, and the man nodded, then addressed her. "Perhaps I can take you somewhere warmer first?"

Normally, Ingrid would avoid going off with people she didn't know, but her choices over the last few days had dwindled to almost nothing. She couldn't walk. The only people she could trust—Karl, Anna, Frau Davies, and maybe a few of the staff at Falcon Point—were all in different countries. She was desperate. "Thank you. That might be best."

The doctor checked a few of her vital signs. "This next part might hurt," he warned.

He slid one arm under her shoulders and the other under her knees. He'd been right. The next part—when he lifted her so he could carry her to the car—was the most excruciating pain she had ever felt. The torture flashed so intensely that her vision spotted, and her stomach roiled. She cried out in agony and bit her lip to stop more whimpers from creeping out. She wasn't a little girl anymore. Young ladies of fifteen didn't cry when they were injured. Except she just had.

Dr. van der Veen carried her across the mud and set her in the back seat of the car. Ingrid could tell he was trying to be gentle, but she would have cried again if she hadn't been biting her lip. Anita handed the doctor a blanket, which he took and laid across her lap. Gerrit placed her knapsack on the car's floor.

Then the doctor and Anita climbed into the front seats. Dr. van der Veen started the engine, and Ingrid held her breath as the car moved along the road. Lying on the Opel's back seat was much preferable to lying in the cold mud, but each bump and vibration made her appreciate the utter stillness of the field.

From her position, sitting with her legs outstretched across the back seat, she could see the countryside pass outside. Occasional trees. Homes in the distance—large ones set far back from the road. Then the homes grew closer together and went from grand to moderate. The car pulled to a gentle stop.

Dr. van der Veen came around to open the car's rear door, revealing a home three levels high sitting beside other homes much like it. "Rather than move you inside, I think I ought to check your legs here. I've a suspicion that we'll need the X-ray machine at the hospital, and I can save you some pain if I don't have to move you so much."

Ingrid nodded.

Dr. van der Veen pulled away the blanket. "Where is it most painful?"

"My legs."

"Yes, which part?"

She pointed to her left thigh, then both calves.

He started with her lower leg, pulling her stockings down to study her bruised and swollen limbs. He said something in Dutch to Anita, and she hurried into the house. Then he gave her a grim smile. "We'll head to St. Elisabeth Hospital. I'll need those X-rays."

Ingrid nodded, trying to be brave. Broken legs. If she couldn't walk, how on earth was she supposed to get to London and find Anna so Karl could find them both?

Gerrit shivered as he pulled his bicycle up to his grandfather's house on Utrechtseweg in Arnhem. Ingrid still had his coat, and riding always made the wind stronger. Anjing greeted him as he tucked the bicycle beside Anita's on the side of the house and went through the door to the kitchen.

His mother stood at the sink, cleaning dishes. She gave him a good look-over. "I left a bowl for you in the dining room. Johan and Nellie are just finishing. You had better wash up before you eat, and you best hurry. We have a train to catch, and your opa took the car to the hospital, so we'll have to walk."

"With our cases?"

"We only came for the weekend. We didn't bring that much."

No, *he* hadn't brought much. No one had, but Gerrit had a feeling that he'd be the one who would have to carry Johan's and Nellie's belongings. Nellie might be only eight years old, but she was not a light packer. Gerrit grunted.

"What was that?" his mother asked.

"Yes, Mam."

"Where's your coat?"

"With the girl we found."

Mam looked at her wristwatch. "We'll have to fetch it the next time we come. You can wear an extra sweater until then. We're past the worst of winter anyway."

"I've almost outgrown it. Maybe I can have a new one?"

Mam went back to the dishes. "Maybe in the autumn, after we've seen how much you grow over the summer."

Anita peered through the doorway. "Come on, slowpoke, your cocoa is getting cold."

By the time Gerrit had washed his hands and face, then changed into trousers without any mud on them, Anita's prediction was correct. His cocoa was tepid.

"Hurry, Gerrit," his mother called.

Gerrit guzzled most of the cocoa and drank the oatmeal from the bowl. Mam might not approve of his table manners, but she was busy gathering Nellie's and Johan's things. Anita rushed about helping her. Getting the entire family to the train station on time was a challenge under the best of circumstances. Having that spy show up and pull Opa and his car away had made it even worse.

"Gerrit!" Mam's voice again.

He took a last swallow of cocoa, ran up the stairs to the room where he and Johan had slept, and shoved his clothes into his bag. Then he ran down the stairs and out the front door.

Anita had strapped the other luggage to the back of a bicycle. Bless Tante Anita. She could carry the luggage on the bicycle and then ride back. There wasn't room for Gerrit's bag, but if he had to carry only his luggage, he wouldn't complain.

Mam saw him and started along the road, holding Nellie's hand. Johan walked beside them, and Gerrit and Anita followed.

Ingrid had managed to ruin Gerrit's morning quite thoroughly. No goodbyes with Opa, no car to take them to the station, no coat. No chance for a rematch with Anita either, though he doubted he could have out-pedaled her for long anyway.

"Where's your coat?" Anita asked.

"With the girl we found. But that's all right. It was getting too small anyway."

"Do you have an extra?"

Gerrit shrugged because he didn't.

"Your opa would buy you a new coat if you asked."

Gerrit shook his head. "Pap wouldn't like it." That would be too much like accepting charity, and for his father to accept it from his father-in-law . . . well, the chances of that happening were slim. Opa hadn't been pleased when Gerrit's mother had run off to marry Gerrit's father six months before Gerrit was born. Father and daughter hadn't spoken for almost ten years, but Gerrit's mother had felt she needed to attend her stepmother's funeral, and time had softened the anger enough to allow a partial reconciliation. Time and Johan's heart murmur and weak lungs that Opa treated from time to time. But though Opa and Mam wrote letters and Mam brought the children for visits, Opa and Pap's relationship remained uneasy. Pap could have come to Arnhem for the visit. He'd preferred to stay home.

Anita glanced in the direction of the hospital. "Maybe I can fetch your coat and still make it to the station on time."

"I'll be fine. Spring's just around the corner anyway. Besides, I didn't have a chance to warn Opa, but I think Ingrid's a spy. You have to warn him."

Anita's brows scrunched together. "She's not old enough to be a spy."

"That's the genius of it. No one would suspect her, but she has two passports with two different names. A third and fourth, too, but they were for other people. Probably more spies. Maybe she's a courier taking false papers around."

Anita looked as if she were trying not to laugh.

"I'm serious, Anita. What type of lawful citizen carries around two passports with two different names?"

Anita shook her head. "Espionage is hardly the only reason a person might have two passports, but I'll warn your opa."

"She had fancy jewelry too. Like a bribe or a payment or something. Will you go to the hospital from the station? Before she hides everything?"

This time, Anita did laugh, but the smile she gave him held too much affection for the laughter to hurt his feelings. "Yes, I'll go directly to the hospital, and I'll warn Pap, or if he's busy, I'll look through the knapsack. I'll even write a letter with an update when I mail your coat. But in exchange, I want you to read fewer comic books about spies."

"I only read comic books when my Oom Antoon passes them on to me. Once or twice a month. And anyway, in case you haven't noticed, that railroad track comes from Germany, and Germany's at war with half of Europe." Gerrit gestured toward the border.

"France, Great Britain, and what's left of Poland are hardly half of Europe. The Netherlands is neutral. We'll stay that way. If there are any spies crossing the border, they're probably German agents heading for France or Britain. Or they're French or British agents returning with information about the Reich. They'd be adults, not youths. There's nothing for us to worry about."

Gerrit hoped Anita was right. Germany had respected Dutch neutrality in the last war. There was no reason to expect that they'd do anything different now. But people weren't found injured off to the side of the train tracks every day. Even if she weren't a spy, Ingrid was hiding something.

Ingrid sat in a clean hospital bed with fresh casts on both her legs and a system of weights and pulleys keeping the more serious of the injured limbs in traction. A nearby window revealed afternoon sunlight turning to evening. What a day it had been. Being threatened by spies, jumping and breaking her two legs in three different places, lying in the cold for hours, and now being stuck in a bed for the foreseeable future in a foreign country. She'd thought there wasn't any way things could remain as awful as they'd been since Papa's murder, but all the longing for her family, all the pain, all the uncertainty—it swirled within her, and tears leaked down her cheeks.

One of the nurses noticed Ingrid's weeping and patted her hand. The nurses were nuns, and most were German, so she could communicate with them. They even helped reduce the physical pain gnawing at her, but the other types of pain—no one could fix those. Ingrid wiped the tears away, wishing she were back in Falcon Point. She'd gladly take Anna's unmelodious piano playing or Karl's teasing instead of the all-consuming loneliness.

Dr. van der Veen approached her bed. He'd explained her three different fractures earlier, before being called away. Now he pulled a chair up and sat where he could best communicate with her while her head rested on a pillow.

"One of the nurses said you were crying. The pain?"

Ingrid shook her head. Her legs hurt, but not as much as her heart.

The doctor looked unconvinced. "I'm sorry I didn't come sooner. Other patients needed my help. But I'm here now. How should I contact your parents so we can let them know what's happened?"

Ingrid's throat felt tight. "They're both dead. Mama died a year and a half ago. Papa was killed a few days ago."

Dr. van der Veen's face softened. "I'm very sorry to hear that. If your parents are gone, who is your next of kin?"

Ingrid swallowed. Her paternal and maternal grandparents were both dead. Papa's brothers had died in the Great War, and her mother had no siblings. "I'm supposed to meet my older brother and younger sister in London, but we were separated."

The doctor glanced at her legs. "I'm afraid any travel will have to be postponed for a time, but I can arrange for a telegram."

"I don't know the street or the number. Just instructions on how to get there." The vague directions Karl had given her wouldn't do a telegram delivery boy any good.

Dr. van der Veen folded his arms and leaned back. "And is your name Ingrid Lang or Ingrid Eckerstorfer?"

Eckerstorfer wasn't a real name, just one Papa had used when he'd somehow procured forged travel papers for all of them. The doctor would only know that name if he'd looked through her things. "Lang."

"And, Mejuffrouw Lang, can you tell me why you have two passports?" The words were spoken with kindness, but even so, she almost told him to mind his own business.

She sighed. Karl would need the assistance of someone like Sherlock Holmes to find her in a hospital in Arnhem. So would Frau Davies. She couldn't trust anyone other than them. Dr. van der Veen had treated her broken legs, but he'd also snooped through her things. Yet she had to trust someone. A Dutch doctor seemed like the best of her extremely limited options. "My father was trying to get us out of the Reich. An old friend wanted him to work for the Nazis, and that went against Papa's conscience. He refused, and then he was murdered."

"So you're an orphan and a refugee."

She nodded. "Papa was worried that the SS would track him, so he arranged for alternate passports for all of us."

"That explains the duplicate." He chuckled. "Gerrit suspected espionage when he saw the pair of them. Given your age and the political situation in Germany, trying to escape the Nazis is a much more reasonable assumption."

Gerrit. He'd been kind enough to find something warm for her, but apparently, he'd also been suspicious enough to snoop through her knapsack. Silly boy, to think her a spy. But espionage wasn't so farfetched. "I overheard spies on the train. One was telling the other what to search for. Information on bridges, train tracks, that sort of thing. They're planning to invade the Netherlands."

"The Netherlands is neutral."

"I only know what I heard. That's why I jumped from the train, because they knew I'd heard them, and they were planning to kill me in order to silence me."

She wasn't sure if the doctor believed her, but he must have reported it, because the next morning, a German-speaking Dutch army officer came to interview her.

"You wish to report a spy?" He kept his clean-shaven face calm, but his voice hinted at skepticism. Regardless of how he felt about the report, he pulled out a pencil and small pad of paper with which to take notes.

"Yes, sir. Two of them. They met in my train car and spoke about their plans."

The officer's nose and upper lip scrunched together. "They spoke in front of you?"

She shook her head. "It was a sleeper car. They couldn't see me, not until the end when I tried to see them. They assumed it was empty because the other passengers had been arrested and taken off the train."

"Arrested?"

"I think they were Jews trying to escape the Nazis."

The office dutifully wrote down her response. "And what did you hear from the spies?"

"One was telling the other what information to gather so they could prepare an invasion of the Netherlands. Mostly, he wanted information on the bridges, canals, train tracks, things like that."

"Did they mention specific locations?"

"Not that I heard."

He huffed. “If they’re real spies, they’re probably just passing through the Netherlands on their way to France.”

“One specifically mentioned that an invasion of the Netherlands could only succeed if an army captured the bridges.”

Another nose wrinkle. Another scratch from the man’s pencil. “I see. I believe that is all I need for my report.”

“But what of the men? Don’t you need a description so you can try to find them?”

The man sighed. “Yes, please go on. What did these two spies look like?”

“One had his back to me, but I’d know his voice again, and he wore a tan fedora. The other wore a black homburg, and he had a large nose and needed a shave. Dark, close-set eyes. Thin lips. His jaw was soft but not fat. The train car wasn’t well lit, but I’d recognize him again.”

She expected the officer to arrange for an artist to come sketch a picture of the spy. Instead, he held back a yawn. “And then your story ends with the men threatening to kill you?”

“Yes. They had a knife, and they spoke of putting the body—me—into a canal or a river so it wouldn’t be discovered as quickly.”

He smirked. “Yes, quite the thrilling story.”

The way he said *story*, it was as if he thought she’d been making it all up. She was trying to help his country, and he was treating her as though she were a waste of time. “It wasn’t thrilling to live through. It was terrifying.”

He glanced at the casts and traction equipment. “I suppose so. Anything else to add to your account?”

The condescension lay thick in his words. Why would she tell him more when he didn’t believe a single word she had already said? She wasn’t a liar. Her face heated as she realized that wasn’t entirely true. She hadn’t been completely honest with Rupert or the train conductors. Maybe the flight from the Nazis had ruined her integrity, and the Dutch officer could somehow detect it. “I just don’t want your country to face what Austria has faced. German spies are nothing to laugh at.”

“Certainly not.” His words were right, but his tone still hinted at disbelief. “Your age?”

“I’ll be sixteen in a few months.”

“Should anyone wish to ask you follow-up questions, where can they find you?” His expression, as if he were holding back a scoff of disbelief, made it clear that he did not foresee anyone asking her further questions.

His attitude rankled, but his question rattled. She had no home. She couldn’t go back to Falcon Point or forward to London. “I . . . I suppose I will be in the hospital until I can walk again.” A quick glance at her casts told her that might be a very long time.

Perhaps an hour later, Dr. van der Veen sat on the chair next to Ingrid's bed, interrupting her thoughts on how infuriating the Dutch officer had been, on how much her legs hurt, and on how much she wanted Karl or Anna and Frau Davies to walk through the hospital door.

"He didn't believe me." Her words sounded childish in her own ears, but at that moment, she felt like a lost little girl, not like a young lady capable of making her way to London. She met the doctor's eyes. He'd passed her report on, but that didn't mean he believed her.

He sighed. "We Dutch have been warriors for centuries. We've made our mark on Europe and on the Indies, but perhaps we trust too much to the protection of neutrality here." He shook his head. "If war comes, we aren't ready. Our military can deal with insurrections in the East Indies, but compared to our German neighbor, well, our equipment is antiquated."

"Do you think Hitler will invade the Netherlands?"

The doctor didn't answer right away. "Were I a betting man, I would bet against it."

Ingrid frowned. She hoped the doctor was right because she didn't want the war to spread. But she also wanted someone to believe her.

He continued. "That doesn't mean German intelligence isn't sending spies out to plan for contingencies. I don't think you jumped from that train because of an overactive imagination. To threaten a girl like you . . ." He shook his head. "Some men are ruthless, even if they're only planning contingencies."

The two of them sat in silence for a time. Nurses rushed past in the hallway, and the rattle and ring of a streetcar echoed in the distance.

"I was wondering, Ingrid, if you might like to stay at my home instead of here in the hospital while you recover."

Ingrid's gaze had gone to the window, but it quickly came back to the doctor. "Do you often take patients home?"

"I don't often have patients with such a long recovery ahead and no family around to help them. I can check on you there as easily as I can check on you here. And you're about the same age as my youngest daughter." He smiled. "I have seven children. The first six were all raised together when we lived in Sumatra. For years, there was never a quiet moment in the house until they were all asleep. Then my first wife died, and I remarried, and Anita came along. Things have been different for her. Quieter. Lonely, even, especially when her mother died. Making friends in Arnhem hasn't been easy for her, but I've noticed the way she cheers up around her nephews and nieces. The home might be less lonely for her if you were to come stay with us. It might be better for your recovery as well so you aren't exposed to everyone who walks in with measles or mumps or some other disease."

"I've had mumps before." Karl had marched about her room with his cheeks puffed full of air to show her what her swollen face had looked like. He'd come down with the same illness three days later, with significantly worse swelling.

She sensed the doctor's offer wasn't merely about avoiding childhood diseases. She felt his compassion, for her, for his daughter. Ingrid was already dreadfully tired of sitting in the hospital bed with the same view all hours of the day. Dr. van der Veen and his daughter had already helped, already shown kindness. It seemed safe to trust them again. "Thank you for your offer. I'd very much like to convalesce with you and your daughter."

CHAPTER 4

May 1940

A warm, summer-like breeze blew through the cracked bathroom window as Ingrid stared at her shrunken legs. After two and a half months in casts, her muscles had grown smaller and weaker. Regardless, she planned to enjoy her first immersive bath since February. Anita had found soap from France for the occasion, and Ingrid inhaled the scent of lavender and almond. She washed her hair, scrubbed every inch of her skin, and tried not to worry about how hard it would be to travel to London on her feeble limbs.

Or how dangerous. The Germans had invaded Norway—a neutral country. The British had tried to help. They'd gained nothing but casualties, and travel to Britain seemed more and more likely to end in a sunken ship or a devastating air raid.

Ingrid finished her bath and pulled on a clean dress, a hand-me-down from Anita. Ingrid's parents had always purchased new clothing for her, but maybe that would have been different if she'd had an older sister. She'd been meant to have more than one younger sister. Mama had lost a baby when Ingrid was three. Ingrid hadn't understood what that meant, not until much later. How could someone lose a baby? They cried often enough that they'd be easy to find. But her sister hadn't been misplaced. She'd been born too early, and that had made the birth of Anna all the more precious. Anna had worn mostly new clothes as well, though a few of Ingrid's outfits had been passed on.

Soon after Ingrid opened the bathroom door, Anita stepped from her bedroom into the hallway.

"Waiting for me?" Ingrid had been learning as much Dutch as she could throughout the last days of February, all of March and April, and the first days of May. On Ingrid's first day in the home, Anita had walked around the bedroom and pointed to objects, telling Ingrid the Dutch words. Then she'd said *hond* and had held Anjing up for Ingrid to pet, and Ingrid and Anita had been fast friends ever since. Ingrid's Dutch pronunciation still needed a great deal of work, and her vocabulary was limited, but she had made steady progress.

"Pap said walking might be harder than you remember for a while. He suggested I stay within earshot in case you needed help." Anita spoke slowly, in Dutch, and Ingrid comprehended each word.

Ingrid looked down at her legs. "They shrank."

Anita walked over and hooked elbows with Ingrid. "That's nothing a daily bike ride won't cure. I can show you all my favorite sights so much more easily now that we won't have to wait for Pap to drive us around."

Dr. van der Veen had driven Ingrid around several times a week throughout her recovery, giving her a glimpse of the countryside and a break from her long convalescence inside the home. Though it was a nice home, it wasn't anywhere near as sprawling as Falcon Point, and the only German books in the library had been on anatomy and infectious diseases. Educational, but not Ingrid's preferred reading material. Far more entertaining were the conversations Anita shared with her when she came home during the school's lunch hour to check on her and the late-night talks that usually ended in giggles and lasted until Dr. van der Veen insisted Anita return to her own room for the sake of Ingrid's recovery and Anita's marks in school.

Ingrid had grown to love them: Anita, with her shy exterior that hid a mischievous streak tempered with compassion. Dr. van der Veen, with his serious expressions and tireless work to help each of his patients. Even Mevrouw Ruysch, the middle-aged cook and housekeeper, had shown Ingrid enough kindness to win her regard. But Arnhem wasn't Ingrid's home, and the van der Veens weren't her family. "Anita, I need to find my brother and sister."

Anita's smile faded. "Pap's working on it. He's been asking friends for a month about taking you to London. He can tell you what he's found, if you think you can manage the stairs."

"He's here?" He'd removed her cast not more than an hour ago, but more evenings than not, a telephone call would summon him back to the hospital.

Anita nodded. "No emergencies so far. And Mevrouw Ruysch made Pap's favorite meal, so that ought to keep him from wandering to St. Elisabeth's without reason."

Ingrid's legs felt wobbly as she and Anita made their way down the stairs from the middle to the bottom level of the house. She didn't release Anita's arm and gripped the railing with her other hand. She'd never had difficulty walking down stairs before. A few times, trying to keep up with Papa and Karl after a long day of cross-country skiing or hiking, she'd felt sore muscles pull and fatigue hinder, but that had always been on the way up the stairs, not on the way down. She could almost hear her brother teasing her. She'd become as weak and wobbly as a toddler.

Movement was scarcely easier when they reached the ground floor, and she had to lean on Anita more than she would have liked. Dr. van der Veen had carried her up and down the stairs several times a week over the last few months. How had he managed that so easily, especially with the weight of her casts?

Most of Ingrid's time in the van der Veen home had been spent in the same bedroom. Meals and books had been brought to her, so despite living in the home for two and a half months, the room Anita led her to was one Ingrid had never seen before. Ingrid suspected that most of the books she'd been reading had been shelved here. Bookshelves lined the walls, just as they did in the Falcon Point library. The room wasn't nearly as large as the one in her family's home, and the shelves were not so neat, but the warm smile from the man sitting at a large desk had a familiar feel to it.

"I would have been happy to come upstairs so you didn't have to walk all the way down." Dr. van der Veen set down the pen he'd been using and took off his glasses. She didn't see him wear them often—only when he read or wrote.

Anita led Ingrid to one of the plush chairs by the window, and Ingrid sank onto it with relief. Anita sat on a matching chair a meter away. "Pap, Ingrid wants to leave us." Anita's voice was level, but Ingrid turned to study her face and caught Dr. van der Veen doing the same.

"It's not that I want to leave you. I just want to find my brother and sister." Ingrid stumbled over the Dutch words, but the doctor's warm, bittersweet smile told her he understood.

Anita nodded and looked out the window.

Dr. van der Veen turned to Ingrid. "Of course you want to find your family. One of my colleagues travels to England every few months. He's leaving tomorrow. He's not familiar with children. No siblings, never married. But he agreed to take you, if you feel up to it so soon after having your casts removed."

Ingrid had barely been able to walk down the stairs. Would Dr. van der Veen's associate be patient enough to help a young lady who could barely walk take the London tube, then find the right church to ask about the right flat for her former nanny? Could she go that far and walk that much starting tomorrow? But how could she not take the first opportunity to find Karl and Anna?

Dr. van der Veen had examined her legs immediately after cutting off the casts, but now he came around his desk to study them again. "I had the casts removed on the early end of how long I expected the healing to take. Did you feel any pain when you walked down the stairs?"

"No pain . . . just weakness." Weakness that was unlikely to clear up by tomorrow morning.

Dr. van der Veen nodded. "I would expect as much. You've been bedridden for several months. You'll recover, but it will take some time. Perhaps you could postpone your trip to England for a week or two, and then Anita and I can take you."

Ingrid felt her mouth open in astonishment. "You'd do that? Travel to London?"

Dr. van der Veen smiled. "After traveling all the way to Java and Sumatra, you don't think I'd balk at a jaunt over to England, do you? I just had to give the hospital appropriate notice and your legs a little more time to recover and plan it so that Anita won't miss too many days of school. What do you say, Ingrid?"

The doctor kept his face cheerful, but open to either answer. Anita's face lit with hope. Travel to London with them after she'd had the chance to prepare physically for walking around the city or travel with a stranger when she wasn't sure she'd be able to keep up? The choice was easy. She hated to make Karl, Anna, and Frau Davies worry about her any longer than they already had, but what was another week or two after two and a half months? "I'd very much like to travel to England with you."

Rupert Altbauer stared at the letter he'd just received from his uncle Wilhelm. *It is with deep regret that I confess my inability to pass on Ingrid Lang's address. Her father died in a horrible accident, and young Karl took his sisters and fled. If you saw her the day you reported for active duty, you would have seen her after her father's death. Did she tell you anything at all about where she and her siblings were going? I've been appointed trustee of the Falcon Point estate, but naturally, it is not just their heritage I wish to protect. As a longtime family friend, I feel it my duty to find the Lang children and do everything I can for them. I must also warn you that Leopold Lang may have been involved in something less than honorable when it comes to our Fatherland's current circumstance. He spread his lies to his son, so you must exercise caution should you meet Karl. He could be dangerous, and his loyalty to the Reich is questionable.*

Karl dangerous? Rupert could imagine Karl playing the role of protective older brother with his fists should Rupert wish to spend an inordinate amount of time with Ingrid, but Karl wasn't even old enough to join the army. He couldn't really be dangerous.

The other news was more unexpected. Herr Lang was dead, maybe a traitor? Herr Lang had always seemed so upright. He had listened with care to everything Rupert had said, with real interest, not the feigned attention adults sometimes gave to juveniles. Rupert had admired Herr Lang in a way that he had admired few others. Why hadn't Ingrid said something when he'd given her money for a train ticket? So close to the death, she must have been reeling from grief.

He skimmed through the letter again. He ought to have purchased the ticket directly for Ingrid; then he would have known her destination. Ingrid had never come across as incapable, but she was three years younger than Rupert; if her father was dead, she needed the help of someone like Uncle Wilhelm. That was who Rupert had always turned to when his father had thrown around sharp words or hard fists. Later, after the divorce, Uncle Wilhelm had been the one to see that Rupert had proper clothing for school, and he'd taken Rupert on holidays—indulgences his mother would have never been able to afford.

Why would Karl have taken his sisters from Falcon Point? And how on earth did the siblings get separated? Months had passed since Rupert had seen Ingrid in Berlin, so he hadn't any hope of tracking down the Lang siblings. He could only hope they would come to their senses and seek out the help Uncle Wilhelm offered them.

"Altbauer?"

Rupert turned to Willi Keller, an enlisted man like him.

"Did you hear?"

"Hear what?"

"We're marching soon. The oberleutnant just received orders."

"Do you know where?" Fighting in Norway continued, but he doubted they needed reinforcements this far into the campaign. Not long ago, Denmark had done the wise thing and surrendered to Germany, so his unit was unlikely to be needed there.

Keller glanced around to make sure no one else in the barracks would overhear them. "Someone said something about Holland."

Ingrid glanced at her alarm clock. Three hours until she needed to wake up, but today was Friday, May 10, and on Saturday, she would travel to England with Dr. van der Veen and Anita. If excitement was already making her wake early, she hated to think about how poorly she would sleep the next night.

Something rumbled in the distance. Was that what had wakened her? A thunderstorm? She slipped from her bed and pulled the curtains back. No rain, but that rumble . . . It had been too loud to ignore. Other sounds broke up the normally quiet night and made her blood run cold. She went across the hall to Anita's room and knocked softly on the door. "Anita?" Her friend pulled the door open immediately, so she must have been awake. "Do you hear all the airplanes?" Ingrid asked.

"That's an awful lot of airplanes." Another door down the corridor opened. "Pap?" Anita called.

He came toward them, tying the belt around his robe. Anita flipped the light switch on.

"No, keep it off." His voice sounded strained.

"But why?" Anita obeyed, plunging them all back into darkness.

Dr. van der Veen swallowed. "Because I'd bet my medical license that the last rumble we heard was the bridge over the Nederrijn. The army wired it for demolition . . . just in case. They wouldn't destroy it unless they had to."

Ingrid's throat felt tight. She could think of only one reason the Dutch Army or the Arnhem authorities might destroy the bridge, and she didn't dare say it out loud, even if the airplanes and the order to keep the lights out seemed to confirm it.

"What's happening, Pap?" Anita asked.

"I didn't think they'd do it," he whispered. "Not to us. To the French, yes. Maybe even to the Belgians. But not to us." He put one hand on Anita's shoulder and the other on Ingrid's back. "We can hope the bridge was a mistake. Someone nervous because too many German troops were moving on the border. Or maybe I'm wrong, and it's something else entirely. But if the German Army is trying to invade, we don't want them to see any lights from our windows. No silhouettes, do you understand? They'll be nervous. They'll shoot first, find out if it was a soldier or a civilian later."

Ingrid nodded, even though an icy fear made it hard to breathe.

"Why would they invade the Netherlands?" Anita asked. "We're neutral."

"We were neutral." Dr. van der Veen turned for the stairs. "Now, I fear, we are at war. Come down to the kitchen, and we'll see if the radio has any information."

Anita followed but shook her head. "The first radio program doesn't begin until eight." That was almost four hours away.

"They might begin earlier on a morning like this," the doctor said.

Ingrid huddled with Anita and the doctor around the radio in the parlor, waiting for the tubes to warm up. They were supposed to have arisen early on Saturday morning for a trip to England, not Friday morning to listen for news of an invasion. Now it would be too late. "I should have left as soon as my casts were cut off."

"Can't we still go?" Anita asked. "I know we aren't as strong as Germany, but surely our army will hold them, at the very least slow them down. Let's leave now, while we can."

Pap shook his head. "You heard all those airplanes?"

Anita nodded.

"Trains will be targets."

"Then, we can drive."

They'd meant to take the train to Rotterdam, then a ship to Folkestone. Dr. van der Veen had the Opel, but Ingrid doubted cars would be safe either.

Dr. van der Veen signaled for Anita to turn up the radio's volume. Someone was broadcasting, and the announcer's voice, normally calm and composed, seemed agitated.

Ingrid struggled to understand the rapid Dutch words, but Anita explained in a voice laced with horror. "The Germans aren't just coming over the border. They've dropped airborne units near The Hague and Rotterdam."

The phone rang, and Dr. Van der Veen answered it. He turned away and lowered his voice, but Ingrid could pick out his words, and she understood most of what he said. "Yes, I understand. But if the Germans really are invading, I can hardly leave two young ladies at the home unprotected."

Somewhere nearby, a siren began its wail, the pitch rising and falling, weaving around Ingrid's chest and warning her that everything had changed, and not for the better. She had heard about the atrocities of German soldiers when they'd invaded Belgium twenty-six years ago. She and Anita were at a vulnerable age should German soldiers be in search of female company and be unwilling to take no for an answer.

"Yes, I expect they'll transfer military casualties over, but I have responsibilities as a father too."

Another pause in the conversation, filled with news from the radio. Ingrid grabbed an atlas and flipped to a map of the Netherlands. Anita looked over her shoulder, helping point out the locations mentioned as sights of attack by land and air.

The doctor hung up the phone. "Anita, Ingrid. Get dressed at once. I'm needed at the hospital, and I don't intend to leave the two of you here by yourselves."

He had left the two of them home by themselves most days since Ingrid's arrival. But this was different. This was fear that the enemy could march inside their home and do anything they wanted with the inhabitants. They were no longer safe, because the Netherlands was now at war.

CHAPTER 5

Gerrit and Johan stood on the roof of their apartment building, surveying the damage to Rotterdam. A ship burned near one of the piers. Smoke from a bombed refinery sent up a steady plume of thick, black smoke, and a combination of sirens, artillery, and airplanes filled the air.

"Johan! Gerrit!" Mam called from the roof's doorway.

Gerrit raised his hand in a wave so she could see them.

"What are you doing up here?" She rushed toward them. "You ought to be in the cellar."

"But, Mam, we saw one of our Fokkers shoot down a Heinkel." Gerrit had cheered, and so had his brother and some boys watching from the top of a nearby building.

He expected some sort of positive emotion—gratitude for the victory, satisfaction that one of the invaders had met his end. Instead, anger wove into Mam's voice. "And what will happen when a stray bullet from a Fokker or a stray bomb from a Heinkel gets you?"

Gerrit shut his eyes so he wouldn't accidentally roll them. "They weren't close enough for that. The paratroopers and most of the planes are near Waalhaven." And the airport was too far away to view from the top of their apartment building in Alkemadeplein. Tante Francisca, Pap's younger sister, lived near the Willemsbrug across the Maas. From there, one could probably see everything exciting.

"Inside," Mam said. "We've bad news enough without you getting injured. If you insist on treating an invasion like a sporting event, you can listen to it on the radio, like you do your football matches."

Cheering that a German bomber had been shot down hardly counted as treating the invasion like a sporting event, but Gerrit knew better than to argue. Mam was upset—but not at him and Johan. Their country was under attack, and they'd been taken completely by surprise. Yes, Gerrit had more than one friend with a brother in the army who had been told to report recently, but the Netherlands had been neutral.

Everyone had assumed Hitler would honor that, and even if the Germans were to attack, Rotterdam wasn't anywhere near the German border. Any attack would have to start in the distance, and the rivers and canals would slow an advance, even that of an overwhelming enemy, to a crawl.

Yet somehow, the Germans had managed to do not only the improbable—ignoring Dutch neutrality—but also the impossible—surprising cities far from the border. Planeloads of invading soldiers had jumped from the sky to seize the bridges of Rotterdam, and if the radio was correct, they had jumped around The Hague too—Rotterdam, the country's largest port, and The Hague, the country's seat of government.

Gerrit glanced along the rooftops. The smoke was too thick to see much of what was happening anyway. Maybe the radio would give him a better picture of how the fight was progressing.

Three days passed. No one went to school. Few people went to work. Gerrit and his family left the apartment only to go to the air-raid shelter. He helped his mother put tape across their windows to prevent glass from shattering inward and cutting them if something nearby exploded. Fear frayed their tempers and made it hard to sleep at night.

Invasion. Gerrit knew the German army was stronger, so he took pride in news coming from The Hague—the royal family had escaped, and hundreds of highly trained German paratroopers had been captured. The news in Rotterdam was less decisive. The Germans held the southern end of most of the bridges. The outnumbered Dutch held the northern ends.

"Holding isn't good enough," Pap mumbled as the announcer on the radio spoke of the brave defenders guarding the bridges over the Nieuwe Maas.

"Why not?" Johan asked. "If it's a standstill, aren't the German troops as likely as our troops to be defeated?"

Pap shook his head. "The German troops are waiting for their tanks to catch up, and every day, they're getting closer. Our men can hold against paratroopers. Holding against tanks is an entirely different matter."

"What will we do?" Nellie looked up from the string of her tangled yo-yo.

Pap forced a smile. "Let your mam and pap worry about that. Either way, I'm sure school will start again soon." The moment Nellie went back to her string, Pap's smile faded.

What would happen if the Germans won? Gerrit didn't dare ask the question aloud, but the Germans had already taken over Austria, Czechoslovakia, Poland, Norway, and Denmark. Would his country, too, be conquered?

"Do you want help?" he asked Nellie. The fate of armies was something Gerrit couldn't do anything to change, but he could solve the small problem of Nellie's tangled yo-yo.

Nellie nodded and handed it to him. She'd made a mess of it, but he undid a small knot, then started work on the larger mass of tangled string. When the yo-yo was untangled, he repaired Johan's broken wind-up car because he needed something to keep him busy. He'd long ago developed a talent for fixing things because the family could rarely afford to buy anything new.

But the next day, neither the broken toaster he fiddled with nor the jigsaw puzzle Johan pieced together was sufficient to keep Gerrit's mind off the news when the radio announced that the city was surrendering.

Gerrit pounded his fists on the kitchen table. Mam looked in his direction but didn't say anything. If she didn't feel the same frustration he did, it was only because there were so many other things to feel: shame, fear, grief. He wasn't sure what Rotterdam's surrender meant, beyond the Dutch army losing, their allies being too busy to help, and the Nazis now taking control.

Nellie started crying, and Mam looked at Gerrit as if he were the cause. Maybe the noise had startled her, but it certainly wasn't Gerrit's fault that the Netherlands had been invaded.

"I'm going out." Pap stood.

"Where?" Mam asked.

"To check on my sister."

"But Francisca lives where the fighting is at its worst!"

"And I haven't heard from her since this nightmare started." Pap grabbed his coat from the small closet by the apartment's entrance. "Then I'll go to the docks. See about work. Regardless of who controls the port, they'll need stevedores."

Gerrit felt his mouth hang open. Pap had spent every day since the invasion following reports of each new development. He'd cursed the Nazis again and again. "You'll cooperate with the Germans?"

Pap's mouth went tight. "We still have to eat, won't we?"

"Can I come with you?" Gerrit didn't want to stay in the apartment.

"Not this time." Pap left without saying anything else. Maybe Gerrit shouldn't have questioned him. Of course Pap would still need a job, but if that involved loading and unloading supplies for the Germans, it seemed somehow wrong. But what else could Pap do? Watch his family starve? Get a different job that would undoubtedly in some indirect way also help the Germans? Everything anyone grew, made, or created might be turned to the use of the enemy, but farmers couldn't stop planting food, or people would go hungry. Tailors couldn't stop making clothing, or people would go naked. And refusing to paint or sing or play an instrument would deprive an already darkened world of those acts most likely to cast light.

"Can I see if there's any news about the schools reopening?" With the exception of one trip to the apartment roof and several to the nearest bomb shelter, Gerrit had been stuck in the apartment for going on five days. He wanted an escape.

Mam looked around their front room. With everyone spending so much time at home and the threat of air raids making it easy to postpone housekeeping, the apartment wasn't up to her normal standards. "Take your brother and sister."

"Yes, Mam."

Johan stood at once, not even finding a location for the puzzle piece he held in his hand. He seemed just as eager as Gerrit to get outside and do something.

Before they left, they had to get Nellie to stop crying. Gerrit could usually make her laugh, yet laughter, now, seemed wrong. But she was only eight. Maybe she needed something to cheer her up as much as he did. "Come on, Nellie. Maybe one of your friends will be out doing the same thing."

Nellie frowned. "Which one?"

"Any of them could be checking the school, but we won't know unless we look." Gerrit offered her his hand, and she took it for the three flights down and through the apartment-building entrance.

As they neared the school, a growing drone caught Gerrit's ears. Airplanes. If the city were surrendering, he doubted he would get to witness any more Dutch Fokkers shoot down German bombers. But surely the fight would go on . . . somewhere. The Germans had managed to take too many pieces of too many bridges too soon in Rotterdam, but Dutch forces might hold out longer in The Hague or in Amsterdam. Maybe that was the real reason Pap had gone to the docks—to find a way of getting his family somewhere else, somewhere safe.

Or maybe Gerrit was grasping at straws because a defeated reality was too bitter to swallow all at once.

"Where do you think the planes are going?" Johan asked.

Gerrit shrugged. "Wherever they're still fighting, I guess."

"Will they bomb us?" Nellie asked.

"We're surrendering," Gerrit said. "They won't bomb us during negotiations."

Nellie looked at the sky and swallowed. "It looks like they're going to bomb us."

Gerrit followed his sister's gaze and studied the flock of Heinkel He 111 bombers. If they were flying to another city, they would be at higher altitude. But why would the Germans bomb a city in the process of surrender?

The bomb bay doors of one of the lead Heinkels opened. For a moment, Gerrit froze. He couldn't move, couldn't think, could do nothing but stare as small dark shapes left the airplane's bomb bay. Then he gripped Nellie's hand. "Run!"

He made for the nearest building with a basement, pulling Nellie and checking to see that Johan followed. Why were the Germans bombing downtown Rotterdam? Their previous attacks had all been on the other side of the harbor, near the military targets.

"What about Mam and Pap?" Nellie was already winded, and her voice carried a note of panic.

If they went all the way back to their apartment for Mam, they wouldn't make it into the shelter before the bombs hit. And Pap's location was uncertain. "They'll find their way."

Explosions shook the ground beneath their feet as Gerrit and his siblings rushed down the stairs to the basement of the restaurant they had entered. They had to slow as the press of others seeking shelter created a bottleneck. Gerrit kept his grip on Nellie with one hand and took hold of Johan with the other, not wanting to get separated in the crowded room with dim lighting.

The rumbles and vibrations were unnerving, and the press of people, most of them taller than him and packed so closely that he couldn't see anything beyond the mass of shoulders and heads that surrounded him, made everything worse. He wished Mam or Pap were present to manage things instead of him, but a quick glance at Nellie and Johan reminded him to stay calm, for their sakes. But it was hard to breathe with so many people about.

"Gerrit, you're hurting me." Nellie tried to tug her hand free.

Gerrit didn't release her, but he met her eyes. "We have to stay together." If they were separated, they might not find each other again. "I'll loosen my grip, but don't let go. Understand?"

Nellie nodded and stopped struggling. Gerrit changed his hold so it wasn't so tight. Someone moved, and Johan's head pushed into Gerrit's shoulder, shoved there by an elbow. Gerrit didn't think it was intentional, but he wormed his way to the space under the stairs. The three of them were short enough that they could sit without hitting their heads, but the adults couldn't, so they had the corner to themselves.

The ground rocked, and his eyes shot to the ceiling as he wondered if it was about to collapse. Johan huddled closer, and a few meters away, someone let out a shrill cry of alarm. Gerrit closed his eyes for a moment and pretended he was somewhere else: Arnhem at sunrise, with verdant grass and the Nederrijn stretched out before him. A field of tulips. A wide pier with gentle waves lapping against the pilings. Not a dark, crowded basement in the middle of a massive bombing raid. Another series of rumbles moved beneath his feet and bombarded his ears. Then the lights snapped off. Nellie whimpered into Gerrit's shirt.

Gerrit wasn't sure how long the raid lasted. Long enough that the air grew foul from so many people, then came to taste of smoke as something nearby burned. A few people had flashlights and oil lamps, so the shelter wasn't completely black, but the dim light played tricks with the shadows. Gradually the rumbles grew less frequent and softer, and then they seemed to stop.

"We need to get out before we suffocate," a nearby man said.

Gerrit had the same concern. It was getting harder and harder to breathe, and the room was growing unpleasantly warm.

"What if more bombers are on their way?" another voice asked.

"What if the building above us is on fire?"

Gerrit's eyes turned toward a ceiling he could barely make out in the murky light. What lay above them? A ruined building? A fire? Or the restaurant, undamaged, waiting for the battle to end so it could reopen?

People shifted toward the stairs. Johan wheezed. Gerrit wasn't sure if it was heart strain, fear, the growing stench of smoke, or simply the overwhelming number of people. Regardless of the wheezing's cause, fresh air was the best solution, so he took his siblings' hands and followed the crowd. But the crowd moved at a glacial pace. An orange glow lit those nearest the exit, but the door seemed very far away.

The building groaned and popped, and somewhere above them, glass shattered. Those on the stairs screamed, and flames flickered in the doorway. Panic turned Gerrit's stomach. If the stairs caught fire, how would anyone escape the basement? Rushing toward the crowd and the flames seemed the logical next step, but pushing through everyone and escaping up the stairs before the fire consumed them seemed impossible.

"Look for another way out," he told his siblings.

The air grew thicker, filled with smoke. He tried to remember how the restaurant was positioned. If the structure was near a canal, one side of the basement might open to the water or an alley. And if there was another exit, it would be on the opposite side of the room from the stairs.

Crashes from above seemed to punctuate each step of their search. Someone shouted. The ceiling creaked ominously in the near darkness. Then something hard pummeled Gerrit on the shoulder, and he fell to the ground, bringing his sister down with him. Nellie screamed. He pulled her under him as the deluge of a collapsing floor poured over him. His body ached with the fury of strikes, and ash and dust choked his throat. Within moments, he and Nellie were buried alive.

He could barely move. Darkness blocked his vision. The air felt too thick to breathe, and panic lapped at him from all sides. He coughed and tried to speak. "Johan?"

He didn't hear an answer, but he doubted his brother had heard his weak voice anyway. A familiar wheezing sounded nearby. Gerrit swallowed and tried to call to his brother again. "Johan, are you all right?"

"Where are you?"

"Under everything."

"We're trapped!" Terror laced Nellie's voice as thoroughly as ash and crumbled plaster choked it.

Gerrit heaved, trying to move something, anything, trying to fight the panic. He pushed a hand free and heard something else shift and give way. One piece at a time. That was what he had to try, and he had to work quickly, before Johan's heart faced too much strain, before the fire caught them, before the rest of the building gave way. Gerrit wasn't strong enough to escape all at once, but bit by bit, he unburied himself and his sister.

At last he could see the hazy, fire-lit room. Only the room was much lighter now because someone else must have found the exit Gerrit had been searching for, and the open doorway seemed to glow. Johan reached for Nellie's hand and pulled her free while Gerrit held the largest piece of rubble off her body. She sobbed as Gerrit crawled from the pile. If she was even half as battered as Gerrit, she was undoubtedly in the worst pain of her life.

They stumbled toward the door. Gerrit had expected the outside air to be better, but when the siblings stepped through the doorway, the pall of smoke was even worse. The sky, though lighter than the dark basement, was shrouded with thick, black billows, and bits of ash and small black debris glowing orange on the edges floated through the air. Bright flames flickered between coiling smoke in buildings to the north. Sticky sweat trickled down Gerrit's neck and under his arms. May felt like July, and it looked . . . He stepped around a building, and his view opened up. Roaring flames raged as far as he could see. It looked like fire and brimstone.

"Where's Mam?" Nellie asked.

Everything looked different, but Gerrit thought he could still find the way home. Yet that would take them closer to the worst of the flames. "She will have gone somewhere safe. And that's what we have to do too."

"Is this what hell looks like?" Johan coughed. In addition to his heart murmur, he had fragile lungs. Mam said it was because he was born too early, and not even Opa had been able to change the way Johan gasped for breath when he overexerted himself. They had to get away from the smoke so Johan could get better air.

Gerrit studied the burning buildings and led his siblings in what he hoped was the safest direction. Johan kept coughing, so Gerrit dug his handkerchief out and helped his brother make a mask of sorts. Maybe it helped, but the coughing didn't stop.

Others rushed past them, but Gerrit hesitated to push Johan too hard. Then, after walking three blocks in what he had assumed was the safest direction, they turned a corner and were surrounded by more burning buildings, all of them creating an inferno that blasted Gerrit with so much heat that even his eyes felt hot. In either direction, flames lapped at the buildings. A home behind them collapsed, and flaming rubble spilled onto the street.

"Run!" Gerrit led Nellie and Johan to the canal, afraid more buildings would implode and trap them in the center of the blaze. The walkway was safe, for now, but the heat was getting worse.

Nellie pointed across the canal. "Only a few of the buildings over there are burning."

Gerrit had become disoriented during their flight. He couldn't name the canal they'd come to, not when all the homes and businesses that lined it were aflame, making the street unrecognizable. The canals in this part of the city were designed for barges, not oceangoing vessels, so they weren't overly wide. Yet it would be deep enough for water traffic, so they'd have to swim rather than wade. Mam had hoped swimming would strengthen Johan's heart and lungs, so Gerrit and Johan had both taken lessons, but that had been years ago, and Nellie had been too young.

Remaining where they were meant all of them would burn to death. Crossing the canal offered a risk of drowning, but of his choices, the canal seemed to give the best chance for survival.

"Can you swim it?" he asked his brother.

Johan nodded, then took off his shoes. "Can you throw them across?"

In six throws, Gerrit tossed all three pairs to the other side.

"Nellie, if you can just float, I'll pull you across," Gerrit said.

Nellie's face showed uncertainty, but after a glance at the fires behind them, she nodded.

Johan pulled off his makeshift mask and jumped into the canal before Gerrit had given him any instructions. His head popped above the water, and he took overhand strokes toward the other side of the canal. The current was light, but it still carried him away from their shoes.

Gerrit wanted to watch to make sure Johan didn't run into any trouble, but even if he did, Gerrit couldn't very well leave Nellie by herself with the burning buildings behind her. Yet he wasn't sure if Johan—or any of them—could climb out once they reached the other side. The gap between the waterline and the top of the canal's embankment was longer than any of their arms and the sides too steep to give their feet any leverage.

Two figures appeared on the other side of the canal, barely visible through the smoke. Gerrit waved and called to them, then pointed to his brother. He doubted his voice carried over the roar of the flames, but the figures—men in uniform, he now saw—seemed to understand. As they approached Johan's destination, Gerrit turned to Nellie. "Hold my hand and don't let go. You understand?"

"Yes."

"Let me guide you. You'll have to get on your back and spread your limbs. Understand?"

She nodded again, but the movement was frantic, panicked. Regardless, they didn't have much time. Gerrit checked on Johan's progress—he was nearing the other bank. Gerrit sat on the edge of the canal and pulled Nellie to sit with him. Dozens of bruises and cuts protested, but hundreds of fires compelled them to act.

"Hold my wrist," he said.

She obeyed, and he held hers in turn.

"Keep your lungs full."

She nodded.

He slid off the embankment, pulling his sister with him. They fell into the water, then bobbed to the surface. The water was cold, a shock after the heat of the flames, but they wouldn't be in it long. Or that was what he thought before Nellie grabbed at him in a panic. She pulled herself closer, trying to climb him to keep her head above water. He tried telling her to lie on her back, but instead, he swallowed a mouthful of water. She wouldn't stop moving, wouldn't relax or release. If she didn't let up, they were both going to die.

None too gently, he pinned both his sister's arms to her side and pulled her against his chest, then kicked to get his head above water. "You have to calm down. Float on your back, flat like a barge."

She whimpered in answer.

"You have to, Nellie. I'm not strong enough otherwise."

He felt her relax just a bit, and he loosened his grip and used a hand to push her into position. "There, keep your hips and legs level with the water. Arms out."

She obeyed, but terror filled her eyes.

Gerrit released her back, and she flailed again, and both of them swallowed water and drifted downstream in the ensuing struggle to stay afloat. When he once again had her on her back, he kept one hand under her shoulders and the other on her wrist. He'd have to kick to the other side because his sister would panic if he let go long enough to use his arms.

The first movement was promising because he pushed off from the canal's side. After that, his kicks seemed to move the two of them barely at all. He inhaled and checked on his sister. Her face was above water, and it wasn't cold enough to worry about exposure, so he could take his time. As long as his hand stayed under Nellie's back, she stayed afloat—not because he was holding her up so much as his hand seemed to assure her that she was safe.

His legs grew tired, and his wrist ached. He made slow progress and drifted with the current. As he neared the opposite bank, one of the soldiers waved him in. The man's uniform was Dutch, not German, which was a relief.

When Gerrit was close enough, the soldier threw one end of his coat to him, keeping the other end in his hand so it could be used like a rope. Gerrit missed the first toss but caught the second, and the soldier pulled him in, then reached down to tug Nellie from the canal. He gave Gerrit his hand next, and though Gerrit tried to use his legs, there was nothing to step on. He wouldn't have made it out of the canal without the man's help.

Johan found them, and the boy clutched all their shoes to his chest. He still coughed, but the air was clearer on this side of the canal.

"Thank you," Gerrit said between gasps. Swimming was hard anyway, harder still when the air was full of smoke.

The man smiled, revealing a crooked front tooth. He towered over Gerrit, but he wore a cadet's uniform, which made Gerrit suspect he was not yet twenty. "Glad you made it."

"Berend, come on," another cadet called.

Berend patted Nellie's wet head, then pointed. "If you continue that way, you should escape the worst of it."

"But our apartment is in the Alkemadeplein. Mam's probably still there." Johan looked around as if uncertain which direction that was.

A sad expression creased Berend's mouth before he seemed to consciously hide it. "Best go somewhere else until the fires are all out. That way is safest." He pointed again.

Despite being wet, Gerrit wasn't cold. He took his shoes from Johan. He wanted to wait until he wasn't dripping before putting them on, but a quick look at the ground covered in ash and broken bits of buildings, including glass, convinced him to put them on at once, and he had his siblings do the same.

"Where will we go?" Johan asked.

"To Tante Francisca." Her apartment was in a different area, probably safe from the fires, and that was where their parents would look, assuming Mam and Pap were still alive.

The sun had long ago set, but fires lit the skyline behind him as Gerrit trudged around a corner and recognized Tante Francisca and Oom Antoon's apartment building. Nellie rode on his back, sniffling every few seconds. Johan walked beside him. He hadn't complained, but his stride had grown slower and slower as they'd made their way from the fires, his steps shorter and shorter. The wheezing hadn't worsened, but nor had it disappeared.

They weren't the only refugees fleeing the fire. Nellie wasn't the only one crying, and Johan wasn't the only one whose emotions seemed frozen in a mask that looked calm at first glance but revealed overwhelming pain if inspected too closely.

"We're almost there." Gerrit hoped his aunt and uncle were in their apartment, because he didn't know where else he and his siblings could go. Their own neighborhood wasn't safe. They had family in Utrecht, Arnhem, Haarlem, Amsterdam, and the Dutch East Indies, but Tante Francisca was the only relative in Rotterdam.

Gerrit was too tired to carry Nellie up the stairs, but she didn't complain when he set her down and took her hand. Hunger twisted his stomach, his eyes burned from smoke, and his clothing that had long been wet still chafed uncomfortably on his skin. Yet relief was only—he hoped—a few flights of stairs away.

When they reached the door and knocked, no sound greeted them in reply. Gerrit tried the door only to find it locked. Johan slid to the ground beside the door, and Nellie soon followed his example. Gerrit wasn't sure what to do. If the building had been evacuated, they shouldn't stay. But he and his siblings were exhausted. He wouldn't be able to get them much farther, so he sat next to them. He would just rest for a while, find a position that didn't hurt his blisters, bruises, or cuts, then go check on the fire to make sure it wasn't approaching this part of Rotterdam.

Falling asleep hadn't been part of Gerrit's plan, but he jerked awake sometime later. Much later, because the window at the end of the hall showed the dim light of approaching dawn. He found himself stretched out in front of the door of his aunt's apartment, with Nellie snuggled next to him and Johan resting with his head against the doorframe.

Voices carried from below. "Gerrit wanted to come with me. I should have let him. Then at least I'd have one of them." The voice was familiar and yet changed. Pap.

"You couldn't have known." Oom Antoon's voice. "I thought the city was surrendering so we could avoid destruction. What's the point in negotiating if the threats are carried out anyway? They should have . . ." Oom Antoon's head came into view, and he met Gerrit's eyes.

Pap appeared next, though he was hard to recognize, covered in soot as he was, with a frown big enough to crack a face in half. Yet the frown softened when he saw Gerrit and the others lying in the hall. "Gerrit?"

Gerrit nodded and stood, slowly, because the hard floor had made all the aches in his body worse.

Pap closed the distance and pulled Gerrit into an embrace, lifting him off the ground in a way that he hadn't done in years. Then something happened that had never happened at all, so long as Gerrit could remember: Pap cried. It started as a shake, then built into a sob.

"I thought you were dead," Pap whispered through his tears, gripping Gerrit as tightly as Nellie had when she'd panicked in the canal. "I thought you were all dead." He released Gerrit only so he could take Johan and Nellie into his arms in turn.

"We've been looking for you all night," Oom Antoon explained. "Francisca, too, but she stayed to help at the hospital." He unlocked his apartment and pushed it open.

"And Mam?" Nellie rubbed her eyes and yawned. "Have you found Mam?"

Both men went quiet. Their eyes met, and Gerrit knew even without words. Oom Antoon had more composure at the moment, so he swallowed and spoke. "I'm afraid your mother won't be coming back."

Nellie looked at the stairs as if she expected Mam to walk up them any moment despite his comment. "She's probably still out looking for us. Or had to go somewhere else until the fires died."

Oom Antoon swallowed. "I'm sorry, Nellie. But we already found your mother."

"Then, where is she?" she asked.

Pap looked like a broken man as he placed a hand on his daughter's shoulders. "She's gone, Nellie. She's gone."

A few days after the official surrender of the Netherlands, Dr. van der Veen brought home a telegram that he'd received at the hospital: his eldest daughter was dead, killed when the Germans had bombed Rotterdam, destroying the entire city center. The rest of her family was homeless.

Ingrid had seen so much tragedy, but that didn't stop her from feeling grief on behalf of the van der Veens. She put an arm around a weeping Anita. "Will the others come stay with you?" Ingrid asked the doctor.

"They would be welcome, but I expect not." Dr. van der Veen sank into a nearby chair. "When Judith married, it wasn't with my approval. She and I reconciled, but her husband has his pride. He forgave me enough to let his wife and children visit. Maybe, eventually, he would have come, but now, with the war on and with Judith gone . . ." He ran a frustrated hand through his hair. "I don't expect he'll reach out very often. He didn't send an address. Doubt he has one yet. A tenth of the city is homeless now."

Anita wiped her eyes. "So we'll lose not just Judith, but also Gerrit and Johan and Nellie?"

Ingrid knew all about loss. Both her parents were dead, and her brother and sister seemed out of reach as long as war raged between Germany and Britain. She had hoped to be back with Karl and Anna by now, and she longed for that, but she expected to see them again. Anita's sister was gone permanently, at least for this life, and now Anita might lose her nephews and niece too.

"I trusted too much in Dutch neutrality." Dr. van der Veen's words were soft, a whisper. "Even when Hitler surprised us and invaded, I didn't think we would fall so swiftly, so completely. Arnhem is near the border, but for them to get past the Grebbe Line and break Fortress Holland so quickly . . ." He shook his head.

No one spoke for a long time. Ingrid couldn't help feeling that the Nazis had caught her for the second time. Would they invade Britain, too, and catch her brother and sister?

"I have patients to check on." The doctor stood.

"Pap . . ." Anita didn't say any more, but tears still streaked her cheeks, and Ingrid could tell that she wanted her father to be with her while she grieved.

In his own grief, he paused for only a moment to give his youngest daughter an embrace. "I'll be back before too long."

"Liar," Anita whispered as he left. "He'll work until he's too tired to feel the pain."

Ingrid understood the doctor's need to distract himself, and she understood Anita's desire for comfort. "Can I make you some tea or something?"

Anita shook her head. "I just want someone to tell me it's all been a nightmare and that I'll wake up again soon."

Ingrid had no such assurance for Anita. She could offer only sympathy and someone to sit beside while Anita grieved.

Ingrid was carrying dirty dishes into the kitchen a few days later when Mevrouw Ruysch, the housekeeper and cook, entered through the kitchen door.

"Good evening," Ingrid said, though she wasn't sure if the *good* part was accurate. The French, British, and Belgian Armies were still fighting the Germans, even after the surrender of the Netherlands, but according to the radio, they weren't winning.

"Evening, Ingrid. Is the doctor home?"

Ingrid shook her head. "He's at the hospital." As Anita had predicted, he was keeping himself busy. Perhaps it helped him process his grief. Regardless, it kept him away from home. Away from Anita as well, who still sat in the dining room, staring at a plate of food she wasn't eating. She'd been like that for days. Usually, she ate something eventually, but she didn't seem to enjoy it.

Mevrouw Ruysch's face was flushed, and she seemed agitated. There were plenty of things to be upset about: the Netherlands had surrendered to the Nazis after a five-day campaign, the Nazis seemed ready to take over most of Western Europe, and no one yet knew how the conquerors would treat the conquered. When the Nazis had taken over Austria, Ingrid had seen few immediate changes, but she thought that was mostly because her father had kept her and her siblings sheltered at Falcon Point. But eventually, the Nazis had taken that haven too.

"I was at the hospital, and they said he'd just left."

As Mevrouw Ruysch spoke, the front door opened.

"Maybe that's him." Ingrid and Mevrouw Ruysch went to see.

Their suspicions were soon proved correct. Dr. van der Veen placed his fedora on the hat rack as the two met him.

"Mevrouw Ruysch, good to see you," he said. She hadn't come by since before the invasion. "Is all well with your family?"

Mevrouw Ruysch bit her lip and shook her head. "You remember my brother, Thomas?"

"Yes, I remember. Working for the general staff, wasn't he?"

Mevrouw Ruysch nodded. "Yesterday, a pair of Germans soldiers came asking about him. I told them he lives in The Hague, but they said he was missing."

"I'm sorry to hear he's missing." Dr. van der Veen tilted his head. "Or maybe not. If he's missing, the Germans can't arrest him."

Mevrouw Ruysch lowered her voice. "They will arrest him if they can find him. And he showed up at my door this morning. I want to help, but I'm terrified that those men will come looking for him again, and my apartment doesn't have any hiding places. But your home—that top floor is a maze. Perfect for hiding someone. And the Germans aren't likely to search your home for my brother, are they?"

The doctor's face grew thoughtful. "Not likely, no." He glanced at Ingrid, then at the doorway into the dining room, where Anita now stood. "But if they did, and if they found him, they might arrest all of us."

Mevrouw Ruysch didn't disagree, but the plea remained on her face.

"Mevrouw Ruysch, will you give me a moment alone with Anita and Ingrid? And, girls, will you join me in my office?"

Ingrid followed the van der Veens into the office. The doctor took his seat, and the girls took theirs. He looked at each of them in turn. "We have the opportunity to help someone." He put his hands together, making a steeple with his fingers. "But before we come to a decision, I want to make sure you both understand the risks. If we hide someone the Nazis wish to arrest, and if they find out, they won't just arrest whomever we're hiding. They could punish us as well. That punishment could be severe."

Ingrid already knew that. Her Papa had said no to an SS officer, and he'd been murdered because of it. "They could kill us."

Anita blinked. "Just for hiding someone?"

"It's possible." Dr. van der Veen shifted in his chair.

"But we can't turn him away," Anita said. "Not when he needs our help."

"Even if it puts your life in danger?" he asked.

Anita shrugged. "You put yourself at risk whenever you work with someone who has an infectious disease. That doesn't stop you."

Dr. van der Veen looked to Ingrid.

"I'm willing to do anything if it will thwart the Nazis." Ingrid crossed her arms. "My Papa always said I needed to do what was right regardless of anything else. Helping someone like this is right."

Dr. van der Veen nodded. "Very well. I'll go tell Mevrouw Ruysch her brother can come by this evening after dark. I suggest the two of you go up to the top floor and find the room with the best access to the drain pipe in case he needs to escape."

CHAPTER 6

August 1944

Gerrit Hendriks hunched his shoulders and turned off the main street to an alley lined with the backs of multistory buildings built close enough to share walls. It had been four years, three months, and thirteen days since the German Army had invaded the Netherlands. Four years of occupation. Four years of fear and want. Four years since his home and most of his city had been destroyed in a firestorm. Four years since his mother had died and his family had come to live with Pap and Tante Francisca's brother in Utrecht.

A lot had happened in four years. Pap had been arrested and sent away after getting involved with the strikes the first winter after the invasion. Oom Nicolaas, Pap's brother, had been taken away two years later because Germany had wanted labor, and they were strong enough to take it. Soon after, Gerrit had joined the resistance. No matter how careful he was, the Nazi occupation meant that each time he ventured outside, he took a risk that he wouldn't return to his aunt and uncle's home.

Gerrit turned into another alley. He still wasn't sure if alleys or main roads were safer. He was more likely to encounter German soldiers on a main road, but he'd also blend in with the rest of the crowd. Fewer people, and fewer Germans, traveled the alleys, but that meant if he did see someone hostile, he was more likely to become their focus.

He meandered along the alley until a nearby clock struck the hour. Then he followed the road along a turn and continued until he reached the main road and crossed the Oudegracht Canal. Not long after, he spotted a newspaper left on a bench and picked it up. Three days old, but it was the only one there, so it had to be the right one. He tucked it under his arm, careful to keep the fold positioned downward.

The hairs on the back of his neck stood on end. He'd been doing this for years, but he still felt the tension every time. Fear wouldn't force him to stop, but he wished it weren't still so potent. He ought to be used to it by now. Or maybe the fear was useful—it kept him sharp, likely to notice anyone watching or following him.

Ten minutes later, he sat on a different bench and pretended to read the paper. When it looked like no one was about, he opened the newspaper to the middle and pocketed the dozen ration coupons that had been left there for him. He wanted to hurry away from the bench, but someone might be watching, so he needed to stay long enough to read an article. He skimmed the words, not really paying attention to their meaning. He was using them as a timer, not as a source of Nazi-approved information.

Today's work had him distributing ration coupons for twelve people who had dived under. People became onderduikers for many reasons: because they were Jewish, because they had the wrong political ideas, because they were the right age to be shipped off to Germany for forced labor. Gerrit wished his father and uncle had become onderduikers before they'd been rounded up and sent away. He missed them. And every day, he was more and more worried that he would either be forced to join them or forced to join the ranks of the onderduikers who depended on the resistance to stay hidden and fed.

When he'd been at the bench long enough, he walked with purpose past street after street of Utrecht's most beautiful buildings. Then he turned into another alley. It wasn't deserted, though the middle-aged woman walking toward him probably wasn't a spy. Just someone going about her business as best she could in the current circumstances. He judged the distance she still had to walk and her current speed. He paused to retie a shoelace that didn't really need adjustment, then slowed his walk to a stroll. A quick glance behind him confirmed the woman had left, and Gerrit took the remaining ten meters to his destination and opened the back door of a flower shop. No one was in the back room. No one ever was, not if he arrived between one and two. He opened a lunch pail set between three others and slipped four ration coupons inside. He didn't know who the lunch pail belonged to or who the lunch pail's owner was hiding. Maybe other members of the resistance. Maybe shot-down airmen. Maybe Jews or Communists.

Gerrit didn't linger. He cracked the door to the alley and made sure no one would see him exit, and then he continued on this way. He had more deliveries to make.

An hour later, Gerrit slipped the last five ration coupons into a bicycle basket between the greens and the bread while he pretended to flirt with the bicycle's owner, a girl of about fifteen. He didn't know the girl's name, and she didn't know his. It was safer that way. She was too young for him anyway, but the way her eyes lingered on his face more and more each time they met . . . Either she didn't mind the age difference, or she was really a Nazi informant, memorizing his features so she could give the Gestapo a detailed description. She giggled and smiled and pushed off, away from the market. That smile—she was a good actress. That or she found the same whispered lines of poetry endearing even after hearing them every week for nearly a year. She was lucky to still have a bicycle. The Germans had been commandeering them for years, but perhaps hers was too small to tempt a German soldier. Even when the Moffen didn't steal bicycles, it was hard to keep them in working condition. Extra parts were hard to come by, and a growing number of people rode on the rims or on wooden blocks because rubber for tires was nearly impossible to procure.

Gerrit should have felt more at ease as he left the market, now that his pockets no longer contained stolen ration coupons. If a member of the Green Police or the Gestapo pulled him aside to search him, he didn't have anything incriminating. But the occupying authorities didn't need evidence of wrongdoing to haul a Dutchman from the streets and send him to a factory in Germany with meager wages, meager food, and meager chances of making it home again.

Gerrit had turned nineteen three months ago, but he looked younger. He would have hated looking younger than his age in other circumstances, but for the time being, he blessed whatever traits had delayed his growth into manhood. Still, he was having to shave more and more frequently, and not even the pitiful rations the Germans set could keep his shoulders from growing broader. Just last month, his aunt had insisted he try on a dozen different pieces of clothing from neighbors, finding the ones that made him look the youngest. They wouldn't be able to do that forever. Some of his contacts in the resistance purposely made themselves look elderly, but he didn't think that would work for him. Those men were already middle-aged, so while looking old took time and effort, it wasn't as much of a stretch. He might have to follow the example of other resistance men and dress as a woman. He'd make an ugly woman, but maybe that was just as well. German soldiers sometimes harassed ugly women, but the pretty ones received far more of their attention.

Gerrit walked several blocks, then circled around one to make sure no one was following him. When he was certain he had no tail, he crossed the canal again and made his way toward his aunt's flat.

One block away, Tante Petronella met him. She took his arm and pulled him off the road, into a bakery.

"What is it?" he whispered.

Tante Petronella's face had been wary on the street, but she smiled brightly at the baker. "Three of your cheap loaves, please."

Gerrit hadn't any idea what his aunt was up to, but he knew better than to ask more questions in front of the baker and his other customers. Tante Petronella had her shopping bag with her. Perhaps the meeting was coincidental.

His aunt gave the baker the appropriate coins and ration coupons, then motioned for Gerrit to pick up the loaves for her. She sometimes had Gerrit accompany her when shopping so he could carry her purchases, but the loaves weren't heavy. She could have easily carried them herself. She led Gerrit through the bakery's back door. Both of them checked each direction to make sure there weren't others about who might overhear.

"Why did you buy three loaves at once?" Everything was rationed—three loaves of bread would need to last almost a week. Occupation bread, a significant downgrade from the prewar days, was best when fresh, so it made far more sense to buy it as the family ate it rather than all on the same day.

Tante Petronella looked around again. "Klaas's brother was arrested."

Gerrit almost dropped the bread. Klaas was his best friend, and Klaas's brother, Niels, was the leader of their resistance cell. He'd set Gerrit's route to distribute the stolen ration coupons, and though he hadn't let Klaas or Gerrit join him yet, he also worked with a group who assassinated Dutch collaborators. "Are you sure?"

"Certain. Klaas came to warn you, but he couldn't wait. Niels must have talked, because they arrested three others today. Everyone they haven't caught yet is going underground."

Gerrit swallowed hard. Niels knew all about Gerrit's work, so if he had cracked under interrogation, the Nazis had all the evidence they needed to arrest Gerrit too. He hadn't been involved in the plots to kill Dutch traitors, but dealing with stolen ration coupons was enough to get him deported. "Where will Klaas go?"

His aunt shook her head. "He didn't say. It's better that I don't know. It would have been better still if you hadn't gotten mixed up in all this in the first place." Her tone changed as she ended her remarks, but Gerrit didn't think it was anger. It was fear.

They'd had this discussion before. Tante Petronella wanted to play it safe, but Gerrit couldn't stand by and do nothing. "You didn't see what they did to Rotterdam."

"I didn't have to see it to know that they could do the same thing to Utrecht, and I have four children to think of."

"I'm not a child anymore."

His aunt sighed. "You might not be a child anymore, but you're not a man yet either. Not that your age will earn you any mercy from the Nazis. You'll have to leave Utrecht so they don't find you."

Gerrit nodded. He didn't want to leave Utrecht. That meant leaving his brother, sister, cousin, and aunt. But he'd known this day might come. "I'll go home and pack, then I'll head out early enough to make it to the countryside before curfew."

Tante Petronella placed a hand on his shoulder. "You can't come back to the flat. They might be watching it. And a suitcase would look suspicious. Here." She took the shopping bag from her shoulder and handed it to him. "The bread is for your journey. I've put some cheese and soused herring in the bag along with socks and underthings. I wish I could send you with more, but there's not a lot of time, and the other children need food too."

Gerrit took the bag and added the bread. That explained why she had bought so much at once. She'd bought it for him.

She pulled thirty guilders from her pocket. "Again, I wish it were more."

"I understand." Her husband was gone, and so was Gerrit's Pap. Tante Petronella had her own son, a niece, and two nephews—one nephew now—to feed. "You'll take good care of Johan and Nellie?"

She nodded. "Like they are my own."

Gerrit hadn't needed to ask. She'd been caring for all of them as if they were her own since the moment his family had arrived from Rotterdam, motherless and needing a place to stay. "I don't suppose I can tell them goodbye."

Her face softened. "I had Nellie wait near the watchmaker's shop in case you came home from the other direction. Go find her, and I'll send Johan with your bicycle. Don't tell any of us where you're going. I assume you have friends in the resistance who can help you. Or someone from your mother's family. She never lived in Utrecht, so I don't think the Gestapo will make the connection. She had several brothers, didn't she?"

Gerrit nodded. Five brothers, one half sister. Scattered across the Netherlands and across the world. Two of the brothers had been working in the Dutch East Indies when the war had broken out. One was a sailor. Oom Cas lived in Amsterdam, and Oom Aart lived in Haarlem—or at least, they had, if they hadn't been shipped to Germany like Pap. Mam's half sister and father lived in Arnhem. Gerrit hadn't heard from any of them in years, not since before the war, but he thought he remembered how to get from the Arnhem train station to Opa's home, and if Opa still worked in the hospital, that was even easier to find.

Utrecht to Arnhem. How far was that? Sixty kilometers? Seventy? With a good bicycle, it wouldn't be too difficult. He wouldn't have a good bicycle, but even one without tires ought to take him there by morning.

Tante Petronella pulled him into a hug and held him tightly. "I wish you didn't have to go. But I'd rather this than have you arrested or have you taken in a roundup. The Nazis are losing. The war will be over soon, and then you can come back. I would tell you to lie low and be careful in the meantime, but you've too much of your father in you for that."

She released him. He knew he needed to dart down the alley and circle around to where Nellie waited, but his throat suddenly felt tight. Niels was probably being tortured, Klaas was on the run, and Gerrit felt as if he were abandoning his aunt just when he was finally old enough to help her keep the other children fed and clothed. "Thank you, Tante Petronella. And I'm sorry."

She blinked and sniffed. "You come back to me when it's safe, Gerrit."

"I will."

She wiped her eyes, turned, and walked away. Gerrit's feet felt stuck to the pavement, but the sight of a Green Policeman reminded him that now wasn't the time to feel sorry for himself. He would have had to leave soon anyway, simply because he was growing taller. He had good memories of Arnhem. He just wished he didn't have to leave the rest of his family behind to go there.

He walked away from the Green Policeman and took the first turn he could. After passing a few businesses, he stopped in front of a tailor's shop to check the reflection in the glass panes. The policeman didn't seem to be following him. Good. German soldiers were dangerous—they were well-trained, and while they'd spoken of Dutch-German brotherhood in the early days of the occupation, that had quickly turned to condescension toward the local population. But the Green Policemen—some of them Dutchmen working with the Nazis—were harder to get past. They knew the cities they patrolled, seemed able to smell lies, and had given their loyalty wholly to the Nazis.

Nellie sat on the stoop of a candle shop across the street from the watchmaker's. She noticed him as he crossed the street toward her and sprang to her feet. Though twelve, she looked younger. He hoped, for Nellie's sake, that the Germans would be long gone before she stopped looking like a child. Guilt flashed through his chest. If he went into hiding, he wouldn't be able to protect her. But he couldn't protect her anyway, not really. Interference with a German soldier, even one committing a crime, would earn Gerrit an arrest or death. The best thing he could do for Nellie was find a way to end the German occupation of the Netherlands. He could no longer do that in Utrecht. He'd have to find a way to do it in Arnhem.

She practically ran to him, and he held a hand out to slow her down. Her frown showed hurt.

When she was closer, he explained, "Too much exuberance might cause suspicion."

Nellie nodded. "Niels was arrested. Tante Petronella says you can't come home, or you might get arrested too."

"I know. She found me."

Tears welled in Nellie's eyes. "First Mam. Then Pap. Now you."

For his siblings, Gerrit would be one more person taken away—in his case, driven away—by the Nazis. He put a hand on Nellie's shoulder and walked her back to the stoop where she'd been sitting before. "I'm leaving now so that I can come back when the war ends."

"And how long will that be?"

Gerrit wished he knew. "The Allies are going to win. I'm sure of it." They were fighting in France now. If the Nazis lost as swiftly as they'd won four years ago, his trip to Arnhem might be only a month. "You'll be good for Tante Petronella?"

"Yes. But I'll miss you."

Gerrit shifted the grocery bag. "I'll miss you too. But it won't be for long."

"Where will you go?"

He almost told her. She'd been only eight the last time they'd visited Opa Christiaan and Tante Anita, but she would remember them. Yet if she knew, she might tell someone. It was better for him to disappear and leave no trace. He just hoped that if the Gestapo or Green Police questioned his family, they would believe that Gerrit had gone underground without telling them anything. "I can't say. Somewhere safe. Away from Utrecht."

Johan appeared not long after. He was fourteen, but like his siblings, he looked younger. The bicycle he rode was too big for him. Not Gerrit's. Tante Petronella's. Johan struggled for breath as he stopped beside Gerrit and Nellie. "She said this bicycle was better."

It was. Despite its age, it still had tires that had been patched only three or four times each. Gerrit had outgrown his bicycle a few years ago, though he still rode it, even without tires. Finding another would have been almost impossible, even if he had the money for it, which he didn't.

"She's giving me her bicycle?" Parting with a bicycle in times like these meant a sacrifice comparable to parting with a wedding ring.

Johan nodded and took off the jacket he wore—Gerrit's, a hand-me-down from Oom Nicolaas—and handed it over. Underneath, Johan wore a second, the one Gerrit had left in Arnhem during his last visit there. Anita had sewn the tear and mailed it to him. She'd also left a few guilders in the pocket. Not enough to attract attention but enough for Gerrit to take Johan and Nellie to the candy store.

Johan swiped the hair off his forehead. "It's hot wearing two coats, but Tante Petronella thought you might need something warm."

Gerrit nodded. He would, if he traveled at night or if the war lasted longer than a few more months. "Thank you." He gripped the bike. "And tell Tante thank you too."

"Who will take care of . . . ?" Johan trailed off and glanced at their little sister. "Who will take care of what you were doing?"

Gerrit shook his head. He didn't know who would pick up the ration coupons and deliver them from now on. He had four routes he did on four different days, distributing enough coupons to feed sixty people. He didn't want sixty people to starve, but the consequences for them were better if he disappeared than if he were arrested and broken. Maybe Klaas had told the right people, and they'd arrange something different. "Something will work out." He wouldn't be the first courier forced into hiding without warning.

"I could take over."

Johan looked young enough to be dismissed by the authorities, young enough that he wouldn't be rounded up and sent to work in Germany. But Gerrit didn't think Johan was ready. He trusted too easily. Wasn't aware of his surroundings. Got distracted far too frequently on his way home from school. How would he maintain the strict timeline the deliveries depended on?

"Not now." Gerrit kept his voice a whisper. "They might be watching our family. If they followed you around, it would lead them . . ." Gerrit glanced at Nellie, then back at Johan. He didn't need to elaborate on how many people might be drawn into the Nazi net if someone were to follow Johan on Gerrit's old route. "You'll probably be under surveillance for a while, and even if that isn't true, I don't have time to explain it all to you. I have to go. The three of us standing here might make someone suspicious."

Johan frowned. "We look like siblings. That's hardly suspicious."

Gerrit studied his brother and sister. Nellie's braids were lighter than Gerrit's and Johan's sandy-brown hair, and Johan's eyes were a more vibrant blue, but the family resemblance was hard to miss. "True enough. But I need to get out of town before curfew."

Nellie threw herself at him and wrapped her arms around his waist. "Be careful, Gerrit."

"Of course I'll be careful. You look after this rascal, eh?" He motioned to Johan.

Nellie nodded.

"I'll be back soon." Gerrit kept his voice low. "The Nazis are losing."

Johan seemed less inclined for an affectionate goodbye. He probably resented being told he couldn't step into Gerrit's shoes and deliver ration coupons for onderduikers. Gerrit extended his hand instead. Something more grown-up. That Johan took without hesitation.

"You'll be the man of the house now. I'm depending on you to take care of everyone."

Tante Petronella would be the one taking care of everyone, and they both knew that, but Johan stood a little straighter and didn't resist when Gerrit pulled him in for a quick hug.

Gerrit climbed onto his aunt's bicycle and headed off. Before he turned the corner, he paused and looked back. Nellie and Johan stood side by side, watching him go. He was going to miss them. As the oldest, he'd felt they were his responsibility from the moment of Pap's arrest. But staying would endanger them, and he couldn't sit out the war—more than anything, he wanted the Nazis defeated and driven from the Netherlands. If separation from the rest of his family was part of the price, he would have to pay it. He gave them a final wave, then rode out of sight.

Rupert Altbauer glanced around Arnhem Centraal. He had almost made it to the Netherlands back in 1940, but his unit had been farther to the south during the campaigns of that spring. Now he could add one more country to the list of places he'd seen, this time without the danger and destruction of a battle to mar it. Occupation duty ought to be a picnic in comparison to the Eastern Front. He stretched his right leg. It was always stiff when he sat too long. Ached when he stood too long. Was pure agony when he overexerted himself. But he was a twenty-two-year-old soldier, not a sixty-something-year-old pensioner. He would not complain. If not for the wound to his leg, he would be dead or in a Soviet prison camp along with the rest of the German Sixth Army.

Though a soldier, a leutnant now, he wore civilian clothing. He wasn't sorry to see the end of his active campaigning days. Intelligence work, according to Onkel Wilhelm, was just the thing for a curious young man with the wisdom that came from battlefield experience and the ambition to make his mark on the world. Sometimes Onkel Wilhelm seemed more intent on Rupert's making a mark on the world than Rupert, but he was grateful that his uncle had arranged a new position. Rupert could have been happy on indefinite convalescent leave with his mother, stepfather, and Heidi, his three-year-old half sister, but the Fatherland was at war. Rupert needed to do his part.

Dawn came early in the Netherlands during the summer, so full sunlight lit the streets as he followed directions to local SD headquarters. With each block, he liked Arnhem more and more. The buildings all looked so tidy, so welcoming. Intelligence headquarters wasn't marked, so it looked like all the other buildings, but when he entered, a guard in a Waffen SS uniform met him.

"I've been told to report to Hauptmann Denhart," Rupert said.

"Identification?"

Rupert handed over his papers.

"Right this way, Leutnant Altbauer."

Rupert followed the guard through a corridor and into a room with a dozen desks manned by a mix of men in uniforms and plainclothes. A few pecked away at typewriters, and someone spoke into a telephone. Others looked through files or listened intently to something via headphones. The guard led Rupert to a closed door and knocked firmly.

"Enter," a voice said from inside.

The guard opened the door and saluted. "Leutnant Altbauer is here, Hauptmann Denhart."

A few seconds later, a hauptmann strolled through the doorway.

Rupert saluted. "Leutnant Altbauer reporting for duty, sir."

The hauptmann motioned for him to stand at ease. "Thank you, Jung. You may return to your post. Welcome to the Netherlands, Leutnant Altbauer."

"Thank you, sir."

"Let's get you settled." Hauptmann Denhart led Rupert to a desk along the outer edge of the enormous room. "Fresh from the Eastern Front, are you?"

"Not quite, sir. I spent most of last year in convalescence, then I was processing recruits until my uncle suggested I try intelligence."

"Obersturmbannführer Sauermann is your uncle?"

"Yes, sir."

"Did he tell you what we do?"

"No, sir."

Hauptmann Denhart perched on the edge of the desk and motioned for Rupert to take the chair. "Perhaps that's just as well because our focus shifts. As does our chain of command."

Rupert nodded. He assumed this office had once been part of Abwehr, but Abwehr had been folded into the SD after the failed plot to assassinate Hitler the month before.

"Our battles also shift," Denhart continued. "In theory, we are assigned counterintelligence, working against enemy agents. That includes any Dutch troublemakers with foreign connections, and don't let the Gestapo tell you otherwise. That's one of our battles—keeping our jurisdiction."

"I see, sir." Rupert didn't really. Weren't the Gestapo, the Kriminalpolizei, and the Sicherheitsdienst all on the same side?

"Most of our associates are ever eager to stamp out our enemies. I assume your uncle is the same way."

"Yes, sir."

"Our priority, however, is defeating our adversaries."

"Isn't that the same thing?"

Hauptmann Denhart shook his head. "Not quite, and that's your first lesson. What would you do if, say, you captured an English agent who had parachuted into the Dutch countryside?"

"Arrest him, interrogate him, and execute him as a spy when we've learned all we can from him."

Denhart's foot swung gently back and forth along Rupert's desk. "You could do it that way, I suppose. And then what?"

"Well, we might gain useful intelligence, and we would prevent the man from sending his reports to the enemy."

"What if, instead, you offer the man a deal? His life, perhaps, for a bit of cooperation. Learn his codes. Tell his friends back in England that all is well—so well, in fact, that he needs more friends to parachute in and help him gather all the information so readily available?"

"I suppose, if he went for the deal, that would be helpful."

"Yes. When we were still part of Abwehr, we managed to convince the British to send us some fifty agents that way. We greeted them as friends, pretended to be their allies. It's amazing what a new agent will say when he thinks he's speaking to associates. We couldn't keep a ruse like that up indefinitely, of course, but we usually kept it up long enough for them to send in reports of safe arrival. Then it was a simple enough matter to take over their next reports."

Telling the enemy what they wanted them to hear rather than what their agents had been sent to find. The possibilities swirled through Rupert's head. It was extraordinary. "That many, and you controlled all of them?"

Hauptmann Denhart shook his head. "Not all. But no one expects every agent to arrive safely. It would have been suspicious if they all had."

"For how long?"

"About a year and a half. The British, unfortunately, are not completely without intelligence. It couldn't last forever, but while it did . . ."

Eighteen months of capturing enemy agents and not only apprehending them but using them to send false intelligence to the enemy. Eighteen months of controlling the enemy's information. "It sounds marvelous, sir."

"Indeed, it was. But our focus has shifted. Lately we've seen a rise in sabotage. Thwarting that is our main objective now. So tell me, Leutnant Altbauer. If you were to see a man doing something that clearly marked him as a foreigner—looking the wrong direction when he crossed the road, as if he were back in England, or grabbing a cigarette like an American instead of like a Dutchman—what would you do?"

Five minutes ago, Rupert would have suggested arresting the man and questioning him. If he were innocent, they could release him. But now that he knew the possibilities . . . "I would follow him, sir, at a safe distance. See where he went, who he met, where he lived."

Denhart nodded. "You're a fast learner, Altbauer. I think you'll do just fine here."

CHAPTER 7

Ingrid carried a pile of breakfast dishes into the van der Veen kitchen and set them in the sink next to the ones she'd already brought in. Breakfast had been late because several of the home's occupants had been up most of the night.

A casual knock sounded on the outside door leading into the kitchen, and then the door pulled open. A young man appeared on the other side, about her height, with light-brown hair and pale-blue eyes. Wrinkled civilian clothing and dirt-smudged hands made her wonder when he had last bathed. Something about him seemed familiar, but she couldn't quite place him. A neighbor perhaps? Regardless, that didn't give him the right to enter the kitchen uninvited.

"Who are you?" Ingrid spoke loudly so the onderduikers in the dining room, a British pilot and a Jewish man, would hear her and sneak away before the stranger saw them. The other illegal residents of the van der Veen home were already upstairs. Everyone, onderduikers and more permanent residents, took turns watching the street by the front entrance when the group came to the ground level, but this man had come to the side of the house, so it was doubtful that the lookout had seen him.

The intruder's face grew wary. "Who are you?"

Politeness dictated that he ought to answer her before asking his own questions, but the longer Ingrid stalled him, the longer the onderduikers would have to hide in the home's upper level and attic. "I live here."

Confusion showed in his pinched eyes. "Isn't this Dr. van der Veen's home?"

"It is. If you wish to see him, you can find him at the hospital."

"Where's Mevrouw Ruysch? Are you the new cook?"

Ingrid took her turns cooking, but she wasn't hired help. Her clothing was ordinary, and she stood beside a sink full of dirty dishes, so maybe she could forgive his confusion. Maybe. "Mevrouw Ruysch hasn't worked here for years." Her grandbabies needed her help, and between Anita, Ingrid, and the onderduikers, there were plenty of people capable of preparing the ever-diminishing rations.

"Is Anita still here?"

Ingrid tried to pinpoint how he knew so much about the home's residents, past and present. Maybe he'd been spying on them. A quick conversation with a few neighbors could have supplied the right names. The Germans paid a bounty on onderduikers, and plenty of unscrupulous Dutchmen and -women made a living by turning the hiders over to the enemy. Ingrid and the van der Veens tried to be so careful with the people they hid, but it would take only one neighbor seeing a light on at the wrong time or mentioning that the curtains in the home were almost always closed to spark suspicion.

On the other hand, Anita had more contacts in the resistance than Ingrid did because she coordinated intelligence from multiple agents, then wrote reports for transmission to Britain. Could this be one of Anita's associates? Ingrid couldn't trust the man, but she couldn't really turn him away either. "Anita is at the hospital."

"Is she ill?" The man seemed genuinely worried.

"She works there."

"I thought all the nurses were nuns from Germany."

The man was either a well-informed spy, or he was a local. He might be both. "She helps with the paperwork." Or at least, that was what she and Dr. van der Veen—Opa, as Ingrid had been calling him for years—told everyone. In reality, most of Anita's work was for the resistance. It was easier, less suspicious for people to come and go from a hospital. Agents could dress as delivery boys and bring their reports to her. Onderduikers could claim they were ill and show up in her office, where she could coordinate sheltering them or smuggling them out of the country.

The man glanced around the kitchen. Was he noticing how many dishes weren't clean? She'd just told him Opa and Anita were at the hospital, so that would imply the dishes in the sink had been used either by someone else, or they had been dirtied over several meals. Only a very poor housekeeper in the Netherlands would let dishes from multiple meals pile up. Yet his expression didn't portray suspicion, just a weariness that seemed to sink in deep.

"May I wash my hands and face before I go looking for them in the hospital? I ran into a bit of trouble with my bicycle." He held out a hand.

Ingrid had noticed some of the dirt, but there was a large smear on his palm, and it looked like it wasn't just mud. Blood, too, soiled his skin. She didn't see an injury serious enough to need a doctor, but she wouldn't call his bluff. She nodded toward the sink and fetched a clean towel for him. Then she grabbed the broomstick and held it beside her just in case the spy planned to escalate from washing his hands to searching the home.

He glanced at the broom, then turned his eyes on her. "Planning to hit me with that?"

Ingrid felt her face grow warm. "Only if you give me reason to."

He turned the water on and felt the temperature. "I just want to clean up before I head to the hospital."

Ingrid didn't reply but studied him while he washed. He had a straight nose, clear skin. Maybe he used his boyish good looks when chatting up gossipy housewives to find out if they'd seen anything suspicious in their neighbors' homes.

He finished, eyed the broom again, and tucked the towel into the basket in the cupboard under the sink. "Thank you, mejuffrouw. I'll continue my search at St. Elisabeth's."

He let himself out the door, and Ingrid peeked after him to make sure he really left. He hadn't gone far before bending over to pet the dog. Anjing normally hated strangers. How had the spy duped the Keeshond into trusting him? Perhaps he'd brought him a scrap of meat on a previous visit to watch the house. Sneaky. Food was scarce enough that it wouldn't take much to impress Anjing. Ingrid whistled, and the dog came running, more than happy to be let inside. The man stood. A deep frown lined his face, and his brow pulled in what looked like anger. Maybe she should have let him play with the dog instead of making an enemy. But Anjing was supposed to warn them when strangers arrived, not lap up attention as if he hadn't been given plenty earlier in the day.

The man stalked off. When he was out of sight, Ingrid bolted the door.

She glanced around the kitchen. How had the man known where to put the dirty towel? She'd lived in this house since 1940, and she'd never seen him before. Could he be one of Mevrouw Ruysch's relatives? But that didn't make sense, because he would have known she no longer worked here. He must have been spying on them for a long time. Long enough to win over Anjing and learn their routines, down to where dirty kitchen towels were kept between wash days. That was no small intelligence coup when the kitchen curtains were open only when all the onderduikers were upstairs. She glanced through the window, into the back garden. Had the man been watching her or Anita cook from one of the neighboring homes?

She inhaled and exhaled deeply several times. The onderduikers needed to be warned, maybe moved, though that would have to wait until nightfall. Ingrid parted the curtains on several windows throughout the bottom level of the house, looking for anything suspicious, but everything seemed normal outside other than a bicycle left to the side of the house. The Germans had commandeered too many Dutch bicycles to leave them in plain sight, so Anita, Opa, and Ingrid had long ago started putting their bicycles in the cellar. She supposed the bicycle belonged to the intruder, and that meant he was coming back.

She climbed the two flights of steps to the home's top floor, then tugged on the rope to bring down the ladder from the attic. "It's clear," she called up.

The five onderduikers climbed down: a British pilot, a Jewish couple, and two members of the resistance, one recovering from a gunshot wound, both wanted by the Gestapo.

"Someone came asking for the doctor and Anita. It might be nothing, but he knew an awful lot about the home and the family. I don't know him, so I think we ought to keep a thorough watch until we learn more." She repeated her words in English for the sake of the pilot. Ingrid's nanny had been British, and with her parents' encouragement, each of the Lang children had learned English. One of the resistance men, Petrus, organized the watch. Ingrid went back to the kitchen. Should anyone return to search the home, she didn't want the pile of dishes giving away the fact that far more people lived in the home than were registered.

Of all the days to have a suspicious visitor. She shook her head while she scrubbed. Tonight she had planned to take three of the onderduikers to the next home in the line, but if the van der Veen house was under suspicion, she ought to move all five of them. They didn't have enough bicycles for that, and without bicycles, they'd have to leave earlier. But so many people might see if they set out during daylight. Waiting until dark would be better, but without bicycles, they'd be late for their rendezvous. Should she go early and risk being seen? Or go after dark and risk missing Cornelis? Whichever choice she made, it seemed that the sandy-haired intruder had ruined her day.

Gerrit paused before St. Elisabeth Hospital and glanced at his hand. He'd cut it while trying to repair a spoke. Just a small cut. Nothing to worry about, but perhaps an excuse if he needed one to see Opa. He didn't dare use his real name lest a diligent German intelligence officer make a connection between Gerrit Hendriks, wanted for questioning in Utrecht, and Gerrit Hendriks, looking for his grandfather in Arnhem.

He'd never actually been inside the hospital, so he hadn't a clue where he might find a specific doctor or a specific clerk. But visiting the home hadn't worked, not with that suspicious housekeeper, or whoever she was. He'd thought her attractive at first glance, but she'd instead proven hostile and petty enough to keep him from Anjing. At least the dog had remembered him, even if, in the end, he'd obeyed the woman rather than Gerrit.

Gerrit scanned the street in front of the hospital, then went inside. He asked the first uniformed nun he saw for Dr. van der Veen, and she directed him to a waiting room. He sat, and drowsiness soon pulled at him. He'd cycled long into the night after leaving Utrecht, until he'd been so tired he couldn't keep his eyes open. He'd slept a few hours in a barn, then been up at first light. The ride that morning should have been shorter, but the broken spoke—and his attempt to repair it without proper tools—had slowed him. He didn't normally have trouble with bicycle repairs, but bad luck had hounded him all morning.

He stood so he wouldn't fall asleep. Not long after, Anita entered the room and scanned those waiting. Her eyes stopped on him for several long seconds. Gerrit smiled but waited for her to lead. She might prefer something more discreet than the jubilant hug he wanted to give her. She was twenty now. He hadn't seen her in more than four years, but she hadn't changed all that much. She was less curvy and more willowy, and her hair was neater, yet her face was the same.

"Follow me, please." Her tone was courteous but not overly warm as she motioned to him. Maybe she hadn't recognized him. He walked behind her down a hall, then down a flight of stairs into the basement. She turned a corner, glanced around to see that they were alone, then stopped. "Gerrit?"

He nodded and felt a grin growing across his face.

She flung her arms around him and pulled him in for an embrace. He was taller than her now. Goodness, it had been a long time.

She released him and punched him playfully in the arm. "Not a single letter or telephone call for four years and you just show up again?"

"Didn't Pap send word when we moved?"

"He told us that Judith died and the entire neighborhood was destroyed, but he didn't say where he was taking you, and he never wrote to us again. And you never wrote either. We didn't know if you were dead or alive."

"Everything in the flat burned: all my letters, the address book. I couldn't remember your house number, and I've never lived in a house with a telephone." Pap had sent a telegram to the hospital, but telegrams were too expensive for social use, especially during a war.

"Nellie and Johan?"

"Fine, as of yesterday. We've been living in Utrecht with Tante Petronella."

"Petronella?"

The two sides of his family had never met. "My father's brother's wife. Oom Nicolaas was sent to Germany in one of the roundups two years ago. And Pap was arrested after the strikes in 1941. We haven't seen or heard of him since."

Sympathy lined Anita's face. "I'm sorry. I'll pray that he returns when the war is over."

Gerrit had almost forgotten that Anita and Opa were even more religious than his mother had been. He wasn't sure how anyone could believe in God in this day and age. Hadn't Anita read about all the awful things men had done in the name of religion throughout history? But he didn't want to talk about that now. "We hope we'll see him again."

"Did you bring Johan and Nellie with you?"

He shook his head and lowered his voice. "I got into a bit of trouble. I needed a new place to live, and with Mam dead, Tante Petronella didn't think they'd trace me to you."

"What type of trouble?"

He wouldn't have come to Arnhem if he didn't trust Tante Anita and Opa Christiaan completely, but now that he had to explain, it was hard to break a habit of secrecy and caution. "One of my associates in the resistance was arrested. They got him to talk, and now they're looking for me. But in Utrecht, not in Arnhem."

Anita gave him half a smile. "Pap won't turn you away. But if you were hoping to stay out of trouble, that might be harder than planned."

"If by 'trouble' you mean 'doing something to defeat the Nazis,' then I want to be right in the middle of it."

Anita's smile faded.

"What?" Had he misinterpreted her words?

She shook her head. "I'm not sure if that means you've grown up or if that means you're still a boy."

He scoffed. "I grew up a long time ago, when Nazi bombs destroyed my city and took my mother." He crossed his arms. "What type of things are you involved in?" There were a great many resistance groups throughout the Netherlands, but they weren't all the same. Niels's group had assassinated Dutch traitors. Other groups hid onderduikers. Still others sabotaged German military installations or gathered intelligence.

"It's better not to discuss it here."

"I tried going to the house, but the woman in the kitchen wasn't very welcoming." The old housekeeper would have offered him something to eat instead of standing guard over him with a broom while he did something as basic as wash his hands.

"Which woman?"

"Blonde. Blue eyes." He would have called them sky blue at first, but now he thought a frigid, glacial blue a better description. "About our age."

"Ingrid?"

"Who?"

"You didn't recognize her? The last time you were here, you found her by the train track with a pair of broken legs. But I suppose that was four years ago, and she was covered in mud."

"The spy from Austria?" Now he remembered. Ingrid, with multiple passports, expensive jewelry, and a host of secrets she hadn't wanted to share with him.

Anita shook her head. "She's not a spy, not for the Nazis, anyway. You just thought she might be. And I suppose she didn't recognize you after all this time."

"No. Threatened me with a broom while I washed my hands. Why is she still here?"

"She couldn't travel with two broken legs, and by the time the casts were removed and we arranged for her to go on to London, the war had started. She was stuck."

"But she's still living with you and Opa?"

"She didn't have anywhere else to go."

"Well, I hope she's been kinder to you than she was to me."

Anita gave him a full smile. "Ingrid is like a sister and a best friend all rolled into one. If she gave you a hard time, it's probably because she was afraid you would search the house and find something you shouldn't."

"Like what?"

Their entire conversation had been spoken in hushed tones, but now Anita lowered her voice even more. "Onderduikers. Once we add you, we'll have six."

When Gerrit returned to the house that evening with Opa and Anita, Ingrid waited, and she still looked at him with suspicion. He wondered if she'd practiced that look: head tilted, eyes narrowed, mouth held tight.

Anita went to stand beside Ingrid. "You might not remember him, but this is my nephew Gerrit. He was visiting the day you broke your legs, and now he's back."

Now that Gerrit knew who she was, curiosity about how the breaks had healed drew his eyes to the skin showing below her skirt, but now wasn't the time. She might think he was looking for other reasons. He forced his eyes to stay on her face rather than on her legs. "I apologize for not recognizing you earlier," he said.

"I supposed I owe you the same apology."

She hadn't actually apologized, and her face hadn't softened, but he wouldn't press it. "I thought you didn't speak Dutch." He still remembered the awkward conversation he'd attempted with her in German, yet when she'd spoken in the kitchen, he hadn't even noticed an accent. She didn't sound like she was from Rotterdam, but no one did, other than the people who had lived there. Like most of the Dutch, her dialect sounded a bit softer, but it hadn't sounded foreign.

"I've had four years to learn," she said.

"And a most diligent student she's been." Opa removed his hat and placed it on the rack near the door. "You'll have plenty of time to hear her. But first, Gerrit, you ought to pull your bicycle into the cellar before it's stolen by a thief or a soldier with a requisition order."

Ingrid's nose tilted up. "I suppose if Gerrit is family, there's no need to change tonight's plans."

"No." Opa smiled. "You can tell them all to come out of hiding. Gerrit can be trusted with everything that happens in this home."

Ingrid headed for the stairs, and as she walked up, Gerrit gave in to curiosity and studied the lower part of her anatomy. Four years later, her legs showed no sign of having been broken, and her stride showed a flair unhampered by any lasting injury. Indeed, he couldn't remember the last pair of legs that were so attractive. How unfortunate that they went with a woman who was quickly proving herself absolutely infuriating.

Anita raised an eyebrow at him. No doubt she'd caught him staring.

"It looks as if the train incident left no lasting damage." Gerrit hoped that would explain it away without him sounding overly defensive. "I'll go see to my bicycle."

Gerrit tried to relax in Opa's dining room after supper finished, but it was hard. The last time he'd been here, Mam had still been alive, Pap had been at work instead of missing, and the Netherlands had been free. Gerrit hadn't been running from the Gestapo, and Anjing's favorite place had been beside him. Now the Keeshond sat with Ingrid, who petted the dog absently while she nodded at something the onderduiker woman said.

The Austrian seemed to have integrated herself firmly into his family. She and Anita had chatted nonstop from the time he'd come into the kitchen after hiding his bicycle until the meal had been served. Opa, too, seemed comfortable with her. Gerrit hoped their trust wasn't misplaced. Plenty of Dutch men and women were turning in their neighbors either because they believed the Nazi lies or because they wanted the bounty on onderduikers. Trusting a girl from Austria when he couldn't trust people who had lived their entire lives in the Netherlands felt wrong, but if he were going to live with Opa and Anita, he had to trust them, and that meant trusting their judgment too. Perhaps Ingrid had really owned all that jewelry in her knapsack because she was wealthy, and maybe she thought she was better than all the Nazis, and that was why she didn't want to work for the Germans.

"Do you think it's safe for Gerrit to be seen?" Anita asked Opa. "It's not so strange for someone to move in with relatives. We could stick with the truth: that his home was destroyed in an air raid, and keep the details of when and by whom a secret."

Opa, sitting next to Gerrit, turned to study him. "If someone asks, we can tell the truth, that he's my grandson. And in that case, you ought to know that Ingrid is your second cousin once removed."

Gerrit glanced at Ingrid. "What?"

"I've told people that she's my cousin's daughter. Her paperwork has van der Veen listed as her surname, and she's called me Opa ever since."

"How did you manage that?" Forgeries were expensive, and for a nom de plume to hold over the course of four years without anyone discovering her real identity seemed too good to be true.

A conspiratorial smile appeared on Opa's face. "I've treated a man a few times when he's been indisposed due to . . . ah, less-than-flattering decisions on his part. He accepted a bribe in exchange for help, and he knew exactly who to approach when someone other than him needed to be involved."

Opa was blackmailing someone? The man in question certainly didn't sound trustworthy, but maybe after four years, he'd proven able to keep the secret.

Opa continued. "He was sent to Germany to work in one of their factories, so we can't approach him again should you need new paperwork, but I'm sure Anita has a contact who can help with that."

Anita didn't answer, but her expression confirmed Opa's prediction. Over the last several years, Gerrit had wondered how the war was affecting his Tante Anita. He had never supposed she was so deeply involved in the resistance, but he was proud of her.

"You'll have to be cautious," Opa told him. "You might be able to pass as sixteen or seventeen, but that's not always young enough to escape a razzia. I suspect things will get worse before the end because the Germans are getting more and more desperate. Stay out of sight as much as you can."

"That's how it is in Utrecht, too, but I managed not to get caught."

"Not yet." Ingrid eyed him.

"Do you suppose it's safe for him to go to church with us on Sunday?" Anita asked.

"I haven't gone to church in a long time." Gerrit hadn't been since the war had started. "No need to risk a razzia over that."

Ingrid looked as if he had personally offended her. "You're not religious?"

"Religion is the opium of the people."

She raised an eyebrow. "I see you have read Marx carefully enough to parrot him."

"Gerrit," Anita broke in before he could snap at Ingrid. "You must be exhausted after such a long journey. I'll show you where you can sleep. And those of you who are leaving tonight, I'm happy to wake you when it's time, if you'd like to nap."

"People are leaving tonight?" He'd assumed the onderduikers were meant to stay for an extended period of time, if not for the war's duration.

"Mynheer and Mevrouw Landmann will be safer in the country." Anita began stacking plates together. "And Flight Lieutenant Rollins can best defeat the Nazis from somewhere other than our attic."

Ingrid was the first to stand. "Thank you, Anita. I had meant to nap earlier, but with the disruption . . ." She glanced at Gerrit. "It didn't feel safe."

"Are you leaving as well?" Gerrit hoped his question sounded neutral rather than hopeful.

"Not for long. I'll most likely be back in the morning." She turned from him to help Mevrouw Landmann stand. The woman didn't look a day over thirty, but it took her a moment to find her balance and take her first few steps.

"You're part of a line?" Gerrit asked.

Opa yawned. "I haven't the slightest idea. These are all friends of Anita and Ingrid. If it so happens that most of the people passing through happen to need a doctor's care, what am I to do other than see that they are treated?"

Gerrit doubted that excuse would be enough to satisfy the Gestapo should they question Opa about his connection to the onderduikers staying in his home, but he felt a swell of esteem and affection. Opa and Anita had found a way to defy the Nazis. "I can help."

Anita looked to Ingrid as if it were her decision to make. Ingrid shook her head. "Not tonight. If Cornelis sees more people than he's expecting, he'll assume it's a trap."

"Then, next time." Gerrit didn't plan to sit out the remainder of the war in Opa's attic.

"We'll see." Ingrid followed Mevrouw Landmann out the door.

Gerrit looked to Anita for sympathy, but she seemed to find the situation comical. He didn't see the humor, but he helped her gather the dishes and take them to the sink.

"I'm quite capable of leading onderduikers from one safe house to the next. I lived near Nijmegen until I was ten. I know Gelderland, probably better than she does." He set the dishes down and put his hands on his hips.

"Maybe you do, but if Ingrid says she doesn't need your help, then having you riding about after curfew will put you at risk without good reason."

"Why should she get to decide? She's petty and vindictive, so she'll say no regardless."

Anita raised an eyebrow. "I would use neither of those adjectives to describe her. She'll do what she thinks is best for the line."

"I'm still wondering why she gets to decide."

"Do I detect resentment?"

He huffed. "You'd be upset, too, if someone you didn't know threatened you with a broom when all you wanted to do was wash your hands in your opa's kitchen."

"You could have identified yourself. It would have saved you her suspicion and saved her an afternoon of worrying that you were planning to turn in the onderduikers for a bounty."

"I didn't know who *she* was, so of course I couldn't tell her who *I* was. And it's ridiculous for her to think I was trying to spy out onderduikers."

Anita filled the sink. "Do you remember the last time you were here?"

He nodded.

"You thought she was a spy. Don't be too hard on her for making the same assumption about you four years later. There's a war on now. Far more reasons to worry about spies."

If Anita had wanted to placate him, it wasn't working.

She chuckled at his expression. "Don't worry, Gerrit. If you want to be involved, there is plenty of work to go around. You can start by bringing in the rest of the dishes."

CHAPTER 8

INGRID CHECKED OVER HER SHOULDER and counted three people cycling behind her in the dark. Flight Lieutenant Rollins was close enough that people would mistake them for a couple, which might come in handy if they were stopped, because he spoke no Dutch. They'd be in trouble regardless if discovered outside after curfew, but Ingrid had talked her way past checkpoints and nosy patrolmen before. She planned to deliver the three onderduikers safely to the destination without anyone seeing them. But if anyone did see, she would tell them she and the airman, dressed in civilian clothing, worked for a bakery, and they'd been sent to the country to collect milk because their normal supplier's truck had broken down. Their employer couldn't go without, not even for a day. Broken-down trucks were believable enough. Few people had them now, and the parts necessary for proper maintenance were in short supply.

Mynheer and Mevrouw Landmann rode behind Flight Lieutenant Rollins, far enough back that no one would assume the four of them traveled together but close enough that they could follow. Ingrid kept a more moderate pace than she normally would because she wasn't sure how Mevrouw Landmann's newly healed ankle would manage the ride. Four years ago, when recovering from her breaks, Ingrid had needed to take it slow on her borrowed bicycle for weeks. Anita had been so accommodating of Ingrid's limitations that Ingrid hadn't any idea how fast Anita was until nearly autumn. Ingrid had improved significantly over the years, but Anita ought to compete in races with the best cyclists in Europe. If they ever had races like that again.

The darkness of the night surrounded them, with only a half moon to reveal the border between road and field. An engine rumbled in the distance, and Ingrid slowed. Sometimes she wished she were still in Austria, where forests and mountains made it easier to hide. But that was an ungrateful thought. The van der Veens had adopted her as one of their own, and as much as she loved Falcon Point, her family no longer lived there, so it wasn't home anymore. Still, the geography of the Netherlands left much to lament when it came to shuttling onderduikers from one safe house to the next.

The engine grew louder. It was an automobile rather than an aircraft, so she headed toward the nearest place they could hide: a house. She didn't know who lived there, but she doubted the Germans, or whoever was driving the vehicle, would stop. Nor were they likely to discover a group of onderduikers hiding behind the home.

She couldn't see the ground as well once off the main road, so she dismounted her bicycle and continued on foot. Hopefully the home didn't have a dog. Food restrictions and rations made pets rarer and rarer but hadn't eliminated them entirely. Ingrid and the other three rushed to the back of the house and waited without a word. The engine noises grew, then reached a crescendo, then fell and faded.

"Was it a German truck?" the pilot asked in a whisper.

"Likely. Hardly anyone else has a vehicle or permission to drive it at night." Opa's automobile had been confiscated years ago despite his arguments that he might need it to tend patients. Other resistance groups might scrounge one up and venture out despite curfew, but unless it was one of her contacts, Ingrid couldn't very well trust them.

The four returned to the road and cycled farther. Ingrid recognized most crossroads, homes, and trees. Perhaps an hour after sneaking out of Arnhem, she led the three onderduikers into the yard of a two-story farmhouse. They rode to the back and rested their bicycles against the wall of the home.

Ingrid approached a door and knocked.

A short, middle-aged man with a rounded stomach and a receding hairline opened the door. Behind him, not a single light showed. He glanced at the moon. "Do you suppose it will rain tomorrow?"

"I hope not because I have three umbrellas, but I left them all at home." The code phrase changed according to how many onderduikers she was guiding. It was a silly phrase. If a stranger knocked on someone's door in the middle of the night, he was unlikely to start a conversation about the next day's weather. But the man's question and her answer confirmed for each of them that neither had been arrested and acted under duress.

"Come in. Cornelis is yet to arrive, but I expect he'll show up soon."

Cornelis coordinated several resistance groups, including Anita's. He usually arrived before Ingrid, but her group had made better time than expected, even with the delay while they hid.

Ingrid led the others inside, and once the door was fastened, the host and his wife switched on a lamp to reveal a tidy room with a sofa, a pair of deep armchairs, and several side tables. A grandfather clock sent out an audible tick from one corner. The hostess brought thick slices of dark bread and a warm drink that vaguely resembled coffee. Ingrid took a sip. She'd never developed a taste for coffee before the war had begun, and since then, it had been hard to come by. But the smell of the acorn substitute, like so many things, stirred memories of her parents. Four years without her family and she still missed them every single day despite finding a kind doctor who treated her like a granddaughter, and a brilliant, daring friend who treated her like a sister.

A knock sounded, and the hostess switched off the lamp before her husband answered the door. He again asked his question about the weather, and a reply about two umbrellas followed. Once the three newcomers were inside, the hostess again switched on the light, then excused herself.

Cornelis removed his hat, revealing fair, slicked-back hair, and gave Ingrid a smile of recognition. He was in his early thirties, the perfect age to be forced to Germany for labor, but he'd somehow managed to escape the razzias thus far and excelled at helping others do the same. With him were two men whom Ingrid hadn't met, but that was normal. She brought onderduikers from the van der Veen home, most of them there because they'd needed a doctor's aid, and Cornelis brought onderduikers from other locations in the Arnhem area. They might have come from the same street as the van der Veen home or from as far away as Velp or Oosterbeek. He knew where she lived and where the men and women were hidden, but the information didn't go both ways. Compartmentalization of information helped prevent disaster. So did keeping their cells small so one arrest didn't lead to dozens. That was one of the reasons Ingrid held reservations about integrating Gerrit into their network. Anita and Opa knew him, but Ingrid didn't. She remembered him being kind enough to lend her his coat when she was injured after leaping from the train, but she also remembered him snooping through her knapsack.

Cornelis gestured to one of the men dressed in blue mechanic's overalls. "Bombardier from a B-17. From California. Doesn't speak Dutch."

Ingrid glanced between the tall, brawny American and his British counterpart. She hoped the two of them would get along. The last time they'd had a combined group of British and American airmen, the Englishman had claimed the American didn't speak real English. The American had called the Englishman a limey snob. Nothing overt had happened, but the tension had been noticeable. Yet previous groups of multinational airmen had formed good working relationships. Perhaps the man from California and Flight Lieutenant Rollins would do the same. They shared a goal of returning to their airbases without getting nabbed by the Nazis.

Cornelis then introduced the second man, who had brunet hair, a narrow face, and a roman nose. He stood a few inches taller than Cornelis, but Ingrid guessed he was a decade younger. "Berend. A colleague. The government-in-exile has been promoting better cooperation between resistance cells, and we'd like our groups to coordinate efforts."

So much for compartmentalizing information. But she could also see the benefit of the plan: More people working together, determined to harry the Nazis until they were forced from the Netherlands, could take on more daring projects.

Cornelis motioned to her. "This is Ingrid. Her family hides people who need a safe haven or a reliable, discreet route from the country. Intelligence gathering as well."

"No sabotage?" Berend asked.

"No, not yet." Her group had never done anything so violent. Anita and Opa just wanted to help people in need, not destroy a part of their homeland.

Berend smiled, revealing white teeth, one of them a little crooked. "Well, I hope you're willing to change. The Germans are losing. Our best efforts can keep it that way."

Ingrid nodded, but she'd heard about the reprisals the Germans enacted for sabotage. Was it worth destroying a trainload of ammunition if it resulted in the execution of innocent people? She would have to talk it through with Anita.

Cornelis handed her a piece of paper with an uncoded address written on it. "I want you and your cell leader to meet Berend there tomorrow at four in the afternoon. It's a residence. The door will be unlocked. Go to the top floor, in the back. The windows there overlook the river. If you take bicycles, pull them inside, but you can leave them at street level."

Ingrid memorized the address, then handed the paper back to Cornelis. She also handed over the report Anita had written after analyzing information from the four agents reporting to her. If someone were to read it, the words formed an ordinary letter about a nonexistent child learning to walk and a housewife's struggle to adjust recipes when so many food items were rationed. If the report fell into the wrong hands, it ought to pass as something innocuous, but it hid coded intelligence the Nazis would kill over should they discover its true meaning.

"You won't be there tomorrow?" Ingrid asked.

Cornelis shook his head. "Can't be, I'm afraid. But I trust Berend completely. You can trust him too."

"Yes, sir." Ingrid studied the new man more thoroughly. Berend studied her in return. His eyes showed intelligence but no emotion. Intentionally or not, he was hard to read.

Their Dutch hostess returned, bringing with her the scent of fried eggs. "Come, eat."

Ingrid translated for Rollins and the American bombardier. They would spend a day at the farm. The Landmanns would likely stay even longer. Then tomorrow night, another courier would lead the two airmen to a safe house across the Waal, closer to the Belgian border. From there, other contacts would be their guides to freedom.

The next afternoon, back in Arnhem, Ingrid tried to keep her voice neutral as she tied a kerchief over her hair. "I'm sorry, but Cornelis only requested that Anita and I attend the meeting."

Gerrit folded his arms. "Yes, but if you didn't tell him about me, he wouldn't know to invite me, would he?"

Ingrid bristled. It wasn't as if she and Cornelis had been given the privacy or the time for a long, in-depth chat about a boy on the run from the Utrecht Gestapo. Gerrit ought to be grateful rather than complaining about everything. Some things took time, including incorporation into a resistance cell.

Anita placed a hand on Gerrit's arm. "Cornelis didn't ask for Petrus or Willem either, and he brought them here, but we'll make sure the new contact knows about you."

"So, I'm to spend the day hiding in the attic in case the Gestapo comes searching for us?" Gerrit's tone made his distaste clear.

Anita sighed. "No. The three of you will spend the day with one of you watching the window or listening for anything suspicious, and the other two of you can do whatever you like."

"Whatever we like inside, you mean."

Anita gave her nephew a sympathetic smile. Ingrid barely suppressed a huff. "None of us want you to be arrested," Anita said. "Staying out of sight is the best thing you can do right now, especially given how recently your previous cell was broken."

Gerrit nodded. He didn't seem happy to be staying behind, but perhaps he was finally done arguing.

"I wish I could stay longer to help you settle in, but we'll be back before you know it." Anita managed to sound suitably apologetic.

An apology was completely unnecessary. Gerrit ought to simply be relieved that his relatives had taken him in so readily. Ingrid took the stairs to the cellar to retrieve their bicycles, and Anita followed. Then they hauled their bicycles up the stairs to the garden.

"Where's the meeting?" Anita asked in a voice soft enough that no one would hear, even if some of the neighbors had open windows, something quite likely given the warm weather.

"By the railway bridge over the Nederrijn." They would cycle through some of the busiest streets in Arnhem, so it was just as well that they were leaving Gerrit behind—if the Germans felt like rounding anyone up, that was the area they were most likely to scavenge. Ingrid might not like Gerrit Hendriks, but she didn't want him sent to Germany. Or worse, executed.

The two rode side by side when traffic allowed, single file when it didn't. Anita led and set the pace as they cycled past tidy brick buildings and tree-lined streets. They slowed in front of a tall home that looked much like the van der Veen home, only it didn't have a side yard because the homes bordered each other along this street.

Ingrid wouldn't normally pull a bicycle through someone's front door, but the instructions had been clear, and as they entered, it seemed they were not the only people using the home's entry for bicycle parking.

The bottom level looked deserted. No furniture occupied the rooms, and nothing but wallpaper hung on the walls. The home location was highly desirable—even Ingrid, who had lived in the city for only four years, could recognize that. Surely anyone trying to rent or sell would quickly find another occupant. Not wanting to walk into a trap, they inspected each room on each level to ensure no one lay in wait for them.

"I suppose this is the place," Anita said when they found the window overlooking the river.

The water below flowed past to the sea Ingrid had once planned to cross on a trip to England. If their trip had been scheduled just a few days earlier, would Ingrid be there now, with Anna and Karl? And might Anita and Opa also have escaped the German occupation? They had discussed joining the Engelandvaarders who fled the Netherlands for England, but the land route to a neutral country was perilous, and the route by sea was even more deadly. Besides, if they left, who would guide the airmen and resistance fighters who would face imprisonment or death if they didn't flee? Ingrid could do more good in Arnhem, but that didn't ease the worry that came from meeting an unknown contact who planned to pull them into even more danger.

"I'll watch the door." Ingrid walked to the landing on the lower set of stairs, where she could see the door but quickly duck around a corner if needed. Even after four years of war, clandestine meetings still made her nervous. But when the door finally opened with a creak, it was Berend.

He strode through the door with an apologetic smile. "Sorry I'm late. Had to lose a tail."

"*Did* you lose him?" An unpleasant worry crept into Ingrid's chest.

"Yes, but it took longer than I thought it would."

The worry didn't leave. Cornelis had promised she could trust Berend, but he'd probably been referring to political commitment, not Berend's ability to lose tails. Regardless, Ingrid led him upstairs.

"This is the man Cornelis introduced me to," Ingrid told Anita.

"Pleased to meet you." Anita didn't introduce herself. She never did unless it was absolutely necessary. "Do you know why this home is empty?"

"The Jewish owners were taken away. So was anything inside worth having." Berend studied both of them. "Cornelis said I could rely on you."

Anita nodded. "We've managed to avoid arrest so far. We've gathered intelligence for years and helped a hundred onderduikers. We look forward to the Nazis leaving and the queen returning."

Berend glanced around the room. "I'm not a royalist, but I do want the Nazis gone, so we have a common cause to work for."

"What did you have in mind?" Anita asked.

"The Allies are advancing. They haven't told me which route they intend to take to Germany, but a path through the Netherlands is likely enough. That's the route the Germans took four years ago."

Ingrid nodded. She remembered the invasion all too well.

"So we help prepare," Berend said.

"We're already doing that." Anita's voice held a hint of question. "If they invade, they'll know which units are where, which bridges are wired to explode, which roads will be easiest to take and which might be blocked . . ."

Countless times, Ingrid had cycled through the countryside to collect the location of German antiaircraft batteries, troop encampments, airfields, and charges for bridge demolitions. Anita worked with a handful of other agents who did the same thing, then compiled the information and sent it to Cornelis, who enciphered the reports and transmitted them to contacts in England.

Berend held up a hand. "Yes, yes, that's all well and good. But when the time comes, don't you think it would be better to destroy the roadblocks for them rather than merely reporting their location? What if we can demolish an antiaircraft battery before it shoots down their planes? Remove key players before they cause problems?"

The muscles around Anita's lips tightened. "Remove key players . . . What do you mean by that?"

Berend folded his arms. "Well, we can't very well put them in jail, can we? Not when the enemy controls all the prisons."

"You're talking about sabotage and assassination." Anita's tone held disapproval.

"How many Dutchmen die every day that the Nazis are in charge?" Berend asked. "We're fighting a ruthless enemy. That requires ruthlessness in return. And if we manage to free ourselves a few weeks or a few days earlier than we otherwise would, we'll save Dutch lives. Think about it. One campaign shortened and a thousand lives spared. One key Nazi dead and a hundred innocent Dutchmen saved. One Dutch traitor executed and a dozen members of the resistance given a reprieve."

Ingrid swallowed. If Anita or Opa were in danger, it would be easy to justify anything, even assassination. But it wasn't always that simple. "What about reprisals?" she asked.

The Germans weren't above taking and executing hostages. They'd cordoned off streets before and forced passersby to watch as they'd gunned down victims arrested before an assassination was made or a sabotage successfully carried out. Killing a German officer might save a few Dutch lives, but if it also resulted in Nazi revenge killings, the cost might outweigh the benefit. Then there were the moral implications.

"That's why we've been so cautious before." Berend walked to the window. "You remember how swiftly the Germans made it through the low countries and France in spring 1940? If the same is about to happen in reverse, then it's time for us to fight for our liberation."

May 10, 1940. Ingrid remembered the date clearly, when she'd woken to the sounds of airplanes and artillery and bridges being destroyed. Less than a month later, the final evacuation ships had sailed from Dunkirk, leaving most of continental Europe in Nazi hands.

"It won't be the same in reverse," she said. "Normandy is farther to the west than Dunkirk. And the Netherlands surrendered so quickly because the Germans destroyed Rotterdam and threatened to do the same to other Dutch cities. I doubt the Allies would make threats like that, and even if they did, it wouldn't sway the Germans. And anyway, it's already taken longer than it did in 1940."

Berend's jaw clenched for a moment. "Yes, I can read both maps and calendars. The point is, if we want to be liberated, it's time for us to do our part. Do either of you have training in sabotage or in tracking down and removing targets?"

Ingrid shook her head.

So did Anita. "I'm willing to learn more about sabotage, but it will have to be around my other duties." Anita worked a consistent schedule so her sources would always know when they could find her at the hospital. All took risks coming to St. Elisabeth's. A missed shift might mean an agent would have to return another time, doubling their danger.

"There's a farmhouse out in the country." Berend slipped his hands into his trouser pockets. "Four days there, maybe three, and you'll be ready."

Anita looked thoughtful. "I can't abandon my agents for four days in a row. I don't suppose you can break it up?"

Berend shrugged. "It's possible, but not every member of every cell needs every skill. If you're meeting with agents, perhaps others could learn to build bombs and find Dutch traitors."

"I can go," Ingrid said. "Courier work can usually be pushed back a day or two. We do that anyway if someone is still healing from an injury or if a patrol has been snooping around the neighborhood." Ingrid had seen the havoc the Nazis had caused in two countries, and she wouldn't be opposed to destroying a supply depot or an antiaircraft battery if the opportunity arose.

"We've a few others hiding near us. They might be interested." Ingrid assumed Anita spoke of the three men currently in the van der Veen home. Petrus had gone underground when a neighbor had told the Gestapo that he wasn't loyal to the Nazis. He hadn't wanted to flee the country, preferring to stay and help. Willem's father had been arrested and held as a hostage, then murdered by the Nazis in one of their reprisal killings. He wanted revenge. And Gerrit had made his burning impatience to help quite clear. "Four total might be available for training."

Berend nodded. "Can you spare all of them without compromising your work? We want to do more to win the war, but we don't want to interrupt existing efforts."

Anita's head tilted as she thought. "When would it be? I can manage care of onderduikers by myself for a few days, if needed, but we can't always predict when they'll arrive."

"Tomorrow. After curfew."

Anita looked at Ingrid. "If you went, would you be back in time for your next rendezvous with Cornelis?"

"Yes, just."

"And you want to do this?" Anita asked.

Ingrid met Anita's eyes. She hoped her friend could see her determination to strike back at the regime that had hounded her since she was a girl. "Yes, I do."

"Four, then," Anita said.

Rupert entered SD headquarters through the back door. He nodded at the guard on duty and reminded himself to keep his head up and his shoulders back. No one expected intelligence work to be a series of uninterrupted victories.

"Altbauer? Back already?"

Rupert stopped and swiveled to face his commanding officer. He saluted sharply. "Yes, Hauptmann Denhart."

Denhart handed a sheet of paper to an enlisted man and motioned to Rupert. "Come, tell me about it."

Rupert followed Denhart into his office. The hauptmann sat in his chair and leaned back, then motioned for Rupert to take the seat across from his desk. The room was filled with paperwork, confiscated radios, and other miscellaneous items. The surface of the desk was full, but the stacks seemed organized, and a pair of framed pictures angled toward the hauptmann in a uniform line.

"You tailed the man in question?"

Rupert nodded. "For an hour. Then I saw him stop at a tree. It wasn't natural, so I checked and found a piece of paper in the hollow. I couldn't read it. It wasn't in German. Not Dutch either." Rupert spoke only a little Dutch, but he could recognize real words versus coded words. "I put it back and waited. And I saw the man who stopped to retrieve the paper."

Denhart leaned forward in interest. "And?"

"I followed him for about four blocks. Then he took a bicycle—not sure if it was his or not—and he disappeared. I couldn't keep up on foot."

"You are authorized to commandeer a bicycle when needed, Leutnant Altbauer."

"Yes, sir. I just . . ." Rupert trailed off and shifted his leg. "He seemed well aware of his surroundings, so there were several people between us. Even if I'd had a bicycle, I doubt I could have outridden a Dutchman. Not anymore."

Hauptmann Denhart glanced at Rupert's leg. "The wound still bothers you?"

"No, but it doesn't bend as well as it used to. I tried a bicycle a few months before I received this transfer, and riding was awkward and slow."

Denhart frowned. "Pity. Your sacrifice for the Fatherland is recognized."

"I only regret that it prevented me from being more useful to the Fatherland today."

Denhart chuckled. "No need to be quite so thick with your devotion. Your loyalty is not in question, only your ability to ride a bicycle. Recognizing the dead drop was useful. They may use it again. I'll assign someone to watch it. I trust you can find it again?"

"Yes, sir."

"Now, why don't you tell me how your leg really feels, Altbauer."

Rupert sighed. Had his lie been so obvious? "Most of the time, it's just a dull ache. Worse when the weather changes or when I spend a lot of time on my feet."

"Do you need a reduction in duty?"

"No, sir."

"Well, you have my condolences."

Rupert hesitated, but he liked Denhart. He was clever and fair, and Rupert suspected he would appreciate honesty. "There's no need for sympathy. This injury was my ticket out of Stalingrad. I'd take it again in a heartbeat."

"Ah. A lucky wound, but one you'll feel the rest of your life."

"The alternative was death in Russia. Either relatively quickly, on the battlefield, or slowly, freezing in a Soviet prison camp. I was on one of the last flights out of Gumrak Airfield, in January 1943. The Red Army captured it the next day."

Denhart nodded. "Do you need to rest your leg now?"

"I don't need special treatment, sir. I can handle a little pain."

"Well, rest it for a while anyway. Jung should be back soon. When he comes, you can show him where that dead drop is. He's not as imaginative as I'd like when it comes to concealment, so please suggest a proper hiding place for surveillance. In the meantime, write down what you can about the man you followed. Height, clothing, any distinguishing characteristics."

"Yes, sir." Rupert still preferred success. But they had a clue. Eventually, they'd catch both of the men and their contacts.

CHAPTER 9

When Petrus and Willem had given Gerrit the first watch, he'd gone to the bedroom where his mother and Nellie had always slept when the family had come to visit. But the formerly well-appointed bedroom had morphed into a storage room of sorts, crowded with accent tables and trunks full of Opa's old things from the Indies. The trunks had all been in the upper level or the attic before, but Gerrit had seen how those areas, too, had changed. It seemed every spare bed or mattress had moved to the top floor and the attic, which was where he had been relegated for his sleeping chambers the night before. The home's top floor wasn't unpleasant. Some of the rooms were small, designed for servants, but they were still larger than the second bedroom in Aunt Petronella's apartment in Utrecht. And his uncles' old rooms on the top floor of Opa's house were even more generous in size.

All the leftover bits of furniture shoved into his mother's old room made it uncomfortable for standing watch, so when Gerrit's second turn for watch came, he went into the room where he and Johan had always slept. This room, too, was different. A desk had taken the place of the second bed, a desk with a feminine scent. Last night, he'd seen Anita go into the same room she'd had before the war, so that meant this room was now Ingrid's. The room offered a good view of the street in front of the home, so he ignored the nagging feeling that he was trespassing. It had been his room long before it had been hers.

He kept an eye on the window, but out of curiosity, he pressed on each floorboard. The last time he'd visited, he had discovered a hiding place beneath a loose one, and he'd hidden a few coins and a comic book there. Which board had it been? He walked along the floor, checking with his toes, trying to remember exactly where the furniture had been before.

A knot in one of the floorboards caught his eye. That was familiar. If the hiding space was still there, it could be a useful place to store ration coupons or false papers. He hadn't been in the home long enough to learn the full extent of Opa's and Anita's clandestine activities, but everyone had to be fed, and without ration coupons, food was hard to come by. Even with ration coupons, it was hard to come by.

Gerrit peeked out the window to make sure the street was clear, then got on his hands and knees and checked under the bed. He moved aside a valise and felt the floorboards. There. That one was loose. He popped it free of the floor and put it aside. He couldn't see the contents from his current angle, so he reached in, hoping any rodents or insects had been frightened away by the sound of the board moving. His fingers brushed a booklet of some sort, but it wasn't a comic book. He pulled the items out. Reich passports. Those could be useful to the resistance. But when Gerrit opened them, they were the same ones he'd seen the day Ingrid had fallen from the train. Curious now, he reached under the bed again. This time, his hands felt something with a smooth cloth surface, and he pulled out a red satin jewelry box.

"What are you doing?" a feminine voice asked.

Gerrit flinched in surprise, hitting his head against the bed frame. He shuffled out from under the bed and turned toward a fuming Ingrid. Her hands rested on her hips, and her face pulled with anger.

Still on the floor, Gerrit massaged his throbbing scalp. "I was looking for my old treasure stash. It seems the space is now otherwise occupied."

Ingrid glared at him. "If by treasure stash, you mean an old comic book and a few cents, those have long ago been cleared away."

"Was it only a few cents?"

"Not even half a guilder. Are you finished here?"

Gerrit wished she wouldn't have sneaked up on him. It looked like he was snooping, but he really had been curious to know if his things were still there. "Let me replace the items, and I will happily leave."

"I can put them back myself, thank you very much."

Gerrit took his hand from his head. He'd have a bruise on the back of his skull, but maybe he deserved it. "Would you like me to move the bed for you so you can reach it easier?"

"No, thank you."

"It would be a good place to hide things we don't want the Germans to find."

Ingrid rolled her eyes. "As are a dozen places in the attic. I assure you that the home's security is well thought out. When whoever is on watch does his job, our precautions have proven entirely adequate."

"I'm just trying to help. I've some experience with hiding things, like ration coupons."

"Yes, and apparently some experience with snooping."

Gerrit stood. He was perhaps an inch taller than Ingrid, something he was glad for when she was scolding him as if he were a misbehaving child. "The comic book is practically worthless, and I'd guess the coins were barely enough to buy a bag of candy, but don't tell me you wouldn't do the same thing if you returned to a family home you hadn't seen in years."

Ingrid inhaled sharply and avoided his eyes, but not before he detected what looked like pain in her pinched mouth and stiff shoulders.

Gerrit left and didn't look back.

Gerrit didn't let his run-in with Ingrid spoil the excitement when news came over the radio that Paris had been liberated. And the evening improved even more when Anita announced that Gerrit, Ingrid, Petrus, and Willem would be leaving the following evening for training in the countryside. Opa was still at the hospital, leaving five of them about the table for supper that night.

"They'll teach us how to sabotage bridges and such?" Gerrit asked. He'd been wanting to do more than distribute illegal ration coupons for onderduikers, and it seemed the opportunity had finally fallen into his lap. Just in time because if Paris was free, liberation had to be coming for the Netherlands too.

"Yes, Berend says it's time to set the Netherlands ablaze." Anita frowned. "I just hope he's right about the timing, because the Germans won't hesitate to take reprisals. Setting the country aflame could burn more than the enemy."

"Maybe that's part of the training." Gerrit leaned forward. "If sabotage is done the right way, it can be blamed on something else. A motor that burns out too quickly—looks like poor maintenance, but it can be forced. A small bomb disguised as coal—ignites a train engine when it's shoveled in far from Arnhem." If destruction looked like an accident or bad luck rather than deliberate destruction, the country ought to be safe from reprisals.

"I had the impression that Berend is a Communist." Ingrid dabbed her mouth with a napkin. Her tone indicated disapproval.

"Is something wrong with that?" Gerrit asked.

"Communists are not so different from Fascists. The needs of each individual is subverted by the needs of the state, and government controls everything."

Gerrit huffed. "Communism and Fascism are diametrically opposed to one another. And the Communists are doing more to win this war than anyone else—on the Eastern Front and here in the Netherlands."

Ingrid stood and began gathering dishes. "I don't doubt the military value of the Red Army or the work of Communist Resistance cells, but I don't expect either to consider the needs of the average civilian. Their goals will outweigh the threat of reprisals and the good of the masses."

Gerrit rolled his eyes. "Winning this war is what's good for the masses. The Communists are the group most likely to keep that in mind."

"Winning the war how? Is victory a month earlier worth widespread slaughter?"

"The Nazis are already slaughtering us. People like my father and my uncle are being worked to death in factories; people like my mother are dying in air raids. People like my aunt's best friend are being shipped to death camps simply because they're Jewish and didn't go into hiding soon enough. And people like Willem's father are being held hostage and shot on the street as punishment for someone else's resistance. The sooner we win our freedom, the sooner the slaughter stops."

"I won't dispute Nazi evil. But I'm not sure I trust the Communists not to snatch our freedom away again should they take power after the war." Ingrid took her stack of plates through the doorway to the kitchen.

Petrus and Willem both looked from Ingrid to him. Amusement lit Petrus's face. Willem's expression reminded Gerrit of a dog owner whose animal had just been reprimanded for biting a passerby; he knew his beloved pet was in the wrong, but that didn't change his sympathies. Gerrit could gather the other dishes, if he wanted, and follow Ingrid into the kitchen to finish their argument, but he had no interest in butting heads with her again today, or in providing Petrus with entertainment and Willem with fodder for contempt. "Do you suppose that means she doesn't wish to go?" he asked his aunt. He wouldn't say so aloud, but he hoped Ingrid would stay in Arnhem.

Anita shook her head. "She wants the training because she wants the Nazis defeated. But she's careful about which allies she trusts."

"We're more of a threat if we work together to defeat the enemy." That included bourgeoisie women like Ingrid, professionals like Opa, and people like Gerrit, who, like his father, considered himself a Socialist. Maybe a Communist like Oom Antoon. "Victory needs to be the current focus, not wrangling for political positions that will only matter if the Nazis are defeated."

Anita gave him an indulgent smile. "Then our cell is incredibly blessed to have someone reminding us to show caution and someone else reminding us of the benefits of cooperation. That will help us keep balance."

Gerrit would have preferred that Anita take his side, but at least she was trying to make peace between him and Ingrid rather than taking Ingrid's side.

Anita stood. "Petrus, would you mind showing Gerrit how our coding system works? I want everyone to be able to use it."

A smile crossed Petrus's face. "I could, but Ingrid is far better at it than I am. She'd be a more effective teacher."

Anita looked toward the kitchen and seemed to hesitate.

"Can you teach me, Anita?" Gerrit asked.

She shook her head. "I need to run food to Pap at the hospital, and then Willem and I are planning to meet a contact. We may have to sneak back after curfew."

Petrus and Willem excused themselves before Gerrit could ask for their help, leaving him with his aunt. "Ingrid might not want to teach me. I'm afraid we've started off on the wrong foot."

Anita patted his cheek. He wasn't used to such aunt-like gestures from her, and frowned. "Then, use this as an opportunity to get on the right foot," she said.

"Won't you have time tomorrow?"

Anita shook her head. "I'll be gone all evening, and tomorrow, I need to be at the hospital early. You and Ingrid will both be here tonight and most of tomorrow. So you'll have to put aside whatever's making the both of you act uncharacteristically hostile and find a way to work together."

"Maybe this evening, a little time apart would be the better option."

"Didn't you say something about working together to defeat the enemy only two minutes ago? You can start by cooperating with the people living under the same roof as you."

When it came time for the lesson, Gerrit joined Ingrid at the dining room table.

She avoided looking at him as she placed a pencil and a blank piece of paper on the table before him. It seemed she wasn't any more pleased to be teaching Gerrit than he was to be learning from her. "To put it simply, we communicate in Morse code."

Morse code? "Wouldn't that be easy for the Gestapo or the Green Police to decipher if they ever got ahold of it?"

"Only if they know what they're looking at. We don't actually use dots and dashes. Each letter has an *A* form—the dot—and a *B* form—the dash. Vertical is a dot, and slanted is a dash. When you know what to look for, it's straightforward enough. But we make sure that whatever we're writing doesn't look like a report. It should read like a normal letter, or notes from a medical appointment."

"Do Opa's notes have hidden messages?"

"Opa will be the first to tell you that he is not a member of the resistance, though I'm not sure the Gestapo could be convinced of that, if any of us were arrested."

Disappointment lodged in Gerrit's chest. "He's not?"

"He'll tell you he is simply helping those who come to him—those in need of medical care, those in need of a place to stay. Enabling all of us to collect information, send reports, and lead people from one safe house to another is illegal under the current regime, but, according to him, in line with a good Christian life."

"I'd forgotten how religious Mam's side of the family is."

"Does that mean your father's side of the family is less religious?" Ingrid's tone was terse.

"On my father's side of the family, we don't have time for old-fashioned beliefs that have been used to oppress the masses for centuries."

"Is that so?" Ingrid stood.

Gerrit assumed his remark had been one offense too many, and he almost wished he hadn't said it. Almost. Only because if Ingrid refused to teach him their coding system, Anita would have to do it, and that would probably involve a sacrifice of her sleep.

"I forgot something," Ingrid said. "I'll be back in a moment." She returned a minute later with two books. The first, she opened to a table listing the Morse code for each letter. The second book was a Bible. "To start, I'll let you copy from an existing source. Then you don't have to work on the *A* and *B* forms while composing a letter at the same time. We use a new word for each letter. Since no letter is longer than four taps, use any word with four or more letters. Don't try burying a code in any of the shorter words. Any questions, or are you ready to try?"

Gerrit picked up the pencil she had placed in front of him. "What should I encode?"

Ingrid flipped through the Bible. She slowed, turned a few pages, and placed the book on the table. "Encode this verse, and use this column as the cover text. I've some work to do in the kitchen. I'll check on you in a while."

Gerrit looked at the verse she'd pointed to. *As long as I am in the world, I am the light of the world.* It seemed Ingrid wasn't one to be offended when someone questioned her faith. She simply took revenge instead. Gerrit worked for the next twenty minutes, trying to hide the verse about light in a story about Jesus healing a blind man. His mother would have liked the story, but Gerrit focused on the way he was writing each letter rather than on the meaning. If Jesus had power to heal the blind man, why hadn't He also healed Johan's heart or protected Mam from the firestorm in Rotterdam?

Ingrid returned before he finished. He assumed that was intentional, to show him how slow he was. He would practice, and he would get faster, of that he was sure.

"May I see?" she asked.

Gerrit handed the paper over.

Ingrid perused his work. "Yes, I can see which one is *A* form and which one is *B* form, but it's too obvious."

"That makes it clear for whoever is reading it. I don't want whoever we pass the reports to having to guess if the letter is a dot or a dash."

Ingrid's mouth pulled in exasperation. "It needs to be more subtle."

"*More subtle* sounds an awful lot like *more confusing*."

"*More subtle* means it won't trip someone's suspicion if the Nazis get their hands on it. It's supposed to look like a normal letter, not like a code hidden in a normal letter."

Gerrit inhaled and exhaled, wishing Anita could have fit a lesson in. She would have explained that in the first place. Gerrit grabbed another sheet of paper, but rather than beginning his letter again immediately, he flipped the old sheet over and practiced some of the more difficult letters, trying to make one style completely upright and the other ever so slightly tilted to the left.

He did his best to ignore Ingrid when she looked over his shoulder. *Nosy, sharp-tongued, arrogant, unyielding.* Those were all good words to describe her. Maybe he'd put that into a code.

"The *O*'s are quite good. Perhaps a little less differentiation between the *T*'s and a bit more between the *S*'s."

Gerrit turned to look at her, then pulled away when he realized how close she was. He took in her profile a moment before going back to his paper. Perhaps his earlier list could include one more adjective: *beautiful.* But beauty didn't matter when it was paired with vindictive disdain and useless devotion to outdated religious stories. Yet Anita needed a team, and that team included Ingrid. For Anita's sake, not for Ingrid's, he would try. While he worked on his *T*'s and *S*'s, Ingrid took a sheet of paper and started copying some of the words from the Bible.

"When you're ready, try again." Ingrid folded her paper in half. "You may have noticed that it can be a bit laborious to write an entire word for each letter that's meant to be part of the report. Tomorrow we'll go over some of our common abbreviations and shortcuts."

Learning that first would have saved his wrist a great deal of effort, but he suspected Ingrid would find a way to indirectly call him lazy if he requested the efficient method without trudging through the more tedious method first.

"When you're done"—she tapped her sheet—"you can practice reading a code."

Gerrit watched as she left the room, grateful to see her go. He spent the next hour practicing his letters, then writing out the passage from the Bible. He was tempted to encode something such as *Ingrid is like one of those tropical flowers. Beautiful and filled with poison.* But that would give Anita more headaches, and she already had enough to worry about. He stuck with the original verse of scripture.

When he was done, he tackled the letter from Ingrid. He used scratch paper to note the dots and dashes, even grudgingly admitting that her penmanship was excellent and her *A* and *B* forms of the letters clear but appropriately subtle when he knew what he was looking for. He supposed that was why she had been asked to teach him. She was good at it.

He didn't have Morse code memorized, so he used the table from the book to transcribe the dots and dashes. Once they were letters, he had to add the appropriate spaces. When he looked at the message, he sighed. *When the world has gone dark, don't turn away from the light.* Ingrid seemed to know how to push his buttons even better than his siblings did.

Ingrid spent most of the next morning training Gerrit on the abbreviations and shortcuts they used in their coding. His second message of the night before had been adequate, but would he be able to make his *A* and *B* forms as well if he had to think up the cover text as well? Ideally, he would have more time to learn. And, she hoped, time to stop being an infuriating snoop. Though truth be told, if she ever went back to Falcon Point, she would want to look to see what was still the same, years later, and what had changed or disappeared. *If* she went back to Falcon Point. When they'd left, she had thought they were only leaving for a little while, not for years. But the Allies were in France now, pressing on the Nazis from the west. And the Soviets were advancing in the east. The Germans would lose this war, and then maybe she would find her brother and her sister and return home to see if the family's paintings had survived and if the book she'd been reading still lay on her bed, right beside where her knapsack had been. Karl had grabbed the bag for her. He'd forgotten the book.

Gerrit found her while she was preparing lunch and handed her a coded message. "Here. Perhaps you can tell me if the coding is acceptable." He glanced at the pot on the stove. "I can watch the soup. Is it just meant to simmer, or do you need anything added?"

"I haven't added salt and pepper yet." She wasn't sure she trusted Gerrit in the kitchen. She knew from experience that learning how to cook could be a messy process. And while it might be a disservice to stand between him and a learning experience, she didn't want to suffer through any culinary mishaps. "Have you seasoned soup before?"

Gerrit nodded. "After the Germans arrested my uncle, I thought about dropping out of school. Tante Petronella wouldn't hear of it, and anyway, she could get a better-paying job than I could at age sixteen. I learned to cook so she didn't have to do it all."

Gerrit was a snoop, he was bristly, and for his practice report, he had copied out part of the Communist Manifesto as his text to hide his code. But he had also lost part of his family, and he seemed to be hurting. The war hadn't been easy on Ingrid, but nor had it been easy on him. Maybe she could give Gerrit another chance because maybe he felt just as lost as she did.

She read the message he'd coded beneath the distasteful political garbage.

> *Dear Ingrid,*
>
> *We seem to have started out on the wrong foot. I apologize for my part in that. Had I known you were hiding anything beneath the floor panels, I wouldn't have looked. We may not agree on everything, but we both care for Opa, Anita, and Anjing. We've both lost family to this war. And we both want the Nazis out of the Netherlands. I hope we can cooperate in that goal, if not for ourselves, then for Anita's sake. Perhaps we can call a truce?*

Ingrid put the letter down. Yes, she would give Gerrit another chance. Tasting his cooking confirmed it. He hadn't ruined her soup. He'd used a tad more pepper than she would have, but today, she enjoyed the burst of flavor.

When Gerrit helped clear the table and followed her into the kitchen, she gave him a smile. "I can agree to a truce."

He nodded. "Good. Anita has enough to worry about without our adding to it. And our training will be more effective if we aren't distracted with petty irritations."

Ingrid wouldn't call the irritations petty, but she had just agreed to a truce, so she didn't say that aloud. "Thank you for helping with the soup."

"Thank you for cooking."

Ingrid was fairly certain that conversation constituted the longest the two of them had gone without resorting to sarcasm or other verbal barbs with each other. She was relieved when he left the room, because she didn't want to ruin it.

CHAPTER 10

Ingrid gave Anita a hug goodbye after supper that night. "Will you be all right without anyone here to help you?"

"Pap will be around."

"You know as well as anyone that he'll spend more time at the hospital than he spends here."

"Then, if I get lonely, I'll join him. I'm sure I can find some paperwork that needs to be done." Anita glanced around the dining room to ensure they were alone. "Will you watch out for Gerrit? I still think of him as if he were fourteen."

Ingrid almost laughed. "The two of us called a truce. We're trying to be polite to each other."

Anita raised both eyebrows. "Really? I'm glad, but I imagine poor Petrus will feel as though he's been cheated out of his entertainment."

"I think we'll be too focused on training to have need for entertainment."

Anita's mouth pulled with sadness.

"What?" Ingrid asked.

"I just hope that when the war ends, we can be happy again. That you won't be so serious all the time. Gerrit too. He used to laugh and smile and, well, act like a normal adolescent."

"He's nineteen, isn't he? Not a boy anymore."

"I suppose not. But do you remember when you had your broken legs and we would stay up for hours finding things to laugh about?"

Ingrid remembered. She'd felt lost then, too, but Anita had made it easy to push the grief and worry aside for a while. And back then, it had been easier to hope that she'd find Karl and Anna again soon. It was harder to hope that now. "After the war, we'll finally take that trip to London. We'll find a teahouse that sells all the sweets we've been craving for years, and we'll laugh until it hurts."

The women joined the men preparing to leave. Two bicycles waited at the safe house, so they would need to bring two more so everyone would have one for the journey to the farm. That meant two of them could ride to the safe house, and the other two would need to walk.

"I've been thinking it through," Petrus said. "We're less likely to be seen if we split up."

Ingrid nodded. That was wise, and if something happened, it was better for two of them to be arrested than all four of them captured.

"And . . ." Petrus glanced at Ingrid, then at Gerrit. "Well, you two are about the same age. If you were caught, you could pretend to be a pair of adolescent lovers, and you could probably talk your way out of any serious trouble."

Ingrid stiffened. She had agreed to a truce with Gerrit, but that didn't mean she wanted to pretend to be his sweetheart. "I'm not sure—"

Petrus continued. "You're not going to get caught, Ingrid. You know Arnhem. You know the routes any patrols are likely to take. But this minimizes the risk to the group as a whole. Willem and I would be the most suspicious, should we be stopped. But that won't happen either. Willem and I will meet you at the safe house."

Ingrid folded her arms. She would rather ride than walk, and the bicycle had been hers since her casts had come off in spring 1940. More than that, pretending to be in a romantic relationship with Gerrit would test her acting abilities. She'd flirted her way past checkpoints when she'd been carrying messages, stolen papers, or money, but flirting with a stranger was easier than flirting with someone who irritated her. She'd never seen any of those guards a second time. Gerrit, on the other hand, seemed likely to live with his opa until the end of the war. "I think you just don't want to walk."

Petrus grinned. "That too."

She glanced at Anita for help, but her friend was busy talking to her nephew. Gerrit's frown suggested that perhaps he, too, was less than thrilled about their cover.

"His plan does have a certain logic to it," Anita said. "Willem's still not completely finished with his convalescence. He should ride. And, well, you and Ingrid are the same age. Petrus isn't old enough to be her father, but he's too old to be her boyfriend. And if the Nazis caught you and Petrus after curfew, they'd assume you were up to no good."

Gerrit met Ingrid's eyes and gave her a cross between a grin and a grimace. "Seeing as how we'll be on foot, I suppose we'll take longer, so the two of us should leave first."

Gerrit wished he knew Arnhem better. He didn't want to ask questions about where Ingrid was leading him—noise might attract attention, and asking Ingrid for help was . . . Well, he'd rather avoid it if he could. He'd already humbled himself when it came to Ingrid. The reduced animosity was no doubt a boon to Anita, and

Gerrit didn't enjoy butting heads with Ingrid. But nor did he want to give her any additional reasons for thinking she was better than him.

The sun had set, but the sky near the western horizon wasn't completely dark. The shadows were deep enough to hide in, but someone could spot them on the sidewalk. He walked beside Ingrid for the sake of their cover, though it might have been easier to walk behind her.

A pair of men appeared in the twilight's gloom, coming toward them, still too far away for Gerrit to see if they wore uniforms. Curfew had begun a few minutes before, so it was late enough that the German authorities or the Dutch who worked with them could detain them, but not so far after curfew that a reasonable man—if there were any of those in the German occupation forces—might let it slide.

Gerrit slipped his arm around Ingrid's waist and recited the Dutch poem he'd used on the girl in the market in Utrecht.

She leaned her head on his shoulder. "I bet you say that to all the girls." She pulled him around a corner.

"I've used it before, yes."

She stopped with her back against a wall, and Gerrit, playing the role, stood close, almost leaning into her. He put a hand on her waist and lowered his forehead until it almost touched hers. Each action was only pantomime, but it wasn't unpleasant.

Ingrid smiled up at him. "I wonder what they would do if I slapped you."

He shifted, giving her more room. "They would probably give my papers more scrutiny than ideal. Or insist on hauling me somewhere with better lighting. Anita would be heartbroken if I were arrested, so for her sake, please don't create a scene."

She held her pose. "I'm curious. Who else have you been reciting Dutch poetry to?"

"Those details will remain secret but involved situations not unlike this one. I'm not foolish enough to fall in love during a war."

Ingrid looked past him. "They're gone."

Gerrit quickly backed away. The last thing he wanted was for her to think he'd enjoyed pretending to be her lover. She was pretty enough, clever enough. Perhaps they could cooperate more and bicker less, become colleagues rather than opponents. Maybe even friends, eventually. Nothing more.

Ingrid led him the rest of the way down the alley so they wouldn't be spotted by the pair of men who had conveniently ignored them. They could hardly hope to be ignored again. This road was more familiar to him, because one of the shops that lined the streets sold ice cream—or it had before the war. He recognized a dress shop, too, where Anita had talked Mam into buying a new dress. The dress she'd been wearing the last time he'd seen her.

Gerrit pulled his mind from the past. Arnhem was a different place now. The Netherlands was a different place now. Maybe the whole world was.

A creak sounded behind them. "You there, where are you going?"

Gerrit flinched at the German words and turned to see a uniformed German soldier standing in the doorway to one of the shops. Just one man, and darkness would likely thwart his aim. Gerrit reached for Ingrid's arm and was about to tell her to run when she spoke instead.

"Good evening, soldat. How are you?" Ingrid used German.

"You're not supposed to be out past curfew. That was twenty minutes ago."

Ingrid made a show of looking at her watch. "But last time I visited my uncle, curfew wasn't until eight. Did it change?"

The soldier walked toward them. "Yes, and I'll need to see your papers."

"Oh, those are at my uncle's home. Perhaps you can escort me there? I didn't think the restrictions applied to Reich citizens."

The soldier glanced along the street. "Where's your uncle's home?"

"Reichskommissar Seyss-Inquart lives on the Parkstraat in Velp." Ingrid patted Gerrit's arm. "This strapping young member of the NSB was planning to see me home, but I think I'd prefer a German escort."

Gerrit held back a gag of disgust at being labeled a member of the Dutch Nazi party, but the soldier seemed far more surprised than Gerrit was. "You're Seyss-Inquart's niece?"

Ingrid nodded. "Yes, visiting from Vienna. I'm sure he'll be in an awful mood to learn that his own niece confused the curfew times."

Gerrit could almost imagine the soldier's train of thought. Like most Dutch school boys, Gerrit had imitated Arthur Seyss-Inquart's distinctive limp as a jest, had called him Six-and-a-Quarter instead of Seyss-Inquart. But as the highest-ranking Nazi in the Netherlands, the man was positively terrifying. Ingrid's German would mark her as Austrian, and that might be enough to make the soldier believe her assertion, or at the very least consider it possible. And if it was true, no ordinary soldier wanted to risk an unpleasant encounter with the reichskommissar.

The soldier glanced along the road, then back the other way. "I've a street to patrol. You best get home to your uncle as soon as possible."

"I'll go there directly. Have a wonderful evening, soldat." Ingrid turned Gerrit around and led him away from the soldier. She didn't cut into the first alley. But she took the second, and with her arm tucked through his, he could feel her trembling.

He, too, was keyed up enough to fear he would vomit. He inhaled deeply and ran a hand over his face as he leaned against a brick wall. "I can't believe you claimed to be Six-and-a-Quarter's niece. And I can't believe we got away with it."

"We're both Austrian. It seemed worth a try. I'm surprised the patrolman didn't say something about us walking all the way to Velp in the dark, but I think even an average German soldier is intimidated by a reichskommissar."

"What were you planning to do if he didn't buy your bluff?"

Ingrid started walking again, and Gerrit took a few quick steps to catch up. "Had that been the case, I was hoping we could outrun him."

When Gerrit and Ingrid arrived at the safe house twenty minutes later, Petrus and Willem were already there along with their bicycles. So was another man, and Gerrit recognized him, even though only a single candle lit the entryway.

"Were you in Rotterdam during the bombing?"

Berend nodded. "I was stationed there as a cadet."

"You might not remember, but you pulled my sister and me out of a canal. If you hadn't, we would have drowned. And if we hadn't crossed the canal, we would have burned. Thank you."

Berend scrutinized Gerrit. But that had been four years ago, and Gerrit had been sopping wet. "I remember pulling a few people from the canals. Glad I could help."

"What happened to you when the city surrendered?"

Berend shifted his feet. "We were war prisoners in Germany for a while. Then we were released, somewhat worse for wear, and allowed to come home. Last year, they asked us to report for internment again, but I wasn't stupid enough to go back. I've been an onderduiker ever since."

"And a resistance man." Gerrit shook Berend's hand. "I'm happy to join you. I've smuggled ration coupons and paperwork, but I've never sabotaged anything, and I'm eager to try my hand."

"Glad to hear it." Berend looked at the others. "We had best leave. We'll ride one person at a time rather than bunching up. I'll lead. Maintain twenty meters between riders." He blew out the light and took his bicycle outside. Willem went next, then Petrus.

"After you," Gerrit said to Ingrid.

One of her eyebrows rose in surprise, but she accepted his invitation and headed off after the others. Gerrit gave her a few seconds to mount her bicycle and pedal from the house, and then he headed after her.

The beginning of their journey lay through busy neighborhoods. He hoped no one watched from windows, especially if the occupants were Germans or sympathizers. Though if anyone did, he wasn't sure how much they would see in the darkness. He could make out Ingrid, but he couldn't see Petrus ahead of her. The moon hadn't yet risen.

For the next hour, the pace was steady but not strenuous. The moon rose, and that made Petrus visible, but not Willem or Berend. Then the pace slowed significantly. Or that was what Gerrit thought until Petrus disappeared from view again, and he realized Ingrid was falling behind.

They were supposed to maintain distance, but they were away from any homes, and something was obviously amiss, so he caught up to her.

"Is everything all right?" Gerrit asked.

"Something's wrong with my bicycle."

Gerrit stepped off his own. "Trade me. See if you can catch Petrus. I'll look at it and catch up. But make sure I see the next turn so I don't go the wrong way."

She took his bicycle. "Thank you."

She'd left him behind the first time she'd gone to meet Berend. He didn't entirely trust her not to do the same thing again. "You'll wait at the next turn, won't you? Or come back?"

"I promise I won't let you get lost." She pushed from the ground and sped away.

Gerrit tried her bicycle to feel what wasn't working. It took him only a single push to diagnose the symptoms: a chain that didn't move smoothly. He backpedaled and watched the chain move along the sprocket until he spotted the frozen links. With tools and lubricant, he could make the bike run as intended, but for now, he flexed the problem links back and forth until the plates opened slightly and the tight link resolved. He'd look at it again in daylight, but for now, he wanted to see if the bicycle would work well enough for him to catch the others.

The chain seemed to slide over the gears well enough now, and Gerrit put on a burst of speed. This bicycle still had rubber tires, as opposed to the other one he'd been riding that had only the rims. The tires probably had a few patches, but the bike was in better shape than any he'd ridden in years, and the open road and the call for speed made Gerrit feel a surge of joy.

Freedom. That was what it felt like, this speeding along in the dark to an unknown location where he could learn how to finally take his revenge on the Nazis. Helping feed onderduikers was all well and good, but he was ready to strike back.

Ingrid waited for him at a crossroads, and he was strangely happy to see her. "You got it working again?" she asked.

"For now. It had a few frozen links. I'm not sure how long the fix will last, but with the right tools, I ought to be able to repair it."

Ingrid began pedaling. "We may as well ride together. We're less likely to be seen out here, and, well, we already convinced one soldier we're a couple. I suspect we could do it again."

They pedaled swiftly, trying to catch the others. Gerrit's bicycle gradually became less and less responsive, so he pedaled harder so as not to be outpaced. "Do they know how far behind we are?" he asked.

"No, but that was the second-to-last turn. Petrus is supposed to wait for us on the road so we know which farm to stop at."

Gerrit hoped it wouldn't be much longer because his legs burned, and he wasn't interested in providing amusement for Petrus if he couldn't keep up with Ingrid. He had to be slowing, but Ingrid matched his pace. She'd also fought with the bicycle, so maybe she was weary too. He doubted she was slowing out of consideration.

Petrus stepped from behind a tree just before they rode past. There wasn't enough warning to slow and make the turn, so Gerrit and Ingrid rode past the driveway, then turned around and rode back. Moonlight revealed a farmhouse surrounded by several smaller structures—probably hutches for rabbits or chickens. It didn't look like a school for saboteurs, but maybe that was what made it so ideal.

As a morning breeze whispered through the farmyard, Ingrid studied the painted paper target near the barn and rubbed at the knots in her shoulders. She hadn't complained—not out loud anyway—when all five of them, her and four men, had been taken to their sleeping quarters the night before. One narrow room in the attic, tucked away behind a wall. Anyone searching the attic would assume the room with the trunks and old furniture was the attic's only space. The secret room beyond was a clever hiding place for a group intent on learning illegal skills like how to make bombs, detect tails, and monitor a target. But the lack of privacy was a new, degrading experience for her. She had always had her own room at Falcon Point. She'd had her own room at the van der Veen home as well, even when the house swelled with guests, because they kept onderduikers on floors farther from the entrance so they'd have more time to hide in the event of a nighttime raid. The farmhouse consisted of a single level, however, so the attic was the only safe option for the resistance students.

"Sleep well, Ingrid?" Petrus asked with a tone of mischief.

Ingrid would have preferred to ignore him, but that would only make him ask more questions. "Reminded me of camping before the war." That wasn't entirely true. She was fairly certain the family tent had more square footage than the room in the attic, and she'd been smaller back then. The cot she'd slept on while camping was far more comfortable than a blanket on the floor. And being in close quarters with siblings and parents had been a fun break from routine. Being in close quarters with four men had been simply uncomfortable.

"You camped?" Petrus's upturned lip suggested he didn't quite believe it.

"My father took me when I was younger, before the war."

"In a tent or in a cabin?"

Ingrid smiled at his persistence. "Both. When you are born in a land of beautiful mountains and breathtaking lakes, it is best to try both." They had usually stayed in cabins when the whole family had gone, but Papa had taken her and Karl for overnight adventures on many summer nights. She missed her brother and father. Her mother and sister too. What she wouldn't give to have been crowded into the tiny attic nook with them instead of the men.

Berend handed her, Petrus, Gerrit, and Willem four different types of pistols. "Those are empty. I want you to practice loading and unloading each kind."

They spent the morning learning as much as they could about the weapons: cleaning them, loading them, aiming at targets, and pulling the trigger. They didn't shoot any rounds. Weapons and ammunition were hard to get, and even if they'd had unlimited rounds, shooting them would create enough noise to attract attention. They worked for hours, and given the ride of the night before—much of it forcing an uncooperative bicycle to keep up with the group—her legs were tired. Given the nature of their sleeping arrangements, most of her other muscles were stiff and tender.

Ingrid wasn't sure she wanted to assassinate anyone. It seemed wrong. And yet, what if killing a traitor would save others in her resistance cell before the traitor turned them over to the Nazis? What if killing a key official would prevent a train full of Jews from being deported to camps they were unlikely to return from? Morality aside, a competitive streak kept her working, improving, practicing. Whether she ever shot anyone or not, she didn't want to fail at her training or give any of the men reason to doubt her. There was an underlying assumption that women were less of a threat. That was what the Nazis thought, and that made Ingrid even more valuable because they were less likely to suspect her. But if she proved less capable than the men, they might think the Nazis, and society as a whole, were right.

Berend was free with his hands as he helped her aim, adjusting her arms, pressing his hand to her back. She subtly shifted positions to create more space between them. He stepped in, patted her hip, and suggested a holster there would be wise because she could hide it with a coat. If a few buttons were undone, the bulge wouldn't show. Or she could put the weapon in the pocket of a jacket, if the pocket was deep enough. He brushed her lower back. "Or you could hide a pistol there, beneath a few loose layers." She shrugged away from his touch.

"Berend?" Gerrit's gaze seemed hostile as he took in Berend's close proximity to Ingrid. "What type of recoil should I expect with this one?" Gerrit held up the 9mm FN pistol. Berend moved on to Gerrit. His hands stayed at his sides, and he used words instead of fingers for instruction. *Men.* If she didn't need Berend to train her, she would have slapped or elbowed him. And Gerrit—glaring at her as if she were intentionally distracting Berend and monopolizing his time. At least Gerrit had pulled Berend away.

Berend continued to give them tips as they worked: the best way to dispose of a weapon if a search seemed likely. The best way to tail a contact without being discovered. The best places to ambush a target.

"And tomorrow we'll practice aiming while riding a bicycle."

"Can I borrow a few tools and work on the bicycles?" Gerrit asked. "One of them needs a better chain repair than I could give it last night."

Berend nodded and went to fetch the tools. Ingrid kept working on loading, unloading, holding the pistol in two hands to aim, lining up the sights, and pressing the trigger. She would have liked to practice with live rounds, but she understood the need to maintain quiet and preserve their limited ammunition.

Petrus and Willem smoked, and Gerrit and Berend chatted over the bicycle that she'd been riding yesterday. Gerrit took pieces of the chain and gears apart as if he'd done it a hundred times before. He adjusted and oiled the links while he and Berend discussed and debated the next steps for driving the Nazis from the Netherlands. Those two shared the same thirst to hurt the Nazis. She understood. She didn't know Berend's story, other than an unpleasant stay in a German camp for war prisoners. But she remembered the day the telegram had come bearing news of destruction in Rotterdam and death for Gerrit's mother. Then the Nazis had taken a father and an uncle from him. She knew what it was like to lose family. Knew the deep, burning fury at the Germans who had stolen them in death or detainment.

Then, while Gerrit put the bicycle back together, he and Berend turned to what they wanted the Netherlands to look like after the war. She rolled her eyes as they spouted off communist drivel about the evils of capitalism and the sins of the wealthy. They wouldn't ever convince her that capitalism and wealth had created the Nazi evil. That was the result of something else entirely. Harsh reparations. Hurt pride. Desperation. Weariness when option after option, election after election, had failed to improve conditions. Then fear, then consent as the evil grew more and more powerful.

She hoped Gerrit didn't know how wealthy her family had been. But that was a silly thought. Why should she care if Gerrit looked down on her because she had been born to privilege? She steadied her pistol, aimed at the target, and pretended to shoot. She had a feeling the next few days would, for her, be a test of endurance.

CHAPTER 11

INGRID RELISHED THE WARMTH OF afternoon sunshine on her face as she cycled back to Arnhem after finishing her three days of training at the farmhouse. Gerrit, Petrus, and Willem had decided to wait until dark before returning to Arnhem to avoid the risk of a razzia, so she rode alone, a pleasant change after so much time with the men. Berend had assigned her a bicycle that didn't have rubber for the tires, so it was slower and harder to pedal, but the gears worked flawlessly because Gerrit had given all the bicycles mechanical overhauls. Someday, someday soon if the Allies kept advancing, she would ride a bicycle that had rubber tires *and* was in excellent mechanical condition. Not only that, but she would ride it without fear that German soldiers or Dutch collaborators would harass or arrest her. Someday, it would be divine.

When she arrived, Ingrid pulled the bicycle into the basement through the cellar door, then took the stairs to the ground level. Given the day and time, Anita ought to be at home, and Ingrid was anxious to see her. She didn't call out in case there were new onderduikers trying to sleep, but after searching the first two levels of the home, she wondered if perhaps Anita had gone to the hospital after all. Ingrid had missed Anita, but she had also missed her bed. A nap would be a worthy consolation.

Distant laughter sounded from above, so Ingrid climbed the stairs to the top floor. The giggle was feminine. It sounded like Anita, but Ingrid hadn't heard Anita laugh in years.

"Now you number them in alphabetical order," a male voice said in Dutch.

"There are two *A*'s." That was Anita.

"In that case, left to right. One, two." The man again.

Ingrid pushed the door open. Anita and an unfamiliar man sat next to each other at a desk with papers spread out before them. Or they did for a fraction of a second. Then the man flipped the desk forward, ducked, and pulled Anita to the floor with him. An instant later, he was aiming a pistol at Ingrid.

Ingrid held her breath and slowly raised her hands, showing that she wasn't armed.

"Don't shoot Ingrid!" Anita laid a hand on the man's arm. "She's family."

The man lowered his weapon.

"Where did you get that?" Anita asked him.

He tucked the pistol into his waistband at the small of his back. "Cornelis left it for me."

Anita stood and walked over to Ingrid. "Are you all right?"

Ingrid nodded, but having a pistol aimed at her was an experience she'd be glad never to repeat. Her heart was beating far too rapidly, and her throat felt dry.

The man stood, grasping his side. "I apologize. I didn't hear anything until you were at the door and . . . well, I'm sorry. You surprised me."

Anita, perhaps sensing how unsettled Ingrid felt, put an arm around her. "Are the others back yet?"

"They're waiting until dark. But training is finished, and I would rather sleep here than in a narrow attic room with four men."

Anita made a face of distaste. "I'm glad you're back. As you can see, we have a new guest. Luitenant Brug is visiting from America. I daresay he'll be on his way again as soon as he recovers from an emergency appendectomy." Anita's eyes homed in on the luitenant's hand still holding his lower right abdomen. "Does it hurt again?"

He gave her a lopsided grimace. "A little."

Anita walked back toward him. "You should have considered that before you started throwing furniture and your nurse around. And Cornelis ought to have told me that he left you with a pistol."

"I was trying to keep the two of us safe." He reached for the desk.

"No, don't try to put it right," Anita said. "That might make one of your stitches pull out, and Pap isn't planning to come home until nearly curfew. Ingrid, will you help me?"

Ingrid nodded and helped Anita lift the desk back into place.

"All right, Luitenant," Anita said. "I'll need to examine your incision site again."

His expression wasn't willing, but when Anita put her hands on her hips, he let out a sigh and untucked his shirt.

Ingrid gathered the scattered papers to give the man a bit of privacy. She glanced at the writing and tried to figure out what it meant. "What are these?" she asked.

"We were helping the luitenant's convalescence pass by comparing methods of encoding." Anita tapped the top sheet. "That's double transposition, using a poem as a code, although Luitenant Brug tells me random numbers are now the preferred key. An agent is less likely to remember them, and thus the Gestapo is less likely to drag it out of them."

Luitenant Brug fixed his shirt and faced Ingrid. "I'm sorry I pointed a weapon at you."

Anita smirked. "For some reason, people have a tendency to assume she's a spy."

The luitenant glanced between the women. "Based on the fact that she lives here and you trust her completely, I think my assumption was reasonable."

"But she's on our side."

"How did you learn to walk so quietly?" he asked Ingrid.

Ingrid shrugged. "I've lived here long enough to know which floorboards creak." Given how close Anita and the luitenant had been sitting and their easy manner with each other, Ingrid suspected that the two of them had been more absorbed in listening to each other than in listening for silent intruders.

"Maybe we can try this again." The luitenant offered Ingrid his hand. "I'm Luitenant Brug." Lieutenant Bridge didn't seem like a real name, but if he preferred to use an alias, she wouldn't insist on anything different.

"Ingrid van der Veen." Ingrid didn't use her real name either, but she shook his hand. "Welcome to Arnhem."

The man looked between Ingrid and Anita. "Not sisters, I would guess. Some other relation?"

Ingrid gave the same reply she'd given countless times before. "Our fathers are cousins."

"You look a little pale." Anita put her hand on the man's forehead, feeling his temperature. "You don't seem feverish, but maybe you should rest."

He nodded. Ingrid didn't know the man's normal appearance, but something about him suggested less-than-perfect health, and the skin around his eyes looked pinched with pain. "I should be gathering information, not napping."

"No one can predict a problem with an appendix." Anita motioned to the bed, and the luitenant sat.

He shook his head. "What a rotten time to be laid up. My fault or not, I'm letting people down. And now I'm late checking in, so they'll worry that I've been compromised and might not believe anything I tell them anyway. Without good intelligence—good intelligence they could trust—the cost in blood for our side will rise."

"Can we help?" Ingrid asked.

"I don't want to drag either of you into more danger."

Anita scoffed. "Don't be silly. We were in danger the moment the Nazis invaded, in more danger the moment I let Cornelis bring you inside the house. And we both very much want the Moffen out of the Netherlands. Their rockets too."

"Rockets? The V-1s?" Ingrid had heard the V-1s thundering toward Britain, sounding like pulsing jackhammers. On clear nights, she had seen their fiery exhaust trails.

Anita nodded. "Luitenant Brug came to the Netherlands to study rocket science."

His serious expression softened. "Not quite. But they're taking a toll on Britain. Mostly aimed at London. Mostly killing civilians. Rumor is Hitler has another version coming along that's even worse. Current countermeasures are having limited success once they're in the air, but if we can prevent their launch altogether, we could save a lot of innocent lives."

"What do you need to know?" Ingrid asked. "Between us and Cornelis and all of his contacts, plus Berend and all of his, we ought to be able to learn something useful."

"Do you trust Berend?" Anita asked.

"To defeat the Nazis? I think so. To restore the queen and the constitution when the Moffen are finally driven out? That's a little more uncertain." Nor would Ingrid trust him to share her sleeping quarters if there weren't three other men around.

"Is he a Communist?" Luitenant Brug asked.

Ingrid nodded.

Luitenant Brug thought for a while. "I don't suppose anyone, Soviet or German, would be surprised to find American intelligence agents poking around to learn more about the rockets. I was trying to determine whether there were any launching facilities in Gorssel when I fell ill. If there are, we can have our bombers destroy the sites before they kill more people in England."

"Gorssel?" Anita straightened. "That's only a few hours away by bicycle."

"I could ride over there now," Ingrid offered. She'd gone on trips of similar length time after time to pinpoint checkpoints, antiaircraft batteries, and supply depots. Opa and Anita spoke so often of helping those in need. Normally that meant onderduikers in Gelderland, but surely it also included innocent British civilians.

"You already had a long ride today," Anita pointed out. "I can go."

Luitenant Brug looked even more ill than he had before. Ingrid hoped he hadn't torn something loose internally when he'd thrown the desk on its side. "Aren't the two of you vulnerable to abuse from the Germans? If you were middle-aged and ugly, I might not worry, but given the fact that the two of you are young and quite good-looking . . ." His cheeks colored slightly. "I don't want either of you harmed."

"If we both went, we could look after each other," Ingrid said.

Anita smiled. "Yes, but then Luitenant Brug might shoot my nephew when he returns."

Luitenant Brug opened his mouth, then shut it again. "Perhaps if you give me a good description of what he and the others look like, I'll recognize them when I see them."

Anita shook her head. "No, I'll go alone. I'm the faster cyclist anyway, and I've been itching to get out of Arnhem. This is the perfect excuse. With any luck, I'll arrive in Gorssel with several hours of daylight left. I might even beat Gerrit and the others home."

Luitenant Brug shook his head. "I don't think it's wise for me to pass my responsibilities off to you when it puts you in danger."

"I'd be grateful for the chance to tell your airplanes where they should drop their bombs. I lost my sister in an air raid. If I can save someone in Britain from going through the same thing . . . You can't very well go. You'd be doubled over in pain within minutes, and even if you weren't, I've seen your papers. They're a good forgery, but they are a forgery, aren't they?"

"The papers are a forgery, yes," Luitenant Brug said. "And though I suspect you're exaggerating about how quickly I'd be doubled over in pain, you're right that I'm not up to several hours on a bike."

"Then, trust me," Anita said. "And tell me what I'm looking for."

When Anita left Luitenant Brug's room, Ingrid followed her down the stairs. "Are you sure you don't want me to come with you?"

"I'd like your company, but I plan to take the best bicycle. That would leave you with a slower one, and like I said before, you've already ridden a great deal today."

Ingrid folded her arms. "And even if I hadn't, and even if we had real rubber for all the tires, you'd still be faster. But you'll be careful, won't you? He's right about German soldiers."

Anita nodded. "I've arranged treatment for more than one of their female victims. I know what they're capable of. But if we're in the city, they'll behave. And when I'm not in the city, I bet I can outride them. Shooting a moving target is harder than it sounds, especially on the way back when it will be dark."

Ingrid wasn't so sure. "Berend had us practice assassination from a bicycle. I didn't pick it up right away, but by the end of day three, we all seemed to have it down. We can hope anyone trying to chase you has had less practice, but there's no guarantee."

Anita hooked her arm through Ingrid's. "I wish I could hear all about your training now, but I think it will have to wait until I'm back. I'll see more if I get there before twilight."

Ingrid nodded. "Yes, we can share news when you return. But be careful?"

"I will be."

While Anita grabbed Opa's field glasses, Ingrid went to the kitchen and placed a few slices of bread and a wedge of cheese into a napkin, then wrapped it into a bundle. She met Anita outside as she was bringing the bicycle out of the cellar. "Put this on top of the binoculars so they aren't so obvious if you're stopped at a checkpoint. And sometimes they put less effort into searching your things if you flirt with them a little."

Anita nodded. "I think I can manage that. I'll just pretend I'm flirting with Luitenant Brug instead of an enemy."

Ingrid laughed. "You were sitting very close to one another when I walked in on you."

"Only so we could work on the same sheet of codes."

"If you say so." There wasn't time for teasing, but the moment Anita returned, Ingrid would insist on the full story.

Anita sighed. "Well, he is very good-looking. And very sweet. And obviously very brave to drop behind the lines like this. And I might as well enjoy his company while he recovers because he won't be here long." A dash of sorrow crept into her voice at the last statement.

Ingrid placed a hand on her arm. "Anita?"

Anita returned the gesture. "Don't worry. I won't let myself get too attached. Will you check on him every few hours? I'm afraid he might have damaged Pap's sutures when he knocked the desk over, and as much as I'd like him to stay longer, I'm not selfish enough to want his care ignored. If his fever returns, you'll need to call the hospital and alert Pap."

"I've never seen you give so much as a fond glance at any of the daring men who have passed through the home before." Ingrid smiled. "Luitenant Brug must be exceptional. So even if he nearly frightened me to death, I'll take good care of him for you."

Anita smiled. "Maybe stomp a little on your way to his room so he's not surprised."

"You won't be there to distract him, so I doubt I could sneak up on him again, even if I wanted to, which I don't. Be careful, Anita."

Anita nodded and then set off for Gorssel.

Ingrid dragged one foot as she walked along the hallway of the upper floor, wanting to make sure she wouldn't surprise the American intelligence officer. She didn't suppose he would shoot her now that they'd met . . . unless he'd developed a fever. The next time she saw Cornelis, she would suggest he not leave patients with firearms until they were well and truly out of danger of delirium.

She knocked on the door and entered when Luitenant Brug told her to come in.

"Is it time for you to take my temperature again already?" he asked.

"It is."

He raised an eyebrow, took the thermometer from her, shook down the mercury, and stuck it under his tongue. "I'm not feverish."

"Good, but if you keep talking, I won't get an accurate reading, and Anita will scold me for neglecting my duties."

He didn't speak for the five minutes needed to take his temperature. He pulled the thermometer from his mouth and glanced at it before handing it to her. "No fever."

"No. How do you feel?"

"Sore."

Ingrid wasn't surprised. "You did have surgery only a few days ago. And moving furniture isn't normally encouraged so soon after a life-threatening infection."

He lay back on the bed. "I'll keep that in mind next time. I don't suppose the other Mejuffrouw van der Veen is back yet?"

"No. Anita is an accomplished cyclist, but she'll want to do a thorough job when she arrives, and neither the roads nor her bicycle are in top shape."

Plane engines had been rumbling in the distance, but they grew louder, and Ingrid walked to the window and parted the curtains to see if they were visible.

"Ours?" Luitenant Brug asked.

"Yes. B-17s. I assume heading back to bases in Britain." The route from Britain to the Ruhr and Berlin passed right over Arnhem.

He went to the adjacent window and peeked out. "My little sister got a job at an aircraft factory. Don't know which planes she's working on. I don't think she can tell me that in a letter. But every time I see one, I wonder if maybe she riveted something into place on that very plane."

"You miss her." Ingrid made it a statement, not a question.

"Yeah. Worry about her too. She's probably grown up a lot in the last few years, but if not, well, I hope she's staying out of trouble." He put his hands in his pockets. "That probably sounds callous. People all over the world are worrying about family being bombed or shot or starved to death. I don't have to worry about any of that for her. I just hope she's not running around with the wrong type of guy while I'm over here unable to talk her out of it."

"I miss my siblings too." Ingrid hadn't told many people, other than the van der Veens, about her missing brother and sister, but the ache to see them again, to know they were well—it hadn't left, despite the years.

"Brothers, sisters?"

"One of each."

"How long since you've seen them?"

"February 1940."

He let out a whistle. "That's a long time. Do you get letters?"

Ingrid shook her head. For all she knew, Karl and Anna were both dead.

"I'm sorry. That's got to be hard."

The planes flew out of sight. Not hearing from her family, not knowing what had happened to them—it was hard, but she didn't want to talk about it with a stranger, not even a model patient with sympathetic brown eyes. "Would you like anything to eat, Luitenant?"

He shook his head. "My appetite isn't back to normal yet. Maybe when the other Mejuffrouw van der Veen or the onderduikers you were training with return."

Ingrid glanced around the room. "I can leave you to rest, or if you'd like, I can find a deck of cards."

"A game of gin rummy sounds like just the thing."

"You'll have to explain the rules."

"I can do that."

Ingrid fetched the cards, and Luitenant Brug taught her how to play. He was partway through shuffling the deck after their practice game when he paused and stared at her for several long seconds.

"Is anything wrong?" she asked.

He shook his head. "No. Earlier today, you reminded me of someone, and I just figured out who. But that doesn't make any sense."

"Who?"

"A sailor I met in London a few years ago. Last I heard, he died at sea. But he wasn't Dutch."

Ingrid wasn't Dutch either. She had a cover to maintain, but if there was any chance the sailor was her brother, she had to know. "What was his name?"

Luitenant Brug placed a hand over his incision. Perhaps it was hurting. "Mr. . . . oh, what was his name? It would be easier to remember without a headache."

"Lang?" Ingrid asked. "I have Lang relatives who were trying to get to England."

"No, it was longer than that, and a bit of a mouthful. Had an ending you hear from time to time . . . not *stein* or *mann* or *burg*, but something like that."

Not Karl, then, and that was a relief. Ingrid was desperate for news of her brother, but she didn't wish to find out he'd been lost at sea. Opa already had that worry. "Opa has a son at sea and two in the East Indies. He hasn't heard from any of them since the Moffen invaded."

"Not knowing sometimes makes it worse."

Ingrid nodded her agreement. Opa also had sons in Amsterdam and Haarlem, but they communicated only through brief letters. If something went wrong with their work in the resistance, Opa and Anita didn't want the Gestapo tracking down Cas or Aart, especially not when they'd already lost Judith, and the three other siblings were missing.

"Does the other Mejuffrouw van der Veen have a beau?" Luitenant Brug asked after placing the queen of hearts in the discard pile.

"No." Ingrid kept her answer simple, but she would be certain to tell Anita that he had asked. "Do you?"

"No."

Ingrid would also be sure to pass that information on to Anita. Maybe it was silly to encourage a romance that couldn't last more than a week or two, but it had been years since Ingrid had seen Anita smile as wide as when she'd been speaking to or about Luitenant Brug. Maybe a week or two of happiness in the midst of war was a miracle worth pushing for.

Ingrid lost three games, then won the fourth. Luitenant Brug explained how the rockets worked and how RAF fighters sometimes managed to fly close enough to make the rocket's wings tip, overriding the gyro and making the V-1 spin and crash to the ground, away from the cities. Night fell while the two played, and in the middle of their fifth game, a door on the bottom level of the home creaked open.

Ingrid stood. "I'll see who it is."

It could be Anita or Opa or the trio of men coming from training. Ingrid hoped it was Anita because that was who she most wanted to speak with, but instead, she glanced down the last staircase to see Gerrit, Petrus, Willem, and Berend. Why was Berend here? He wasn't supposed to know where they lived. She understood the need to cooperate with other cells, but Berend's arrival breached normal security precautions.

"Hello, Berend." She did her best to be polite. "I didn't know you were joining us here."

Berend surveyed the entry. "Plans changed. I have an assignment for you. Gerrit too."

Any assignment for her ought to go through Anita, but Anita wasn't here. "What assignment?"

"A target." Berend made his way to the dining room. "I'll explain more over supper."

Ingrid hadn't yet made supper because she'd known in advance that everyone from Opa to Anita to the new trainees would be late. "I'll prepare something to eat as soon as I assure our newest onderduiker that the new arrivals aren't hostile."

"Someone else is here?" Berend seemed unhappy.

Ingrid nodded.

"Can he be trusted?"

"Yes." She wasn't ready to tell Luitenant Brug all her secrets, but Anita certainly trusted him, and Ingrid trusted Anita. "Cornelis brought him."

"Well, we can always use another man to help."

"He just had an appendectomy, so I think it's too early to incorporate him into any of your plans quite yet." And Luitenant Brug seemed focused on his primary mission. She didn't think he'd let Berend distract him from his rockets.

Ingrid walked the two sets of stairs and found Luitenant Brug waiting just around the corner on the top floor, his pistol out, but at his side rather than pointed at her.

"You won't need that." She gestured to the firearm. "The arrivals are friends. Three of them currently live here, so I expect you'll meet them soon. I'm planning to work on supper now. Shall I bring it up to you in a while? Anita might skin us both if I let you try the stairs this soon after surgery."

Luitenant Brug smiled slightly at the mention of Anita. "I can wait and eat when she gets back."

"If I let you go that long without food, she'll definitely skin me."

Luitenant Brug put his pistol away. "All right. For your sake, I'll continue to be a cooperative patient and eat my meal on time, in my room, at least for tonight."

"And tomorrow?"

He put a hand over what she assumed was his incision site. "For now, let's take it one day at a time."

"Hmm. Well, it's time to take your temperature again. Can I trust you to do that yourself?"

"Yes, ma'am."

Ingrid left the luitenant and went to the kitchen. Even before she entered, she could smell eggs frying, and the sizzle met her ears soon after the scent met her nose. Willem and Petrus never cooked.

Gerrit, standing in front of the stovetop, glanced over his shoulder at her. "Will you slice the rest of that bread?"

Ingrid didn't like being relegated to helper rather than master of the kitchen, but she held her tongue and grabbed the knife, aiming it at the bread despite the temptation to aim it at the usurper. But maybe having someone usurp her plans in the kitchen wasn't so awful when he did part of the work.

"Where did you get the eggs?" she asked. The price of eggs, like the price of everything, had shot up as the war dragged on. The last time she'd shopped, a single egg had been the extravagant price of one and a half gilders.

"The farm we stayed at." Gerrit flipped one of the eggs over. "I fixed a radio for the owners. I wasn't planning to charge them, but they insisted. Is Anita around?"

"She went on an errand for our new onderduiker."

Gerrit looked away from the frying pan for a moment. "What's she doing?"

Ingrid focused on slicing the bread. She wasn't sure how much Luitenant Brug wanted others to know of his mission. He'd been reluctant to tell Ingrid and Anita and likely wouldn't have said anything at all had he not been too ill to do the work himself. "I'm sure she'll tell you when she gets back."

Gerrit huffed and turned back to the eggs. "Will she be gone long?"

"I expect her before midnight. She took the bicycle you fixed at the farm. It worked very well on my ride, and I assume it will do the same for her." Ingrid snuck a glance at Gerrit. He fairly bristled with irritation, but that was hardly a rarity. "Our onderduiker isn't supposed to use stairs yet. I was planning to bring his food to him, unless you'd rather." Gerrit had cooked the food, so he deserved to deliver it, if he wanted to.

"You trust me to feed him?"

"Why wouldn't I?"

Gerrit shrugged. "You don't seem to trust me to do anything else, other than cook eggs and fix bicycles. Or maybe you just don't trust me to keep secrets."

If he was going to act like a child and be upset because she hadn't told him where Anita was, Ingrid was finished in the kitchen. "Maybe it's not my secret to tell."

"She's my aunt." Gerrit didn't shout, but his voice was louder than it had been before. "I've already lost both my parents—one of them permanently, maybe both of them—most of my uncles are missing, and I have no idea what happened to my brother and sister and cousin when I had to leave Utrecht. I just want to know that Anita's not about to get arrested or shot or otherwise taken away from me."

Ingrid swallowed. Maybe, were she in a similar position, she'd feel the same edge of desperation that carried through his voice. "I'll finish the eggs. Go talk to Luitenant Brug. Maybe he'll tell you."

Gerrit stared at her for a few moments, as if trying to determine whether she was trying to help. Finally, he took a plate, added an egg and a slice of bread to it, and headed toward the exit.

"Be sure you make noise going up the stairs. He's a bit jumpy. And be sure to tell him you're Anita's nephew." Gerrit had a way of getting on her nerves, but she didn't want Luitenant Brug accidentally shooting him. And she suspected Luitenant Brug would be more cooperative if he knew Gerrit's concern for Anita was familial attachment rather than anything romantic.

Gerrit nodded and left.

Gerrit liked Luitenant Brug. The man hadn't told Gerrit much, but he'd been nice about it rather than rubbing it in the way *some* of the home's residents liked to do. Luitenant Brug seemed to think Anita's assignment carried no more risk than a normal bicycle ride through occupied Gelderland. Gerrit hoped the man was right. Gerrit hadn't meant to sound so desperate in the kitchen, but he was tired of goodbyes. Not that he always had a goodbye. He'd been able to bid farewell to Johan and Nellie, but Mam's death had been sudden, Pap had been arrested at work, and Oom Nicolaas had left one morning and never returned. They knew he'd been taken in a razzia only because a neighbor had seen it.

Gerrit took the luitenant's dishes to the kitchen, then joined the others in the dining room. He sat beside Berend and across from Ingrid. Gerrit's egg was lukewarm now rather than hot, but he was hungry enough that he didn't really care.

Berend took a picture from his pocket and placed it in front of Gerrit. It showed a man with thin-rimmed glasses, fair hair, and a long, straight nose. "That's our target."

"Who is he?" Gerrit assumed he was Dutch since the man wore no uniform.

"Dirk Daalmans. Founding member of the NSB. Makes his living by turning in onderduikers. Gained the trust of a resistance member and that led to the arrest of an entire cell. We suspect it's not the first time he's befriended and betrayed someone."

Gerrit passed the picture to Ingrid, who studied the image.

"When you say target, what exactly do you mean?" she asked.

Berend leaned back in his seat. "I want you to find him, tail him, see where he lives, what his patterns are. Then I want you to plan a hit and take him out."

Ingrid looked up from the photo. "You want us to kill a Dutchman?"

"I want you to kill a traitor," Berend said. "I'd prefer to kill Germans, but the reprisals for that make it a tactic to be used only selectively."

"Aren't there reprisals for killing collaborators too?" Ingrid still held the photo.

Berend nodded. "Yes, but not as severe. Believe me, there are others I'd like to punish, but we limit this type of operation to targets who are likely to cause more harm by living than we would expect from a reprisal."

Gerrit wasn't sure he wanted to kill someone, even if Daalmans deserved it, and Ingrid's pallor suggested similar reluctance.

"We only have two options." Berend's voice was firm. "We can kill him. Or we can let him continue hunting down anyone who's gone into hiding because they're Jewish or because they're trying to avoid slaving away in a German factory or because they've been working for the resistance. We can't arrest him because we don't control any of the jails. We can't tell him to stop, because he'd have us arrested. Killing him is guaranteed to save more lives than it costs."

Ingrid folded her arms. "That will be small comfort to anyone rounded up and shot in reprisal."

"Then, make it look like an accident instead of an assassination." Berend pointed to the picture. "He's responsible for twenty arrests, probably more, and of those, we can assume the overwhelming majority will be executed or sent to a camp they won't return from. Most are probably dead already." Berend glanced to where Willem and Petrus sat listening but not participating in the discussion. "Petrus and Willem can assist after nightfall. During daylight, Ingrid is the least suspicious." Berend's eyes fell on Gerrit. "And you look enough like a schoolboy that the danger to you is acceptable."

Acceptable danger. Gerrit wasn't sure where Berend drew the line between acceptable danger and unacceptable danger. Gerrit swallowed. He wanted to fight back at the Nazis, and it sounded as if trailing and targeting Dirk Daalmans was his best option for that.

"Have you anywhere to hide a pistol?" Berend asked.

Gerrit thought of the loose floor panel under Ingrid's bed. He met her eyes but didn't open his mouth. He'd already interfered once with her hiding place. He wouldn't make the mistake of volunteering it without her permission.

She didn't speak immediately, but eventually she nodded. "I can think of several places."

"I'll bring one by in a few days, and you can share your plans then," Berend said. "He's been seen often at Arnhem Centraal in the mornings. That's where I'd start looking for him."

Petrus seemed to have recognized Ingrid's reservations about the assignment. He touched her elbow. "If you figure out where he sleeps, I can help with the rest."

The sound of someone unlocking the front door drew Willem from the room. He reappeared a few moments later. "It's Dr. van der Veen."

Ingrid slipped the picture of their target off the table. "He won't want to know about this."

Gerrit nodded. Opa had devoted his entire life to healing people. What would he think about an assassination? No matter who the target, Gerrit didn't think Opa would approve. But that didn't seem fair. If Gerrit escaped to the Allied lines and joined the Dutch forces in exile, no one would condemn him for shooting an enemy soldier on the battlefield. That was war. And this was also war . . . but something about the assignment felt different. Regardless, Opa had to eat. "I'll go fry him an egg."

Ingrid lay awake, the image of Dirk Daalmans in her mind. A traitor. A villain. A target. None of the titles meant she was willing to kill him. Moral scruples aside—and those might be insurmountable—four days of rigorous training might not be enough to turn her into a competent assassin.

The floorboards outside her doorway creaked, and she tensed. Probably just one of the men walking to the end of the hall to use the water closet because someone else was using the one upstairs. Still, after the way Berend had found so many excuses to touch her during training, she wished she would have locked her door. She didn't think he would be so bold as to enter her bedroom uninvited, but he was a godless Communist who planned assassinations. He might think nothing of attempted seduction.

She relaxed when Anita called softly at the door, quietly enough that she wouldn't have woken Ingrid had she been asleep.

Ingrid slipped from bed and pulled the door open. "I'm glad you're back. You're later than I expected."

Anita came inside and switched on a lamp. "Gerrit was waiting in the kitchen when I arrived. He fried an egg for me. And then I checked on Henry because Gerrit said that his temperature was higher when Opa checked on him last."

"Henry?"

"Luitenant Brug. Seeing as how you and I are both Mejuffrouw van der Veen, I told him he could call me Anita, and then he suggested I call him Hendrik, but that's too confusing when Gerrit's surname is Hendriks, so I suggested Henri or Heinrich or Henry. I imagine Henry is the one an American would use." Anita smiled.

"And how exactly did Luitenant Brug come to be here?" He'd told her a little over their card games but had also confessed that he didn't remember large portions of his stay.

Anita sat on the edge of Ingrid's bed. "Cornelis brought him by the day after you left. They were pretending to be drunk. I doubt Cornelis has ever been drunk a day in his life, but by the time Cornelis got him here, Henry could barely walk. I wanted to take him to the hospital, but Cornelis wouldn't allow it. Henry speaks marvelous Dutch, but when he's delirious—and he was then—he mutters in English. Pap listed all the reasons the hospital was the better place for surgery, but Cornelis wouldn't risk it. He said Henry knew too much, and if he were questioned while so sick and vulnerable . . . well, he might not be able to keep his secrets. Given the circumstances, the choices were doing the best he could here or letting Henry die."

"Then, where was the surgery?"

"In Pap's bedroom. Cornelis and I assisted."

Ingrid glanced in the direction of Opa's room. "I'm glad it worked."

"Me too."

"Our patient taught me how to play gin rummy while you were gone." Ingrid ran her toe along the floorboards. "He asked if you had a beau."

"Did he?" Anita's voice was still soft, but the excitement there was impossible to miss.

"Yes, and he has no beau himself."

Anita's smile grew to a grin. "I'm being ridiculous. I only met him a few days ago. But . . . well, sometimes you just know."

Ingrid nodded, not because she had experience with falling in love but because her father had said much the same thing about meeting her mother.

"So, um, which of my dresses do you think is most flattering?"

Ingrid laughed. "The blue one that you gave to me because you didn't like the way that Green Policeman eyed you the last time you wore it." She gestured to her closet. "Take it back. It's shorter than is fashionable on me anyhow." That was true of most of Ingrid's clothing. She and Anita had been sharing for the past four years, and Ingrid was now taller and had longer legs.

"You don't mind?"

"No. I just wish I had some lipstick to loan you. How was Luitenant Brug when you checked on him?"

"Sleepy but interested in hearing all about my trip to Gorssel. I tried to sketch the rockets for him. They're like small airplanes but without windows. Fatter than a torpedo, and the engine attached to the back is shaped like an enormous spyglass. I couldn't get the engine quite right, but the ramps and wooden sheds of the launchers were easy enough to draw."

"How close were you?" The rocket sites were carefully guarded.

"About a hundred meters away. For the most part, the area is cleared so trees don't interfere with the launch, so I think I saw enough, with the aid of Pap's field glasses."

"Did you run into any trouble?"

"No. But after a ride that long, I'm feeling it in my legs. I'll feel it even more tomorrow."

"Well, I'm glad you're back." Ingrid hesitated before turning the subject to something far less cheerful than mysterious American intelligence officers recuperating from appendectomies. "Did you hear that Berend is staying the night? He plans to leave in the morning."

Anita nodded. "Gerrit told me. And it's not that I suspect Berend, but now there's one more person who can give us away if the Germans catch him. And I heard about the assignment."

Ingrid frowned. "I don't want to be an assassin."

"Then, don't be. That's not what we agreed to. Berend can't make you do it."

"Will Gerrit do it?"

Anita folded her arms. "Maybe. He has so much built-up hatred for the Nazis. And he thinks stopping Daalmans from hurting anyone else will save people in the final tally." She swallowed. "Maybe he's right, but I hate how much the war has changed him. He used to be so sweet, and now he's discussing plans for an execution. I suppose the bombing of Rotterdam stole away the last bit of his childhood, but he's lost more than that. His faith. His innocence. His innate sense of right and wrong. And I don't like Berend's suggestion that he look for Daalmans at Arnhem Centraal. It's too close to Gestapo headquarters, and no matter what Berend says, Gerrit does not look like a schoolboy anymore. Even if he did, I don't suppose a German soldier who's been told to collect a hundred men will be too careful about who he loads onto those trucks. And if they see Gerrit's papers, they'll wonder why he has an Utrecht address, and if they start asking questions . . ."

Ingrid took Anita's hand and squeezed it.

Anita shook her head. "I'm sorry. I was so happy to see Gerrit again. But now I'm just worried about him. I tried to talk him out of the assassination, but he's determined."

"Maybe tomorrow he'll change his mind. I can do the tailing near the station. I don't want to kill anyone, but I can help locate a traitor."

Anita nodded. "I should let you sleep. I'll talk to Berend tomorrow. Tell him what my cell is and isn't to be used for." She stood and was almost to the door before their earlier conversation flitted through Ingrid's mind.

"Don't forget that blue dress."

CHAPTER 12

Early-morning sunlight rushed through the windows when Ingrid pulled back the blackout curtains. She hadn't been squeezed into a small hidden room in an attic, hearing the men and smelling their cigarette smoke, yet despite being in her own bed in her own room, she'd had trouble sleeping. Where was the line between right and wrong when it came to thwarting a deadly Dutch traitor? She had thought about it most of the night and all of that morning. Did agreeing to find the man cross that line, even if she wouldn't be the one pulling the trigger?

The house was quiet when she left her room. The men, other than Opa, had little reason to rise early. Ingrid used the water closet to tidy up, and when she left, Berend stood in the hallway.

"Are you heading to Arnhem Centraal soon?" he asked.

"About that . . ." Sometime during the night, she'd concluded that anyone involved would bear some of the guilt. "I don't want to be involved with making hits on targets."

Berend raised one eyebrow. "We're at war. We all have to do a great many things we don't *want* to do. It's for the greater good, for our freedom. And being a woman, you're less likely to draw suspicion." He pointed toward the stairs leading to where the other men slept. "If I sent one of them, they'd likely be picked up before they even found him."

"I understand that, but . . . isn't there another way?"

Berend shook his head. "We already went through this. We control no jails, no prisons. Elimination is the only option. Think of it as an execution."

Ingrid looked away. "Most executions occur after a trial and conviction."

"We don't control the courts either. Trust me, he's guilty. He has blood on his hands, and taking him out will save lives. Lots of them."

Ingrid tried to remember all that her parents had taught her. They had believed in justice, but they'd also believed in rule of law. Papa had always told them to do what was right, but what happened when she wasn't sure which choice was right and which was wrong? She didn't want to disappoint Berend or force others to take risks that would be far smaller if she took them. Nor did she want Dirk Daalmans to continue turning innocent people over to the Nazis. But killing another person, even someone who was guilty, still felt wrong.

Berend placed a hand on her shoulder. "I know you're not Dutch."

Ingrid met his eyes, not denying it but also wondering how he knew. Two years ago, Opa had congratulated her on sounding like a native, and the language came even easier now. Had Gerrit told him? Anita?

Berend lowered his voice. "Germans often have trouble pronouncing a few Dutch words. Overall, you have a competent grasp of the language, and Cornelis has vouched for you. But sometimes your *s-c-h* comes out like an *s-k*. You weren't born in the Netherlands, were you?"

"My identity papers say I was."

Berend tightened his grip. Before, his touch had been unwelcome. Now it was painful. "I don't know how you obtained your papers, but it will take more than falsified identification to keep you safe if you prove disloyal to the resistance. I'm not interested in your bourgeoisie scruples. I'm interested in results. If you want to prove your loyalty, let your actions say what your tongue can't—that you're willing to do anything for the liberation of the Netherlands. That includes the assignment I've given you. Don't try to weasel out of this. And don't try to sway your cell leader either."

No one in the van der Veen home had ever questioned Ingrid's loyalty before. She tugged her shoulder free of his grip. For a moment, Berend had reminded her of Herr Sauermann, and that thought made her stomach roil. So did his question. Was she loyal to the Netherlands? She'd fallen in love with the van der Veens, the canals, the artwork. But at heart, she was still Austrian, still an exile who wanted to return home. Yet she was loyal to liberty, committed to working against the Nazis and driving them from power. Berend had no reason to think her untrustworthy . . . other than the fact that she wasn't Dutch.

Footsteps sounded on the stairs from the upper floor, and Gerrit appeared, yawning and pulling his suspenders over his shoulders.

He looked from Berend to Ingrid. "Is everything all right?"

Berend's posture and proximity *felt* threatening to Ingrid. Maybe it also *looked* threatening from Gerrit's viewpoint.

Ingrid swallowed. "Everything is fine. I was about to leave for the station to find our target." She would have liked an ally against Berend, but she couldn't count on Gerrit. He'd probably told Berend about her Reich passport, and he'd made it perfectly clear that he shared Berend's distrust for anyone born with money. Any discussion would result in the two of them uniting against her.

She returned briefly to her room to fetch a jacket—not because she anticipated cold weather but because it would give her a way to quickly adjust her appearance, which she might need if she found and tailed Daalmans for an extended period of time. She also grabbed a book, so she'd have a reason to loiter, if needed.

Gerrit stood outside her door when she left her room. "Are you sure you're all right?" he asked.

"I'm sure." The two of them may have called a truce, but that didn't make them friends or confidants. He wouldn't take her side anyway, not against Berend. And if Anita hadn't changed his mind about targeting Daalmans, it would be folly to think that Ingrid could.

Gerrit's mouth pulled in frustration. She didn't think he believed her, but he nodded. "I'll walk toward the station in a while, see if you need any help. If I time it when schools are about to start, maybe I can blend in."

"I don't want help if it will put you in danger."

"This isn't a solo job, Ingrid, and we're the two least likely to get arrested for it."

He was right. If she tailed Daalmans by herself, she'd be seen eventually. Even two people might not be enough, but it was an improvement over one. "All right. Good luck finding me if I've followed the target away from the station."

Ingrid left before Berend could threaten her again. She didn't take a bicycle. If Daalmans was frequently seen riding the tram, she suspected he, too, would be on foot.

The entire walk, one burning question wouldn't leave her mind: Did loyalty to the Dutch Resistance require assassination? She didn't have to decide today. Today, she just needed to find Dirk Daalmans. Later, when they knew more about him and his patterns, the larger decision would loom.

She'd left the van der Veen home just as curfew had lifted, so the streets were not yet crowded. Their home lay on one of the largest streets in Arnhem. The Utrechtseweg passed St. Elisabeth Hospital, Arnhem Station Square, Koepel prison, and Gestapo headquarters. Places she loved and places she dreaded.

When she reached the station, she did her best to blend in with people coming and going by train and tram, something that grew easier as the morning progressed. Two hours passed. Daalmans might have slipped past her. Or maybe he wouldn't come until later. Or not at all.

A young man approached her with thick spectacles and three school books tucked under his arms. Gerrit, though she hadn't recognized him at first glance.

"Have you seen anything?" he asked.

Ingrid shook her head. "You shouldn't stay. Train stations are favorite roundup locations."

Gerrit looked around. "I don't see too many soldiers at the moment."

"They rarely give warning before descending on crowds."

He nodded. "I'll walk around and check in with you again later."

She kept him in her peripheral vision until he was out of sight. The last thing she wanted was to tell Anita that she'd seen Gerrit get arrested. That might be as bad as having to kill Daalmans.

Newly arrived passengers disembarked from a streetcar, and Ingrid strode along the edge of the crowd, as if preparing to board. She scanned the faces walking toward her, ignoring the women, children, and men who were too old or too young. Then she saw him. Daalmans didn't look particularly evil, but she hadn't really expected him to. His photograph hadn't revealed his treachery; neither did his mien. Ingrid made an inconspicuous turn and followed. She would allow more space between her and Daalmans later. For now, she used the other passengers to shield herself from view.

People scattered as they left the station. Ingrid matched Daalmans's pace but kept a middle-aged woman between her and the target. When the woman's pace slowed, Ingrid's did, too, until Daalmans lengthened the distance between them more than she was comfortable with. Ingrid hurried to catch up, caught him turning a corner, and followed.

His walk led him to Gestapo headquarters, and her stomach churned with fear. She wouldn't follow him inside, so she continued walking past the building until she found a convenient place to wait for him. Sitting on a wooden bench, she removed her coat and unpinned her hair. She hoped that would be enough of a change to prevent him from recognizing her when he came out again.

She tried not to think about how many Gestapo agents walked past her while she pretended to read a book. Any of them could arrest her on the slightest hint of suspicion, then torture her until she confessed to something that would earn her deportation or death.

Gerrit slid into the seat beside her. "Pretend you like me," he whispered.

She leaned closer to him and smiled. She didn't mind the proximity, not when fear of the Gestapo was making her throat tight and her hands moist. "He's been inside Gestapo headquarters for forty-three minutes. I'm not sure which exit he'll take when he leaves."

Gerrit nodded. He reached for her hair and ran his fingers through it. "Do you still have your hair pins?"

"Yes. Why?"

"Let me fix your hair."

Gerrit wanted to play with her hair? She understood pretending to be sweethearts, but having him work on her hair seemed to be taking it too far, and it might backfire. "I want it to look different from what it did when I followed him from the station."

He brought his face closer to hers, so close that she could see the small freckles on his nose. "I won't duplicate what you did this morning, but the left side is untidy enough to be more memorable than you want."

When tailing someone, she wanted to blend in, not stand out because of messy hair. Embarrassment heated her face as she handed over her hairpins. Years had passed since someone had arranged Ingrid's hair for her, and Gerrit's hands were gentle and oddly comforting. He finished quickly and gave her a little space, leaning forward and looking at her with a smile.

"I hope you aren't smiling because you've done something awful with it," she said.

He shook his head and put a hand on her knee, which should have been irritating, but it worked with their current cover. And for a moment, it calmed her fear. "It looks very average now. Neither glamorous nor neglected."

"Where did you learn how to arrange women's hair?"

His smile, which she assumed was fake, fell for a moment. "After my mam died, someone needed to help my sister with her hair."

She took the leftover hairpins when he handed them back to her, a twinge of compassion hitting her as she imagined a younger version of Gerrit helping a little girl when they'd just lost their mother. Gerrit had his failings, but she admired the way he cared for his family. "You should stay here in case he comes this way when he leaves." Ingrid didn't want to walk past Gestapo headquarters again, but she could do it with less risk than Gerrit could. "I'll go to the other side in case he goes that way."

Gerrit nodded. "Be careful."

"You too." She walked slowly away, then turned back and gave him a flirty wave in case anyone was watching. She didn't like leaving him sitting around doing nothing so near a main thoroughfare. But maybe no one would notice.

Ingrid meandered to the other side of the street so Gerrit would have an easier time seeing her, and she would have an easier time seeing him. She stopped to admire trees and flowers, hoping Daalmans would exit the building soon, before her loitering became suspicious.

She strolled past the Gelderland Provincial Electricity Board and tried to look unremarkable. She examined more plants, more windows, all the while getting farther from Gestapo headquarters. She kept an eye on reflections in windows, and finally, she saw Daalmans leave and turn toward Gerrit. Ingrid crossed the street and followed.

Gerrit tailed Daalmans, and Ingrid tailed them both for several blocks. Maybe a bicycle would have been a good idea after all so she could try to get ahead of them. Gerrit glanced back and motioned for her to catch up. She accomplished it fairly quickly.

"Don't stop," Gerrit said as she passed. "He's seen me at least twice. Maybe I was following too closely. But if you'll take over for a while, I think that would be best."

Ingrid nodded. "Take off your glasses and leave your books. You don't have a different shirt you could change into, do you?"

"Not with me."

Ingrid kept walking, allowing the distance between her and Gerrit to increase so he could slip out of view. She wished more people walked the streets. The sidewalks weren't deserted, but crowds would have made her job easier. Daalmans turned onto a side street, and that would make the problem even worse because even fewer people would be about. She hoped whatever Gerrit had done to her hair made her look different from how she had looked at the train station because if Daalmans was checking reflections in the windows as he passed or using his untied shoelace as a reason to stop and look behind him, he would have seen her.

He kept a normal pace, and Ingrid made sure hers matched his, for the most part. She stopped to admire a few store windows when the distance between them grew too close, and she constantly scanned the street for anything that looked like a sign that he was drawing her into a trap.

Another turn, another block. He was heading to Arnhem Centraal as though his sole purpose in getting off the streetcar were to visit Gestapo headquarters. She forced herself not to shiver as she pondered what he might have been doing and who he might have been betraying on his visit. But why had he taken a different route back? A precaution? Or had he noticed he was being tailed?

She glanced ahead at a group of patrons sitting outside a café, and in an instant, Daalmans became the least of her worries. What was Rupert Altbauer doing in Arnhem, wearing civilian clothing? Rupert would recognize her, and Daalmans had just passed the café. If she followed, would Rupert check her papers? Tell his murdering uncle that he'd seen her? At the very least, he'd pretend to be an old friend, and even if that didn't draw Daalmans's attention, it would delay her long enough that she would lose him.

Panic rippled through her. Rupert stood, and Ingrid ducked into the nearest shop to avoid his gaze.

Gerrit bit back a curse when Ingrid disappeared inside a tobacco shop. What was she thinking? She was supposed to tail Daalmans. When Gerrit reached the shop, he slowed, thinking she might join him, but a glance through the windows showed that if she was in the shop, she wasn't near the front waiting for him. He clenched his jaw and continued past the tobacco shop and a bakery with tantalizing smells, then around the tables of a café full of patrons, half of them in German uniform.

Daalmans wasn't in sight, but given the route they had taken thus far, Gerrit suspected the target planned to return to Arnhem Centraal. He scanned the growing crowds as he neared the station and spotted Daalmans. Gerrit gave him a wide berth, not wanting the man to notice him.

The wait for the next streetcar was short. Daalmans was among the first to board the tram headed to Oranjestraat. Gerrit was among the last and slipped the appropriate coins to the conductor. He avoided looking at the target as he passed him on his way to the back of the streetcar. He hated walking so close to the man, but maybe Gerrit was worrying over nothing. Daalmans might very well assume Gerrit had simply been walking the same direction. Plenty of people went to the station.

They passed one stop, then another. As the streetcar slowed for the next stop, Daalmans made no move to leave. Outside, the station came into view. Moderate traffic, a few German soldiers, but not enough to cause alarm. Only after the line of ten people exiting had left the streetcar did Daalmans rise to leave. Gerrit cursed under his breath and followed, hurrying to exit before the car loaded new passengers and Daalmans got too far ahead.

Gerrit needn't have worried about that. Daalmans hadn't gone far at all, just far enough to walk up to a Green Policeman, show him a paper, and then point to Gerrit.

Gerrit turned on his heels. A line had formed for the streetcar, so he couldn't get back on, not without being stopped before he reached the front of the line.

"Excuse me." He ducked through the line so the string of passengers stood between him and the patrolman, and then he walked as quickly as he dared.

"Halt," someone called.

Gerrit looked back, confirmed the patrolman's orders were for him, and then he ran, cutting across the road and into an alley. His heart beat in his ears, and fear fueled his feet. The shouts continued, as did the slap of running boots. Gerrit kept his eyes forward, scanning the backs of buildings, hoping he hadn't run into a dead end. Gerrit had only a vague knowledge of this part of Arnhem. Any moment, he expected the patrolman to shoot him.

He ran by a middle-aged man with a wheelbarrow full of bricks. After Gerrit ran past, a rumble and crash sounded behind him. He peeked over his shoulder to see the bricks now spread across the narrow alley. He hadn't touched the man or the wheelbarrow, but maybe the man had guessed what was happening and spilled the bricks as a way to help. They wouldn't slow the patrolman for long, but even a few seconds could make a difference.

Gerrit ran around a corner and cursed. The alley continued on for a while, but it ran to a dead end. He would soon be trapped.

"In here, lad." The woman who whispered to him might have been a member of the NSB, might have been planning to stall him and turn him over with hopes of payment for her work, but Gerrit's other choice was waiting for the patrolman to catch up, so he ran through the open door.

The woman shut it behind him. She was middle-aged, with wrinkles around her eyes, and she wore well-worn clothes.

"This way." She led him around a hallway, through a room, and then to another door that exited on a different side of the house. "They took my son away when he was about your age. If I can save one person that fate . . ." Through a window, she pointed at a building across the street from hers and two doors over. "Go there. Follow the hallway through the building to the other side. That should be far enough away that they won't find you. Then keep your head down. A healthy lad like you shouldn't be out on the streets."

"Thank you, ma'am." He'd have to share the woman's advice with Berend, who still seemed to think Gerrit young enough to pass for an adolescent. But that wasn't fair to Berend—the patrolman didn't want him for labor. He wanted him because Ingrid had disappeared, leaving Gerrit to do their assignment by himself, and then Daalmans had noticed Gerrit's pursuit.

The woman opened the door and looked both ways. No soldiers. Just a few Dutch civilians going about their business, mostly women.

"Go now, but don't run—that will draw too much attention."

Gerrit heeded her advice and crossed the street to the door in question. He pulled it open and stepped into the murky hallway. Small offices lined either side. A lawyer, a dentist, an architect. Gerrit rushed past them, slowing only as he reached another exit—the building's main entry point, based on the spacious lobby with potted plants and an older gentleman at a desk.

"Can I help you?" the man asked.

Ignoring the man might make Gerrit stick in his memory, and he wasn't sure how many people the German patrolman might question in search of a runaway suspect. Gerrit remembered the name on one of the windows he'd passed. "I had a delivery for Mynheer Janssen."

The man raised one gray eyebrow at Gerrit. "Mynheer Janssen is Jewish. He was deported two years ago."

Gerrit swallowed. Maybe ignoring the building concierge would have been the better option after all. He backed away toward the door. "My mistake. I must have confused my deliveries."

The man scoffed but didn't move to follow Gerrit or to try detaining him. Instead, he lifted a telephone. Gerrit didn't stay long enough to hear who the man called. He rushed from the building and turned away from the alley he'd almost been trapped in. At least he thought it was away from the alley and the patrolman chasing him. He'd never seen this street before, but that didn't matter. He had to put space between him and the suspicious concierge without stumbling back toward the streetcar stop and the patrolman.

He took the next turn he came to, so the concierge wouldn't be able to step outside his building and report which direction Gerrit had gone. Gerrit kept that pattern up, not staying on any street long, weaving his way across Arnhem for fifteen minutes before the vice that had clamped around his lungs finally eased enough that it felt like he could fully breathe. That was also about the time he realized he was lost.

"Altbauer, do you have a minute?" Hauptmann Denhart asked when Rupert came into headquarters.

"Of course, sir."

Denhart seemed less jovial than usual. Rupert hoped he wasn't about to be reprimanded. He was doing his best, but few members of the resistance had fallen into his net lately. They'd arrested people in hiding because they were Jewish or because they didn't want to work in Germany, but finding people in hiding wasn't very satisfying, not when their history included catching British agents and using them to capture even more.

The hauptmann gestured to a seat and closed the door of his office. "Any luck at the café today?" Denhart asked.

"From an intelligence perspective, no. I don't think the proprietor is involved in anything illegal. I'd like to go back again, learn which patrons are regulars, observe them again, but had I lingered much longer, I think I would have drawn suspicion. Now, from a culinary perspective, it was a success. The snegl was as good as I've had in quite some time." It reminded him of the fresh-baked zimtschnecken he'd enjoyed when he'd stayed at Falcon Point manor. As had that flash of blonde hair. For a moment, he had thought he'd seen Ingrid Lang. But that was ridiculous. Ingrid Lang had disappeared, her siblings with her. She wouldn't be in Arnhem. She was probably on his mind because he'd received a letter from his uncle Wilhelm recently.

"Perhaps I'll try it myself, if there's good snegl to be had." Denhart paused. He seemed finished, but he didn't dismiss Rupert, so Rupert stayed seated, forcing his spine into an upright position and doing his best to ignore the ache in his leg. It hurt more than usual today.

Denhart reached for one of the framed photographs on his desk and studied it for a while, then turned it so Rupert could see. Four couples, all smiling, all in formal attire. One of the women wore what looked like a wedding dress. For a moment, Rupert thought it was a picture of Hauptmann Denhart's wedding, but the groom, though he looked a great deal like Hauptmann Denhart, was shorter, and he wore glasses. A younger version of Hauptmann Denhart stood in the left of the photograph.

"That's from my youngest brother's wedding," Denhart said. "Right before we all went off to war. My parents should be easy to pick out. And you'll recognize me. My wife is to my right. Then there's Horst and Ingeborg, Rolf and Freida."

"Three brothers?"

Hauptmann Denhart nodded. "Yes. Horst died in Northern Africa, and Rolf's U-boat never returned to port."

"My condolences, sir." Rupert didn't have any brothers, but his three-year-old half sister, Heidi, held his heart completely, and he hadn't even grown up with her. He could imagine the pain that would come with losing two brothers.

Denhart replaced the photograph. "I don't show you the picture of my family because I want your sympathy. I show it to you because I want you to know that I understand."

"Sir?" Dread snaked through Rupert's gut.

Denhart stood and took a piece of paper from his desk. A paper the size of a telegram. He tapped the paper against one palm a few times. "I'm afraid you have bad news from home. Take your time reading it and . . . I won't be needing my office for a while, if you'd like to be alone." Denhart handed the telegram to Rupert and left, closing the door behind him.

Rupert inhaled against a growing tightness in his throat. He checked the sender: his uncle. Onkel Wilhelm wrote to Rupert regularly, but no one sent telegrams for ordinary news. Rupert's hand started to shake even before he read the words. *Regret to inform you that your mother and stepfather were killed in an air raid. Have taken custody of Heidi.*

If his chest had felt tight before, now it felt as if all his breath had been stolen away from him. His mother and stepfather, dead? Heidi left all alone? He shook his head in denial, as if the motion might somehow make the words untrue. But Rupert had seen enough of war to know just how easy it was for a couple to simply cease existing. Most of his army group had disappeared into the snow outside Stalingrad. He could well imagine an entire family, an entire block of homes, an entire air-raid shelter disappearing into death.

He let the telegram fall to Denhart's desk and squeezed his hands into fists. His uncle hadn't given details, but he could guess that responsibility lay with either the British or the Americans. Were any of them hiding in the attics of Arnhem's inhabitants? For a moment, Rupert had been certain he would cry, but now anger changed his grief into determination. He would punish any terror-fliers who fell into his hands and anyone hiding them.

Gerrit had only needed a glimpse of the Nederrijn to reorient himself and find his way back to Opa's home. He entered through the kitchen and found it empty. Then he went to the dining room, where Ingrid and Anita waited, huddled together speaking in low tones.

Irritation at Ingrid bubbled up inside him. "What were you thinking?" He'd stolen a hat on his way back to use as a disguise, and now he slapped it onto the table. "You almost got me arrested!"

Ingrid's mouth was pinched, and her eyes looked red. Had she been weeping? For a heartbeat, he regretted his outburst, but then her eyes narrowed, and all sympathy for her vanished.

"What happened, Gerrit?" Anita asked.

He didn't want Anita to have to play peacemaker again. He wanted Ingrid to apologize for abandoning him. Had he been caught, the Germans might very well have shot him. "I told her he saw me, so I needed her to tail him for a while. Then she disappeared into a tobacco shop and left me to tail him all by myself. I followed him onto a streetcar, and when he got off, he pointed the Green Police my way, and I had to run for my life!"

Anita stood and put a hand on his arm. "I'm glad you're safe."

"No thanks to her." Gerrit met Ingrid's defiant eyes, and his jaw clamped shut in anger.

Anita sighed. "She had her reasons."

Gerrit put a hand on his hip and turned a glare on Ingrid. "Then, by all means, please explain why you abandoned both me and our assignment."

"I would have explained immediately if you hadn't been so busy berating me. If you're quite finished now." Ingrid's chin tilted up, as if in question. Gerrit didn't respond. Silence hung in the room, and only when Anita cleared her throat did Ingrid speak again. "I recognized someone sitting at the café, and I'm certain he would have recognized me had I walked past. At best, it would have involved a conversation long enough for Daalmans to get away. More likely, it would have involved close scrutiny of my papers, and he would know they're false."

"I thought Opa blackmailed someone for real papers."

Ingrid nodded. "The papers are real, but the information on them isn't. That man knows my name is Ingrid Lang, not Ingrid van der Veen, and he knows I'm not Dutch because he visited my family's Austrian estate while on holiday more than once."

Some of Gerrit's anger eased. It didn't change the fact that he'd almost been arrested, but she'd had a good reason to break off. "So you wanted to avoid an old friend?"

"He's not an old friend." Ingrid's response was terse. "His uncle murdered my father."

Gerrit had assumed Ingrid's father was trapped in another country. He hadn't known he was dead. "Your father was murdered?"

Ingrid nodded.

Having a father murdered sounded even worse than having a father hauled away for work duty in Germany, though Gerrit had heard enough about Moffen camps to know that he, like Ingrid, might never see his father again. "I'm sorry."

Ingrid didn't respond, but her face held less anger now.

"One of the soldiers?" Gerrit asked. If the man was Austrian, he was probably in uniform.

Ingrid shook her head. "When I last saw him, he had just completed training and was reporting to his army unit. That was just before I came to Arnhem. But he wasn't wearing a uniform at the café today."

Average German soldiers weren't allowed to visit cafés in plainclothes. So that meant her old acquaintance wasn't a normal soldier. "It sounds as if he's deserting. Or he's in intelligence."

"I would guess the latter."

"Not a man to tangle with, then."

She could have motioned Gerrit into the tobacco shop and explained, but maybe she'd panicked. Gerrit had felt his share of panic that day. It had left him tired and, he was starting to realize, hungry, but he didn't go back to the kitchen. He headed for his room instead. Anger at Ingrid had disappeared, leaving him with nothing but the bitter taste of failure.

At the sound of footsteps, he turned to see Anita. "How did you get away?" she asked.

"A middle-aged woman let me into her building."

Anita closed her eyes and nodded. "I'm glad you ran into someone who helped you instead of turning you in. God was watching out for you."

Gerrit doubted it was divine protection, but he had been lucky. "I owe her, but I doubt I could find the house again to thank her. The target left the streetcar at a stop I wasn't familiar with, and then I ran wherever I could."

"Ingrid tried to catch you both at the streetcar, but she couldn't get there fast enough." Anita searched his face as if she wanted to know how angry he still was. "She was worried about you. Probably would have apologized if you hadn't barged in yelling."

"I didn't yell." He knew better than to risk raising his voice loud enough for the neighbors to hear.

"Hmm. Close enough."

Gerrit rubbed his eyes in frustration. "It's been a rotten day all around. Our target will be harder to find now. And I had to walk past him on the streetcar, so he'll recognize me."

"We'll figure something out," Anita said. "Or if we don't, maybe it's just as well. We have intelligence to gather and people to hide. Cornelis sent word to the hospital this morning that there's a shot-down airman who needs Opa's help."

CHAPTER 13

INGRID KNOCKED ON THE DOOR to Luitenant Brug's room.

"Come in."

"Anita said you needed a courier." Ingrid glanced at the papers covering the top of his desk. Most were blank or facedown.

"I do. Wish I could do it myself, but I don't think I'm up to it yet, even if Anita and Dr. van der Veen hadn't threatened me with loss of life or limb if I tried anything so reckless so soon after surgery."

Ingrid bit back a smile. He'd referred to Anita by her Christian name rather than *Mejuffrouw van der Veen.*

Luitenant Brug tapped the paper in front of him. "I'm almost done. Could I trouble you for an ashtray and a match?"

Ingrid hadn't seen Luitenant Brug smoke yet, but most people in the Netherlands did. Maybe the same was true for Americans. She slipped from the room and went across the hall. Willem and Petrus were in the middle of a card game.

"May I borrow an ashtray and a match?" she asked.

Petrus raised an eyebrow. "Given Gerrit's utter silence about the mission, I assume it was a rough day. Must have been absolutely beastly to drive you to start smoking."

Ingrid walked to a mostly full ashtray. "It's not for me."

Willem glanced at the door. "For the American?"

Ingrid nodded. Willem passed her a small book of matches, which she slipped into her pocket. "Thank you."

Rather than going directly back to Luitenant Brug, Ingrid took the ashtray downstairs to empty it. The men weren't supposed to let them get so full—if there was a raid, full ashtrays would make the rooms look occupied. The home had good hiding places in the attic and a reinforced rain gutter that anyone wanting to escape could slide down, assuming the Germans didn't leave anyone outside to watch the garden. Yet even if the ashtrays were empty, even if the raiders found no one in the attic, the rooms upstairs looked lived in. Why couldn't men clean up after themselves and put things back exactly where they belonged?

As she climbed back to Luitenant Brug's room, she remembered that Opa had put her legs back together, and they had healed completely enough that she could walk up two flights of stairs without pain. She ought not be so hard on the home's inhabitants. It wasn't as if they'd asked for the war that had forced them from their homes and made them live in a state of unending danger. Maybe making the rooms feel like home, even if they appeared inhabited, was more important to them than living in a place that wouldn't cause any suspicion.

She knocked again before entering because she hadn't forgotten that Luitenant Brug could be dangerous when startled. He told her to come in, then thanked her when she handed him the ashtray and the matches. She expected him to pull a cigarette from his pocket, but instead, he lit the ends of his papers on fire and let them burn, putting them on the ashtray when they shrank and the flame approached his hand. He added a small strip of a handkerchief with a series of numbers printed on it.

He noticed the direction of her gaze. "The encoding key. It's random, so even if the Germans tortured me and made me want to confess, I wouldn't be able to. I might remember most of the message, but not the numbers."

He slid the one paper he hadn't burned toward her. She spoke German, Dutch, English, and a little French, but the five-letter groups didn't form words in any of those languages, not even if she mentally rearranged the spaces. Nor did they follow the normal patterns about vowel and consonant use.

"It's ready to be transmitted." Luitenant Brug gave her a smile that seemed to hold guilt. "Unfortunately, if the Germans find it, they'll know it's not innocent. So hide it well or destroy it if you run into any scrutiny."

For now, Ingrid folded the paper and put it in her pocket. Before she left, she would hide it in her shoe or her brassiere. "I've some experience with hiding things."

He nodded. "Good. I'll pray you have a run with no surprises and no unpleasantries."

"Thank you."

He checked that everything in the ashtray was sufficiently burned. "I didn't mean to eavesdrop, but from your conversation with the men across the hall, I take it your earlier work today wasn't completely smooth?"

Looking for Daalmans, finding him, leaving Gerrit to manage by himself, and nearly coming face-to-face with Rupert Altbauer had left her shaken, but she didn't want to admit that. "As an intelligence officer hiding in an occupied country, I would expect you to eavesdrop as often as you can."

He smiled. "All right. You caught me. I gather you were tailing someone and lost him?"

She nodded.

"Someone important?"

She shrugged. Daalmans was finding people in hiding and turning them over to the Nazis. That was dangerous, evil, disloyal . . . Did that make Daalmans important?

"Are you ready to go back out again?" he asked.

"I am." She patted her pocket. "I assume your report is time-sensitive, or you would have saved it until you were better."

"It is urgent. Maybe. Depends a little on the weather." He glanced out the window. "Do you want to talk about it, whatever it is that's bothering you?"

"Who said anything is bothering me?"

He turned back toward her with his kind brown eyes. "I don't know you well, Mejuffrouw van der Veen, but sometimes, words aren't needed."

She sighed. She wanted to talk to Mama or Papa, not with a near stranger. "I won't let it get in the way of delivering your message."

"I don't suspect you will, but I don't want to make whatever it is worse."

She crossed her arms. "Delivering a report from an American intelligence officer so it can be transmitted back to whoever needs it in Britain won't weigh on my conscience."

"And your other mission does?"

She nodded. "The man we're tracking has turned in members of the resistance, onderduikers—anyone he can get a reward for betraying. And he isn't likely to stop, and we can't put him in jail, so that leaves us one solution."

"I see." His tone held neither approval nor disapproval.

"I know we're at war," she whispered. "And I know he's evil, but it feels like murder."

Luitenant Brug gestured to a nearby chair. "Have a seat."

She sat.

"You're right, we are at war. And that means doing things we wouldn't normally do. The Nazis have to be stopped, even though it will cost us, even though it has cost us." He poked at the final glowing embers of his burned coding material. "If you kill a target to keep him from killing others, are you taking a life or saving a life? Both? Does a soldier in the middle of a battle ask himself the same question?"

He gestured to the window. "Is it wrong for American bombers to drop bombs that will kill civilians?" His voice grew softer. "And if the bombings are wrong, does the fault lie with the crew of the aircraft? Their commanders? The intelligence officer telling them where to drop their bombs? The factory workers across the Atlantic creating the airplanes and the munitions?"

Ingrid swallowed. "I don't know. I've never thought of soldiers or airmen as murderers. Nor intelligence officers or factory workers. But what Berend asked me to do feels different."

Luitenant Brug bit his lip. "I don't know where that line is, that line that if we cross it, we've turned into the same evil we're trying to fight. But I do know that when it's all over, when we've beaten Hitler and we go back to peace, we'll have to live with what we've done. Regardless of what Berend or Anita or I or anyone else says, you can't let your soul be another casualty of this war."

An hour later, Ingrid batted her eyelashes at the Green Policeman checking her papers. She wasn't smuggling ration coupons or identity papers for onderduikers today, just Luitenant Brug's report nestled next to her skin, so she expected to make it through the checkpoint easily. Only the boldest of patrolmen would search where she had it hidden.

"Purpose of leaving Arnhem?" the man asked.

"Visiting a friend and hoping to find some fresh food."

He handed her identity papers back and turned to the next person in line. Ingrid pushed off on her wooden-wheeled bicycle and tried not to let the relief show. Maybe relief wouldn't be that suspicious anyway. The Moffen had to know the Dutch weren't happy under occupation.

She rode along the main road, enjoying the sunlight, hoping she wouldn't run into Rupert Altbauer again. What a mess that morning had been. Finding Daalmans. Spotting Rupert. Worrying about Gerrit.

The more she thought about it, the more she was sure that she couldn't kill anyone. Daalmans might deserve death, but should she be forced to carry out his sentence, she didn't think she could live with that weight. Yet if she refused, Berend might mark her a collaborator and carry out his threats. Anita trusted her. So did Cornelis. Would that be enough to counter Berend? And even if he trusted her, could she trust Berend enough to work with him when something in her gut told her he was dangerous—not just to the Nazis but also to her?

Eventually, she arrived at the barn where she was to meet Cornelis. She rode past, then looked over her shoulder to see if anything looked amiss. All looked as it ought to, so she turned around, rode to the barn's door, and let herself in.

Cornelis stepped from behind a stall not long after. "Any trouble?"

"Not that I've seen."

"And how was Berend's training?"

"Effective."

"Has he given you any assignments?"

Ingrid nodded. "He wants us to assassinate someone."

Cornelis kept his face neutral. "How does Anita feel about that?"

After Ingrid had returned from the disastrous attempt to tail Daalmans, most of her conversation with Anita had revolved around the new risk with Altbauer and worry for Gerrit. Yet they'd spoken of Daalmans too. "She doesn't like it, but she hasn't stopped it. Today, we were looking for the target, gathering information to plan. We're not ready to act." And Ingrid didn't think she ever would be ready to act.

"I know it's hard, having another cell shifting assignments to you. He might take some of your assets, too, if he gets the chance."

"I'd prefer to remain with Anita."

Cornelis nodded. "It makes sense for you to stay in Arnhem. You can move about without suspicion. One of his other projects involves work where people are less likely to be seen. It could give those in hiding a chance to go outside and see the sun from time to time."

Ingrid assumed that meant Berend would want Petrus. Probably Willem, if the work didn't involve anything that would put too much strain on his arm, where he'd been shot. Maybe Gerrit. He seemed enthusiastic about all of Berend's plans. Just as well if he went. She wouldn't miss him, as long as he gave the bicycles a tune-up before he left. "About Berend . . . Do you trust him, really trust him?"

"I wouldn't have introduced him to you if I didn't. Berend and I met through one of my cousins. They were both cadets when the war started, spent time in a prison camp in Germany together. Berend is devoted to defeating the Nazis. Effective, too, even if his techniques are different from Anita's."

A hint of defensiveness wove through Ingrid's chest. "Anita has also been effective."

"She has, and I don't wish her to stop or change her work." Cornelis smiled. "I'm not asking you to dance with Berend or elect him to Parliament. But when it comes to winning our freedom, I'm willing to work with any loyal Dutchman, even if we don't agree on everything. We all want the Reich defeated. That's enough for me."

Ingrid tried to let go of the suspicion she'd been harboring toward Berend. She couldn't find any fault with Cornelis's conclusion, that they needed to work together instead of letting differences divide them. Anita had said much the same thing. "It's enough for me too. Give me a moment." She turned her back to Cornelis, retrieved Luitenant Brug's report, then handed it over. "That's from the American intelligence officer you brought to us. He would prefer to deliver it himself, but he's still recovering."

"I'll take it to the radio operator he worked with last time." Cornelis took off a shoe and slid the heel to one side, then stored the paper in the hollowed-out space. "I wish I could tell you that I knew when the Allies would arrive and this would all be over soon, but that depends on the battles taking place in France. Maybe, eventually, they'll be close enough that our efforts can help them along. But we're not there yet."

"I hope it comes soon." She wanted peace. She wanted to find her siblings. She wanted to live without constant fear hanging over her.

"As do I. Come. I'll introduce you to the airman."

He walked to the stall he'd been hiding behind when she arrived. She followed, finding the American sitting on a pile of straw. The first thing she noticed was the sling around the man's arm. That might make it hard for him to ride a bicycle. He wore civilian clothing, and apprehension showed in his dark-brown eyes as he looked from Cornelis to her. The American's skin was olive, and his hair black. She guessed he was either American Indian or Latino, and that might make it more difficult for him to blend in. She'd need to sneak him into Arnhem under cover of darkness or try to pass him off as a native of the Dutch Indies.

"He doesn't speak Dutch," Cornelis said. "English and Spanish."

"Hello," Ingrid said in English.

"You speak English?" His dialect sounded American but a bit softer. "What a relief. I picked up something about visiting a hospital, but he was speaking French, I think."

"Not a hospital." Her words felt sloppy; she'd never achieved fluency, and occasional conversations with onderduikers hadn't changed that. "But I'll take you to a doctor you can trust. What are your injuries?"

He gestured to his arm. "We had to bail out of our plane. I think something's in my arm still. Bit of flak maybe, or part of the plane that splintered when a German fighter shot us up."

"May I see it?"

He nodded.

She supported the arm while she removed the sling, then unwrapped the bandage. A long line ran along his biceps, red around the edges. Opa had taught her how to spot signs of infection, and the wound looked suspect. "May I feel your forehead?"

"Uh, sure."

He felt a little warm. Maybe a low-grade fever, or maybe Ingrid's hands were cold.

"Are you up for a bit of a walk tonight?" They could wait until the next day, but if his wound grew worse, he'd be harder to transport.

"If that's what's needed." He glanced at Cornelis. "Does either of you have news about the rest of my crew? There were ten of us. Pilot, copilot, navigator, bombardier, radio operator, and four other gunners."

She repeated his question to Cornelis, who shook his head. "I haven't heard anything. He was lucky. The Moffen were searching the area. A farmer hid him, and that farmer knew one of my contacts. That's how I became involved. Did he see the others leave the plane?"

Ingrid translated, and the man's face fell. "I counted four other parachutes, but between the smoke and my arm and everything . . . I'm not sure how many bailed out."

"We'll help your friends if we find them," she promised. "Maybe they found farmers to hide them, as you did, but they'd try to keep it quiet, so we would only hear about it if they needed medical care."

"What did he say?" Cornelis asked.

"He thinks at least four others made it out."

"Probably rounded up by the Germans, but no need to tell him that. I should be on my way. Meet me again in five days. Same time. Do you remember passing a house about a mile back with a broken-down chicken coop? Line of trees to the west?"

Ingrid searched her memory. "A little. I'll see it again on my way back."

"Meet there."

"All right."

Cornelis shook the airman's hand. "Tell him I wish him the best of luck. If any of his friends show up, I'll do what I can for them."

Ingrid changed the words from Dutch to English.

"*Bedankt.*" Dutch didn't roll easily from the airman's tongue, but he'd made an effort, and Cornelis smiled in response.

"See you in a few days, Ingrid. Good luck."

Ingrid watched Cornelis go, then turned to the pilot. "What shall I call you?" She wanted to give him the chance to use an alias, should he prefer that.

He struggled to his feet. "Sergeant Cervantes."

"Pleased to meet you, Sergeant Cervantes. I'm Ingrid." An alias for her would only work until someone at the van der Veen home addressed her by her real name.

He nodded. "Ingrid. Like the movie star. Maybe I should call you Miss Bergman."

Ingrid chuckled. "I suppose I can answer to that. Shall we be on our way? It's a long walk, and I think it best if we arrive before sunrise."

His eyes widened slightly. "Long enough that it might take us all night?"

"Probably not, but we might need to take a few breaks, and I don't suppose you can ride a bicycle the whole way with only one hand."

He glanced at his arm. "No, I guess not." He gestured to the door. "Lead the way, Miss Bergman."

Gerrit paced across the kitchen floor. Was this how Tante Petronella had felt in Utrecht when Gerrit had been out delivering ration coupons? Last night, he'd waited up for Anita. Tonight, he waited up for Ingrid. He didn't even like Ingrid—not really—but she was part of the team, and what if his words earlier in the day had driven her to do something reckless to prove herself?

He stilled when a knock sounded on the door. He turned out the light, set his face so he didn't appear as if he'd been going mad waiting, and pulled the door open.

It wasn't Ingrid. It was Berend. Gerrit let him inside and turned the light back on.

"How did it go today?" Berend asked.

Gerrit had been hoping Ingrid would be at the door with the airman so he could stop worrying about her. Now he also wished it had been her because he didn't want to explain what had happened to Berend. "Ingrid found him. Tailed him to Gestapo headquarters. Then I followed him to a streetcar, but he must have grown suspicious because when he stepped off, he pointed me out to the police. I had to run." That was a simplified version of events, but something about how Berend treated Ingrid was off. Ingrid hadn't welcomed Berend's touches during pistol training, so Gerrit had invented a question to pull him away. And earlier that morning, Berend's posture as he'd stood over Ingrid had seemed threatening. So even though Gerrit didn't really want to take the blame, his gut told him Berend would be easier on him than he'd be on Ingrid.

Berend frowned. "So you don't know where he lives?"

Gerrit shook his head. "I'm not even sure if that's the stop he meant to get off on or if it was a test to see if I would follow."

"Can you try again tomorrow?"

Gerrit shrugged. "I think if I try again, he'll recognize me."

"Ingrid, then?"

"She's out on other work tonight. I doubt she can stalk the station again tomorrow. And Daalmans might have seen her too."

Berend nodded, but he didn't seem pleased. "I need help with another project. I want to talk with the others."

Gerrit motioned Berend into the dining room, then he went to wake Anita, Petrus, and Willem. Soon, all were gathered to listen to Berend.

"The Allies are getting closer," Berend said. "If we stay busy, maybe our liberation will come sooner rather than later. I'd like help with an assignment that's not in the city."

Willem moved his arm around. "My wound hardly troubles me at all anymore." He glanced at Anita. "I'm grateful for your hospitality, but I'm itching to get to work. I've had enough hiding."

"I feel the same," Petrus said. "I'm ready to take on a new assignment."

Anita nodded. "You'll both be missed, but I understand. I'll be staying, of course."

Gerrit wasn't surprised by any of the answers. Anita could leave the house, so restlessness didn't haunt her the way it haunted Willem and Petrus. Gerrit might feel the same as the other two men if he were stuck inside as often as they were. And if he stayed, that might be the case. The Utrecht authorities were looking for him by name. Now the Arnhem authorities might be looking for him by description.

All eyes turned on him, waiting to hear his decision. Anita put a hand on his forearm, and her eyes pleaded with him to stay.

Part of him wanted to leave, to fight back at the Nazis however Berend suggested. But Opa and Anita were family, and he'd already lost so many others. And what if Ingrid needed to tail someone else? Gerrit had learned the hard way that one person wasn't enough for an assignment like that. "I think I have unfinished work here," he said.

Berend frowned. "You're good with your hands. Give me a few weeks and I could turn you into the best saboteur in the Low Countries."

Berend's offer was tempting. Something about the man appealed to Gerrit. He was bold and willing to fight, regardless of the risks. But something else about him repelled Gerrit. Maybe it was his casual dismissal of reprisals that might come as a consequence of their work. Maybe it was the way he treated Ingrid. Gerrit wanted to be bold, wanted to make a difference, but he didn't want to turn into a bully.

Anita broke in. "I expect I can carry on with my work with two assistants rather than four, but if you take all three of my men, it might cause a hardship for my cell. Your work is important, Berend, but if there's a way you can do it without sacrificing the effectiveness of my cell, I'd prefer that."

Berend nodded. "Right. Willem, Petrus, we should leave tonight."

The two of them stood and went to gather their belongings.

"Is Ingrid here?" Berend asked.

"No." Gerrit looked at a nearby clock. It was two in the morning.

"She's not?" Anita's mouth pulled in worry. "I would have expected her back by midnight at the latest."

Berend stood. "That's another reason for me to take Willem and Petrus. If she's been picked up, I don't suppose she'll last long under interrogation. You might have the Gestapo at your door by dawn."

An image of a cold, menacing Gestapo officer beating Ingrid until she was bruised and bloody passed through Gerrit's mind, and a chill brushed past his ribs. He swallowed. Maybe he liked Ingrid after all, because the thought of her being tortured made some deep part of him twist with agony.

Anita folded her arms. "Her traveling companion needs a doctor, so maybe his pace is slower than planned. She's probably fine, and even if she isn't, she knows not to say anything for twenty-four hours. Don't underestimate her. She's tougher than you give her credit for."

Willem and Petrus returned, and all of them said their goodbyes. They turned off all the lights before the three men left, and then it was just Gerrit and Anita standing in the kitchen in the dark, with Opa and Luitenant Brug sleeping upstairs and Ingrid somewhere out there, either slowly guiding an injured airmen to their home or being beaten by the Gestapo.

Anita sighed. "I guess we better get some sleep."

Gerrit didn't think he'd sleep at all with the nagging worry about Ingrid hanging over him. "You go. I'll wait up to see if they need anything when they come . . . If they come."

Anita took his arm. "She's probably fine."

Her assurance did little to relieve the fear that all wasn't right. Anita went to bed, and Gerrit went back to pacing the kitchen.

Sergeant Cervantes was neither lazy nor slow, but early in their walk, Ingrid drew out that he hadn't slept in almost thirty-six hours, and she suspected the wound in his arm wasn't the only one he carried after bailing out of his airplane. So they had stopped for frequent breaks. She'd placed a small amount of food in her bicycle's basket before leaving Arnhem, so they'd also eaten. And once, while they'd stopped to rest, Sergeant Cervantes had drifted to sleep, and she'd given him an hour before waking him and encouraging him to continue. She pushed the bicycle and hoped they wouldn't have to resort to her pushing him if he grew too weary to continue.

Dawn came early in August, though not as early as June or July. Because of the curfew and the distance between farms, they saw no one for most of their journey, but as she tried to sneak the airman into the city without anyone spotting them, she was grateful for the extra minutes of darkness. They might end up needing them.

An engine rattled in the distance, and she motioned the American to a nearby clump of trees. Whatever had made the sound was distant, but some stretches of road offered very few places to hide. By the time she could identify the vehicle, it would be too late to escape its view.

"I don't suppose there's much chance that someone friendly is driving that and can give us a lift, is there?" Sergeant Cervantes whispered.

"Not likely. Only Germans, collaborators of some importance, and thieves can get fuel."

"That's what I thought."

"Do you need another rest?"

"How much longer will it take?"

"Less than an hour."

The sergeant nodded. "Then, let's go as soon as the way is clear."

The last hour was the hardest. Their legs were worn out, sleep grew more tempting, and the homes grew closer and closer to one another, making it more and more likely that someone would see them. The dimmer stars disappeared with the approaching dawn, and Ingrid longed for the safety and rest of the van der Veen home.

She led Sergeant Cervantes along remote streets with trees that provided shadows, ones farther from the main roads, where German patrols were more frequent.

They had to hide several times when early risers stepped from homes, and once, Ingrid was certain a man letting his dog outside saw them, but Sergeant Cervantes wore civilian clothing, so from across the street in the murky light, she assumed the airman looked like a Dutchman.

When she turned on the Utrechtseweg, her nerves were worn, a blister pained her right foot, and her stomach knotted with a mixture of fear and hunger. Relief embraced her when they finally reached the van der Veen home.

She had Sergeant Cervantes follow her into the cellar so she could leave her bicycle there, then led him up another set of stairs into the home, then into the kitchen. She flipped the light switch and stiffened when she saw Gerrit leaning forward on the small table. She hadn't expected anyone to be in the kitchen at this hour. He didn't move, and a sudden burst of panic had her rushing over to make sure he wasn't injured. Had Daalmans somehow tracked him down and shot him? But when she came around the table, Gerrit didn't seem to be injured. Just sleeping. He looked different asleep. While awake, his fiery hatred of the Nazis seemed to consume him, but now, all that was gone, and he looked . . . sweet.

Why had he fallen asleep at the kitchen table instead of in a perfectly good bed upstairs? If he were that tired, she wouldn't intentionally wake him, though the position looked likely to give him a formidable neck ache.

She pulled her eyes from Gerrit and addressed Sergeant Cervantes. "I suggest we eat first." She glanced at the clock. Nearly five thirty in the morning. Opa would be up in the next half hour. "After we eat, I'll wake the doctor, and we can both sleep after he removes that piece of metal from your arm."

"Is he all right?" Sergeant Cervantes motioned to Gerrit.

"Just sleeping. I'm not sure why he decided to use a table instead of a bed." He had waited up for Anita to get home the night before, but surely he hadn't been waiting up for Ingrid. He didn't like her, especially not after she'd left him to tail Daalmans by himself. His loyalty to his aunt was admirable, but she couldn't claim the same from him. Loyalty like that . . . She would be glad to have it.

She found a loaf of bread and sliced it so she could make cold cheese sandwiches. Or maybe she would grill them. It would take longer, but the dark night had left her chilled. "Are you cold?" she asked the American.

"A little."

She nodded. That settled it. She would make warm sandwiches. The frying pan knocked against the soup pot as she pulled it out of the cupboard, and Gerrit jerked awake. He looked around in confusion for several seconds before his eyes locked on Ingrid.

He actually smiled and seemed pleased to see her. "Oh, you're back."

"Yes, sorry to wake you." She put the frying pan on the stovetop and lit the burner. "Why were you sleeping in the kitchen?"

"I didn't mean to fall asleep." He yawned and pushed his hair back from his face in a motion that was almost endearing. "I was just worried that something unexpected had come up and you were in trouble."

"There wasn't any reason to worry." That was a bald-faced lie. They lived under Nazi rule. The day before, she'd almost run into a childhood acquaintance who was now most likely an enemy intelligence officer. And Gerrit had been chased by a policeman who might very well have shot him. "The airman has an injured arm, so we had to walk instead of ride. And he's had a rough few days, so we took it at a slow pace."

Gerrit nodded. Then he stood and offered his hand to Sergeant Cervantes. "Welcome."

Sergeant Cervantes gripped Gerrit's hand but looked to Ingrid for a translation.

Ingrid switched back to English. "He's welcoming you." Ingrid placed several slices of bread in the frying pan. "Are you hungry, Gerrit?"

"No, thank you."

"Do you speak English or Spanish?"

Gerrit shook his head. "Just Dutch and some German."

Ingrid hadn't expected that he did. "Then, you'll have to use gestures to communicate with our airman."

Gerrit pushed his hair out of his eyes again. "Between you and Luitenant Brug, we'll manage. Willem and Petrus went with Berend for another assignment, so there are plenty of extra rooms. I'll prepare one for our new guest."

"Cornelis said Berend might want help." She finished assembling the sandwiches in the pan. "I half expected you to go with him."

"I can't leave all the work for you and Anita. Besides, this is home now."

Home. Ingrid had lived with the van der Veens since early 1940, but this house still didn't feel like home. She envied Gerrit, that he could settle in so easily. Maybe it was because of his blood ties to Opa and Anita. Maybe it was because of his history of peacetime visits. Regardless, Gerrit had come home, but Ingrid still felt lost.

CHAPTER 14

Gerrit sat in his room with his arms folded across his chest while Ingrid cut his hair. Sergeant Cervantes stood, giving Ingrid tips on hair styling in a language Gerrit didn't understand, and Luitenant Brug looked on in amusement from where he sat on the bed.

Footsteps sounded the moment before Anita looked in. "What are you all up to?"

Gerrit gritted his teeth. "We thought a new hairstyle would make it harder for Daalmans to recognize me."

Anita went to sit beside Luitenant Brug. "So, a new haircut and some dye?"

Gerrit nodded.

"Hold still," Ingrid said. "I was about to cut, and you just pulled the hair from my grip."

Gerrit rolled his eyes. "Sergeant Cervantes's father-in-law is a barber, so Cervantes knows a little about hair, and he's telling Ingrid how to cut it. He would do it himself, but it's a challenge when one arm is in a sling."

"I've cut your aunt's hair before." Ingrid's fingers moved over his scalp again. "Yours is just more difficult because it's shorter."

"What did you use for dye?" Anita asked.

"We boiled walnut shells and nettle. It might not last more than a few days, but we can reapply a few times a week." Ingrid made a few snips, then let out a worried hmm.

Luitenant Brug glanced at Gerrit's head and winced.

"What did you do to it?" Gerrit asked. Ingrid had assured him that she was capable of modifying his hair, but she had apparently been mistaken. He never should have agreed to it. First had been the strange pleasure of Ingrid's fingers in his hair—and irritation that any part of her held any power over him. Now came a ruined haircut.

"It will be fine. We'll just go shorter." Ingrid consulted with Sergeant Cervantes.

In Gerrit's periphery, the airman used his left fingers as if they were scissors and pointed, showing the correct angle.

Gerrit kept his voice level. "The plan is to make me look different. If that also means I look ugly, I suppose we've accomplished our goal."

"Wouldn't a hat have been simpler?" Anita asked.

"If he has a hat and altered hair, that gives him two options that are different from how he last looked." Ingrid's scissors made a few more snips.

Anita pulled a folded paper from her pocket.

"What's that?" Gerrit asked.

"Berend *accidentally* bumped into me as I left the hospital and slipped it into my pocket. I haven't decoded it yet." She grabbed a book to put behind the paper and began turning the letters into dots and dashes.

"Do you mind if I watch?" Luitenant Brug asked, much to Gerrit's relief. If he was paying attention to Anita, there would be one less pair of eyes on his current predicament.

"Not at all." Anita scooted closer so Luitenant Brug could see over her shoulder.

Sergeant Cervantes spoke for a while, and then Ingrid laughed.

"What?" Gerrit asked.

Luitenant Brug smiled. "He's telling her a story about when he almost blew up his grandmother's kitchen because he forgot to turn the gas off on the stove. I think as a way to help her know that there are worse things than a bad haircut."

Gerrit grunted. "It's not his hair, is it?"

Anita glanced up. "You've never been vain before. When did you start caring so much about your hair?"

"Wanting a haircut that looks neat and tidy rather than looking like something done with a knife in an alley is hardly vanity." Gerrit brushed a bit of trimmed hair from his trousers. "An obviously bad one will draw notice. That's not useful for someone in my position."

Anita put aside her message to walk around and see the other side of Gerrit's head. "All hope is not lost. One side is shorter than the other, but I'm sure Ingrid will make them match, and then your hair will be quite average."

Gerrit grunted as Ingrid began snipping again. Anita returned to her message with an amused expression on her face, but then she scanned the page, and all mirth dissipated.

"What does it say?" Gerrit asked.

She met his eyes, then glanced at Ingrid and Sergeant Cervantes, who were finishing the hair around Gerrit's left ear. "It can wait."

Ingrid made a few final snips, then she and Sergeant Cervantes looked over the results, Ingrid ruffling the hair to look for uneven spots. Gerrit almost enjoyed the sensation. Almost.

"I think we're finished," Ingrid said. "Other than the cleanup."

Anita looked up from her paper. "Berend has two airmen who he wants us to hide. Tonight. And one of his contacts found out where your target lives. He wants Ingrid to take care of him."

A quick glance showed that Ingrid's face had gone pale, and her posture had gone stiff.

"You don't have to take orders from him," Anita said gently. "He's not your commander. And while I'm sure he has his reasons, acting as both judge and jury could be overstep."

Ingrid stared at the pair of scissors in her hands. She didn't want to take the assignment, Gerrit could tell. But refusing Berend . . . If they refused, would he make things difficult for them? And if no one did anything about Daalmans, how many more people would he betray?

Gerrit swallowed. "I'll do it."

Anita frowned. "You don't have to accept the assignment either."

"Maybe not. But it needs to be done, and I'm willing." Gerrit brushed more hair from his clothing. "I can make it look like an accident so we avoid reprisals." One of Gerrit's hands trembled, but he quickly pressed it against his leg so no one else would see.

"I'll fetch the broom and dustpan." Ingrid set the scissors down and rushed from the room.

Gerrit watched her go, then looked at the dark pieces of hair scattered around him. "If I need parts to build something, am I right to assume that I can use anything in my mother's old room or the basement?"

"Yes," Anita said. "And if you need something in another room, I'm sure we can do without."

Gerrit nodded and excused himself. He checked the results of the haircut—much shorter, and darker because of the dye, but rather average. Ingrid's work would be adequate. It wouldn't attract undue attention, and maybe it would prevent Daalmans from recognizing him.

Sergeant Cervantes's story during the trim had sparked an idea, so Gerrit spent the rest of the afternoon and evening looking for the parts he needed and modifying a few of them. It would have been easier if he knew exactly what Daalmans's stove looked like, but he tried to be prepared for multiple possibilities. Hopefully, that would be enough.

Bits of hair itched his neck, but showering might wash out some of the dye, so he was stuck with any pieces he couldn't brush off. Maybe that was for the best anyway. The discomfort balanced out the pleasant memory of Ingrid's fingers touching his skin.

A knock sounded on the door, and he looked around to see Anita standing in the doorway.

"I suppose you have a plan?" she asked.

He looked at the fuel control valve, filler plug, and fuel line he'd scavenged. "I couldn't understand Sergeant Cervantes's story about his grandma's stove, but it got me thinking. If there were a problem with the gas in Daalmans's home, it would look like an accident, not an assassination."

Anita crossed her arms. "What if he doesn't live alone?"

Gerrit considered the possibility. "If it looks like he has a family, I can reassess."

A frown grew on her face. "Gerrit, you don't have to do this."

He ran his thumb over a piece of corrugated tubing. If no one acted against Daalmans, the man would keep betraying onderduikers for the bounty. "Berend is expecting someone to do it. Ingrid doesn't want to."

"That doesn't mean you have to. When Berend asked for volunteers to work directly for him, I wanted you to stay." Anita sat on a trunk. "Partly because I worry about you, and not just about whether you'll come home after each assignment. If you get involved with this, there's a cost. Do you want to bear the burden of killing someone for the rest of your life? What will that do to your soul?"

Gerrit had been trying not to think about that. Besides, thinking about the future seemed a waste of time when all the uncertainties of war swirled round him. "I think it would do more harm to Ingrid's soul than to mine."

"Berend has other contacts. If it's so important, he can have someone else do it or do it himself."

Gerrit studied his aunt. "Let someone else do it? Is that what you'd tell me if there were a way for me to enlist in the Dutch Army and I were about to march off to war?"

"That would be different."

"We're fighting the same war. Just in different ways."

Anita bit her lip and looked away, all out of fight. After a long silence, she spoke again. "Do you need anything other than those parts?"

He didn't want to ask, but if he were really going after Daalmans, he wanted his efforts to succeed. "I could use a lookout."

An hour later, Gerrit and Ingrid set out on bicycles. Ingrid hadn't seemed eager to join him, but nor had she hesitated when he and Anita had asked if she could be a lookout. He let Ingrid lead the way because she was more familiar with the streets of Arnhem. When she slowed, he pulled up beside her.

"I think we'll want to leave our bicycles here rather than right beside his home," she said.

Gerrit nodded. "I can go on foot from here. But if you see him coming . . ."

"I'll ring the bell, and you'll sneak out the back."

That was what they'd planned before leaving, and to blend in, Gerrit wore a utility belt and carried a tool bag slung across his shoulder. Now that he was here, perspiration made his palms slick, and an unpleasant lump grew in the pit of his abdomen. He nodded again. His throat felt dry, and he didn't want to risk speaking and having it come out wrong.

"You don't have to do this." Ingrid's voice was soft, and part of him wanted to listen to it, obey it, turn around, and make up a reason to tell Berend why it wasn't possible. But it was a quiet street. No one suspicious waited, watching the house in an effort to protect it. Fear was the only reason not to proceed—and Gerrit wasn't a coward. Or maybe because it was wrong—but during war, this seemed the only way of protecting those Daalmans threatened. Gerrit suspected Berend had made some sort of threat to Ingrid, too, and that was another reason for him to forge ahead, regardless of how much Anita and Ingrid fretted over morality.

He swallowed and hoped the words would come without any hint of the emotions battling in his chest. "I need to do this."

He left his bicycle with Ingrid and approached the address as if he were just another repairman called to fix something in the two-story rowhome. He knocked, just in case Daalmans was home, and put his hand into the tool bag so he could grip the pistol he'd hidden there. If Daalmans answered his knock and recognized him, a quick shot at close range would be Gerrit's best chance of escaping death tonight. Earlier, when they'd made their plans, he'd told Ingrid to ride away if she heard a gunshot.

No one answered, so Gerrit pulled the lockpicking tools from the bag. In Utrecht, back when he'd been distributing ration cards for onderduikers instead of assassinating their hunters, he'd needed to pick open a locked door every Wednesday. Daalmans's lock wasn't as familiar as the other one, but Gerrit soon pried it opened.

Once inside, with the door locked behind him, he checked all the rooms. Everything suggested that Daalmans lived alone. Only one room was furnished with a bed, and the closets there held no clothes for a wife or girlfriend. Most of the walls were decorated with artwork rather than photographs, and the few exceptions showed Daalmans alone. Some of the artwork was extraordinary. Probably stolen from people who had been arrested. It seemed a pity to damage any of it, but it would be far more of a pity to allow Daalmans to continue hunting down onderduikers.

In the kitchen, Gerrit went to work on the stove, examining the fittings. He replaced one of the valves and made sure everything was exactly as he'd left it, from the kettle on one of the burners to the breadcrumbs on the floor. His heart rate had been beating a staccato tempo since his arrival, and it scarcely slowed now, even as he finished. He left out the back door and made his way to Ingrid.

"Did you see anything?" he asked.

"A few neighbors." Her words were soft. "No sign of Daalmans."

Gerrit nodded. Berend was right. It was easy to kill someone. "I'm staying to see if it works, but you can go back, if you prefer."

Ingrid studied his face for a few moments. He wasn't sure what she was thinking, but he wished she would look at him and smile instead of look at him as if they were strangers. Neutrality was better than contempt, but he wouldn't have minded some gratitude. If he hadn't done what needed to be done in Daalmans's home, Berend would be hounding Ingrid to ride past Daalmans and shoot him from her bicycle, just as they'd practiced at the farm.

Ingrid swallowed. "If you don't need me for cover, I think I'll go back."

He didn't want to feign a romantic relationship again, and his clothing and tools gave him a reason to loiter near pipes or meters. "I'll see you later, then."

She slowly pulled her eyes from him to her bicycle. "When do you think you'll be back?"

"That depends on him." If Daalmans came home in the next hour and began preparing tea or coffee or a meal . . . In that case, Gerrit might be home soon. But if he didn't return until curfew and went to bed instead of the kitchen, Gerrit might be watching and waiting all night. Could he stay awake that long? Last night, he'd been tired enough to fall asleep at the kitchen table, and he was hardly more rested now. "I don't plan to spend the night here."

Ingrid bit at her bottom lip. "Be careful." Then she rode away.

Gerrit watched her disappear. Then he walked to a group of pipes in an alley with a view of Daalmans's home and spent the next few hours pretending to work on them, using a loose wrench to fiddle with them, digging through his bag to compare fittings of similar diameter, making measurements. Bits of hair still scratched his neck. His heart still beat quickly enough to leave his hands with tremors. A few people walked past, one of them in a German uniform, but no one seemed to find him suspicious.

Daalmans strode by the alley at a quarter to six. His gaze scanned past Gerrit, who turned his head to examine the pipes again. When Gerrit looked around, Daalmans had continued across the road. The man's gaze kept moving, always on the lookout. Gerrit had been right: he was more cautious now. He hoped that caution didn't include inspecting all the pieces of his oven before lighting the burner beneath the tea kettle.

The waiting was worse now. Gerrit slowly packed up his tools, wondering how long he should wait. Time passed slowly, as if it had turned to a frozen bicycle chain. He couldn't wait forever. He had just put away his last tool when a blast rattled the window panes and set no fewer than three nearby dogs barking.

Daalmans had turned on the stove. The part of the oven Gerrit had replaced would have failed, as intended, and the explosion had most likely killed Daalmans instantly. Curiosity kept Gerrit in the alley a few seconds more. One of Daalmans's windows looked cracked, but it hadn't shattered. Despite a desire to see more, self-preservation quickly won over curiosity, and Gerrit mounted his bicycle and rode from the disaster.

His body had been so keyed up for so long that it was hard to ride. Long before he made it back to the Utrechtseweg, the muscles in his limbs began to shake, and nausea twisted his stomach. Riding a bicycle like a drunkard might have been good cover if the sun hadn't still been up. As it was—nearly curfew, with plenty of daylight to make him visible—he wished his body would cooperate.

What was wrong with him? He was perfectly capable of riding a bicycle, even one with wooden blocks instead of rubber on the wheels. Physically, he was fine, other than a ridiculously short haircut and an excess of adrenaline that needed to work its way through his system. But the thought that he'd been trying to push aside all day kept intruding into his mind.

He had killed a man.

A man who deserved death after betraying the innocent and members of the resistance. Besides his treachery, he had nearly gotten Gerrit arrested, and that arrest would have likely led to death. Daalmans had been a traitor, and that was even worse than a Nazi.

The death was justified, wasn't it?

Anita hadn't been convinced. Opa wouldn't have liked it. Ingrid's hesitation had seemed to be more about morality than about feasibility or fear. Pap would have approved, wouldn't he? Pap had lost a wife to the Nazis, and he'd gone on strike—even when it had been risky—to protest Nazi discrimination against the Jews. But as far as Gerrit knew, Pap hadn't ever killed anyone. And Mam . . . Gerrit's gut twisted. He slowed his bicycle and stumbled off, toward a bush, and vomited into its green leaves.

He panted for breath. Dread swirled in his chest because no matter what the circumstance, Mam would never have approved of assassination.

Gerrit climbed back on his bicycle and forced himself to ride the three remaining blocks to Opa's home. He focused on the handlebars, on the pedestrians, on anything other than his mother and the horror she would feel if she knew her son had killed someone.

He held off the tears until he arrived at Opa's house and pulled his bicycle into the basement. He placed it next to the one Ingrid had used, so she must have made it home safely. Safe and unsullied with the blood of Dirk Daalmans.

Gerrit couldn't see any blood on his hands. Of course he couldn't. He'd used a sabotaged oven, not a knife, to commit his execution. Or was it murder? He wasn't even sure he believed in souls and God and a life beyond this one, but either way, it felt like he'd lost a piece of his soul, and tears quickly grew into sobs. Sometimes, he wished he did believe because that meant his mother wasn't gone forever. But if she still existed, she wouldn't want to see him now. And if she still existed, that meant there was a God, and Gerrit had accompanied Mam to church enough to know that one of the ten commandments said, *Thou shalt not kill.*

Ingrid waited in the corner of the cellar, where she'd come to fetch potatoes. A shelf of preserved fruit and stored root vegetables hid her from the entrance and the bicycles. She listened to the weeping that echoed along the walls, as if Gerrit's heart had been crushed and his soul ripped apart. Was it because he had failed? Or because he had succeeded?

She wanted to comfort him, but something held her back. He'd undoubtedly stayed in the cellar so no one would see his tears. Wouldn't joining him now, even if she meant to be kind, embarrass him rather than help him? And she did want to help him, a feeling that grew more and more with each cry of anguish. She would never accuse him of being unfeeling again. Obviously, he did feel—deeply. He simply didn't trust her with the part of him that was vulnerable.

And why would he? She hadn't exactly been warm in their other interactions. She'd been critical, secretive, maybe even arrogant. There was a need for secrecy sometimes, but the arrogance hurt them both. When it came to criticism, it seemed that Gerrit was hard enough on himself. He didn't need her reminding him of his mistakes.

Maybe Gerrit needed a friend more than Ingrid needed to . . . Why did she always seem to butt heads with him? Where did her need to point out all his flaws come from? His politics were ridiculous, of course, but he seemed to sincerely think a government could solve most of society's ills. How he could still think that after being under the massive control of the Nazis made no sense to her, but that didn't make him evil or stupid, just hopeful about something she didn't think would ever work. Misplaced hope. She had a little of that. Not hope in an economy successfully run by a central committee, but hope that she'd one day find Anna and Karl. Hope that Anita and Luitenant Brug wouldn't have to say goodbye. Hope that the boy sobbing on the other side of the cellar could find some peace, even in the middle of a war.

She prayed, begging God to comfort Gerrit and asking for guidance so she could help without fighting him or embarrassing him. Gradually, the weeping stopped, and his breathing grew quiet. Ingrid's legs ached with standing in the same spot for so long, but she didn't dare move and risk making a sound. Being discovered now would be far worse than if she had made her presence known when he'd first entered the cellar. Eventually, all went quiet, but she stayed where she was until she heard the familiar creak on the stairs, then the door opening. She waited a few more minutes before following him into the house.

Gerrit tensed when someone knocked on his bedroom door that evening. A soft knock. Anita or Ingrid. Maybe Luitenant Brug. Not someone from the Gestapo. "Who is it?"

"Anita."

He pulled the door open. Her eyes ran over his head. "I'm still not used to seeing you with hair so short, but it doesn't look as dark as it did before."

"Some of it washed out in the shower. Did you get the airmen?"

"Yes. Ingrid's making them something to eat." Anita walked in and closed the door behind her. "Berend asked about Daalmans tonight when he handed the airmen over."

Gerrit swallowed and folded his arms. "What did you tell him?"

"I told him Daalmans would no longer be hunting onderduikers. Berend no doubt assumed that is because Daalmans is dead, but really, Daalmans is a patient under care for intense burns in St. Elisabeth Hospital."

Gerrit's jaw relaxed, and his arms fell open. "Daalmans is still alive?"

Anita nodded.

Gerrit ran a shaky hand over his face. "So I didn't kill him?"

"No. By all appearances, he was severely injured in a gas explosion. An accident. He's not dead, but his stay in the hospital will be lengthy, so the threat he posed is significantly reduced. We might be liberated before he's back to his treason."

Gerrit sat hard on his bed and tried not to cry with relief. "I'm glad. I didn't . . . at least, well . . . I started out wanting him dead, but after, when I thought I'd killed him . . . I started to regret it. A great deal."

Anita sat beside Gerrit and put a hand on his back. "In that case, I'm glad he survived. And I'm glad I didn't tell Berend the full truth, or he might have wanted someone to finish the job."

Gerrit squeezed his eyes shut. "Killing a helpless patient . . . I think that would crush my conscience, even with a target as evil as Daalmans. It already feels heavy, even when he was dangerous and I didn't kill him."

"If that's how you felt, why did you agree to it?"

Gerrit shrugged. "It needed to be done. And it didn't feel like murder when I was sabotaging his oven. It felt like working on any other task, solving a problem. It didn't hit me until I rode away. And . . . well, Ingrid didn't want to do it. I could tell. And I didn't hear most of what Berend said to her, but it sounded like he made some sort of threat. I thought if Daalmans were taken out, Berend would back off a little."

"I thought you liked Berend."

"I do. He's fighting the Nazis, and he's not afraid to hurt them as much as they're hurting everyone else. But if I became like him . . . what would my mother think?"

"Judith would love you regardless." Anita gave Gerrit a one-armed hug. "She always did, and nothing you do will ever change that. But I think she would mourn what you've had to do in order to resist the Nazis."

"I miss her." Gerrit's words were a whisper, but he felt each one of them more deeply than normal.

Anita swallowed. "I do too."

Gerrit translated Ingrid's latest message written for decoding practice the day after the disastrous events at Daalmans's home. *The bicycles you have repaired operate very well. If you ever need a project to help you pass the time, there are several broken lamps in your mother's old room.* He'd expected something from the Bible, and given the guilt he'd felt the last time he had recalled a verse of scripture, he was grateful for this instead.

Did the lamps just need new lightbulbs, or was something else wrong with them? He found the lamps in question and ended up spending all afternoon fiddling with one until he found the corroded wire. Figuring out how to make the lamp shine again was easier than wondering if Daalmans suspected what had really happened to his oven.

He encoded a message for Ingrid, reporting that the blue lamp now functioned and the red-and-gold lamp could be fixed if the right spare part were found.

Days passed that way, with Ingrid finding things for Gerrit to fix, then coding the suggestion in a message, and Gerrit being grateful for the distraction the decoding and the repairs provided.

Anita and Ingrid said Gerrit's shorter hair made him look older, more at risk of being hauled away to work in a German factory, so he was largely stuck inside. The two women stayed busy cycling around to make observations for Luitenant Brug.

The Allied armies liberated Brussels and Antwerp, and hope that the Netherlands would be next grew and grew. The airmen spent their days playing cards and waiting for Sergeant Cervantes's arm to heal. Luitenant Brug compiled information and experimented with how many times he could climb up and down the stairs without making his incision burn. The number increased daily, so Gerrit wasn't sure why the luitenant's progress seemed to make Anita unhappy rather than pleased.

He asked Ingrid about it one day. "Anita seemed sad when Luitenant Brug said he thought he'd be able to leave in a day or two. Shouldn't she be glad that he's getting better?"

Ingrid looked up from the toaster Gerrit had just repaired. It seemed Opa never threw anything away, so the attic and spare rooms were packed with items Gerrit could tinker with. "She's happy he's recovering, but she's going to miss him. They spend hours talking every day."

"And you think it's more than friendship?" For Gerrit, understanding appliances was easier than understanding relationships.

"I have strong suspicions that it is."

Gerrit nodded. "Well, I like him well enough. And I've always thought Anita was extraordinary, so I can see why he would like her, but with the war on . . . Poor Anita."

Ingrid pushed the toaster to the back of the countertop. "When he leaves, do you expect her to be like all the people she's related to, who throw themselves into work when they're hurting, or do you think she'll mope and cry?"

Gerrit studied Ingrid's face, looking for clues about what she was thinking. It was a pleasant face, with pleasant features, surrounded by pleasant blonde hair Gerrit could still remember pulling into a low chignon that day when they had trailed Daalmans. He looked away. Ingrid hadn't insulted him for days. She'd actually been friendly, but that didn't mean he ought to stare at her, pleasant face or not. "I don't expect she'll shirk her work."

"No, I don't suspect that either."

He folded his arms. "What did you mean about all the people she's related to?"

Ingrid fingered the newly repaired toaster. "When your mother died, Opa showed few outward signs of grief. He just stayed at the hospital longer."

"That was when the war started. The number of patients undoubtedly rose. Mam said more than once that Opa could never say no to someone who needed his care."

"I'm sure that was part of it, but I also think it kept him too busy to feel his pain. And I'm sure all your tinkering is partially to relieve boredom, partially because you're helpful and like to fix things. If it also distracts you from your pain, then—"

"Who said I'm in pain?" He was, and it was crushing if he let himself think too much about Daalmans.

"Aren't you?" she asked very quietly.

A week ago, Gerrit would have denied it. But pretending to be invincible didn't make him any stronger or wiser or able than he really was. "There's a war on. My family is scattered, and I've done things I regret. Of course I have pain."

He studied Ingrid's profile again. Her skin looked so smooth that for a moment, he was tempted to run his fingers over the curve of her cheekbone. He pulled his hands behind his back so he wouldn't accidentally indulge in something so foolish. Caressing Ingrid's cheek would be like caressing hemlock blossoms. Pretty but poisonous. Or maybe *poisonous* was too strong a term. Regardless, it was a risk he wouldn't take. "The war has given you pain, too, though, hasn't it?"

Ingrid nodded, and he caught sight of the expression he'd seen on her a time or two before, with stiff shoulders and a mouth pinched in pain. "I miss my parents. They're both gone. And I miss my brother and sister. I don't know what happened to them. I don't even know if they're alive. The uncertainty . . . the fear . . ." She glanced at him and looked away as if she hadn't meant to confide in him, even if they were something close to friends now.

Gerrit wasn't sure he ought to, but he put a gentle hand on her shoulder. "I miss my brother and sister too. It's been weeks instead of years since I last saw them, but I have an inkling of how desperate you must be for word of your family. The Allies are getting closer. The war is going to end soon. And then we'll figure out a way for you to find your brother and sister again. I promise."

She turned to look at him. "How?"

Gerrit shrugged. "I don't know yet. And I know others are more intelligent and more educated than me, but I'm willing to try it the wrong way twenty times—or a hundred—if that's what it takes. And Opa's a lot wiser than I am, and you won't be the only one trying to find someone when this war is over. We'll listen to what others try, and we'll learn what works."

"You'll help me?"

He nodded. Didn't she believe him?

"Why?"

He didn't answer right away. Didn't say how part of him wanted to see her smile, really smile—at him—because he'd proven capable of solving her problems instead of creating them. He didn't talk about the need to atone for that day when he'd nearly become an assassin or the time he'd criticized her for making the best choice in a bad situation. "We're friends, aren't we? And friends help each other."

Looking into her blue eyes, it hit him that his feelings for her were pushing beyond mere friendship, and he couldn't indulge in something so reckless. Not now. Not with Ingrid. He pulled his gaze away. "Maybe before we tackle that problem, we ought to figure out what to do for Anita when Luitenant Brug leaves."

CHAPTER 15

RUPERT GLANCED AROUND THE HOSPITAL wing to make sure none of the nurses was paying him anything other than superficial attention. His office had heard rumors, mostly unsubstantiated, that members of the Dutch Resistance used the hospital as a meeting point. The nuns who tended the patients were German, but some of them had been in the Netherlands for a long time, and not everyone who spoke German was loyal to the Reich. Leopold Lang had proven a traitor. So had his son. Maybe Ingrid too—regardless of her political beliefs, she'd proven a liar in Berlin.

Rupert pushed the Langs from his mind and leaned closer to the patient. "Mynheer Daalmans? Do you remember me?"

Rupert barely recognized Dirk Daalmans. Bandages still covered his burns, obscuring most of his face. Daalmans nodded and answered in German. "*Ja.*"

"The last time we met, you suspected that several of your associates had resistance connections. I would very much like to learn their names and anything else you can tell me about them."

"That was days ago. Almost a week. They may have moved on by now."

"I know. We weren't aware of what happened to you until recently. An accident in the kitchen?"

"My oven exploded." Daalmans's voice was strained. "I don't think it was an accident. Everything in my home was in perfect working order, and the resistance was targeting me. I pointed out a man following me only the day before."

Rupert had read the report of Daalmans's last meeting with Hauptman Denhart. The patrolman hadn't caught the suspect, but the man had run, so he was probably guilty of something. He'd clearly followed Daalmans. Targeting Daalmans felt less certain. Why would the resistance target someone like Daalmans when they could instead target someone far more important? Yet Daalmans had led to a significant number of arrests over the past months: usually Jews, or men trying to resist the opportunity to serve the Reich in one of its factories across the border in Germany, or people en route to Allied lines. But some of the catches had been more useful, from an intelligence perspective. Airmen who could be tricked or forced into telling who had hid them previously. Members of the resistance who had found themselves under suspicion and had, therefore, gone into hiding. Daalmans had proved a useful source. "Can you describe the man who followed you?" Rupert asked.

"Average height and size. Late teens, I think. Wore glasses one of the times I saw him but not the other time. Light-brown hair."

Rupert took notes, but the description was too vague to be useful. "Hairstyle?"

"Parted on the side. Combed back into a bit of a wave."

"Eyes?"

"Don't know."

"Clothing?"

"Working class."

"We'll keep our eyes out." Rupert had interviewed the patrolman who had unsuccessfully chased the boy. His description wasn't any more helpful. "Do you have any onderduikers for me?"

"They've probably move on by now, but I had two leads."

Rupert bent to pick up a cigarette butt in the attic of the Velp home that Daalmans had marked as suspicious. Rupert smelled the stub. Real tobacco, not the ersatz items Dutch civilians had been making do with for years, normally made of oak or beech leaves. Manufactured, not rolled by hand. It wasn't proof that enemy airmen had been hiding in the attic, but it made Daalmans's claim more credible. Not that Rupert had doubted. Daalmans had handed them too many successes for Rupert to discount anything the man said.

He slid the cigarette butt into his pocket and finished his search of the attic. No further clues. No proof that the home's Dutch occupants had been involved in anything illegal. He could arrest them anyway but thought it better to keep the house under surveillance. Maybe they'd open their attic to another enemy airman or to a member of the resistance, and maybe next time, Rupert would be able to capture someone, interrogate them, and roll up more of the network. He'd discuss it with Hauptmann Denhart before making a decision. The homeowners, too, might have information that would lead to more arrests. Yet sometimes, the safe-house operators knew only the couriers who brought onderduikers to their homes or led them away. Recognizing a face might be useful, but it didn't guarantee more arrests.

A patrolman waited in the parlor with the middle-aged couple who owned the home.

"My apologies." Rupert kept his voice calm and apologetic when he returned to the main level. He wanted them to think they were above suspicion so they would once again welcome enemies and criminals into their midst. Then he would arrest them all.

"It appears I was misinformed. I hope it wasn't a great inconvenience. Please, enjoy your evening."

Rupert and the patrolman left the house. "Keep an eye on things. I'll arrange for your relief. I want this house watched around the clock. If they have visitors, arrest everyone."

"Yes, sir."

When Rupert reached SD headquarters, Hauptmann Denhart had already gone home for the night, but Jung arrived at about the same time Rupert did.

"Did you find anyone?" he asked.

"No." Rupert took the cigarette butt from his pocket. "But I'm guessing this came from someone other than the home's owners."

Jung fingered it. Sniffed it. "American. Did you arrest them?"

"Not yet. But I left them under surveillance. You?"

"Nothing. It doesn't look like anyone lives in the home, not now. But that doesn't mean someone wasn't there a week ago."

Neither of Daalmans's leads looked urgent enough to interrupt Denhart's evening, so after arranging relief for the patrolman he'd left at the suspected home, Rupert retired for the night.

Rupert woke early the next morning, sweating and out of breath as images from his nightmare swirled around him. He closed his eyes, almost seeing the bombs that had rained from the sky, crashing into his mother's apartment, killing most of its occupants. The nightmares had come every few nights since the telegram from Onkel Wilhelm. Rupert swallowed and told himself it was just a dream. And it was, but it was a dream of something that had really happened, robbing him of two people he loved and admired. Heidi and Uncle Wilhelm were the only family he had left now. He opened the small drawer in the table beside his bed and pulled out the pendant of St. George his mother had given him before he'd joined the Sixth Army. It had brought his grandfather back from the Great War. It had brought Rupert back from Stalingrad. If he had left it in Berlin, might it have protected his mother?

He checked the clock and the calendar. It was 5:00 a.m. on September 5. A week since his mother and stepfather had died. Rather than trying to go back to sleep, Rupert washed, dressed, ate, and headed to SD headquarters.

What he found there was chaos. Before he went inside, he passed three men carrying boxes outside to a waiting car. Given the posture of the men, the boxes were heavy. Inside was just as full of commotion. Most of the staff were there. Some packed items into crates. Some carried on animated conversations via the telephone.

"Altbauer, I'm glad you came early."

Rupert turned to Hauptmann Denhart and saluted. "Sir, what's going on?"

"The British broke out of Belgium. We're evacuating. Today. Before noon, if we can make it happen."

Rupert was stunned. He'd heard about the battles in France and how dire the situation was on the front lines. But to evacuate so quickly? The Allies had landed in Normandy in early June, and they'd been fighting in France for three months. Surely they wouldn't take the Netherlands in mere days. "What about current leads?"

"Secure any files or notes. I hope we can take everything with us. If not, we'll have to burn them so they don't fall into the wrong hands."

"Not so loud." Ingrid reached for the volume dial on the radio. Gerrit had turned it up far too high. Having a radio was illegal, and if the neighbors heard . . .

Gerrit grinned. "It sounds like that's not going to matter anymore. They're finally coming!"

Ingrid was gathered with all the onderduikers in the attic: Gerrit, three airmen, and Luitenant Brug. According to the news—most of it in English, with Luitenant Brug translating for Gerrit—German forces were withdrawing from France and Belgium, retreating through the Netherlands. Queen Wilhelmina addressed the nation in their native tongue, as did her son-in-law, Prince Bernhard, who had been given command of all Dutch forces, including the resistance.

"They're on the run." Gerrit sat on the mattress near the radio, almost pulsing with excitement. "I assume Berend or Cornelis will have ideas on how to keep them that way."

Ingrid looked out the small attic window. All day, traffic had been busier than usual. Some of the vehicles were military, but civilians were out in greater numbers too. Gerrit bent down next to her to peer through the window pane. A week ago, she would have resented sharing the view with him, but now she was glad for his presence. Extraordinary events were best experienced with friends.

"He's NSB." Ingrid pointed to a man with a large suitcase in one hand and a bundle of bedding in the other. A woman, probably his wife, pushed a baby carriage loaded with household items, and two children trailed behind them.

"Doesn't surprise me. If the Nazis are leaving, anyone who's worked with them has got to be scared. They won't have many friends left when the Allies roll in."

Ingrid studied the homes she could see from the window. Orange banners representing the royal House of Orange. The red, white, and blue flag of the Netherlands. "Those flags!" No one had been bold enough to show those for years, not without fear of immediate arrest. Excitement and disbelief pulled at her in equal measures.

Gerrit's grin hadn't faded, and his excitement was contagious. "I don't suppose things will calm down right away. And travel might be rough for a while, but maybe we can both plan to spend Christmas with our siblings."

Ingrid nodded. It was the first week of September, giving the Allies plenty of time to defeat the Nazis in the Netherlands and reestablish transport before year's end, probably before All Saints' Day. Once the Germans left, she would find a way to get to London. She still remembered the directions on how to get to her old nanny's apartment. Anna would be there, and Karl was bound to have found Anna and Frau Davies by now, if he'd escaped that SS officer in Vienna. If he hadn't, surely he'd make his way to London as soon as the war ended. Their parents would still be gone, but after more than four years apart, a reunion with her brother and sister might be only weeks away.

Anita's lithe form crossed into view, heading toward the home. Her somber attitude of the last few days was now replaced with a bounce in her step, something that had first shown up at about the same time as the American intelligence officer, then disappeared, temporarily, when he spoke about leaving.

Ingrid raced down the stairs and reached the front entry only moments after Anita entered. "Can you believe it?" Ingrid asked.

Anita gave Ingrid a heartfelt embrace. "The Allies are only a hundred and twenty kilometers away. The Moffen are leaving, and all the traitors with them, and then this ghastly war will be over."

"What are things like in the hospital?"

Anita unbuttoned her jacket. "Things are about to change, and everyone can feel it. A handful of staff are leaving, and a few patients too. All eager to escape before the Germans disappear and can no longer protect them. Daalmans is among those evacuating. I'm not sure it's wise for him to leave at this stage of his recovery, but I won't be sad to see him go."

Daalmans. His mere name made something cold wrap around Ingrid's spine, but she wouldn't let him ruin the otherwise good news.

Anita gazed past Ingrid, and the bittersweet expression on her friend's face told Ingrid that Luitenant Brug had made his way downstairs, even before she heard his footsteps. She turned and verified it, then excused herself to the kitchen. She hadn't been planning to start cooking so early, but Anita's time with Luitenant Brug was limited. She didn't want to intrude.

"Will the chaos make it harder or easier for you to sneak back to Allied lines?" Anita asked as Ingrid walked away.

"I'm not sure."

"You could stay and wait for them to come to you."

"I could, but if they're advancing, I ought to take them as much information as I can."

Ingrid didn't hear the rest of the conversation. If the Germans were all focused on retreat to the east, it might be less dangerous for Luitenant Brug and the airmen to leave for the west. But with all the enemy troops entering the Netherlands from Belgium and France, it could instead be more dangerous.

She was halfway through kneading bread dough when Anita and Luitenant Brug came into the kitchen. They held hands, but the expressions on their faces made Ingrid suspect Luitenant Brug wasn't staying much longer.

"Mejuffrouw van der Veen," Luitenant Brug began. "I wondered if I could trouble you for another favor."

Another favor would be another trip to observe the enemy or identify a bombing target. "Where to?"

"Deelen Air Base. Or as close to it as you can get without getting into trouble."

Ingrid nodded. She'd crept through the forests of the Veluwe several times in the last few weeks, trying to assess damage from recent air raids. "Want to know if they're evacuating?"

"Please."

"I assume you'll still be here in the morning if I take all night?"

He nodded. "I'd offer to finish whatever you're baking, but I'd probably burn it."

"I'm sure Anita or Gerrit can bake it, after it's had time to rise." But it seemed Ingrid wouldn't be around to eat any of it while it was warm.

Gerrit watched Ingrid ride away until the view from the window in his mother's old room no longer showed her progress. Civilians could be shot for trespassing on Deelen Air Base. Ingrid had completed reconnaissance there before, so there was every reason to assume she could do it again without getting caught. Maybe if the Germans were retreating anyway, they wouldn't be as cruel as normal. Or maybe they'd be worse. Were he the praying sort, he would say a prayer for her safety. Instead, he watched and hoped she wasn't riding off for the last time.

"Does it still look like they're retreating?" Luitenant Brug stepped in from the hallway.

Gerrit had been paying attention to only one of the many people on the street below. He glanced at the crowds still streaming past, trying to make it to Germany before the Allies arrived. "Yes. Seems almost too easy for them to slip away like this. Like they're outrunning justice, too, not just the Allies."

"Justice will come. If not in this life, then in the next."

Gerrit shrugged. If justice were so important to God, why did so many unjust things happen? But maybe it was better for the enemy to escape, if it meant Arnhem wouldn't suffer the same destruction Rotterdam had. A flash of memory hit him: him and Nellie trapped in a dark pile of rubble, the city around them burning, the air hot and thick and choking, the wheezing of Johan's lungs. Gerrit shook his head and cleared his throat. The memory hadn't been that strong for over a year.

"Are you all right?" Luitenant Brug asked.

Gerrit nodded.

"Worry for Mejuffrouw van der Veen?"

"She's good at what she does. I don't expect her to run into any problems." Not that such clear logic could wipe away his worry.

"Nor do I. Otherwise, I wouldn't have asked her."

Another flash of memory: a group of civilians, Gerrit included, stopped on a street in Utrecht and compelled to form an audience of sorts. A Nazi truck pulled to a halt, and twelve men were pulled from the back, shoved against a wall, and shot. Gerrit hadn't known any of them, but that didn't stop the horror from sinking in anew. And it didn't stop the loathing for the men who had occupied his country for four years, three months, and twenty-five days. He sat on a trunk as more memories swirled through his head.

"You sure you're all right?"

"I'm just remembering things. Hostages killed in reprisal. Homes destroyed. People arrested and sent away. What if the war ends and all the rats fleeing the Netherlands get to go home, but all the people they took away don't get to come back?"

Luitenant Brug frowned. "Not everyone will come back. They've been ruthless here and everywhere else they've invaded. They won't be any kinder to people they've taken away."

Gerrit hated the Nazis. He wanted them punished, but more than that, he wanted all their wrongs righted, all their evils reversed. He looked out the window again. So many people passing through Arnhem, fleeing justice. He turned back to the American. "I guess you'll stick around long enough for Ingrid's report?"

Luitenant Brug nodded. "Maybe longer. Depends on how things develop. The border with Belgium isn't all that far away, but that doesn't mean they'll advance to Arnhem this week. Could take a lot longer. If the information I bring them can shorten that time, I don't want to dally."

"Cornelis could send it by radio."

"He could, and it would be helpful, but it might be more effective for me to sit in with the field officers planning all this. I can't give them answers if I'm not there to hear their questions."

"And Anita?"

Luitenant Brug's face softened. "Maybe someday, when the war's over . . . But even when the war with Germany ends, my country is at war with Japan too. I'm in for the duration."

"My country is also at war with Japan." Gerrit didn't want to go halfway around the world to fight them, not if his siblings needed him, but if he were a soldier or a sailor, he could send part of his wages to Tante Petronella. And fighting the Japanese might help family. Two of Mam's brothers had lived in the Netherlands East Indies with their families. No one had heard from them since the Japanese occupation had begun.

"What do you want to do when the war ends?" Luitenant Brug asked.

What would it be like when peace came? Gerrit wouldn't have called himself a child when he was fourteen, almost fifteen, but looking back, that was what he had been. War had forced him to grow up quickly. Maybe over the course of a single, massive air raid. "I'll go back to Utrecht, I think, and help with my siblings—hope that Pap and Oom Nicolaas come back. I'll stay in better touch with Anita and Opa than we did during most of the war. Try to find work, but I dropped out of school when all the real teachers were fired and replaced with parrots who spouted nothing but Nazi propaganda. I wouldn't have been a star pupil anyway, but that's one more thing the Nazis ruined." Limited schooling would mean limited options, but he'd figure something out.

A familiar form appeared on the street outside and caught Gerrit's attention. "I don't think Cornelis has ever come in daylight before."

"Must be something important."

The two went downstairs, and soon everyone was gathered in the dining room, save Sergeant Cervantes, who stood watch at one of the windows, and Opa, who was still at the hospital.

A smile lit Cornelis's face. "Prince Bernhard has asked all loyal resistance groups to combine into the Forces of the Interior. For a long time, we've played it safe, garnering our strength for the time when we could be of greatest assistance. That time is now."

"Have you any sense of how safe it might be for my colleagues and me to head west now?" Luitenant Brug asked.

"No worse than usual, though I would still recommend traveling at night. And the time may come when it would be better to hide until the Allies overrun your area, but I see no reason not to head west tonight."

Luitenant Brug glanced at the airmen and at Anita. "I'm waiting on a report from Ingrid."

"Tomorrow night, then."

Luitenant Brug nodded.

Cornelis turned to Gerrit next. "I hear you're handy with explosives. I've a list of targets we are to prioritize."

"Targets?" Gerrit had almost become an assassin once. He wasn't ready to try it again.

"Rail lines, vehicles, antiaircraft guns, that sort of thing."

Relief spread through him like a warm drink on a cold day. "As long as the leader of my cell approves it"—he glanced at Anita—"I'd be happy to help."

Anita nodded her consent.

Cornelis smiled, his face more at ease than Gerrit had ever before seen. "We'll leave at nightfall."

Gerrit gathered his few items and kept hoping to hear Ingrid returning, but the door opened only once, for Opa.

In the hallway outside their rooms on the top floor, Luitenant Brug shook Gerrit's hand. "Good luck."

"To you as well."

"Can I give you some advice, Mynheer Hendriks?"

Gerrit nodded. Most people wouldn't ask first; they'd just give it.

"Don't underestimate the Germans, even when they're on the run. Limit how long you're at any site, but take your time in the preparation."

"I will." Gerrit would put the utmost care into the explosives he planned to make, and strike a balance of bold and cautious when it came time to plant them.

"You're holding on to a lot of anger, and I understand why. Just make sure you aren't holding on to the bad so tightly that you end up fighting the good."

"I'm not fighting the good." He assumed the American was talking about religion. Not believing in it wasn't the same as fighting it.

"Just in case you haven't realized it yet, love is part of the good."

Gerrit felt his face heating. "I have no idea who or what you're talking about."

The intelligence officer lowered his voice. "Then, I won't beat around the bush. The blonde Mejuffrouw van der Veen."

"I'm not . . . That would never work." Gerrit's voice squeaked slightly. How had the man guessed? Gerrit had barely admitted it to himself.

Luitenant Brug shrugged. "Maybe. Maybe not. Definitely not if you keep fighting it."

Gerrit pulled on a knapsack Anita had given him. "I'm going to be too busy fighting the Nazis to try to fight Ingrid too. But it won't make much of a difference anyhow. War doesn't leave time for romance."

The luitenant's lips pulled as if he disagreed. "I'm not so sure. Maybe when everything else is so dark, we need love more than ever."

Gerrit thought of his aunt and didn't argue. "I suppose you're the expert."

Luitenant Brug shook his head. "No. Before my appendectomy, I was in love once. Maybe. For about an hour."

"An hour?"

The American nodded. "I knew her when we were children. In Amsterdam, actually. Our fathers were both diplomats. Spent a lot of time together. I saw her again years later. Would have liked to take her dancing or something, but then her boyfriend showed up, and it was clear her heart was already taken."

"And since your appendectomy?"

Luitenant Brug looked away. "Once, and it's lasted longer than an hour."

Gerrit adjusted the straps of his knapsack. "You seem to be giving advice that you aren't taking yourself."

"My situation is different. The United States Army owns me until the war is over, and the difference in nationalities makes it a little more complicated."

Gerrit opened his mouth to point out that Ingrid was Austrian and Gerrit Dutch, but if Ingrid hadn't told Luitenant Brug that herself, he wasn't going to share her secrets. "Whatever happens, I'm glad Opa got that rotten appendix out of you so you can go back to prying the Moffen out of the Netherlands. But I better get going because I'm eager to do my part too."

CHAPTER 16

Wednesday morning, Ingrid reported her findings on the air base to Luitenant Brug. The enemy did not seem to be evacuating Deelen, but recent damage from Allied bombings made it hard to judge if all the activity was an attempt to repair the airfield or a prelude to demolishing it before the Allies could seize it from them.

Others were retreating in the same way they had in Arnhem: Civilians who didn't want to be left behind should the Nazis no longer be present to protect them from the resentful Dutch population they'd betrayed. Soldiers, too, but they were different from the men who had marched in four and a half years ago. They were younger, or older, but rarely of prime military age, nor did they look of prime health. Most walked. Some rode bicycles that she suspected were stolen. Others hitched rides in horse-drawn carts, probably also stolen.

Wednesday night, Ingrid led the four Americans through the dark countryside to a farmhouse near Nijmegen, but not until after Luitenant Brug had planted a soft goodbye kiss on Anita's cheek.

Thursday and Friday, Ingrid watched rail traffic and recorded it for Cornelis, whom she was trying not to feel any resentment toward, even if he had taken Gerrit away without giving her a chance to say goodbye.

Saturday, she gathered information about demolition charges on a bridge. Sunday, she went to church with the van der Veens and tried to distract Anita after finding her standing in the empty hallway on the uppermost floor of their home, staring at the room where Luitenant Brug had stayed.

Monday, Ingrid scouted the location of an antiaircraft battery, and when a German soldier—one who wasn't retreating—asked her what she was doing, she found herself pretending he looked like Gerrit so it would be easier to flirt her way out of a potential interrogation. The flirting worked. She didn't want to think about the fact that Gerrit had somehow been the man she had imagined when she'd needed to feign interest. It was probably because they'd pretended to be a couple before. In no way because he was still away with Cornelis, and she found that she missed him.

Tuesday, it was back to the rail line, and then on Wednesday, when she had no assignment, she noticed a couple who lived down the street returning to their home after fleeing it the week before in what was coming to be known as Dolle Dinsdag or Mad Tuesday.

"I think the NSB is coming back," she told Anita and Opa at supper that night. The table was set for only three places, and the home felt almost empty, undoubtedly because onderduikers had been a near constant feature since the start of the war. Certainly not because Anita was mourning the departure of one onderduiker in particular, and Ingrid's mind kept wondering when a different onderduiker would return to them.

"I saw a few at the hospital too," Opa said. "Returning German officials as well."

"Maybe the Allies won't arrive quite as soon as we hoped." Anita wiped her mouth and set her napkin down.

The dazed euphoria of Dolle Dinsdag and the days right after it had been fading, and now it seemed to have vanished completely.

After supper, Anita and Ingrid took the dishes to the kitchen. "Cornelis heard that some of the Panzers passing through are regrouping rather than retreating," Anita said. "He wants you to see what you can find."

Ingrid nodded. "Maybe now that the Germans aren't retreating quite so fast, I can use my bicycle without them stealing it."

As it turned out, her bicycle was safe, but the situation was less so. The 9th and 10th Panzer divisions did not appear to be passing through, not in the same way the other German units had. From what Ingrid could observe, neither division was full strength, but they were refitting and resting. They weren't retreating.

Anita frowned when Ingrid finished her report in the kitchen Thursday night. "Another contact said they've been requisitioning buildings near the Openluchtmuseum."

"Do you want me to look into it tomorrow?"

"Maybe, but first I have some detonators I need you to deliver to Cornelis or one of his men. You're to meet him near the Hotel Naeff in Velp tomorrow morning at ten twenty."

"Isn't there a group of Dutch SS commanders staying in the Hotel Naeff?"

Anita nodded. "There's a bench around a corner, out of sight." Anita drew a map, and after Ingrid memorized it, they burned it. "Your contact will be on the bench. You're supposed to stop and fix something with your shoe. Then ask if the contact thinks it will rain. He or she will say not until next week, and then you can hand over the detonators and leave."

Ingrid nodded. The instructions were straightforward enough, and despite its proximity to the Dutch SS, it seemed safer than snooping around looking for more information on Panzers.

Gerrit sat on a bench in Velp, pretending to read a newspaper. He knew enough about the detonators Cornelis had requested and where they would come from that he wasn't surprised when Ingrid turned onto the street, walking toward him. Because it was Ingrid and he hadn't seen her in a week, it would be all the more difficult to pretend she was a stranger, but he was determined not to draw any unnecessary attention to their meeting.

Sunlight turned her sleek blonde hair to gold, and something about her last few awkward steps as she approached the bench filled him with delight. She wasn't really clumsy; the missteps were meant to make her stop at the bench more believable. But her smile was far too large for a meeting between strangers.

She sat beside him and adjusted her shoe. "Do you think it will rain today?"

Good, she was following protocol, in case Gerrit had somehow been compromised, but the way she looked at him—it was as if they were dear friends. That wasn't part of the script. He stumbled through his reply. "Not until next week." He folded his paper and put it on the bench between them.

"How have you been?" she asked with far too much warmth in her expression.

She was supposed to slide the detonators under the newspaper and walk on. Gerrit was supposed to keep the contraband tucked into the paper, wait an appropriate amount of time, and walk the other way. They weren't supposed to have a conversation, but he responded anyway. "Busy. Not much action. Just preparation so far. How have you been?"

She shrugged. "There's been plenty to do. Our guests left the day after you did."

"And Anita?"

"She's carrying on, though she's certainly missing someone."

Gerrit felt the detonators slip beneath the newspaper. "Tell her I miss her. I know I'm not the one she wants to hear from, but it's the best I can do."

"I'll pass that on." Ingrid waited.

"And I've missed you." Maybe he shouldn't have admitted as much, but it was true. He fiddled with the newspaper and slid the detonators into his jacket's inside pocket. "But we shouldn't be seen together."

Ingrid slid closer to him. "On the contrary, I think you'll look a great deal less suspicious with an adoring woman on your arm."

Something in Gerrit's chest caught. Was Ingrid suggesting she adored him, or was she merely promising that she could *look* as if she adored him? He swallowed. Undoubtedly, her statement was a promise that she could *act* the part, not an indication that she would *feel* the part.

She continued. "Do you have any checkpoints you have to go through?"

Gerrit nodded.

"Let me see you through. If needed, I'll play the role of a reckless flirt with the guard, and you can play the role of a resentful boyfriend."

Gerrit wanted more time with her, and getting past the checkpoint would be easier with her help, but only because some of the risk he faced would transfer to her. "It's probably safest for you if we part ways now."

"But far safer for you if we don't. Come on." She stood, taking one of his hands to pull him up.

Arguing would draw even more attention, so he stood and let her loop her elbow through his. The weather and company were both pleasant. If he could have pushed aside his fear of arrest, it might have been a lovely way to spend the rest of the morning, but as it was, the extra weight in his jacket pocket felt heavier than it should have.

"The Dutch Nazis seem to be coming back," Ingrid said. "The German ones too."

"I've noticed. As has Cornelis."

They joined the line waiting to pass through the checkpoint, and all conversation between them ceased. The group was a sober, quiet contrast to the jubilant crowds who had celebrated on Dolle Dinsdag. Except the Dutch Nazis. Their desperation had turned to contempt. Green Policemen questioned people passing through, sometimes checking papers, sometimes performing searches that would undoubtedly reveal contraband like detonators, occasionally waving people past.

Ingrid stepped closer to Gerrit. He assumed the proximity wasn't about fear but was instead because she wanted it to be clear to the guards that they were a couple. In Gerrit's mind, he reworded that: They weren't a couple. They were merely *pretending* to be a couple.

The middle-aged man in front of them was frisked. A policeman turned to Gerrit. "Papers, please."

Gerrit slid his papers out and handed them over.

"You're registered in Utrecht?" The man looked from Gerrit's papers to his face. For a moment, Gerrit regretted the haircut Ingrid had given him. If it had changed his appearance too much, it might cast suspicion on him. "Why are you in Velp?"

Gerrit cast a sidelong glance at Ingrid and pretended to be smitten. Or maybe it wasn't pretending. Maybe it was simply a cessation of hiding it. "Calling on a friend."

Ingrid elbowed him gently and giggled. "A friend? You've taken an awful lot of liberties the last few days if we are merely friends."

He'd scarcely seen her at all the last few days, and he found that a significant cause of regret. The soldier glanced at Ingrid, and either jealousy, irritation, or a desire to finish up made him shove the papers back to Gerrit, who returned them to the pocket not already full of detonators. Ingrid, a smile still lighting her face, tugged on his elbow, and they passed through the checkpoint.

He expected Ingrid to drop his arm and her smile once they were through. Instead, she chuckled. "I do believe the guard had a case of sour grapes."

"You were convincing enough. Pretty enough. Perhaps he'd feel better if he knew we were acting."

Ingrid's smile faded. "Of course we were acting. But the home has been rather quiet without you."

"I'm not loud."

"No, but so many people left all at once. I suppose I'll be glad to see you back whenever Cornelis is finished with you. Do you know how long he'll want your help?"

Gerrit hadn't any idea. With the way the front line was changing, he suspected he would be needed until the Netherlands was liberated. And after that . . . well, he was of age to be a soldier, and the Nazis needed to be defeated. The Japanese too. Maybe he ought to enlist once the Dutch were back in control of the Netherlands. "Until the Germans all leave, I would guess."

The last remnants of Ingrid's smile disappeared. "A week ago, it seemed like they would all be gone so soon. Now . . . now I'm not so sure."

"If they leave as fast as they came in . . ." Gerrit preferred not to dwell on the horrors of May 1940, nor on the losses for him, for Rotterdam, or for the country as a whole. But he couldn't forget those days either. "Sometimes the situation can change quickly." He hoped that the next time the situation shifted, it would be for the better.

They turned a corner, out of sight of the checkpoint. The houses they passed appeared neat and comfortable, more spacious than any of the apartments his parents had lived in or the farmhouse where he'd spent his early boyhood. Some of them were larger than Opa's home. Cornelis said some of the top Nazis in the Netherlands had commandeered homes in Velp, but he didn't know what neighborhoods they had congregated in.

"You!" someone shouted. "Halt."

Ingrid stiffened and looked back. "Green Policeman, and he's heading toward us."

Gerrit turned and recognized the same patrolman who Daalmans had spoken with the day they'd been tracking the traitor, the one who had chased Gerrit from the tram station. Only a few meters separated them. Gerrit released Ingrid's arm. "What is it?" he asked the patrolman striding toward him.

"You're wanted for questioning."

Gerrit nodded and ducked his head in submission. The man kept coming toward him, and the moment he was close enough, Gerrit balled his hand into a fist and swung a swift right cross into the man's jaw. Pain flared in Gerrit's fist, but the patrolman must have experienced something similar because he stumbled back. Ingrid hooked a foot behind the patrolman's knee, and he crashed to the ground.

Gerrit reached for Ingrid's hand and tugged her away. "Run!"

As Ingrid ran along the sidewalk with Gerrit, she wished she were more familiar with Velp's streets and that she'd worn shoes easier to run in. She also wished they hadn't bumped into someone who found Gerrit so suspicious. A glance showed the street was clear, so she tugged Gerrit's hand and cut across the road, then into an alley.

An alley without an exit. The patrolman had chased them, of course, and he'd gathered another man as reinforcement.

Gerrit, breathing hard, motioned to an eight-foot-tall iron fence. It led into someone's garden. "Step on my knee, then on my shoulder. Over the top, that's the only way."

"How will you get over?"

"I'll manage."

He bent into a crouch, and when she didn't step on him immediately, he pulled her foot toward his knee. Delay would turn a good idea into a bad one and a bad idea into a worse one, so she cooperated. She stepped on his knee, then shoulder, using the long, vertical bars of the fence to balance. When he straightened beneath her, she gripped the top of the fence and did her best to pull herself over. She wouldn't have made it if Gerrit hadn't helped from below, putting his hands under her shoes until she could lift a leg over the top, undoubtedly exposing far too much skin in the process. She swung to the other side in an undignified flop, hung for a moment, and let go, landing hard but staying upright.

Gerrit passed the detonators through the gap between bars. "Take these and run."

"But they'll arrest you!" If he thought she was going to run off without him, he hadn't any clue how stubborn—and loyal—she could be.

"Better one of us than both. Go!"

Ingrid looked at the height of the fence. If Gerrit thought he could make it over, he would have tried. Ingrid went down on one knee, like he had. "Put your foot through the bars and climb."

"Ingrid, run!"

"No! Climb! Or I'll stay here, and they'll take us both."

After a quick glance behind him, Gerrit obeyed. He was heavier on her knee than she'd expected, and she felt his weight even more on her shoulder. She hadn't any hope of rising beneath him the way he had for her, but she didn't have to. He could grab the top from his perch on her shoulder, and he had enough upper-body strength to pull himself up and over. A moment later, he dropped beside her, and they started running again.

Gunshots pierced the air, and Ingrid instinctively ducked. Gerrit grabbed her hand, not letting his stride slow at all. They ran around the side of a house, and two more gunshots sounded, but the house blocked the line of fire.

They escaped the home's yard through a gate, then rushed along the road, through a park, and into another neighborhood. She couldn't see either of the men chasing them, but they couldn't be more than a minute behind, and the search party would only grow larger. Ingrid saw a white carnation tucked into the lamppost of a nearby home and took a risk, opening the door and leading Gerrit inside.

A gray-haired woman looked up from her knitting, startled to have two intruders dart into her front room.

"Can you hide us?" Ingrid asked. The woman might very well say no. Or say yes, then turn them over for the bounty. But a white carnation was Prince Bernhard's favorite flower. Ingrid didn't think the woman had placed it on the lamppost as a mere decoration. It was also a symbol.

The woman set her knitting aside. "Yes."

She led Ingrid and Gerrit through a corridor to a closet. Ingrid almost asked for directions to the back door. If the Nazis searched the home, they would look through all closets. A four-year-old could find a better hiding spot. But the woman removed a broom, mop, and bucket, then knelt to pull part of the paneling forward.

"Through there. You'll have to duck to get in, but you can stand once you're inside. I've never hidden two before, but you're both small."

Ingrid nudged Gerrit forward, but he seemed frozen in place. "Ladies first," he got out with a stutter. They were both breathing hard from their running and climbing, but this was something else.

She didn't know what had gotten into him, but there wasn't time to argue, so she knelt and climbed through the dark hole in the back of the broom cupboard. Her leg just above her knee was sore from Gerrit's climb, and the palms of her hands stung from hanging on the wrought-iron fence. As she stood, she kept a hand raised so she wouldn't bash her head into a board. When she reached her full height, she could feel the ceiling a foot over her head, so Gerrit, too, would be able to stand. Good thing, that, since it didn't seem they would have any excess room otherwise. She moved as far to the side as she could. "Come on, Gerrit."

He began crawling inside. She should have insisted he go first. She kept her legs together and held the loose bit of her skirt tight so he wouldn't look up and see more of her leg than he ought to. If he hadn't already seen far more than he ought to when she tumbled over the fence.

Maybe she had gotten off easier, being the first one in. The moment Gerrit squeezed inside, the woman closed the panel behind them. There was hardly an inch to spare inside the hiding space, and Ingrid felt rather than saw how hard it was to straighten with someone already occupying half the space.

"It's tall enough that you can stand," she whispered.

On the other side of the panel, something knocked against the wall with a sharp rap. Probably the handle of the broom or the mop.

Gerrit straightened, brushing up against her until he was standing. Ingrid gave him as much space as she could, and she imagined he did the same, but they were still close enough that Ingrid could feel his breath not far from her cheek, still rapid from their run, and her left shoulder pressed into his right.

The muffled sounds of Beethoven's "Choral Fantasy" came from the other room. Good German music, perhaps played on purpose to cover any noise from the broom cupboard and to suggest to anyone searching that the woman had a sympathetic taste in music and, therefore, also in politics. Gerrit's arm quivered. Was he afraid? Ingrid was, but something about the woman seemed trustworthy.

Ingrid dared a whisper. "If she was going to turn us in, she would have put us *in* the closet, not *behind* it. She wouldn't have a nook like this unless she were hiding onderduikers."

"It's not that." She could barely hear his voice, but she picked out what sounded like the swallow following it.

"Then, what?"

"When Rotterdam was bombed, Nellie and I were trapped in rubble. It almost became our coffin."

A rap sounded over the music, and Gerrit's arm shook even more against hers. She felt for one of his hands and gripped it, hoping that would help. She didn't mind confined spaces—they had always been her best hiding spots in Falcon Point Manor when playing hide-and-seek with her siblings or friends. But she had never been trapped in a cataclysmic bombing raid.

"Close your eyes, and pretend you're somewhere else," Ingrid whispered. "It's a sunny day, and you're standing by a canal. The war's over, and the wind is blowing through your hair."

Footsteps stomped along the hallway and passed overhead. Either Gerrit's imagination wasn't robust enough to picture a windy day along a canal, or his memory of the bombing was too overpowering. His breathing was growing heavier, more audible, more dangerous, given their situation.

She did the only thing she could think that might help. She threaded her arms around him and pulled him into an embrace. Maybe his imagination, if not strong enough to imagine wind and sunshine, could imagine a different woman held him. Someone he wanted to be near rather than someone he'd been forced against. He didn't fight her—either because he wanted to stay silent or because he needed the comfort she was trying to give. Gradually, his shaking slowed.

She hadn't expected his torso to be so firm. It was rare to find anyone overweight when rations were so restricted, but still . . . Maybe if they had met under different circumstances, she would have noticed his boyish charm and cut figure a little earlier. Regardless, she'd realized something important at the fence, when he'd told her to run away without him: she cared about him too much to leave him behind. He'd been kind when she was injured as a refugee. Also overly suspicious, though given what had happened to his country a few months later and given her suspicions of him four years later when he'd returned to Arnhem, well, maybe she could forgive him for thinking she was a spy. Reluctant partners or not, they had made a good team today. His swift punch and quick decision-making at the fence had saved them.

The footfalls of searching policemen drew near again. They must have finished searching the upper floors. Ingrid flinched when the closet door opened, and Gerrit held her more tightly. She silently prayed that the patrolman wouldn't search the closet too thoroughly, not closely enough to find the panel that opened to reveal a hiding place.

Something ran over the wood separating the two of them from the rest of the closet. A hand, perhaps, searching for latches? Whatever the woman had pushed wasn't on the top half of the wall, and though Ingrid hadn't enjoyed crawling through the bottom, she now saw the wisdom in it. If the policeman or soldier searching the closet had to stoop, his search might miss something he would otherwise see at eye level.

Ingrid tried to keep her breathing as quiet as possible. Now she was the one trembling. She blessed the woman who had hidden them and turned music on to cover any sound, because Ingrid could hear both her heartbeat and Gerrit's. Or maybe she was feeling his, not hearing it, because they were so close to each other and to the danger on the opposite side of the panel.

After what seemed like a very long time, the closet door slammed shut, and the footsteps moved away. Their arms relaxed, and it felt easier to breathe, even in such tight quarters. More footsteps from the patrolman moving farther and farther away. And then a bang that sounded like the front door closing. The patrolman was gone.

Gerrit's head brushed against Ingrid's. "Sorry," he said in the softest of whispers. "I've been trying not to accidentally kiss you."

Avoiding contact with each other was difficult in their confined space. The nook was hardly bigger than a coffin. What a morbid thought. She tried to think of something more cheerful. "When I am kissed, I hope it won't be an accident."

"Has it happened before? Someone kissing you?"

Ingrid felt her face heat, but there wasn't any way Gerrit would be able to see that in the darkness, so she answered honestly. "No."

A soft grunt sounded on the other side of the space. "Trust me, Ingrid, when someone kisses you, really kisses you, it won't be an accident. If you're lucky, he'll kiss you because he knows all about the bravery beneath the beauty and the strength beneath the stubbornness."

"You think I'm beautiful and brave and strong?" She did her best to make it sound like she was teasing, but that was hard with a whisper. Harder still when he'd given her the most thorough compliment she'd ever heard.

"And stubborn. Don't forget that. You should have run at the gate. I probably left a bruise on your shoulder."

Her shoulder, knee, and palms were sore, but they weren't as sore as her heart would have been had she left Gerrit to be arrested. "I probably left similar bruises on you."

He shifted. "My hand is sore from the punch, but everything else is fine." A few audible breaths. "Do you think she'll let us out soon?"

"Probably after the police finish searching the street. They could backtrack."

"That might not be for hours." His breathing started to grow a bit ragged.

"Did it help before, when I held you?"

He didn't answer until he had taken several more inhalations. "Yes, but I don't think we should try that again."

Ingrid laid a hand where she thought his arm was, but it ended up being his chest. She could feel one of his buttons along with the border of his jacket. Below that, the steady thrum of his heart. "Why not?"

"Because I don't want to accidentally kiss you."

"I'll duck my head, and you can lift yours. And if something happens, I promise in advance to forgive you."

"I don't want to kiss you on purpose either." He shifted, probably trying to back away, but there wasn't anywhere for him to go.

Ingrid tried to give him space, but she could still feel each breath on her cheek. An accidental kiss from Gerrit didn't sound so awful. Nor did an intentional kiss.

Time was hard to measure in the dark. Ingrid's legs were sore, so she eased one of them into a different position. She didn't mean to bump into Gerrit, but it was nearly impossible to move without touching him somewhere. His breaths and his limbs trembled. She had to do something to help.

"Gerrit?" She put a hand on his arm—his real arm this time. "Let me help."

"I don't think that's such a good idea."

"Standing here doing nothing doesn't seem to be working."

"I can handle it," he mumbled. "I have enough willpower to breathe in and breathe out and not scream or shout or try to break out of this closet, even if we have to stay until nightfall. And I have enough willpower to be next to someone like you and not do anything we both might regret."

"Regret? Would holding each other be so awful? We're practically in each other's arms anyway."

He swallowed audibly. "A selfish man might take advantage of being in a space like this with you. And a weak man might succumb to temptation, but I am not selfish or weak, and I am not going to kiss you."

"I'm not asking you to kiss me." Ingrid's mouth felt dry. She hadn't mentioned anything about kissing, but Gerrit kept bringing it up. And each time he did, the idea appealed to her a little more. She wouldn't beg for a kiss, but part of her wished Gerrit weren't so determined to avoid one. She liked him more than she wanted to admit, and knowing a squad of police officers was even now searching for them and might find them and haul them off to be executed gave the growing desire a sense of urgency. She didn't say anything for as long as she could, focusing instead on the muted music and Gerrit's labored breathing. "A kiss might be a good distraction. And if we're going to be arrested, this could be our last chance."

His next inhalation sounded ragged. "I know it might be hard to believe at present, but when I am not in small, dark spaces, I have a will of iron."

"I see. And your iron will does not allow kisses to be used for distraction?"

Silence. Several artificially slow breaths from across the hiding space yet so close she could feel the movement in the air.

"There's a war on. Any romance, whether it means nothing or whether it means everything, is a distraction," he said.

Ingrid shifted again. Standing perfectly still was uncomfortable, but so were all the other positions she tried. Part of her wanted to change the subject or stop speaking altogether, but whispering with Gerrit helped the time pass. Silence combined with the darkness seemed to let despair creep in and remind Gerrit of almost dying in Rotterdam. When his breathing grew ragged again, she spoke. "Would kissing me mean nothing, or would it mean everything?" If he said it would mean nothing, she might very well punch him. Or kiss him. She couldn't decide.

Gerrit sighed. "It's a continuum. Nothing on one side. Everything on the other. Innumerable points in between."

"And where would I fall on the continuum?"

He shifted, and she felt his fingers on her neck. "You're making this harder than it should be."

His touch seemed to set her skin alight, and it took her several long moments to come up with a response. "You're avoiding the question."

Another sigh, one that melted across her cheek. "Close to everything, Ingrid. Close to everything."

"Then, why won't you kiss me?" Something brushed against her cheek, but in the dark, she couldn't tell if it was his chin or nose or jaw. Regardless, she leaned closer, threading her arms around him. He wasn't trembling anymore, and he didn't resist when the scant space between them disappeared.

His whisper was near her ear now. "If I did, what would it mean to you?"

Something inside her that she couldn't quite name wound itself tight and pulled toward him. Affection? Desire? Longing? Fate? "Close to everything, Gerrit. It would mean close to everything."

She shifted her head, ever so slightly. He must have done the same, because she'd been tracking the heat of his breath across her cheek, and that warmth stirred and paused, hovering above her mouth.

When their lips met, his mouth warmed her like a fire. A long, slow fire that burned steady and strong. His lips whispered against hers over and over again. Each sensation was vivid, sweet, and deliberate. Each new angle, each new touch set off a need for more kisses, more closeness, more of Gerrit and her. She'd never before felt so cherished, wanted, and adored.

Now she was the one trembling because this unfamiliar sensation was absolutely beautiful. The fact that they were shoved into a tiny hiding place didn't matter. The fact that a patrol was searching for them didn't matter. Together they imbibed the heady addiction of new desire. Ingrid lost all track of time. Maybe time no longer mattered because Gerrit was cradling her in his arms and kissing her with a desperation that seemed to sear her soul.

Only the sound of the closet door being opened brought them apart. Their cramped space had grown warm, and the air seemed thicker. As the panel by their legs pulled free and the woman told them the police had left the area, Ingrid watched Gerrit's face in the new, dim lighting. She saw reflected in his eyes the same thing she felt all the way to her core: something had changed between them, something vital, and neither would ever be the same again.

Night had fallen by the time Gerrit took the detonators from Ingrid and they parted near the outskirts of Arnhem.

"Are you sure you'll be all right getting home?" he asked.

"Yes. You're already hours late with the detonators. And anyone searching for us will be looking for a couple. It's probably safer if we part. For now." Her hand reached for his and rested lightly on the knuckles he'd smashed into the patrolman's face earlier.

Gerrit slid the detonators back into his pocket. "I'll try to come back sooner rather than later. If it's safe." He leaned in for a kiss. Goodness, Ingrid's lips were a wonder. One he would happily spend another hour or so exploring.

He felt her mouth smile beneath his. She sighed. "You're right. This is distracting. But maybe distractions aren't so bad."

Somewhere nearby, a door slammed. Gerrit straightened to look around and make sure they were still safe. "I should go. I don't want to."

"But you need to." Ingrid pulled away. "Be careful."

"You as well." He watched her disappear into the nearest shadow. She'd been out after curfew time after time and arrived home safely. He had no reason to think tonight would be different. Yet if she felt even half as swept up in what had happened between them as he did . . . He closed his eyes for a moment, inhaled deeply, and tried to focus on his next task, not on the way Ingrid's mouth had felt against his lips or the way her body had felt when nestled close. Romance was dangerous at a time like this, but it was, oh, so needed.

It took several hours to walk back to the farmhouse where he'd been working with Cornelis. When he arrived, all was dark. He let himself into the cellar, grabbed a flashlight from where he'd placed it on a nearby shelf, and switched it on. As he shone the light around the room, an uneasiness spread in his stomach. All evidence that he and Cornelis had turned the cellar into a munitions workshop had vanished. Everything suspicious was gone, but the rest of the cellar's contents remained undisturbed. Had the Germans searched the cellar as part of an arrest, they wouldn't have left everything so tidy. Had Cornelis left?

Gerrit turned the flashlight off and replaced it. Then he left the cellar. Maybe Cornelis had left a message with the farmer. Gerrit had just closed the cellar doors when a shadow stepped in front of him. A shadow armed with a handgun.

"Are you alone?"

Gerrit knew that voice. Cornelis. "Yes."

"Why are you so late?"

"Someone recognized me. A Green Policeman who tried to catch me once before. I had to hide for a few hours while they tore the neighborhood apart looking for us."

"Us? Who was with you?"

"The courier who brought the detonators." Gerrit could have simply said Ingrid's name, but for Cornelis, he felt her role was the more vital part of the discussion.

"And she also escaped?"

Gerrit nodded. "Ingrid was fine." Better than fine, but that wasn't what Cornelis was asking. "I didn't see her all the way home, but she wasn't being tailed when we parted. Though I suspect that patrolman will recognize her if he sees her again." Maybe she'd need to dye her hair.

"I'm glad she made it out all right because she would have found a few airmen waiting for her when she returned home. You have the detonators?"

"Yes."

Cornelis put his weapon away. "I hid the other parts in a field. I'll retrieve them and meet you in the cellar. We need to work fast because we have a railroad viaduct to put out of commission tonight."

"Tonight?"

"Yes."

"Where?"

"Between Arnhem and Velp."

Gerrit had scouted several railway viaducts, including one between Arnhem and Velp. He knew the area, was familiar with the patrol schedules that kept them secure. He also knew the consequences of failure or of success. "There will be reprisals."

"I have my orders. It sounds like this one will be worth the price."

Two hours later, Gerrit and Cornelis had gathered their explosives, met their contacts, and positioned the charges where they would do the most damage. One of the other men set the timer, and then they pulled back to where they'd be out of immediate danger.

When the explosion went off, the boom shook the ground beneath Gerrit's feet and no doubt alerted every German soldier within a mile that the Dutch Resistance was up to something. Regardless, Cornelis was convinced that this was a necessary task. Gerrit knew fewer details, but he trusted Cornelis.

They said their farewells to the other resistance contacts, whom Gerrit knew only as Jan Smit and Daan Smit. Given their looks, he doubted they were related, but people often failed to see much family resemblance between Gerrit and Anita, so maybe that wasn't an entirely fair assumption. Still, the names were undoubtedly noms de plume.

Cornelis and Gerrit headed west, back to the farmhouse.

"Any news from the front?" Gerrit asked. He hadn't heard a broadcast or a news summary since the morning before.

"Nothing has changed. Not yet." Cornelis looked to the sky. "I think the Germans were losing faster than the Allies could win for a few weeks. Logistical problems, I would wager. The farther they get from their ports, the harder it is to stay supplied. Maybe now our friends are ready to start winning again."

"The Netherlands happens to have several world-class ports, if the Allies would be so good as to kick the Moffen out and claim them."

Darkness masked any expression on Cornelis's face, but a wistful tone made its way into his voice. "Soon, I expect. They've had enough time to gather supplies by now. And that viaduct we damaged will make it harder for the Germans to bring any troops or equipment from the east. But if the Allies don't act soon, the Germans will repair it. Or force Dutchmen to repair it, more likely. That tells me something will happen soon."

"I hope you're right."

"So do I. It's about time our uninvited guests were sent back to Moffrica."

CHAPTER 17

Ingrid declined a second fried egg when the farmer's wife offered it to her late Saturday night. Or maybe it was early Sunday morning by now. Ingrid wouldn't have minded more food, but she didn't want to put the family out. The airmen she'd brought had no such compunctions, but they'd had a harrowing journey, and they weren't used to the rations she and the other civilians in the Netherlands had become accustomed to.

The woman smiled and put another two eggs in her hot frying pan. "Will you stay the rest of the night?" she asked Ingrid.

"It's probably best if I go back now." Ingrid preferred her own bed rather than sleeping in the same room as the airmen. Besides, there might be more sites to scout or onderduikers to smuggle, and she didn't want to leave it all to Anita, who had all her cover work as well as her clandestine work to keep her busy. And she'd be sad to miss Gerrit if he managed a trip to the house and she wasn't there. "The last group I brought, did they make it off all right?"

The woman nodded. "Yes, but not until yesterday. A courier went missing, so another had to be found."

Something cold swept along the back of Ingrid's neck. "Do you know what happened?" If the Gestapo captured whoever took onderduikers from this home to the next, then the farmer and his wife were in danger, as was anyone staying with them. Ingrid's risk was smaller. The home's inhabitants didn't know her real name or where she lived, and she doubted any of the airmen could find the van der Veen home again without assistance, even if they were tortured and forced to reveal all they knew. But some of them had come through the hospital, which was far easier to remember. And if the Gestapo set a trap for Ingrid, what would she say under torture?

"No one told me any details."

"And the new courier," Ingrid whispered, "are you sure he or she isn't a Gestapo plant?"

"She's completely trustworthy. Someone I've known her whole life."

Ingrid nodded, assuming the replacement was a relative, not an informant. That would mean Luitenant Brug, Sergeant Cervantes, and the other two Americans had safely advanced to the next location on the route to freedom. They were probably in Nijmegen now, maybe a night's journey past it. Ingrid didn't know the route beyond her small role in it. "I better go so I can make it home before daylight." She said her goodbyes to the two airmen and set off.

The missing courier worried her. Gerrit worried her. What had she been thinking, kissing him like that? She'd thrown all caution to the wind. That was foolish in the best of times, and September 1944 was certainly not the best of times. And yet she didn't regret her first kiss, courtesy of Gerrit Hendriks. Nor did she regret the second, third, fourth, fifth, or however many kisses they had shared on Friday. Still, the timing couldn't have been worse. Something in the Netherlands was about to change, she could feel it.

The rumble of a truck caught her by surprise. She'd been listening as she rode her bicycle, but the truck must have been parked nearby because all of a sudden, the sound was right behind her. She rode off the road at once. Like many of the roads in the Netherlands, it was built up higher than the soggy fields that surrounded it. Normally, she slowed before riding into the ditches along the roadside, but there hadn't been time, and the wooden blocks on the tires caught at the foliage and pulled her to an abrupt stop. She toppled, skidded, and stayed still until the engine noises passed and faded. Even then, she stayed put, trying to catch her breath and hoping that the pain in her leg was simply a worsening of the bruise Gerrit had given her climbing the wrought-iron fence and not another broken limb.

She hadn't fallen off a bicycle in years. It would have been mortifying had anyone been around to see her. She stretched her leg and tried to put weight on it. It held. The pain was strong enough that she couldn't ignore it, but it wasn't nearly as agonizing as when she'd broken her legs. She plucked her bicycle from the ground and slipped one leg over the frame. But when she pushed off, it wobbled, and she nearly fell again. She gave the bicycle a closer examination. The fork holding the front wheel hub in place was severely misaligned.

It seemed that she would be walking back to Arnhem.

Gerrit woke with a start. It took him a moment to recognize his room in Opa's house, where he'd come the night before with a coded report from Cornelis. A cacophony of airplane engines, shrieks, and explosions had roused him. The air raid was close enough that he ought to go to the cellar, even though his muscles were weary and a dull ache had taken up residence in his head.

Someone knocked on his bedroom door. He turned over and sat up. "Come in."

Anita entered wearing her best dress for church. "I suppose you can hear all that racket?"

He nodded.

"Well, come on, let's go to the cellar and hope it passes."

"Is Ingrid back?" he asked as he pulled on a shirt and joined Anita in the hallway. Had he arrived a few hours earlier, Cornelis's report could have gone with Ingrid and the onderduikers. Gerrit would have tried to catch up to her, but Cornelis expected to gather more information today, and Cornelis's instructions had specified that one of them—Ingrid or Gerrit—was to be available for a courier run Sunday night.

Anita shook her head.

Worry tightened Gerrit's gut, but failing to return by morning was rarely reason for panic. She might have simply spent the night at the safe house. But there were a number of less innocuous reasons why she might have been delayed, and they included death and arrest. "I hope she's all right."

"So do I." As they rushed down the stairs, Anita studied him closely enough that he felt the need to brush a hand through his short hair in an attempt to straighten it. The way she was looking at him, something must be amiss. "She said you collected the detonators on Friday, and you were almost arrested."

Gerrit nodded. "Yes, but we ended up being a good team when it came time to outsmart the patrolman. And we got lucky and found someone to hide us." He wondered if Ingrid had said anything else about their encounter, and if Anita knew, would she be happy for them or feel like they had done something wrong?

They joined Opa in the basement and listened for the booms to fade. The explosions tapered off relatively quickly, but that didn't mean more weren't coming.

"Those were close." Anita looked at the ceiling. "What do you suppose they're targeting?"

"Maybe one of the airfields," Opa said. "Or one of those other military targets you and your friends tell the Allies about. Whatever they're aiming for, I'd better see what the damage is and if anyone has been wounded."

Gerrit and Anita followed Opa up from the cellar.

"You'll be careful, won't you?" Anita asked as Opa grabbed his hat and doctor's bag.

"I don't suppose they'll have me pulling people from rubble for long, not if there are wounds to tend." Opa nodded his goodbye, then rushed out the door.

Anita rested a hand on her hip. "I was worried about another air raid more than I was worried about rubble collapsing on him. Now I'm worried about both."

"The hospital isn't a military target. He ought to be all right."

Anita frowned. "I hope so. I don't suppose you want to join me for church now that my planned escort has headed off to the hospital?"

Gerrit shook his head. "I'd rather not risk a razzia or a patrolman recognizing me again. I'll wait to see if Ingrid needs help when she gets back."

"You won't rush off before I return?" she asked.

"I doubt it. Cornelis said to take his report on if he hasn't sent anything by midnight. That's a long while yet. It sounded like he was planning to pick up something from a contact in his congregation. Maybe his service is at the same time as yours."

Anita gave him a halfhearted smile. "I suppose you can catch up on sleep, then. I'll see you later. I should go so I'm not late."

After she left, part of Gerrit wanted to go back to sleep, but a nagging worry about Ingrid wouldn't leave, so he washed up, then managed to avoid pacing by finding a sauce pan with a loose handle to tinker with. He'd just secured the handle firmly in place when a slight sound from outside caught his attention, and Anjing scratched at the door.

Gerrit let the dog out, then followed when he saw Ingrid opening the cellar doors. Relief that she had safely returned had him by her side in a moment. "Let me get that for you."

She gave him a weary smile. Dirt clung to one side of her skirt and her left sock, her hair was limp, and a scratch marred her left cheek.

"What happened?" he asked.

She brushed at the dirt on her clothes. "A truck surprised me. I didn't hear it, and then, all of a sudden, there it was. I rode into a ditch and damaged the bicycle. Then I had to stop and hide during that air raid."

He stepped closer and ran a light thumb under her scratch. "It looks like you damaged yourself too. I'll put the bicycle away and meet you in the kitchen."

She nodded and limped inside. Gerrit put the bicycle in the cellar and gave it a quick look-over. He'd have to straighten part of the frame, but he would worry about that later. For the moment, Ingrid looked exhausted, and he wanted to make sure she was taken care of.

He shut the cellar doors and went into the kitchen. "Did you do something to your leg?"

"It's just a bruise. Maybe a sprain."

He knelt in front of the chair she sat in and held up both her ankles. The left one was swollen significantly. The way her skirt rested, he could also see a large bruise just above her knee. He pulled the fabric away for a better view. "Is that from me or from the crash?"

"Both, I think."

He pulled her skirt back over her knee. "I'm sorry. I didn't mean to hurt you."

"Better a bruise than witnessing you shot or arrested. Did I leave any bruises on you?"

Gerrit's knee and shoulder in question were slightly tender but not excruciating. "I haven't really noticed. Are you hungry? I can make some breakfast for you."

She shook her head. "I'm more tired than hungry. I've been up all night." She stood, wincing as her left ankle touched the floor.

"I'll help you upstairs, but let me wrap it first."

"I've already walked several kilometers on it."

"Yes, but those several kilometers didn't include stairs. And I would have helped you with that walk, too, if I'd been there."

She sat back down while he found a long bandage and wrapped it around her ankle. "Is it too snug?" Opa and Anita both had more experience with wrapping injured ankles, but as Gerrit's fingers moved over the smooth skin of Ingrid's leg, he realized he would relinquish the task only with reluctance.

Ingrid flexed and pointed her ankle, making the muscles of her calf perform an eye-catching dance. "I think it's all right. Thank you."

She cooperated when he helped her rise. He held her for a moment, admiring her profile and her mouth. Then he pulled one of her arms across his shoulders and put an arm around her waist to help her up the stairs. He did his best to make sure no weight fell on her injured leg and was grateful when they reached the last step because half-carrying a person upstairs, even a lithe, pretty person, was a lot of hard work.

He helped her to her room, then rested his forearm along the doorframe. "I'm glad you made it back. I've been wanting to see you again."

She looked away. Light from her window reflected off her hair. Goodness, she was beautiful, even with her hair a mess from a bicycle crash, but something about her expression . . .

"What's wrong?" he asked.

"I just had a lot of time to think while I was walking home."

"About how much you want me to kiss you again?" She'd practically begged him to kiss her when they'd been hiding, and once he'd finally given in, he'd wondered why on earth he had resisted so long.

A blush colored her cheeks. "Gerrit, what if what happened in that closet was a moment of weakness for us both? A mistake because we were so close, and we knew we might get dragged out and shot at any moment? It was a good distraction, but we have to focus on winning the war."

Two days ago, holding Ingrid in his arms and clinging to her, he'd felt the most exquisite form of pleasure. Now pain replaced it. She'd promised a kiss would mean something to her. She'd kissed him like she'd been in love with him, and he'd seen the look on her face when the light had returned. She'd felt a connection, a power, a binding—he knew she had. Had all that faded? "You're telling me that what happened didn't mean anything to you?"

"It's not that it didn't mean anything . . . but it all happened so fast, and we weren't exactly in a position to stop and think it through, and don't you regret it?"

"Not even a little." He'd fallen asleep thinking about that kiss, wanting to try it again.

Her eyes held his, and she swallowed. "But I can't be in love with you, Gerrit Hendriks. You have radical political ideas. You're not a man of faith. You're a year younger than me. And . . . and . . ." She glanced at his mouth, then away.

Why had she tempted him in the hiding place only to pull away now? Was she having second thoughts, or was the connection he'd thought they'd formed an illusion? Something in the way she held herself spoke of uncertainty, not rejection. "No other reasons?"

She glanced at his mouth again. "I am certain I can think of more, so long as you aren't distracting me."

All he was doing was standing in front of her. If she thought being near each other, not even touching, was a distraction, then he wasn't quite ready to end this discussion. He wanted to get to the bottom of why she was hesitating now after being so eager before. Painful or not, he needed that knowledge. Or needed to chase away her doubts. "Perhaps I can help. Maybe you can't love me because when we met in 1940, I jumped to false conclusions about your collection of Reich passports."

She shook her head. "Given what happened to your country later that spring, I can hardly fault you for being suspicious. Trust must be rationed in wartime."

Gerrit nodded gravely. "Then, maybe I didn't apologize well enough after discovering that you and I used the same hiding spot in the floorboards." He could apologize again if that would fix everything.

A hint of mischief lit her eyes. "That incident has been forgiven."

"Perhaps I am too simple and uneducated." He was touching more serious fears now because if his intellect were the problem, it couldn't quickly be changed.

"I would have dropped out of school, too, if Nazis had taken over the classrooms as thoroughly as they did in your lyceum."

"Then, maybe you can't love me because my face is too thin or my hair is too short or I have some other physical defect that you find repulsive." Other things he couldn't change, but the hair was mostly her fault.

She looked away with another blush coloring her cheeks. "I can assure you that your face and form are perfectly adequate to catch a woman's eye."

"Maybe it's the claustrophobia." Another more serious issue. "You know my weakness, and that kills any chance of me sweeping you off your feet."

"No, it's not that." She rested her hand on his chest. "I understand. Some of my memories have left scars. I would never hold that against you, not any more than you would hold it against me that I couldn't climb over that fence into the garden without your help."

"Then, why do you regret what happened? If you don't want me, I think I deserve to hear a better reason than the excuses you've given, because none of them is convincing. You are only nine months older than me, not a year, and my political beliefs have moderated as of late, and I may be lost spiritually, but I am looking for light, Ingrid, I promise."

"It's hard to come up with a real list when you're still distracting me." Her hand traveled down his chest a few inches before she pulled it away. He instantly missed her touch.

For forty-eight hours, he'd been convinced that he was more to her than simply an associate working toward the common goal of defeating the Nazis. Now he doubted, and those ruptured hopes clawed at his heart. "Is that all I am to you? A distraction?"

She kept her eyes on the floor. "You said it yourself—there's a war on. Romance can't pull us away from our duty. And I . . . well, I never thought it would be like this."

"You never thought what would be like this?"

She glanced up. "Love. When Anita met Luitenant Brug, she said she just knew. And that's what my father said about meeting my mother. But love is most certainly not the first feeling I had for you. And maybe whatever happened in that closet wasn't love either. Maybe it was just attraction and danger and a tight space we couldn't escape from."

Gerrit put his hand on the other side of the doorframe and shifted so he was right in front of her. His heart had been completely captured by Ingrid Lang, and if she was tottering about on the fence as to whether she loved him or not, he would do what he could to haul her down on the side of feeling the same way he did. "Maybe we should try it again, without the threat of death, with plenty of space, just to see what happens. An experiment, if you will."

She didn't answer, but her gaze flitted from his eyes to his mouth no fewer than three times. She swallowed, but she didn't retreat into her room. "That might be dangerous."

"Thursday, you spied on two Panzer divisions. Friday, you were the quarry in a Nazi manhunt. Yesterday, you led a pair of downed airmen across fifteen kilometers of enemy-held territory. And this morning, you broke curfew, crashed your bicycle, and endured an air raid. Kissing me will be the safest thing you've done in days."

A small smile graced her exquisite lips. He wanted to kiss her with a longing that brought physical pain. He leaned in, hovering mere inches from her lips. "Shall we?" he whispered.

She gave him the smallest nod of surrender, and he met her mouth in the next moment. The fire from two days ago returned in a heartbeat. He'd meant to leave his arms on the doorframe, but that resolution didn't last. He pulled her near, trying to convince her with each kiss, each caress, that she could trust him, could care for him as deeply as he cared for her. She kissed him back, clinging to him as if he were as vital to her as the air she breathed.

Something wet ran along his cheek. He wasn't crying, but when he pulled away, he saw that she was. "What's wrong?"

"Nothing." Yet when she inhaled, there seemed to be a catch in her throat.

"Then, why are you crying?" He'd thought he was holding her gently, but maybe he'd aggravated one of her bruises. He wiped at her cheeks, smearing her tears.

"Because ever since I was separated from my brother and sister, I've felt adrift. Your grandpa and your aunt have been like family, but that lost feeling never went away, not even with them. But something about you . . . I think I felt it Friday, but I couldn't name it. I've been lost for so long . . . except when you're near me. Then I feel like I've found a home."

He wrapped his arms around her again, then planted a kiss on her forehead. "I'll happily be your home, Ingrid. I'll be anything you need me to be."

He could have held her like that, snuggled next to him, for hours. And he could have spent the entire day kissing her. He ran one hand over her back and fingered the ends of her blonde hair. "I suppose you still want to go to bed?"

She nodded, and a small laugh escaped her throat. "Yes, but not together."

"I wasn't suggesting I join you." He relaxed his hold on her. "Maybe I'll go fix that bicycle."

She stood on her toes and kissed his cheek. Then, when he turned his head slightly, she planted one lingering kiss on his mouth.

As she ended the kiss, he put his palm on her cheek. "Sleep well, Ingrid."

She had to be exhausted, so he stepped back from the doorway, even though he gladly would have stayed as long as she would let him. But he did care about her, not just about her kisses, and she needed to rest.

He hadn't even reached the staircase when she called after him. "Gerrit? Do you hear that?"

He'd tuned it out before, but now it became obvious. Airplane engines, and they seemed to be growing louder. "Not B-17s or B-24s." He'd heard the heavy American bombers pass overhead many times, and he recognized the whine of their engines. Nor did it sound like a German Junkers or Focke-Wulf or Messerschmitt. British bombers flew their missions during the night, so it wasn't a Lancaster or a Halifax either.

He went to the window in his mother's old room, and despite the risk of neighbors sympathetic to the Nazis seeing him, he pulled the curtains open wide and looked out. Ingrid joined him.

The planes had American roundels on them. They didn't sound or look like the heavy bombers or fly at as high an altitude. "Mitchells?"

"Are they bombing Arnhem?" Ingrid asked.

Gerrit watched their flight paths. "Nearby, otherwise they'd be higher. And the Germans have created enough military objectives around here . . . I helped Cornelis take care of a rail viaduct, but there are plenty of targets left."

Antiaircraft guns began firing, and the noise was almost deafening. They were close. Gerrit grabbed Ingrid's hand and helped her to the basement to wait out the latest air raid. An hour later, after only a brief reprieve in the kitchen, they went back to the cellar as British de Havilland Mosquitoes zipped through the sky for another low-level bombing, though that raid didn't last as long.

As the afternoon wore on, neither Anita nor Opa returned. They were probably busy caring for the wounded. When Gerrit and Ingrid ventured upstairs, the windows showed smoke plumes all over the city as parts of Arnhem burned.

"Do you think the fire will spread here?" Ingrid's eyelids drooped with fatigue, but she'd been too tense during the air raids to nap.

"Not unless there's another raid. If you want to sleep, I'll wake you if we need to go back to the basement."

Ingrid shook her head. "It feels like something big is going to happen."

More engine noises drew him back to the window, and he let out a slow whistle. He hadn't seen so many planes flying so near the earth since Rotterdam was destroyed, and fear, for a moment, made him feel like a child again. But these planes, some of them tugging gliders behind them, had American markings on them.

"Another air raid?"

He shook his head. They didn't look like bombers. And those gliders . . . Radio Oranje broadcasted for only fifteen minutes at a time at five set times each day, but Gerrit had listened to the illegal news often enough to know the basics of each campaign, and he remembered how the Germans had dropped airborne soldiers around the Hague and Rotterdam when they'd invaded Holland. "They aren't dropping bombs. They're dropping paratroopers." A laugh of joy and wonder escaped his lips. "We aren't going to have to wait for the Allied armies to fight their way from the border. They're going to drop right on top of us."

CHAPTER 18

Gerrit's eyes snapped open hours later to a nudge on the bottom of his shoe. He hadn't meant to fall asleep, but after sitting out several air raids in the cellar, then trying the view from the attic windows and listening to the radio reports, exhaustion had caught up with him. Ingrid had fallen asleep first, as soon as the Dutch-language broadcast on the BBC had finished. And she'd fallen asleep on him. He hadn't wanted to wake her after she'd gone so long without rest. Now Anita stood over them both, and he suspected the nudge that had awakened him had not been the first.

He'd been leaning against the wall with one arm wrapped around Ingrid, whose head still rested on his chest. He scanned the attic. No one other than him, Ingrid, and Anita was there, so he gently shifted Ingrid onto the mattress, where they'd sat. He covered her with a blanket and smoothed the hair away from her face. Then he stood, switched off the radio, and motioned for Anita to follow him from the attic.

"You two are the last people I expected to sleep through the liberation." Anita's eyes were narrowed with surprise. "Especially not"—she waved a hand toward the attic—"not like that."

Gerrit chuckled. No, he didn't suppose anyone would have expected to find him and Ingrid together like that. "We were using Opa's field glasses from the roof, but we couldn't see much. We thought the radio might have more information."

"The Radio Oranje broadcast would have ended an hour ago."

"Ingrid didn't sleep at all last night. She crashed her bicycle on the way back from her courier run and fell asleep as soon as she stopped moving. I didn't want to wake her, and I didn't sleep much either last night . . . I didn't mean to fall asleep, but I'm not surprised."

"What exactly is going on between you and Ingrid?" Anita didn't sound unhappy, just confused.

He supposed that meant Ingrid hadn't told Anita about the change that had started when they'd hid inside that closet. Because Ingrid was uncertain about what it meant? Or because she and Anita had been too busy to discuss anything other than resistance work? "You mean, Is she my sweetheart now?"

"Is she?"

"I suppose so."

"For how long?"

"Um, since Friday. Or maybe just since today." As wonderful as the change was, explaining it felt complicated. "You can understand, can't you? Ingrid's brave and beautiful and clever and, well, you already know how wonderful she is."

Anita nodded slowly. "I do. But those are not the adjectives you would have used a few weeks ago. Then, you would have tried to find fault with anything coming from her mouth."

He grinned. "I might not have used those words before, but I don't expect I'll be complaining about Ingrid's mouth anymore."

Anita put a hand on her hip. "I certainly hope you haven't been taking advantage of her when the house is empty and she's had no sleep for a day and a half."

Gerrit's jaw clenched at the insinuation. Did Anita have so little faith in his sense of propriety? "When I was a boy, I had the fact that the date of my birth is only six months after the date of my parents' wedding rubbed in my face more often than I like to recall. Trust me, I'll not ever risk putting someone else in that position. Besides, you know Ingrid. It isn't likely that I or anyone else could talk her into going against her principles, is it?"

"Berend almost did."

Gerrit sobered. "Yes, I suppose he did." Ingrid had been strong enough in the end to refuse. Gerrit hadn't been, and only luck had kept him from having a man's death on his hands. He could add that to the things he admired about Ingrid: She'd been strong when he'd been weak. "Look, I care about Ingrid a great deal. I don't want to do anything she's going to regret."

Anita looked back at the attic. "I had hoped the two of you would start to get along better, but this . . ."

Hurt tugged at his chest. "You don't approve?"

"I don't mind the idea of you and Ingrid together as long as your conduct is proper, but the timing . . . Gerrit, your timing is absolutely awful."

Gerrit nodded. "I won't argue with that. Could you see the paratroopers?"

"A bit, from the roof of the hospital via field glasses." She smiled softly. "It was extraordinary. Men just stepping out of an airplane, and then their parachutes spreading out above them."

"Any word from Cornelis?"

"From one of his couriers." Anita patted her pocket. "I'm not sure it's still relevant, but we should include it with the other reports meant to move on tonight."

"Did you see where the paras landed?" He wished he could have seen it better from Opa's attic.

"West of Oosterbeek. Which seems too far from the air base or Arnhem to take either by surprise, but maybe those aren't their targets."

Some of the awe and excitement in knowing that airborne troops were nearby faded into worry. "That's awfully close to where those Panzer units were regrouping."

"It is, but we've been sending reports on the Panzer units for days. Surely they knew."

Gerrit tried to figure out what their plan might be. "I would have thought they'd want the bridge." He gestured toward it, only a block away, where the road crossed the Nederrijn. But the Germans didn't call it the Nederrijn. To them, it was the Rhine, and no matter how disorganized the Germans had been at the beginning of September, Gerrit didn't think they would abandon it without a fight. Cords of fear wove through his stomach. Liberation was here . . . but it wouldn't come without a battle.

As if to prove Gerrit's fears true, an enormous boom shook the floor beneath them and assaulted their ears. They stood in silence for a moment, then Gerrit dashed into one of the bedrooms to look out a window.

"What was that?" Anita asked.

"If I were to guess, I'd say a bridge." Gerrit pulled open a curtain. Outside, the road bridge was visible, undamaged. But in the distance, a plume of smoke rolled and dissipated. The railroad bridge, or part of it, was gone. He'd seen Rotterdam destroyed at the war's beginning. Would he now see Arnhem destroyed too?

Anita looked over his shoulder to see out the window. "I should go back to the hospital. If Cornelis has more information for me, I expect he'll send it there. And they might need an extra set of hands before the evening is through."

Gerrit pulled his eyes from the smoke coming from the railway bridge. "Let me walk you there."

Anita shook her head. "You could still be rounded up. The Moffen might need manpower now more than ever if they need foxholes dug or barricades built."

"And you could be shot between here and the hospital." If Arnhem was turning into a war zone, he didn't want Anita out in the middle of it.

"So could you. More easily than I could because you're the right age to be a soldier."

"But I'm not wearing a uniform."

"That might not protect you."

"And the fact that you're a woman might not protect you." He crossed his arms. "If Allied troops are landing near Oosterbeek, the Nazis will be rushing toward them, and I don't want you to be among the casualties."

Anita smiled, a gesture that took Gerrit by surprise. "When did my nephew grow up to become so protective of his aunt? I'll be careful. I've walked the street from here to the hospital more times than I can count. I know several paths through gardens that will take me off the main road, and I'm planning to leave now, before twilight makes it harder for people to see that I'm a woman, not a soldier. I'll call to let you know I've arrived. And I'll call again if there's anything to add to the reports from Cornelis."

Gerrit thought for a long moment before agreeing. "Cornelis said the report he gave me yesterday needed to leave tonight, by midnight, even if he hadn't sent anything else. Everything changed when those airplanes flew overhead, but maybe that means they need our information more than ever." His eyes went to the attic again. "Ingrid needs to rest her ankle. I suppose I'll take the reports tonight."

Anita's gaze strayed to the attic. "Another reason for you not to accompany me to the hospital. No matter how tired she is, I don't suppose Ingrid slept through that blast. She's probably wondering what happened."

Ingrid fell back asleep after Gerrit told her about the railroad bridge, then woke much later to the sound of small-arms fire. Did that mean the paratroopers were approaching Arnhem? She rolled over on the mattress in the attic. She'd been so eager to sleep in her own bed, but falling asleep while Gerrit cradled her in his arms—that was something she wouldn't mind doing again. Soon. Not that she'd meant to fall asleep, but the moment she'd sat down, everything had caught up with her. Physically, she was exhausted. Emotionally, too, even though the emotions—the thrill of first love and the exaltation of coming liberation—were of the best sort. She had no right to be falling in love here, now, in the middle of a war. Or maybe it was the end of the war. Regardless, she planned to enjoy every moment of it.

She made her way to the trap door leading from the attic. The window showed a smoky, twilight sky. Her ankle didn't feel quite as painful as before, but she still used trusses for balance when available. Yet after climbing down the attic ladder, the pain had returned in force. She shouldn't have gone up, but she'd wanted to know what was happening.

The hallway below was dark, and nothing happened when she flipped on a light switch, so the electricity was out. That wasn't so surprising, given all the air raids. She checked the bathroom, and it seemed the water had also stopped. Someone—probably Gerrit—had filled up the bathtub so there would be something to wash with. She slowly made her way down to the bottom floor, looking for Gerrit, Anita, or Opa.

She found Gerrit in the dining room with Cornelis. Their faces were lit by a single candle.

"They aren't listening to me, to anyone." Cornelis shook his head in frustration. "Their transmitters aren't working, so I told them to use the telephone, and they wouldn't. We're ready to help them—ready to die with them, if need be, but they keep saying, 'No, thank you.' They're polite but quite firm."

Gerrit noticed Ingrid and pulled out a chair for her, then grabbed another chair for a footrest. "Why wouldn't they want help?"

"They don't trust us." Cornelis rested his forearms on the table. "But the rest of the network trusts us. That information still needs to be taken on."

"I'll leave as soon as it's dark," Gerrit said.

Worry flared in a hot wave. "But I've done that route a hundred times." Ingrid swallowed. "I should be the one to go."

Gerrit and Cornelis both glanced at her ankle. Ingrid pulled it off the chair it rested on. "If it's wrapped tightly, I'm sure I can manage, especially with a good bicycle."

Gerrit shook his head. "That needs more time. And things might be different tonight. I don't want you caught in the crossfire if the British or the Germans spot you and think you're one of the enemy."

"They're far more likely to think you're the enemy, seeing as you're a man and I'm a woman. There's far less risk if I go."

Gerrit's mouth pulled in a sad sort of smile. "You've used that type of reasoning before, and it may have helped us get through a checkpoint, but when the patrolman recognized me, it backfired and ended up putting you in danger. Besides, at night, I don't think they'll see much of a difference between you and me."

Ingrid felt her eyes sting. She couldn't break down about this. Gerrit had done plenty of dangerous things before, but now the thought of losing him hurt more than ever. Especially if he were arrested or killed doing the courier route that was her responsibility.

Cornelis glanced between the two of them. "I'll let myself out. Maybe the British will come to their senses soon and accept our help. In the meantime, Gerrit, get that information to the next safe house."

"Yes, sir."

When Cornelis left, Gerrit crouched beside Ingrid's chair and slipped his hand over hers. "Can I assume this reaction means you want me to come back?"

She nodded.

Gerrit tucked a strand of her hair behind her ear. "Ingrid Lang, you are one of the bravest women I've ever met, and I'm flattered by your concern, but if I let you go in my place, I would be just as worried about you as you are about me. Maybe more because you're injured, and that would slow you down, no matter how stubborn you are about insisting you're just fine."

"Will you come back right away?" The suspense of waiting to know he was safe would be a form of torture.

"I'm not sure. From what Cornelis says, Arnhem isn't the only place with a little action right now. The British don't seem to want much help from the Dutch Resistance, but American paratroopers dropped to the south, and maybe they'll be more willing to work with us." His thumb ran over her knuckles, and his smile held real joy. "This is what we've been waiting for, Ingrid. The Nazis will have to leave now, and then the war will finally be over, and . . ." His voice suddenly trailed off, and the hope she'd seen in his eyes disappeared, and he glanced away. "And then you can return to your real family and your real home."

She didn't miss what he'd implied. When the war ended, finding her family would be her most important task, and whether they were in London or back in Austria, they weren't even in the same country as Gerrit.

He stood. He should have been thrilled with the prospect of the Nazis being forced out of his homeland, but something else—the thought of losing her?—kept him sober. "Take care of yourself, Ingrid. Stay off the streets and away from the windows. I expect I'll see you again soon, even if it's not for very long."

She stood and took his arm before he could leave.

He glanced at her feet. "You should be resting that sprain."

She put a hand on his cheek and guided his face around until he was looking at her again. "Gerrit, the end of the war doesn't have to mean goodbye."

He swallowed. "Maybe. Maybe not." He smiled, but it looked forced. "And we have to win before we worry about that, don't we?"

She nodded.

One of his arms wrapped across her back. "Whatever happens, thank you for these last few days."

Ingrid didn't want the last few days to be the only time they had together. "Will you kiss me again? Not a kiss goodbye. Something that says, '*See you later.*'"

He nodded and leaned into her lips. The kiss that followed wasn't as fiery as the one in the closet or the one in the doorway, but it was just as beautiful. It was more controlled, more intentional, a calm, tender expression of affection. It warmed her from the inside out, and she vowed then and there that she would figure out a way to find her family *and* keep Gerrit.

"I'll see you later, Ingrid." His lips brushed across her cheek, and his whispered words caressed her ears. "Be careful. If my task were any less important, I'd skip it and stay here to make sure you are safe."

"Gerrit, I . . ." She swallowed, wrapped her arms more securely around his torso, and held him tight. "You be careful too."

He nodded. "While you were sleeping, I pulled some mattresses into the basement. Just in case things heat up. You'll go down there if the fighting gets close?"

"Yes. And you won't do anything reckless, will you?"

A smile shifted his expression. "Only if it will help drive the Moffen from my country."

"That sounds much closer to reckless than careful."

"I said I'd see you later." He held her hand. "I meant it. But I better go now."

He kissed her again, and she wished she were going with him. Only moments before, her ankle had throbbed, but the sensation his mouth created on hers made it easy to ignore petty things like sprained ankles.

When he ended the kiss, he started to pull away, but a burst of rifle fire instead had him holding her more tightly. "Maybe I should walk you to the hospital. I don't want to leave you in the middle of a battle all by yourself."

Ingrid shook her head. "That's the opposite way from where you're going. I'll stay here and rest my ankle. You take those reports on because that information you're carrying might be important. Vital. I'll see you in a few days. Maybe tomorrow."

"You're sure you'll be all right?"

She put a hand on her hip. "Ask again and I'll think you question my competence."

He took her hand again and pressed his lips into her palm. "See you later, Ingrid."

Despite her bravado, something inside her did ache when he left. The dark night, punctuated by rifle fire, made the blacked-out home seem spooky. Death might come to anyone that night: to her, to Gerrit, to Opa and Anita, to the British troops who had fallen from the sky.

Ingrid went to the kitchen. She suspected worry was the real reason behind the tension in her stomach, but perhaps eating something would help—if not with the worry, then maybe with the headache forming in the back of her skull, growing more noticeable with every sharp crack that echoed through the streets.

She sliced a piece of bread and took two bites before a sharp rap on the front door interrupted her lonely meal. That type of knock . . . urgent and loud and unsettling. She went to see who it was. The rap came again as she reached the entryway, and then the door burst open to reveal four British soldiers. Bits of twigs stuck from the netting over their helmets. It would have been effective camouflage in a forest; along a road in central Arnhem, it was significantly less so.

One of the men had an arm in a sling. Another had a bandage wrapped around his leg and leaned on one of his comrades for support.

"We need a place for the wounded," one of them said in English. His diction sounded a great deal like her former nanny's.

"Come in." She stepped back so they could enter more easily. "We have rooms upstairs or in the basement."

"The basement."

"I'll show you the way." She lit a lantern and led them down the stairs. It seemed Gerrit's worry about leaving her alone had been for naught. She would have the company of at least two wounded paratroopers. What she didn't know was whether that would make her situation safer or more dangerous.

Gerrit approached the dark farmhouse with caution. Ingrid had told him about the missing courier. If the person in question had been arrested, they seemed to have stayed silent long enough for Luitenant Brug and the airmen to wait for a replacement and then move on. But what if that had changed? No one could hold out under torture indefinitely.

Freedom seemed so close. Gerrit didn't want to be captured right before liberation. And things were so promising with Ingrid—he would hate to miss that. Or maybe his future with her wasn't so promising, because he didn't think her religious, bourgeoisie family would approve of him. He was still amazed that *she* approved of him, and he still worried that it wouldn't last.

But Ingrid was fifteen kilometers away, and the future was unpredictable. He needed to focus on the present. He stepped off his bicycle and circled the house, looking for anyone who might be hiding, waiting to ambush a courier. Nothing outside seemed amiss. That didn't mean someone wasn't waiting inside to arrest him. As a precaution, he took the reports from his pocket and put them beneath a rock at the foot of a tree. If the location was safe, he'd come back for them. If he was arrested, he could hope no one—especially not the Gestapo—would ever find them. The papers looked like harmless letters, but if found on him, they would be scrutinized with suspicion. And there was a chance they could be broken because the code was simple enough that it depended on looking innocent for most of its safety.

He left the papers and knocked on the home's back door. A man answered and looked him over from head to foot. He was probably expecting Ingrid, and in a time of war, no one wanted a stranger knocking on their door in the middle of the night.

"Do you suppose it will rain tomorrow?" the farmer asked.

"I hope not," Gerrit said. "I still need to purchase an umbrella." No umbrella, no onderduikers, just information that needed to be passed on.

The man cracked a smile. "I saw what came out of the sky today, and I'm hoping for more."

"Airborne troops? We saw their planes over Arnhem, but their landing zone was too far away for me to see details. They're here too?"

The man nodded. "Close. They dropped south of Nijmegen. Come in."

Gerrit's muscles tensed, but he followed the man's instructions. If the Gestapo was waiting, surely enthusiasm for paratroopers wasn't anything so suspicious as to lead to torture. Not that the Gestapo really needed a reason to arrest and torture someone. "I have reports."

"I'll take you tonight so we don't have to wait for the next courier. I don't want to risk delay, not when we're so close to freedom. I'm ready to leave now."

"Me, too, though I'd be grateful for a glass of water."

The man complied, and the delay not only slaked Gerrit's thirst but also gave him the chance to confirm no one hid in the other room.

"I expected the other courier," the farmer said. "Is she all right?"

Gerrit finished his water. "Bicycle trouble. She injured her ankle. Ought to recover in time for the parades we throw when the Moffen finally march out. She mentioned that another courier had gone missing. Any word on that?"

"No."

"Are you taking precautions, in case the courier fell into the wrong hands?"

"I sent my wife to stay with family, and I'm going to do everything I can to make sure those paratroopers make it to this side of the Waal so the Gestapo won't ever have a chance to visit my home."

The farmer led Gerrit outside, and Gerrit went to retrieve his reports.

"Do the Germans still have the bridge over the Waal?" Gerrit asked.

"Yes, and after today, you can bet they'll be extra alert."

"So, how will we cross the river?"

"I have a friend with a small boat. It's how we usually move onderduikers since it's too dangerous to use the bridge. Even when they aren't under attack, the Germans keep a close eye on it. But there isn't room for bicycles, so we'll have to walk."

The river was just over a kilometer away, so they reached it in good time. Gerrit would have never found the boat on his own, but the farmer knew exactly where to look, and together they rowed across. They took it slowly so as to stay silent, and no one seemed to notice the two men slipping across the dark, wide Waal River.

Gerrit grunted as they pulled the heavy boat onto shore. He helped the farmer cover the craft with brush, and then they walked into Nijmegen.

The farmer pointed to a large building. "A transformer factory. Underground headquarters."

Before they were within ten meters, an armed guard stepped in front of them. He didn't wear a uniform, but he held a rifle. He nodded in recognition to the farmer, then gestured to Gerrit. "He's with you?"

"Yes."

"Worked with him long?"

"No, but he knew all the right passwords. He's down from Arnhem. Said the normal courier is injured."

The guard motioned for another man to step from the shadows. "We'll have to frisk you."

Gerrit held his hands out while the other man patted him down.

"He's clean."

The guards let Gerrit and the farmer pass. Inside the factory, a small group had gathered. And in the center of the group, before a large table covered in maps, stood Luitenant Brug.

He smiled when he saw Gerrit and the farmer. "Glad to see a few familiar faces."

"What are you doing here?" Gerrit asked. "Even with the delay, I thought you would be closer to the border by now."

"We made it almost to Grave last night." Luitenant Brug gestured to the sky. "Then this happened. You have information from Arnhem?"

"Yes."

"Let me finish organizing these patrols, then I'd love to see it."

Gerrit watched as Luitenant Brug gave the other men their assignments. Gerrit gathered that they were part of a warning system for any German counterattack in the area. Each of the men wore an orange band around their arms. Orange for the House of Oranje. Not so long ago, the royal house had felt distant and unnecessary, but now Gerrit considered them a vital ally in the war against the Nazis. Royal rule had its faults, but not nearly as many as Nazi rule.

When Luitenant Brug finished, he walked over to Gerrit and gripped his hand in a hearty shake. "I'm glad to see you again, Gerrit. Is everything well with your family?"

"Anita misses you. Ingrid sprained her ankle; otherwise, I think she would have come instead of me. I would have had my doubts about her entering a war zone, but I left her in a war zone. I'm not sure which is worse."

"Have they made any progress in Arnhem?"

"The Germans blew the rail bridge. Don't know if the paras have taken the road bridge or not. If they have, I don't know how well they'll hold against the Panzers."

Luitenant Brug nodded. "I saw the reports. But I'm not sure whoever planned this did."

"What is the plan?" It all felt a little incredible to Gerrit—an army falling by parachute from the sky into the middle of a German occupation.

"Airborne troops were dropped along a corridor from Eindhoven to Arnhem. They're to hold the main bridges and roads for a British armored column pushing north from the border."

"Are paratroopers in Nijmegen?"

"Not in force." Luitenant Brug frowned. "They didn't have enough airplanes and gliders to drop all the troops the same day. More should drop in tomorrow and Tuesday."

"But now the Germans will be looking for them, won't they?"

"Yes. So in addition to taking the bridges, each airborne division also has to make sure their drop zones aren't overrun." Luitenant Brug ran his finger along the map, starting near the border with Belgium. "The American 101st is to the south, with Eindhoven, Son, and Veghel. American 82nd in the center, with Grave, the Groesbeek Heights, and Nijmegen. British 1st to the north, in Arnhem. The Poles are to reinforce them later." He gestured to the resistance men he'd been speaking with before. "We're in the 82nd's zone. Only a third of their division arrived today, so these men are helping keep an eye out for German counterattacks."

"Aren't you still recovering from a major surgery? Opa cleared you to leave but only because hiding always carries a risk. He wouldn't have cleared you for military operations."

Luitenant Brug's lips twisted in amusement. "A few hours ago, I found General Gavin's intelligence officer. I explained my mission and the delays due to illness and missing guides. He didn't ask for details about my illness. I didn't volunteer them. I expect others will need the hospital space more than I do."

"Anita would scold you for doing too much too soon."

The American smiled. "If this works, she'll be able to scold me in person as a citizen of the liberated Netherlands. I care about this country. I care about the people who hid me and healed me and gathered information for me when I couldn't do it myself. I don't want to sit this out, not when I know the language and the resistance and can help the operation along."

"I don't want to sit it out either." Gerrit had been waiting for this moment for years. "Cornelis contacted the British, but they wouldn't take help from the resistance. They don't trust us. But you know me. You can use me, and I'm ready to do all I can to drive the Moffen out."

"You know the danger?"

Gerrit nodded. "I've been living with that danger for four years, four months, and eight days. If you care about the Netherlands and about my family in Arnhem, how much do you imagine I care?"

"I don't doubt your courage or your commitment. But battles are a different type of war from the one you've been fighting, and you haven't had the same training the paratroopers have."

"You said you need people." Gerrit gestured to the remaining resistance men preparing for their assignments. "I've had as much training as them."

Luitenant Brug handed Gerrit an orange band for his arm. "The difference is that I don't know their aunts. But you're right, we can use some help. And whatever information you've brought. I'm cycling back to headquarters tonight. I'll bring you with me. First, let me tie up a few things here."

Maybe an hour later, Gerrit set out with Luitenant Brug and four other members of the resistance. He had yet to see any paratroopers, but he had a feeling that would change before much longer. Small arms sounded. Rifles, then a machine gun. Somewhere nearby, the Americans were skirmishing with the Germans. Maybe the Dutch were too. He hoped it would be enough.

Gerrit pictured a map in his mind, weighing the distances to travel, the bridges over canals and rivers to secure, the drop zones to maintain, and the threat of German troops that could come from any direction. Nijmegen was even closer to the German border than Arnhem was.

"Will the plan really work?" he asked.

"If it does, it will be brilliant," Luitenant Brug said. "If anything major goes wrong or if too many small things don't go right, it will be a disaster."

"Do two understrength panzer divisions count as something major?"

Luitenant Brug was quiet for a moment. "I'm not sure. Either way, we're going to be right in the middle of it."

CHAPTER 19

Ingrid rubbed the soot from a British paratrooper's face and rinsed the cloth in a bowl of water. Eight wounded soldiers now resided in the van der Veen basement. She wished Opa or Anita could help because she wasn't capable of removing bullets or shrapnel and then stitching the wounds closed. She controlled the bleeding and kept the men as comfortable as possible, but she wasn't a nurse. Anita wasn't either, but she had taken classes and worked in the hospital since completing school. Ingrid, too, had graduated the lyceum, a year after Anita, but by then, there had been so many onderduikers to care for that further education had been postponed. She hadn't regretted it at the time, but now that an army had fallen from the sky to liberate Arnhem, she wished she'd been given instruction beyond the basics needed to be a Red Cross volunteer.

"Can you light a cigarette for me, miss?" The man who spoke had burns on both hands from a phosphorus grenade that had caught fire. He'd been lucky it hadn't burned more of him. When he had first come to the basement, his clothing had glowed. Ingrid had fetched some of Opa's clothes and insisted he change. The civilian clothing might be a problem if the Germans captured the building and found him out of uniform, but the British soldiers had told her many times that they were going to win this battle.

Ingrid obliged the man. "Here you are, Riker." There was little else she could do to comfort him or the others, just light cigarettes, brew up the tea some of them had in their packs, and scrounge food from the van der Veen kitchen when things were quiet enough to venture aboveground.

Things hadn't been that calm for some hours. The crack of rifle fire burst from above, where several paratroopers dueled from the upper stories of the van der Veen home with enemy soldiers on the streets outside. She tried not to think what state the rest of the home must be in. The soldiers had knocked out window panes to prevent cuts from flying glass. Curtains had been torn down so they wouldn't catch fire, furniture had been piled into barricades that would stop bullets and shell fragments, and hobnailed shoes had left scratches on the wooden floors. She was certain Opa or Anita would have opened the door to the British, but Ingrid still worried over their reaction to their damaged home. Even more than that, she worried about whether they were safe. The battle had turned the normal walk between the van der Veen home and the hospital into a dangerous gauntlet she hadn't yet attempted. Were Opa and Anita still at the hospital, trying to help a flood of casualties, or had one of them tried to come home and not made it?

According to the soldiers, a British armored division was driving up from the south and ought to arrive Tuesday. Tomorrow. Some of the troops who had parachuted in on Sunday had seized the north end of the Arnhem bridge. She'd felt the quake when the bridge had been destroyed to slow the German invasion in 1940, then had watched the arched steel supports be rebuilt over the last four and a half years. She understood its military importance. What she didn't understand was why more men hadn't come to reinforce the vanguard who had taken the bridge on Sunday. Some of their forces, the men had explained, needed to guard the drop zones so the rest of the division could safely land and reinforce them. But all the men had expected more of their comrades to have reached the bridge by now. They no longer had the element of surprise, and fear that the Germans would cut the small force in half—those at the bridge separated from those closer to the drop zones—sank in with each burst of artillery fire. The explosions caused trembles in the ground and hammered their ears, even in the basement.

As it had so many times before, the basement door burst open, and another wounded man staggered toward them, blood gushing from his upper arm. Ingrid rushed to assist him. He'd lost his helmet and nearly fell down the stairs before Ingrid could reach him.

"Let me help." She put an arm around his waist to help him balance.

She didn't worry about the blood dripping onto her, because her clothing was already stained. She led him to an open spot of floor—something growing far too scarce—and examined the wound. She sprinkled it with sulfa powder from another soldier's first-aid kit, then used part of the destroyed curtain from one of the bedrooms as a dressing. It would control the bleeding, but this soldier, like six of the others, needed care beyond what Ingrid could give. St. Elisabeth Hospital was only ten minutes away by bicycle, but with the battle raging above them, it might as well be in Belgium.

"What's your name, soldier?" she asked.

He'd been clenching his jaw together while she bandaged him, and surprise touched his face as he focused on her.

"If you don't have one, I'll stick with Tommy," she said.

"Lancaster." His voice was deep and so quiet she could barely hear him.

He might be going into shock. She grabbed an extra blanket and laid it over him. "Welcome to the basement, Corporal Lancaster."

The bandage seemed to have stopped the worst of his bleeding, but bullets had to come out, and she didn't dare dig around in the man's wounded flesh on her own, trying to retrieve what she guessed was a 9mm or 7.92mm slug.

Nine wounded men. Five in certain need of hands more skilled than hers. Two probably in need of more than she could offer. One lucky enough to be stitched up before he arrived. The battle noises above continued unabated, but Ingrid didn't think she could postpone what needed to be done any longer.

She crept up the stairs and peeked around the corner, well aware that if the Germans had recently taken over the home or if she surprised one of the British soldiers, she could be shot. Smoke drifted on the air. Rifle fire sounded from the floor above. An artillery whistle grew louder, then shook the entire home and knocked her to the floor.

"You shouldn't be up 'ere." A paratrooper glanced over his shoulder at her, then pivoted away from the window. As he moved, glass crunched beneath his boots. Another soldier kept his gaze on the street beyond the broken-out window.

"The men in the basement need a doctor. I've done what I can, but I don't have training to extract bullets or shrapnel."

"I ain't seen a medic since yesterday."

Ingrid stayed low to the ground and moved along the corridor.

"Where are you goin'?" the paratrooper asked.

"To see if the telephone works." She doubted it did. Electricity and water had both been cut. "If I can't call, I'll ride to the hospital."

"Through a battle? You'll be dead in minutes."

"Then, I'll wait for dark, but if I wait much longer, some of those men in the basement will die." She brushed a few pieces of glass out of the way and crawled to the telephone. As she suspected, no operator answered when she picked up the line. "It's dead."

"So is our wireless set," one of the men said.

"I'll go as soon as it's dark," Ingrid said.

"We'll try to find a medic by then. Don't want to add your body to the pile in the back."

Bodies? Ingrid hadn't seen any dead soldiers—yet. No doubt she would find several along the Utrechtseweg if she peered through the window, but the threat of German sniper fire drove away any curiosity about the street outside. But in the back . . . She needed to go to the kitchen anyway to find more food. A glance through the window—this one still whole because it offered a view of the yard rather than the street—revealed that the van der Veen garden, normally a model of Dutch tidiness, now held four unmoving forms. Two lay beneath a sheet, their boots sticking out the bottom. Two were covered only by their parachute smocks.

Had they died trying to free her street? She returned to the basement with a large pot, a paring knife, the remainder of her butter and salt, and a sense of loss. Four men. And how many others lay dead throughout the city?

She checked Corporal Lancaster's wound again, all the while praying that, by some miracle, Opa would return home to care for the men in the basement. It wasn't just because she was frightened to make the trip to the hospital. It was more a realization that any attempt to make it to St. Elisabeth's was probably doomed. She would die, and the men would be no better off. If the wounded were to receive help, it had to come to them.

She added potatoes and carrots from the basement to the pot she'd brought, along with meat paste from one of the men's rations. She added water and heated it over a portable stove, also from one of the men's kits, made of a square can, half full of gasoline-soaked sand. She prayed and stirred the meal and washed nine grimy faces with a washcloth that was only marginally clean.

The door between the basement and the rest of the home banged open again. Ingrid hurried to help. Three men, but one of them wasn't injured, and around his arm, he wore a brassard displaying a red cross.

Tears pricked Ingrid's eyes. It wasn't an exact answer to her prayer for Opa's return, but for the men in need of care, the medic's arrival would provide the help Ingrid couldn't. She and the wounded men were still in the middle of a battle, in a crowded basement growing more and more dirty with each passing hour. But now she wouldn't have to attempt a trip through the battle lines to the hospital, nor would the men have to wait until nightfall before getting the help they so desperately needed.

Gerrit gripped the unconscious American soldier under the arms and dragged him from the Waco glider. All morning, Gerrit and other members of the Dutch Resistance had waited for the 82nd Airborne Division's promised reinforcements. Poor weather in England meant the drop was four hours late, but now the sky to the south filled with billowing parachutes as men jumped from planes in a tight line and floated to the ground. Others came via gliders tugged behind other aircraft. Some of the gliders landed on the field in a graceful, gentle motion. Far more arrived with thuds and jerks that suggested a very unpleasant landing for those inside. And some, like the one in front of Gerrit, seemed to have crashed as much as landed. Eight men had exited without needing help. Three were dead. Gerrit and the others were dragging the remainder to safety.

One of the Americans grabbed the legs of the man Gerrit dragged. He said something, but Gerrit didn't understand. He did, however, let the soldier direct their path—toward an aid station.

Once the wounded man was settled, Gerrit hurried back to help again. The Wacos disgorged both men and materials. Gerrit worked with a group removing the tail of a glider to reveal a jeep. Then he unloaded boxes full of items whose English names he didn't recognize.

It was extraordinary how much could be flown in—an entire army with food, medical equipment, artillery, ammunition, and vehicles. Yet Gerrit had survived German occupation long enough to recognize that despite the impressive amounts of men and materiel being flown in, the Germans would be assembling a force equal to or larger than the American one.

Luitenant Brug—or Lieutenant Bridger, as the other Americans called him—helped coordinate the Dutch efforts.

"Any updates?" Gerrit asked.

Bridger frowned. "The 101st Airborne Division, south of us, ran into larger-than-expected German forces. And the Germans blew a bridge over the Wilhelmina Canal at Son. Our engineers are repairing it, but that will delay the advance."

Gerrit knew what that meant: The 82nd Airborne Division, in the middle of the operation, would have to hold longer than planned. And the British 1st Airborne Division, on the northern end of the operation at Arnhem, would have to hold even longer. He hoped Ingrid and the rest of them were safe.

Another resistance man arrived to report on a position he'd been monitoring. He was tall and fit, with gray hair and a neatly trimmed mustache. He'd been in a quiet area, so Bridger checked the position on a map and made a note on a paper.

The man scrutinized Gerrit. "You from around here?"

"Not since I was a boy. Most recently, I'm from Arnhem. Had a message to bring down and ended up staying."

He offered his hand. "Arends."

Gerrit shook the man's hand. "Hendriks."

"Son of Georg?"

"Yes."

"You look just like him. I suppose you're the cause of that big scandal all those years ago?" The man chuckled.

Gerrit cringed. Rumors and condescending looks had been the primary reason the family had moved to Rotterdam soon after Nellie's birth. Hearing them again shouldn't have surprised Gerrit, but it still stung.

"Whatever happened to the doctor's daughter?"

"My mother died when the Germans destroyed Rotterdam, and my father was sent to Germany when he went on strike to protest the mistreatment of Jews."

Arends had the decency to stop smiling. "My condolences. Sounds like Georg was on the right side of the war when it came . . . even if his son was born on the wrong side of the blanket."

Rage heated Gerrit's face, but he kept his voice even. "My parents were married before I was born."

"Barely."

Six months wasn't Gerrit's definition of *barely*. His jaw clenched shut. He'd survived four years of German occupation. He could survive a few snide remarks.

Besides, he loved his parents. They might not have been perfect, but they were good people.

"Mynheer Arends," Bridger broke in. "I need you back at your post in case the Germans decide to attack through there."

"I left an associate to cover it. He's thorough, I assure you."

Bridger nodded. "But we need both of you there in case one of you needs to bring me a message." He looked at his watch. "Have your associate report back the moment you see anything. Or in two hours if things stay quiet."

Arends gave a quick nod of agreement and left.

Bridger crossed his arms when Arends was far enough away that he wouldn't hear them. "With allies like that, who needs the Germans?"

Gerrit relaxed a little, grateful that Bridger had sent Arends back to his post. "It's nothing I haven't heard before."

"This world is hard enough without people rubbing our faces in our mistakes years and years later. Or our parents' mistakes."

Gerrit tried to breathe away the anger. "It just doesn't seem fair that people remember *that* about my father instead of how he always spoke against injustice or how hard he worked or how anyone could always come to him if they needed something in their apartment fixed and the landlord wouldn't do it. The way he could make my mam smile through almost anything. The fact that he never lost his temper with me or my brother or my sister."

"He sounds like a good man. I'd like to meet him someday." Bridger's eyes held no condemnation, no pity. Just a sincere willingness to look beyond old mistakes and see the good in someone.

"I hope you have the chance. I hope all the people sent away—especially Pap—get to come home when this war is over."

"So do I." Bridger handed Gerrit a rifle.

Gerrit hesitated only a moment before taking the weapon. Berend had taught him how to use a number of handguns, but Gerrit didn't have much experience with rifles, and thus far, the Americans had accepted their Dutch allies as guides, lookouts, and stevedores but had been reluctant to use the Dutch as part of any military operation.

"The MPs can use a little help guarding the German prisons."

Gerrit smiled with satisfaction. After four years, four months, and ten days of the Germans pointing weapons of all types at the Dutch population, Gerrit looked forward to a reversal.

Hauptmann Denhart frowned as Rupert approached. Since Sunday, they had been wearing uniforms and guarding headquarters to ensure the airborne troops didn't seize their offices. Rupert had been assigned the task of preparing all documents for burning, but he hadn't yet lit the match. It reminded him of Dolle Dinsdag, when rumors of an Allied breakthrough on the border had caused panic and a near evacuation. Some of the men with some of the files had left. They'd returned only to be startled less than two weeks later by an airborne assault.

"The papers are prepared, Hauptmann."

Denhart nodded. "Hold off a while longer. From what I hear, we've managed to box in most of them. The group on the northern end of the bridge is still holding, but we'll clear them out."

Rupert had seen the homes in that area, and he suspected the effort to take the bridge back from the British would devolve into a house-to-house effort. Like Stalingrad, only the Dutch homes were sturdier than their Soviet counterparts. "Any news of the group at Oosterbeek?" They had managed to split the British troops into pockets: the group at the bridge, the group near the landing zones, and scattered units strung out in between.

"Surrounded. Though that might not be good enough. Reinforcements dropped in today. Four hours late, just in time for the Luftwaffe to have returned to base."

"You knew when reinforcements were to arrive?"

Denhart folded his arms. "Someone found plans in a crashed aircraft. But they were wrong, so they must have been meant to trick us."

"Or something delayed them."

"Maybe. Either way, more troops could drop in tomorrow. We need to weed them out. Then arrest anyone who is helping them. This whole plan . . . If those papers were right, it is far more daring than I would have expected from the British."

"Does far more daring mean far more likely to fail?"

Denhart smiled. "We can hope. Assuming we triumph, we'll have a rare opportunity to round up the resistance terrorists. This is the moment they've been waiting for. They might let their guard down."

Rupert mulled over Denhart's words. They would root out the British soldiers at the bridge, contain the other British soldiers into an ever-smaller ring in Oosterbeek, and find all the Dutch men and women who had been so quick to help the Reich's enemies. The Allies had launched a daring assault and taken Rupert and his colleagues by surprise. But when they failed, that failure would be absolute.

CHAPTER 20

Tuesday morning, Ingrid limped down the steps to the basement, where twenty-one wounded British paratroopers and one medic waited. Blood stained the stairs, leaving one step in particular wet and slick. They were running out of blankets. They were running out of water. They were running out of food. Opa and Anita were still missing, and the paratroopers in this part of the Utrechtseweg had received no reinforcements from the drop zone or from the promised tank column.

Ingrid sat beside the medic, Corporal Collins, and began cutting the sheets she'd gone upstairs to fetch into bandages because there seemed to be a never-ending need for those. Corporal Collins extracted a bullet from one of the men's arms, then stitched it closed, and Ingrid wrapped the wound. When the bandage was secure, she replaced the bandages on several other wounded soldiers with her new supply.

Footsteps pounded down the basement stairs. Two British airborne troops, but she didn't see any visible wounds.

"None of us have slept since Sunday morning, so I handed around Benzedrine pills, and Harris here started hallucinating. He needs to sleep it off."

Collins looked up from the infected wound he was examining. "If you gave him Benzedrine, he's not likely to sleep anytime soon."

"Just take him," the other man said.

Ingrid stood and approached Private Harris. "Come along. I have a lovely bed for you."

"Are we dancing, miss? On our way in, a pretty Dutch girl gave me a pear. I would have liked to take her dancing." He hummed a song, but the tune sounded erratic.

"Monty's on his way." That was what everyone had told her, so she repeated it. "Then the Moffen will be gone, and we'll have a grand dance."

"Moffen?"

"Jerry. The krauts. The boche. Swastikas. Hitlerites." It seems every group had a different name for the enemy, none of them flattering. Unlike the name for the British. Everyone called them Tommies, but it wasn't meant as an insult.

Harris allowed Ingrid to lead him across the room to a pallet. She wished he would lie down and sleep, but agitation rolled off him in waves. Little wonder since he hadn't slept in ages, and danger would have been constant since before he'd even landed.

"You rest here, and I'll see if I can fetch a book to read to you."

She hoped no one was firing into Opa's office. Most of the home's books were stored there, though they might be part of a barricade now. She needed to find paper too. She'd been writing letters for some of the injured men, but earlier that morning, she had used the last sheet writing a letter to the wife of a soldier wounded in the shoulder. Writing in English was a challenge for her anyway, with so many words spelled differently from how they ought to be spelled, but the emotion behind the dictation—what the soldier clearly felt might be his last letter—had made it even more difficult.

The battle was even louder when she left the basement. Rifles cracked, and artillery whistled and swooshed and boomed. Most of the noise seemed distant, so she made her way toward the office.

"Tanks!" a Scottish voice called from the second story. "Thirty Corps is here!"

That meant the battle was about to shift. Ingrid rushed to the window, wanting to see the arrival of the liberators.

"Careful, miss," a paratrooper in a red beret said. "There's a German sniper shooting at anything that moves."

That dampened her enthusiasm, and her initial burst of euphoria sobered into something more practical. The British armored division's arrival wouldn't mean complete liberation any more than the arrival of the paratroopers had. It was one more step toward freedom, but that didn't mean the danger had passed.

The paratrooper swore. "Get back to the basement! Now! Those aren't British tanks. They're German."

Ingrid followed the man's orders. She slipped on one of the blood-soaked steps and only barely caught herself before hitting the floor.

"What's all the commotion?" Collins asked.

"German tanks." Only then did Ingrid realized she had forgotten the book. The paper too.

"Will you light a cigarette for me?" one of the wounded asked.

Ingrid nodded. Private Harris hovered. The poor man still looked just as agitated. She hated to think what the tank could do to the paratroopers above. And to the van der Veen home, but freedom was better than having a nice home. That was what Papa had thought when he'd made plans for Ingrid and her siblings to flee Falcon Point all those years ago. She assumed Opa and Anita would agree with him.

She had no book, but some stories she knew by heart. The one Papa and Mama had told her so often, the one she'd told Anna the last day they'd been together. A fairy tale about an Austrian princess slaying a dragon might not be the best choice for a collection of British airborne soldiers, but it had to be better than doing nothing while enemy tanks attacked the block above them, especially for Private Harris.

So when the cigarettes were lit and the bandages all tied, she began. "Once upon a time, an Austrian princess went on an adventure."

Gerrit found Lieutenant Bridger near the power factory Wednesday afternoon. Paratroopers milled around where the curve of the river and the levee would make them difficult for the Germans to see. Bridger waved his recognition.

"Any updates?" Gerrit asked. He couldn't remember ever living through something so exhilarating, frightening, and exhausting. The battle so far hadn't been easy. Faster than American troops could drop from the sky, the Germans had counterattacked. It went against regulations, but members of the resistance had begged the Americans to give them the weapons of their dead and wounded so they could fight by their allies' side. Yet even with help from the Dutch, the American positions remained precarious.

"The British armored division pushing up from the south made contact with the 82nd yesterday. But we've been so busy holding Grave and Groesbeek Heights that we haven't taken those bridges yet." Lieutenant Bridger gestured to the River Waal. Seventeen kilometers beyond its waters lay Arnhem. Around it, huge swaths of Nijmegen burned from the ongoing fight for the city.

"So how will we take them?"

"Hopefully from both sides at once." Lieutenant Bridger looked at his watch. "They're supposed to be sending up boats. They're late."

When a convoy of Allied trucks drove into view and halted, the troops waiting by the river sprang into action and began unloading the contents. Gerrit stepped in to help. The boats were flimsy things with plywood bottoms, short canvas sides, and far too few paddles. Boats like that would have a decent chance of crossing the river in peacetime. But when the Germans were doing everything they could to hold the Nijmegen bridge and the Allies were doing everything they could to take it, crossing in those boats sounded like a sure way to die.

Gerrit didn't understand most of the English words the American paratroopers spoke, but he could guess the meaning. They, too, considered the boats inadequate to the task. Some of the boats had four oars, but some had only three or two or none.

Gerrit helped Bridger and two other soldiers unload another boat.

"How will they row across?" Gerrit asked. "The current will sweep them away if they don't have more paddles." It might sweep them away anyhow.

"They've been told to use the butts of their rifles." Bridger's face seemed calm other than the tension in his jaw.

"Are you joking?"

"I wish I were."

"Can't they find anything better?" There were limits to what equipment an airborne army could bring on a mission, but surely there were more oars somewhere. If not with the armored division, then with civilians in the city.

Bridger looked at his watch again. Gerrit snuck a glance too. It was almost three o'clock.

"We've been waiting for those boats all morning," Bridger said. "The Germans counterattacked Son as they were bringing them up. They're calling the road Hell's Highway now, and it's earning its name." Bridger helped Gerrit pull the canvas over one boat's wooden frame. "The armored division was supposed to be in Arnhem yesterday, and word is the 1st Airborne Division is having a rough time of it. They can't be relieved if we don't have that bridge."

Arnhem. Gerrit wanted the armored division to get there soon, for the sake of the battle and because he needed to know Ingrid and his family were safe. "Do they need volunteers?"

"Do you have any training in amphibious assaults?"

"No. Do they?"

Bridger shrugged. "I sure hope so. They aren't taking Dutch volunteers for this, but there'll be plenty of work for you on this side of the river."

The men checked their equipment and stubbed out cigarettes. Some joked. One puked. When the order was given, paratroopers on either side of the boats lifted them to their shoulders and lugged them to the levee and down the forty-five-meter floodplain on the other side. Then the men climbed into the boats—Gerrit counted twenty-six of them—and began rowing across.

A boom sounded, and smoke from British tank shells floated along the river's surface like low, gray clouds. The Waal looked like it was boiling. For a moment, Gerrit couldn't understand. Then his mind flashed to hail, but that wasn't why the water was so pockmarked. German bullets were tearing into the water, growing ever more frequent. The wind pulled the smokescreen into tendrils that failed to mask the men's movements.

"Are they trying to zigzag?" Gerrit asked Bridger. "Or are they just bad at rowing?"

"I don't know if they covered rowing during training." Bridger's face showed horror as the bullets hit the men in the boats. Some fell overboard; others slumped to the bottom of their vessels.

The men's journey across the Waal, a river one hundred seventy-five meters wide around Nijmegen, was agonizingly slow for Gerrit, and he imagined it was much worse for the men rowing. Relief flooded Gerrit when the first boat made it to the opposite shore. The soldiers disembarked and immediately began attacking across the wide, exposed ground between the river's edge and the levee.

As the troops emptied each boat, the men piloting the crafts began the return journey. That made their task perhaps the most dangerous of all. When they arrived back on the south bank, Gerrit, Bridger, and dozens of resistance volunteers helped with the dead and wounded while the next wave of paratroopers climbed into the boats lined with bullet holes and headed toward the far shore.

Gerrit left a dead body on the floodplain. It could be picked up later. Then he helped Bridger with a man shot through the cheek. The next man was shot through the shoulder. That was all the wounded they could reach on this side of the river, so Gerrit stayed with the last injured man they'd retrieved and held a handkerchief over the gunshot wound while waiting for a medic.

With his good arm, the soldier pulled a rosary from his pocket. His fingers fumbled with the beads, and his lips moved in a soundless prayer. A medic came and took over for Gerrit.

Since Gerrit wasn't needed with the wounded anymore, he watched the second wave of men cross the Waal. Like the first, they disembarked and immediately ran across the open ground, stopping only if shot. It was as if the helplessness of the crossing had galvanized something inside them, and the men were now driven to take revenge on the enemy that had hit so many of their comrades on the river. Fear had morphed and erupted into a controlled rage.

When the boats returned for the third group, Gerrit again helped with the wounded. Then they gathered the dead. Among them was the soldier with the rosary. He didn't look any older than Gerrit. Just in case the overwhelmed medics had been too hasty, Gerrit checked the man's pulse, but it was gone.

Gerrit went back to the levee. Across the river, rifles had been stuck into the earth where paratroopers had fallen. So many casualties. He could see few details of the battle, but he could hear every rifle crack and every burst of fire from a machine gun. So many soldiers dying in his country. And for the moment, he could do nothing to help them.

Bridger joined him.

"Any word on progress?" Gerrit asked.

Bridger shook his head. "Someone took a spool of telephone wire across, but the brass in the power station has priority on using it. In any case, they're probably too busy fighting to make a report."

Gerrit thought of the soldier with the rosary. He hoped the man had found comfort in his prayers during his final moments. Gerrit even hoped that whatever the man had believed was true, because it seemed a shame for a man to die so young, so far from home, and have that be the end. Gerrit glanced at Bridger, who seemed deep in thought. He didn't know Bridger all that well, but what he had seen, he admired, and Anita was fond of him. That counted for a lot.

"What do you suppose happens to all the men who die today?" Gerrit asked.

Bridger thought for a while. "I suppose those who were mostly good go to heaven. And those who were mostly bad go somewhere far less pleasant."

"You're sure there's something else after death?"

Bridger nodded. "As sure as I can be without seeing it."

Gerrit watched the disappearing paratroopers rush toward the north side of the Nijmegen bridge, while the British fought from the south. Some of the Allied troops wouldn't make it. All their bravery, their willingness to fight for another country's freedom—surely that made them mostly good. But they'd also fought and killed, and Gerrit didn't know what they'd been up to on their last leave—he doubted they'd been saints. And what of Gerrit? If some part of him continued after he died, what judgment awaited him? "What about people who want to be good but end up doing things they regret during the war?"

Bridger pulled his eyes from the firefight. "God knows everything, so He understands war. And it's never too late to repent."

Gerrit frowned. He hungered for redemption, but some things couldn't be undone.

Bridger's voice was soft but full of conviction as he continued. "I believe the Lord Jesus paid the price for all our sins so we don't have to."

That sounded too good to be true. Why would an immortal being come to earth and take the punishment for every wrong thing anyone had ever done? It was a fairy tale. Something meant to appease the poor masses who lived lives of misery. Something to turn to when bleeding to death and waiting for a medic. And yet, as another American soldier fell to the ground across the river—either wounded or dead—that reasoning fell apart. The Americans were fighting—and some of them were dying—to rid the Netherlands and the rest of Europe of the Nazis. Maybe it wasn't so farfetched to believe that someone far more powerful, far more righteous would suffer and die to rid humankind of the consequence of sin. Gerrit didn't believe it, not really, but he understood why Mam and her family did, why Ingrid did, why Bridger did.

He didn't have time to ponder further because the boats had returned to the southern shore again. There were more wounded to help.

CHAPTER 21

Ingrid's head hurt, and her throat ached. She and the twenty-seven British paratroopers in the van der Veen basement had finished the last of the water—drained from the radiators—earlier that day. The battle was three days old. It felt as if she'd been hiding in the basement much, much longer. No word from Anita or Opa. No water. No clean bandages. Little food. And little hope as the Germans went house to house, digging out the British soldiers who fought as long as they could.

The faces surrounding her were pinched and dirty, yet most were also determined. They were losing the battle but not their defiance. She probably looked just as filthy as they did. She no longer washed faces or hands—that required water they didn't have—but she did the best she could for the wounded.

An enormous boom shook the entire house, all the way to the basement. It was followed by sharp groans and cracks. All eyes drew upward. Had that been a direct hit? Moments later, someone yelled down from the floor above. "That shell caught the attic on fire. Anyone who can move had best scamper out now."

Ingrid looked at the men around her. Many could no longer walk. Those with arm wounds stood and helped those with leg wounds, but even when they had all paired up, even when Ingrid and the medic had helped a man each, too many still lay on the basement floor.

"Where will we take them?" she asked.

The fire above meant they had to leave, but the sounds from outside—rifles, machine guns, artillery—meant outside wasn't safe either. In the basement, they'd been marginally protected because the turrets of German tanks couldn't aim that low. At ground level and above, they'd be targets.

"The garden, for now." Collins brought one of the men with a leg wound to the foot of the cellar doors. Evacuation from the basement would keep the wounded from burning, but it wouldn't be long until German snipers repositioned themselves so they could target anyone behind the house. "Help me take down the door, and we can use it as a stretcher."

She followed him up the stairs that led into the home and removed the door from its hinges while some of the wounded made their way outside.

"The garden won't be safe for long." She kept her voice a whisper so only Collins would hear.

"They're working on that." Collins motioned to the front of the house. Another of the paratroopers stood before a window and waved a filthy cloth that had undoubtedly been white the last time Ingrid had washed it, though it would be a stretch to call it that color now.

"Does he speak German?" she asked, referring to the man she assumed was trying to negotiate a ceasefire.

Collins didn't need to answer because when the man shouted and cursed, it was entirely in English. Unless the men shooting at the house understood, they were unlikely to reach an agreement, and they needed to reach an agreement quickly.

Ingrid joined the British soldier.

"Back, miss. They're still shooting at us."

"But I speak German. I can help."

He studied her for a moment until a crash from above seemed to remind them both that time was limited.

Ingrid grasped the white flag when he handed it over. "Hello? I need to speak with your officer," she called in German.

A German voice called back. "Why?"

"We wish to call a ceasefire while we evacuate the wounded."

When the reply came, the voice was different. Louder and deeper. "If everyone surrenders, we will allow the civilians to leave, and we will take the wounded to a hospital."

If the Germans were offering to take the wounded to the hospital, she supposed that meant St. Elisabeth's was in German hands. She hoped they were treating Opa and Anita with courtesy. And that would be one more reason—in addition to the battle raging in Arnhem's streets—that they hadn't been able to contact her. Ingrid switched to English and turned to the British paratrooper. "They say they'll take the wounded to the hospital if the rest of you surrender."

He huffed. "The rest of us will fight on till the last bullet."

That was what she had thought. "And the wounded?" If they went to a hospital, they'd become war prisoners. It was, in a sense, a surrender, but the alternative for most of them was death.

Collins had been organizing the evacuation from the basement, but he must have heard the key parts of the conversation. "We don't have much of a choice. We'll take any medical care, even from the Germans, as long as we can be sure they won't massacre us."

Ingrid raised her voice to be heard outside. "Can you guarantee the wounded will be cared for?"

"On my honor as an officer."

Ingrid translated. It wasn't much to go on, a stranger's claim of honor. An enemy, no less, who fought for a regime responsible for countless atrocities. Yet both paratroopers nodded, and Ingrid spoke again. "We accept your offer of safe passage for the wounded. The others decline to surrender." She wasn't sure if the man would let her accept one of his conditions and not the other, but she prayed he would.

He didn't answer right away, and each moment made the overwhelming fear more and more painful. "Very well," he finally said.

Relief filled Ingrid's chest. She didn't want any more of her would-be liberators to die. "They agree."

"You come out first," the man shouted, and that tainted her relief.

"I'm to go first."

Collins frowned. "I'll come with you."

"There's no need for both of us to take that risk." She turned to the other soldier. "If you go through the garden, there's a bin you can pull to the wall to help you climb over. Or there was last time I checked. Trying to go east is no good. They'll see you. But if you get very low and try to head west, the house in that direction has a gate in the back. If you leave now, they might not realize you've left until the wounded are all out."

He nodded. "I'd tell you to take your time, but given those fires, that's something we don't have. I'll pass the word along."

Ingrid gripped the flag of truce and slowly opened the front door. She had opened that door a thousand times before, but this time, she feared, would be her last. Slowly, she stepped outside with both hands raised. Rifle fire hadn't ceased, but it seemed the nearest enemy had stopped shooting at the van der Veen home. In the hazy afternoon light, she glanced at the house. Every window pane was broken, bullet holes had bitten into much of the facade, and the top floors burned. Perhaps if she hadn't come outside to finalize the truce, she would have had time to grab her jewelry, a clean dress, and a coat. But saving as many paratroopers as she could took priority.

She stepped slowly, hoping the Germans would think she was scared, which was true enough, but the real reason for her sluggish progress was a hope that the unwounded paratroopers would have enough time to evacuate.

"Halt!" someone shouted.

Ingrid obeyed, standing in the middle of the street. Tidy, well-cared for homes on both sides of the road had morphed into ruins. Cinders and smoke billowed through the sky. A dozen bodies lay within view. A British paratrooper propped against a fence. Another fallen behind a tree. A great many Germans scattered in heaps. And one civilian: Mevrouw Rolloos, an elderly woman Ingrid had often accompanied to the market.

A uniformed SS officer approached Ingrid. She swallowed. Her father's one-time friend and ultimate murderer, Sauermann, had been an SS officer. Everyone knew the SS was ruthless. Yet if he was going to shoot her, she thought he would have done it from a concealed position, where no one could shoot back at him.

"How many wounded?" he asked.

Twenty-seven had been in the basement with her. She wasn't sure if Collins would escape or join the wounded, and some of the walking wounded might prefer to sneak away rather than surrender. "I'm not sure. Perhaps a score."

"Can they walk?"

"Some of them cannot."

The officer called for stretchers to be brought and men to carry them. Good. That would take time. Although she didn't want it to take too long because flames still licked the attic, where she had fallen asleep in Gerrit's arms, and the floor below, where she had cut Gerrit's hair while Sergeant Cervantes had walked her through each step. The flames would probably spread to the floor where Gerrit had kissed her in the doorway. She hoped he was all right, wherever he was.

As the stretcher bearers arrived, Ingrid moved to go with them. The officer seemed about to stop her, but she spoke before he could prevent it. "They know me. A few may need calming when they see your men."

The officer nodded.

Ingrid had wanted to delay the men further, but the Germans wouldn't be slowed. When she led the enemy troops around the side of the home to the garden, nineteen men waited. Most had grim faces. Others were unconscious. Something crashed in the attic, and those who could walk followed the German orderlies, who took three trips to remove all the wounded and load them into a truck.

The SS officer watched it all with a dispassionate expression, but when his men reported that the wounded were all removed from the garden and the basement, he saluted the wounded. "You have been worthy adversaries." Then he turned to the house and raised his voice. "There is no reason for us to continue this fight. You cannot win. Surrender, and you will be treated with respect."

Ingrid did not translate. She climbed into the back of the truck for the journey to the hospital. Yet as the truck drove away, she could hear the rallying cry of the British 1st Airborne Division.

"Whoa Muhammad!"

One of the men had explained the call to her on Tuesday. They'd picked the phrase up in the deserts of Northern Africa, and it had the benefit of being difficult for German tongues to pronounce. Now, as it rang out from ruined building to ruined building, tears stung her eyes. She had seen courage before but never in such a high concentration.

Ingrid helped the wounded men out when the truck arrived at St. Elisabeth's, and none of the German soldiers guarding the hospital stopped her. When the men were unloaded, she went in search of the van der Veens, praying they were still safe, hoping they were still here.

She spotted Anita carrying supplies up a flight of steps, and despite everything she'd been through, Ingrid felt a rush of relief and joy. "Anita!" Ingrid raced up the steps after her.

Anita turned and studied her for several long seconds before recognition dawned. Ingrid didn't let that hurt her feelings. She was probably just as soiled as the men she'd evacuated with. Anita met her halfway down the stairs and wrapped her in a tight embrace. "I've been so worried about you." Anita's voice cracked.

"I was terrified for you. And Opa. Is he here? Is he all right?"

"Yes. Working around the clock. Where's Gerrit?"

"I haven't heard from him since Sunday night when he took Cornelis's reports south." She told Anita all about the battle and how the home had been shot, shelled, and burned.

Anita's face fell. "I'm not surprised. We heard about the Tommies holding out near the bridge, and our home is along the approaches." Anita motioned for Ingrid to follow her. "I've lost track of how many times the hospital has changed hands. Patients sometimes don't know whether they're currently prisoners or victors. And we're running out of supplies. The Allies have been dropping equipment almost daily, but they're dropping their packs in areas the Germans control, so none of it is getting through to the British."

Ingrid knew all about the frustration of not having the proper supplies to treat the wounded, and how that shortage could hamper recovery and lead to death. She imagined it in an above-capacity hospital, like St. Elisabeth's, and the magnitude of the problem felt overwhelming. These men might be losing the battle, but she didn't want any of them to die when they could instead live with adequate sulfa powder and clean bandages. "It seems the hospital doesn't have electricity either?"

"No. Nor water. We've been walking to the river to fetch it in buckets. So far, no one has fired on us. I'm glad you're here because I was worried, but I'm also glad we'll have an extra pair of hands. I've never seen so many wounded before. But we can spare a moment to find Pap. He'll want to know you're safe. Relatively."

Ingrid followed Anita to one of the operating rooms. Luck was with them, and they didn't have to wait long until Opa stepped out for a break between surgeries.

He smiled when he saw Ingrid and hugged her to his chest. "Seeing you again is an answer to many, many prayers."

Ingrid was quickly incorporated into the hospital staff, and given the high number of casualties, there was always something for her to do. She spent most of Thursday morning sterilizing surgical instruments by boiling them over a portable stove. The sounds of battle continued outside the hospital, a constant mix of boom and pop, blast and screech.

"No, no, you'll have to leave your weapons here. You can't have them while we treat you," one of the nuns told a wounded German soldier. He reluctantly handed his rifle over. "That way." The nun pointed him toward the section of the hospital treating Germans.

Everyone who came received care, whether they were British, Dutch, or German, but when the first casualties had arrived on Sunday, someone had separated the combatants.

"I'll take it for you." Ingrid gestured to the rifle. The resistance had struggled to obtain weapons throughout the war, so earlier that morning, Anita had shown Ingrid where to hide them. When the British armored division arrived, they wouldn't need to stockpile them anymore, but the constant sound of battle coming from the street seemed to suggest that nothing was yet certain. They might need the confiscated MP 40s, Mauser carbines, and MG 42s.

The nun seemed relieved. "I'll trade you. I can take the instruments to the stove after I get this man settled."

Ingrid swapped the scalpels, forceps, retractors, and needle holders for the rifle, then took the weapon to the basement, where she added it to a pile hidden beneath a canvas cloth. They would figure out how to smuggle the weapons from the hospital later.

On her way back to the operating room to gather more tools to wash, one of the paratroopers tugged on her sleeve. "Is Frosty still holding the bridge?"

"Frosty?"

"Colonel Frost. His group made it to the Arnhem bridge, but none of us could get through to reinforce him."

Ingrid swallowed. "I haven't heard news of Colonel Frost, but I was near the bridge. German tanks were destroying each building, one story at a time. The Tommies were holding out as of yesterday, but without reinforcements, I don't see how they can last much longer."

"How hard . . . ?" He looked around. "How hard would it be for me and some of my friends to leave the hospital if we wanted to rejoin our mates before we're shipped to a prison camp?"

Ingrid lowered her voice so no one but the soldier could hear her. "I'll see what I can do."

It wasn't until after dark that Ingrid and Anita returned to the ward and told the soldier in question and two of his friends to follow them. One was injured in his leg, but he walked with only a slight limp. The others had arm injuries, so they could move under their own power.

"Do any of you speak Dutch?" Anita asked.

Their expressions showed that they didn't, so Ingrid translated as Anita explained. "She's done something like this before, but with airmen, before we were in the middle of a battle."

Anita led them to the morgue. The room's pungent, slightly sweet odor made one of the paratrooper's noses twitch. Cornelis waited for them. After everything that had happened with the battle, Ingrid was glad he was safe. He'd brought civilian clothing for each of the soldiers. Once the men had pulled the work clothes over their uniforms, Anita handed them stretchers. "You'll have to pretend to be gravediggers. And the Germans are monitoring all exits, so you'll need to carry real corpses. Cornelis dug the holes already, but you'll have to work at burying the men until it's safe to sneak away."

Ingrid translated, and though the men with arm injuries winced once they picked up their load, determination to avoid a prisoner-of-war camp silenced any complaints. The names of the dead men had already been recorded and their personal effects saved for next of kin. Burial was needed anyway, and if interment could earn freedom for a few of their comrades, Ingrid didn't think the fallen soldiers would complain.

Anita stayed in the morgue. Ingrid led the others away, because her German was fluent. Cornelis and the three paratroopers carried the two bodies behind her. As expected, a German sentry manned the exit.

"Burial, this late?"

Ingrid nodded. "Yes. The corpses are infected. We don't want it to spread. We're already overcrowded, and with no water and the electricity out . . ."

The sentry nodded and pulled back both blankets to verify that the corpses were, in fact, dead. In the past, Anita had smuggled live men on the stretchers, but that wasn't possible now. The guard waved them forward. Ingrid led the men to the hospital graveyard. They passed three other German soldiers guarding the hospital, but burials had been frequent enough this week that her group was given only the normal scrutiny. When they arrived at the open graves, Cornelis and the paratroopers laid the bodies in the bottom, then used nearby shovels to begin burying them in dirt.

Ingrid approached the guard with the best view of the group. "Excuse me?"

"Yes?"

"We're running out of supplies." Ingrid continued moving, slowly, praying the man would maintain eye contact and soon be looking away from Cornelis and the others. "Do you think you might be able to arrange any help for us? We've heard the British are dropping supplies, including medicine and bandages. Surely you've retrieved them."

"Why would we help the enemy?"

"We are treating German soldiers, too, as well as civilians."

He shook his head. "I can't arrange anything like that."

"But one of your superiors, perhaps? Can you tell me which officer might be most open to assisting the sick and the wounded?" Ingrid forced herself to keep her gaze on the man's face. In her periphery, Cornelis and three paratroopers disappeared from view. "We're only trying to help as many of the injured as we can."

He huffed. "I hear Arnhem's to be evacuated anyway. All the prisoners to be sent to Apeldoorn, then Germany. And the civilians are to leave too."

"But where will we go?"

The sentry shrugged. "You should have thought of that before you welcomed the British in."

Rupert had fought in battles before, ones even worse than this, but the frustration still mounted with every piece of bad news. The British paratroops holding one end of the Arnhem bridge had eventually been driven off, but they'd held for days. An even larger group of British paratroopers had gathered in Oosterbeek, and Polish airborne troops were in Driel. Those groups still clung to the buildings with a tenacity that even Tiger tanks seemed unable to dislodge. The German forces fighting them were needed for a counterattack to the south because the enemy had taken the bridge at Nijmegen before it could be destroyed. Now the Arnhem bridge was back in German hands, but they couldn't drive the enemy from Nijmegen until the enemy was driven from Oosterbeek and Driel.

In Arnhem, at least, the British soldiers would soon be rooted out completely. On order, all civilians were to evacuate Arnhem. They'd been told it was for their safety, and that wasn't entirely a lie. Civilians had already died in the fighting. And if all the civilians left, the airborne troops still hiding in the city—soon to be without help from Dutch civilians—would be easier for the Germans to find.

Another reason, too, existed for the evacuation. An absence of civilians made looting much, much easier. Several of Rupert's comrades had already expressed their intention to find Christmas gifts for family back in Germany by looting the homes of Arnhem. Standard Reich policy included using items from occupied lands to compensate victims of bombings in Germany, and the need there was great.

So, too, would be the needs in every city where the refugees fled. The exiled queen of the Netherlands had called for a railroad strike as the airborne operation had begun, so movement of food and supplies had largely ceased. As planned, the strike had crippled German logistics and stalled their reinforcements, but civilians would soon feel the disruption just as harshly. Reichskommissar Seyss-Inquart had been so furious, he'd requested all railway workers be shot, but Berlin had opted for restraint rather than the execution of thirty thousand Dutch railway workers, most of whom had gone into hiding. The reichskommissar had come up with an alternative punishment: no food would be shipped on canals or waterways, and large swaths of Dutch farmland would be flooded. Rupert remembered how rations had been cut repeatedly when he and the Sixth Army had been trapped in the Kessel around Stalingrad. He'd seen hunger before, and he suspected he would soon see it again.

A cold rain soaked into the refugees filing past on the street before him. The adults wore white armbands to mark them as noncombatants, or they carried white flags. Pillowcases, most often, tied to broom handles. The children used sticks and handkerchiefs. Some had carts or baby perambulators to move their possessions, but most had only what they could carry. Rupert's task was to watch for anything suspicious, but he saw only desperation.

A mother with four children, one of them a baby tied to her front, paused when a toddler began crying. She put the small dog she had been carrying on the ground and picked up the child instead. The dog followed for a while but eventually failed to keep up, and the mother and children continued on their way without it.

Another German soldier monitoring the refugees pulled a man out of line. Rupert immediately recognized why. The man wore civilian clothing, but his boots were those of a soldier. Rupert's comrade separated the man and his traveling companions from the other refugees, placing them against a wall, and another soldier went over to help.

A small girl, about Heidi's age, cried five paces away from Rupert. She must have been separated from her family. In the distance, he could see older children, a woman in her thirties, and an elderly couple searching. Rupert lifted the girl up so she could see over the crowd. She cried harder.

"Don't cry." Rupert wasn't fluent in Dutch, but he knew simple phrases. "Is that your grandmother?" Rupert pointed.

The little girl nodded, and Rupert took her back to her family.

As he handed her off, three shots rang out in rapid succession. Rupert turned at the noise. The airborne soldier had been arrested. The three people who had been trying to smuggle him out of Arnhem lay on the ground, shot through the head.

It was illegal to help the enemy. The Dutch all knew that, so there was no reason for Rupert to feel any remorse. Still, he turned away from the bodies. Surely the civilians had already seen how disastrous it was to help the British. Their city was destroyed, and they were being forced from their homes.

More civilians filed past. He scrutinized the men, focusing on their shoes because after so many years of war, few Dutch civilians had extra shoes to use for a disguise. The little girl and her family disappeared from view. The rain continued to fall, the bodies of the executed remained where they were, and the refugees kept their distance.

Except one middle-aged man, who approached the German soldiers and spoke to them. He carried a black case. A medical bag? The soldiers laughed but didn't stop the doctor or whoever he was from bending over the corpses to check their pulses. They must have all been dead, because soon the doctor continued on his way with his two traveling companions.

Rupert glanced at the women with the doctor and forgot to breathe for a moment. Ingrid Lang? What on earth was Ingrid Lang doing in Arnhem?

"Ingrid?" He stepped toward her.

She stopped abruptly and stared at him. Any doubts he'd had about whether it was really her vanished. She had the unforced elegance of her mother, and her eyes had the same color and intelligence that Rupert had always admired in her father, until Leopold Lang had become a traitor. Her clothing was far more worn that he would have expected from a Lang, but she still wore the same pearl earrings she'd worn in Berlin.

"How do you do, Leutnant Altbauer?" she said.

She didn't wait for an answer but continued with the stream of refugees. Four years since their last meeting and that was all she was going to say?

He limped to catch up to her. "What are you doing here?"

She lifted a bag that must have contained very few belongings. "I'm evacuating Arnhem with all the others."

"But how did you get to Arnhem?" He fell into step beside her.

She glanced at the doctor and the other woman, who had the dark hair and rich tan skin of someone from the Indies. "Do you remember when we ran into each other in Berlin?"

"Of course. Right after your father died, but you didn't mention that at the time."

"Yes . . . well, I was frightened, and I hadn't slept in ages, and . . . Well, after that, I hurt my leg and ended up convalescing in Arnhem, and then the war came, and it was hard to travel."

It would have been hard to travel in the months following their last meeting, but as a citizen of the Reich, she could have gone home. "Why didn't you go back to Falcon Point?"

She didn't answer right away. "I wanted to stay with the family who helped me after my accident." She motioned to her companions. "By then, I'd already started the school year, and well, it never seemed like the right time to go back. But it's wonderful to see you again, Rupert, and to see you looking so healthy. You'll have to excuse me. We have a long way to travel."

"Where are you going?"

Ingrid shrugged. "Velp, for now."

Rupert wanted more from her—a better explanation, time to study the grace of her neck and the sculpted shape of her cheekbones, more of her Austrian accent in his ears—but he was to watch the crowds and find hidden British paratroopers, not chat up old friends who had morphed from pretty to intoxicatingly beautiful.

He went back to the men standing by the executed Dutch. "Did you catch the doctor's name?" He pointed in the direction Ingrid's group had gone.

"Yes. Dr. van der Veen."

Rupert nodded his thanks. When things settled, he imagined it wouldn't be so difficult to track down a Dr. van der Veen and his traveling companions in Velp.

CHAPTER 22

GERRIT KNEW HIS EDUCATION WAS lacking, but he normally understood concepts quickly when they were explained to him. Yet when it came to the battle that had raged for a week, so many questions remained. All morning on Wednesday, he had heard of the desperate state of the British paratroopers holding the north end of the Nederrijn bridge in Arnhem. Knowledge that every hour mattered to the men in Arnhem had prompted the American airborne forces in Nijmegen to cross the Waal River in flimsy boats in daylight rather than waiting until dark, when casualties would have been significantly lower. But after the Allies had taken the bridge, the British armored division had not immediately set off for Arnhem, only seventeen kilometers away. They had simply stopped. Gerrit had traveled the road between Nijmegen and Arnhem often enough to realize it was a vulnerable road for tanks, raised and bordered on both sides by polder. Tanks couldn't leave the road without getting stuck in the soggy ground, and while they were on the raised highway, German artillery could hardly fail to see them. But the Allies should have known that when they'd planned their attack, long before desperate paratroopers had been trying to hold a bridge against overwhelming odds, waiting for promised relief that had never come.

And what of the civilians Gerrit had left behind? What had the battle done to Ingrid, Anita, and Opa?

Bridger sat next to Gerrit.

"What a mess." Gerrit gazed at the road to Arnhem.

Bridger grasped Gerrit's meaning quickly. "One of the Dutch liaison officers tells me that on the staff college exams, anyone who writes that the best way to take Arnhem from Nijmegen is by going straight up the road automatically fails."

Gerrit nodded. He'd heard the same thing, and now experience had confirmed it. "How did the other roads fare today?"

"Oh, the usual. We're advancing along a one-tank front, and the Germans are attacking from both sides." Bridger shook his head. "Everything is bordering on disaster."

"Any word from Arnhem?"

"They're holding in Oosterbeek. Barely." Oosterbeek. One of the suburbs closer to the drop zones. Bridger took a sip from his canteen. "If the tanks could get there, maybe they could work with the stranded men to retake the Arnhem bridge, but advancing now . . . Everyone along the corridor, from the border with Belgium up to Oosterbeek is fighting for their lives. We lost surprise a week ago. The German forces are getting stronger and stronger, and we don't have any reinforcements coming to help us."

Gerrit felt the frustration and the pain in his friend's voice. The attack, once so promising, had stalled.

As the battle continued, Gerrit took shifts guarding German POWs and Dutch collaborators. Over the second week of the battle, the Germans attacked, and the Allies did their best to hold. The paratroopers in Oosterbeek withdrew, some by small boat, some by swimming across the Nederrijn. They left behind any wounded who couldn't travel to the mercy of the enemy.

Bridger approached Gerrit late one afternoon. "A lot of men are still hiding in the Arnhem area. In attics, chicken coops, places like that. I've volunteered to go back and guide them out of enemy territory."

Gerrit thought for only a moment before asking, "Can I go with you?"

Bridger nodded. "I was hoping you would."

The two of them gathered supplies and bicycles and set off at nightfall. Darkness hid the worst of the destruction, but the scent of death and spent munitions permeated the land. For much of the way, they had to walk, and they had to stop often to hide, especially when they reached the abandoned city and the ruined remains of the Utrechtseweg. They would start their search at the van der Veen home. They didn't expect anyone to still be there after the evacuation of Arnhem, but it seemed the best place to begin.

When they arrived, Gerrit stared at the remnants of Opa's house. Moonlight softened the details, but still revealed massive damage. The top levels were gone, and of the partial walls remaining, every single window was broken.

"Is this the right house?" Bridger whispered, because Arnhem was a ghost city, and no one was allowed in other than the enemy. If caught, the two men could expect death.

"I'm sure." With every building along the street in ruin, Gerrit had barely recognized the remaining structure, but he knew the location of the bushes, some of them now burned, knew the view from the front entrance.

He walked to the kitchen door, which still hung on its hinges. He didn't dare turn on a flashlight when the windows weren't shielded by blackout curtains, but the crunch of broken crockery beneath his feet told him the kitchen was a mess. Panic grew with each step. What had Ingrid faced when he'd left her here?

If anyone remained in the home, they would have gone to the basement, so he headed there. The door was missing, but he assumed he was far enough inside the house that he could switch on his flashlight. The beam caught on stairs stained a red-brown. Dried blood? At the bottom of the steps, a sweep of the flashlight revealed disaster: discarded cloth bandages, most of them soiled, an empty pot and mess tins, empty shelves that had once held potatoes and preserved food, a helmet, a single boot.

Opa's home had been a battlefield.

Bridger stood beside Gerrit. "I pray none of the blood came from the home's inhabitants."

Gerrit nodded his agreement because his throat felt too tight for words. He headed for the stairs and switched off the light. Above, the ground floor was abandoned, and he had to climb only a few steps up to the next level before he could see stars because the roof was gone. Still, he carried on by moonlight until he reached Ingrid's room. Spent casings littered the floor before the window, and the furniture was all overturned and broken. Curious, Gerrit bent to feel along the floorboards until he found a hole where the loose board had been pulled away. He reached inside to discover bits of burned wood, then the passports and jewelry. Was Ingrid dead? Was that why she hadn't retrieved her most valuable belongings? Or had she simply not had time to fetch them because of the battle or the fires or some other circumstance? The small jewelry box showed a stain, even in the dark, and some of the papers had been damaged by fire or rainwater. He tucked them all into his jacket pocket. If he ever saw her again, he would give them back.

"Did you find anything?" Bridger asked.

"Some of Ingrid's things. Now we just need to find her. The others too."

Ingrid sat around a carved dining table in a house in Velp with Cornelis, Anita, and the home's owner. The De Groot home was modest but cozy, and it had escaped the battle. Like the rest of Velp, it had no electricity and no water. She leaned in so she could hear Cornelis better.

"There might be hundreds of paratroopers in hiding still. I'm at my wit's end trying to find food for them. The chaos with the evacuations helps in some ways, but in other ways, it makes it worse."

Ingrid thought of all the British paratroopers she'd met. Men who had fought and bled for Arnhem. Five currently hid in the De Groot attic two floors above her. "Do you need guides?"

"Maybe, but some of them are wounded and can't be moved. What I really need is a way to buy food."

Anita sighed. "I left Arnhem with nothing but a bag of bandages and the clothes I wore. Our home is gone, and so are any valuables that could buy something on the black market."

"I could try to steal ration cards." Ingrid didn't like stealing and wasn't even sure she'd be any good at it. Nor did she want to cause hardship for whoever lost their ration book. But if it meant the British soldiers who hadn't been able to withdraw wouldn't have to starve, she would risk it.

"It may come to that." Cornelis propped an elbow on the table.

Mevrouw De Groot entered the dining room. "Two men are outside claiming to know Anita and Ingrid."

Anita was nearest the door, so she went with Mevrouw De Groot to verify that the men were friends rather than foes. No one resumed the conversation in her absence. There was no mirth for idle chatter. Liberation had seemed so near, but now they had no freedom, no home, no money. Only a destroyed city, crushed hopes, and an occupying power that had grown even more cruel as September passed into October.

A grin graced Anita's face when she returned, an expression Ingrid hadn't expected. "You'll never guess who's here." Anita held someone's hand, and when she tugged him into the candlelight, Ingrid recognized Luitenant Brug.

Another shadow, not as tall, slipped into the room and came toward her. His stride gave him away before the lighting was good enough to reveal his face: Gerrit. Ingrid stood, and an instant later, Gerrit's arms were around her.

"I was so worried about you!" she mumbled into his neck.

"I was worried about you, too, especially after seeing Opa's home. I didn't mean to leave you on a battlefield."

"How did you find us?" As far as Ingrid knew, Gerrit had never met the De Groots.

"I found Opa at the Velp hospital." Gerrit still hadn't loosened his hold on her, and she didn't mind at all. "He was easy enough to track down."

He told her about what he'd seen in Nijmegen. She told him what she'd seen in Arnhem. Across the table, Cornelis, Anita, and Luitenant Brug had much the same conversation.

"Are you back to stay?" Ingrid asked.

Gerrit shook his head. "We're trying to find any paratroopers who need a way back. Thirty Corps won't make it all the way to Arnhem. They're barely holding where they are."

Ingrid had seen the failure at the Arnhem bridge. She'd heard the devastating quiet when the guns had finally fallen silent in Oosterbeek. But hearing it from Gerrit, who had been in liberated territory, seemed to seal the painful reality that freedom, so close, still eluded this part of the Netherlands.

"I found a few things for you." Gerrit pulled items from his pocket that Ingrid recognized at once. Karl's mittens, slightly singed, one with a brooch and one with the pearls. Her two passports, one for Ingrid Lang and one for Ingrid Eckerstorfer. A passport for Leopold Eckerstorfer and one for Karl Lang, though her brother's was burned badly enough that not even the picture remained. And then Gerrit handed her the box her father had given her the day he had died, the one with Mama's sapphire-and-diamond earrings. Ingrid fingered them, then pulled the cushion out to verify that the mysterious key she'd noticed a few years ago was still hidden behind the black velvet cushion.

Tears stung her eyes. It wasn't just the value of the jewelry, though she could hardly forget that, especially now, when she'd thought she'd lost everything. These were the only things she had left of her family, from before they'd all been separated. She kissed Gerrit on the cheek in front of everyone. "Thank you for coming back to me. And thank you for bringing me these."

Soon the group made their plans. Gerrit and Luitenant Brug hadn't just brought some of Ingrid's jewelry with them. They'd also brought hope and a way forward. As the group began to break up, Ingrid pulled the pearls that had belonged to her mother from her brother's mitten. She handed them to Cornelis. Now they also had a way to feed all the hidden paratroopers who were too injured to follow Gerrit and Luitenant Brug to the Allied lines.

Rupert knocked on the door of the Dutch home in Velp. He never would have found the address if he hadn't asked for the name of Dr. van der Veen during the evacuation of Arnhem. Before coming, Rupert had searched Abwehr and SD files for information on the Dutch family. Months ago, Daalmans had reported his suspicion that Dr. van der Veen held anti-German sympathies, but the past month had shown that to be true for most of the Dutch population.

Regardless of Dutch perfidy, recent events had proved that the German war machine was still a mighty force, one the Allies wouldn't be defeating anytime soon. Certainly, the German position was vulnerable, with the Allies closing in from the west and the Soviet hordes closing in from the east, but all was not lost. The führer's new weapons now in development would save the Reich. Rupert and the others simply had to buy the führer as much time as they could and extract as many resources as possible to keep the Fatherland supplied, despite its reduced borders. And while he waited for a military victory, he would pursue an old friend.

A woman answered the door. The one with black hair and honey-colored skin whom he'd seen with Ingrid and the doctor. "May I help you?" she asked in Dutch.

Rupert hadn't been in the Netherlands long enough to carry on a complete conversation in Dutch, but he knew a few words. "I'm looking for Ingrid Lang."

Her posture stiffened with what Rupert suspected was fear. "I will check. The home is full of refugees, and it's not ready for visitors. Please, wait here."

Rupert could have insisted on entering the home and searching for Ingrid himself, but the full clotheslines and piles of items in the yard provided evidence that the home was indeed hosting a crowd.

The door opened again, and Ingrid stepped outside. "Leutnant Altbauer, to what do I owe this unexpected visit?" Her voice still spoke the polished German she had learned from educated parents and expensive tutors.

"Please, call me Rupert. I know things have been hard for civilians lately, so I'm here to check on an old friend."

He studied her expression. She was gorgeous, but a defeated air hung about her, a mix of shattered hopes, exhaustion, and too little to eat. She looked at the ground while he scrutinized her.

"Things have been hard lately. The family that took me in has lost their home. Now we're living with twenty other people, and one of the babies is ill and cries most of the night. Food is scarce, and there are many mouths to feed."

"That's the Allies' fault. They requested the railway workers go on strike, and that led to supply problems." Rupert had found two railway men yesterday and shipped them off to Germany. Didn't the Dutch recognize how merciful the Germans had been to them? Let them spend time in Poland or Ukraine and they'd learn how lucky they were and how wrong it had been to turn against the benevolent German occupation force.

"Hunger is still hunger, regardless of who's to blame." Ingrid's tentative smile seemed forced. "I'm pleased to see that you survived the battle of Arnhem unscathed."

Rupert's feelings about the battle were mixed. So much death. So much destruction. The British paratroopers had fought well, as had the German troops gathered to fight against them, some injured, most from units not at full strength. The determination of the men and the brutal contest that waged over each house, each block, reminded him of Stalingrad, though it hadn't lasted nearly as long. "Yes, I am fortunate."

"Will they allow civilians back to their homes?"

"Not at present."

"I see." The forced smile disappeared. "Perhaps in a few weeks?"

"I'm not in charge of those decisions. But I have walked the Utrechtseweg. Parts are destroyed. I believe the van der Veen cellar is intact, and most of the ground floor but none of the windows."

"Thank you for checking on our home for us."

He'd searched it for contraband or evidence of treason, not to see if Ingrid and her friends would be able to return, but she didn't need to know that. He looked at the home where she now lived. Compared to the van der Veen home in Arnhem, it was small. Compared to Falcon Point Manor, it was teeny.

"I am fortunate enough to have my own quarters. Men with higher rank than I have taken all the more luxurious suites, but my room is serviceable and not quite so crowded as this home is, I imagine. And food is adequate. You are welcome to come stay as my guest."

Her eyes widened in surprise, and her cheeks flushed a lovely shade of pink. "I'm not sure that would be proper, Rupert."

He hadn't really thought she would accept. Maybe if the food situation grew worse and her desperation grew larger. Or maybe not, because the Langs were a religious family, and Rupert might have invited Ingrid to stay as a guest, but had she agreed, he would have wanted more than friendship from her. He wouldn't be the only soldier in the German Army to take a foreign mistress for the length of his assignment. Some of the men left their women when they moved to a new location, but if Ingrid became his, he didn't plan on letting her go. "In normal times, no, but the situation lately is far from normal. I could ensure your needs were met and offer you protection."

"Your offer is kind, but the van der Veens are like family to me. Propriety and gratitude will keep me with them, at least for now."

He'd been foolish to invite her into a relationship so brazen without more of a lead-up. Before the war, he wouldn't have suggested it at all. But during a battle . . . entire cities could be destroyed in a matter of days. Surely that meant normal rules didn't apply, especially not when he offered her security and she'd invaded his thoughts day and night since the evacuation of Arnhem. He gathered up his disappointment and tucked it away. There would be another day, another invitation. Eventually, the response would be different. "I understand. Perhaps I can call on you again?"

She didn't answer right away, and that hesitation was almost an answer in itself. "I appreciate the gesture, Rupert, but I wouldn't want to distract you from your duties, and with all of us crammed in this small home, there simply isn't anywhere for me to host you, and—"

"Your thoughtfulness is appreciated." He interrupted her before she could give him a more definitive no. "I will keep future visits brief. And I'll not expect you to welcome me into your host's home. Until then, I wish you well."

"I think you can take your finger off the trigger now." Lieutenant Bridger kept his voice a whisper, but Gerrit understood well enough. He even complied, slipping his finger off the trigger of the Colt .45 pistol he'd borrowed from the American, but he wasn't able to release his unease at a German soldier coming to question Ingrid quite so easily.

Lieutenant Bridger told the seven paratroopers hiding in the attic that the German officer was leaving, and most of the men visibly relaxed. One kept his eye next to a crack in the boards, probably watching the street where the German leutnant had gone. Another polished his rifle, though Gerrit didn't imagine it had become fouled in any way since the man had last cleaned it an hour ago.

"I don't like it," Gerrit said.

"I don't either." Bridger nodded at the window. "His stride is off. Right leg. That's the weak spot if you find yourself closer to him."

Gerrit wouldn't forget the man's face, not after pointing a pistol at it for an entire conversation. Weakness in the right leg. He wouldn't forget that either. "I'll go ask what happened." He handed the weapon back to Lieutenant Bridger and pushed out the attic stairs.

The floor below was occupied by four families who had been forced from their homes in Arnhem, either when their homes had become part of the battle or when the Germans had evicted them. A baby whimpered somewhere, and a little boy sat outside one of the rooms, his knees pulled up and his arms wrapped around them.

Gerrit crouched next to the boy. "Are you all right?"

"I don't know where Peper is."

"Who is Peper?"

"My dog." The boy sniffed.

Gerrit hadn't had a chance to ask about Anjing. Opa's Keeshond was probably missing too. "Dogs are clever. He's just gone somewhere safe, and when you go back home, he'll find you again."

"We don't have a home anymore."

"I lost my home too. But I stayed with an uncle, then with an aunt. It's been a grand adventure." *Grand adventure* made it sound as though Gerrit had enjoyed the war, and that was most certainly not true. But maybe the boy was young enough to be excited about the prospects of something new.

"My aunt and uncle lost their home too. I don't know who we'll stay with."

"Your mam will figure it out."

"And then will we have enough to eat?"

Gerrit nodded, though he hadn't any right to make a promise like that. He left the boy and went to the crowded parlor, where he found Ingrid and Anita.

"What did he want?" Gerrit asked when he reached them.

"I know him, from before the war. He's the one I saw that day when we were tailing . . ." Ingrid looked around. "He saw me when we were leaving Arnhem, and he acted like we were old friends. Maybe we were, before we ended up on different sides of the war. Now I think . . ." Ingrid swallowed and looked away. "I think he's trying to court me."

Gerrit had been worried about Ingrid before, when he'd assumed the soldier was suspicious of something he'd seen or heard. Fear that she would be arrested was bad, but knowing she was being pursued by the enemy for romantic reasons was hardly better. "Well, did you tell him you aren't interested?"

"I wasn't quite so blunt. I didn't want to make him angry." She bit her lip. "I think he might come back."

"Then, you have to leave." Gerrit wasn't sure where she would go, but just about any location would be an improvement if it meant getting her away.

She shook her head. "If I'm not here, he might search the home." She glanced at the ceiling, where paratroopers were hiding two floors up.

Gerrit folded his arms. Ingrid couldn't stay here. But before she left, the men in the attic had to be moved. Then the refugees ought to be all right if a lovesick German officer searched the home for a missing woman. "I'll work on a plan for tonight. Then you can leave tomorrow. We have family in Utrecht and Rotterdam and Haarlem. I can help you get there."

Ingrid looked to Anita, then back at Gerrit. "We're not running away just because Rupert Altbauer wants to take me on a stroll along a canal. If he suspected me of subversion, that would be something else entirely, but he's not going to arrest me for refusing to kiss him."

Gerrit supposed jealousy was what caused the burning sensation in his chest, so strong he wanted to go after the man and smash his snub nose. Naming the feeling didn't make it abate. "You will refuse him, won't you?"

Ingrid looked amused, and so did Anita. Ingrid put her hand on Gerrit's arm. "I have no plans to kiss him, no matter how persistent he is, unless it's going to result in an intelligence coup of some significance. I won't kiss him for fun, I can promise you that."

"He might want more than a kiss before he tells you any secrets." Gerrit tried to keep his voice level, but he growled as much as spoke.

"He won't get more. It's doubtful he'll even get a kiss. He doesn't strike me as careless with his information."

"German soldiers don't always ask."

One of Ingrid's hands trembled ever so slightly. "The boy I knew before the war wouldn't do something like that."

"What about the man who's been at war for five years?" Something in her posture told Gerrit that she didn't completely trust that the boy from before the war hadn't changed.

Anita inhaled sharply before Ingrid could answer. "He's coming back."

"Rupert?" Ingrid looked out the window.

Gerrit wanted to look out the window, too, but it was better if he remained unseen.

At the rap on the door, all conversation in the parlor ceased. Ingrid blew out a long breath, straightened her dress, and went to the door. Gerrit followed, staying out of sight but close enough to intervene if needed.

Ingrid opened the door and stepped outside. Gerrit would have preferred she stay in the doorway, where he could hear the conversation, but he understood why Ingrid had left. The Germans had reason to arrest half the people in the house. He glanced at Anita, who watched through the window.

"They're just talking," Anita told him. "He handed her something wrapped in paper."

The man had been gone only a few minutes, and now he was returning with a gift? Gerrit didn't like it. Not one bit.

It seemed like a long time until Ingrid came back inside, but the grandfather clock down the hall from the door said it had been only five minutes. Five minutes of torture. Ingrid didn't seem overly upset.

"What did he want?" Gerrit asked.

Ingrid looked at the object in her hands and unwrapped the paper to reveal a loaf of bread. Not the kind civilians ate. The high-quality kind only Germans could buy nowadays. "I mentioned that food was hard to come by, so he brought me this."

Gerrit studied Ingrid's face, but he couldn't read it. He followed her into the kitchen. "What if he's using romance as a cover to investigate?"

"It's possible." Ingrid put the bread on the counter and frowned.

Anita, too, had come into the small kitchen. "Even if he's not investigating you now, if he spends enough time around you, something is bound to make him suspicious."

Ingrid nodded. "So, what do I do?"

"You leave."

Ingrid shook her head at Gerrit's suggestion. "We already talked about that. If I provoke a search, everyone else will suffer."

Anita looked at the ceiling. "Let's talk to Henry."

They gathered in the attic: Gerrit, Ingrid, Anita, Lieutenant Bridger, and seven British paratroopers, but Gerrit doubted they understood much of the Dutch conversation.

Anita explained their dilemma, and hearing everything again made the danger seem even worse.

"We could eliminate him." Gerrit didn't want to target anyone ever again, but if Ingrid's safety were at stake, he could plan and carry out another hit. This time, he wouldn't fail.

"And the reprisals?" Anita asked.

"I could make it look like an accident."

Ingrid's face grew pale, and she shook her head. "Only as a last resort. I don't want you to have to do that, Gerrit." She took his hand and squeezed it as though she suspected just how much almost killing Daalmans had cost him. "I don't trust Rupert, but he did buy me a train ticket when I needed one, and the bread he brought will be a significant portion of our supper. He's an enemy, but he's not evil."

Gerrit wasn't so sure. Regardless, the man didn't have to be evil to be dangerous. "The more often he comes, the more likely he is to notice something he shouldn't."

"I should leave tonight." Lieutenant Bridger gestured to the British paratroopers. "I'll take these men to the Allied lines. Then there won't be anything for him to find if one of his courting trips leads him inside." He looked at Ingrid. "You should leave, too, as soon as you can."

Anita's face pinched, as if in pain. "Do you know the way?"

Lieutenant Bridger shrugged. "I have a compass and a vague memory of traveling the route twice before. It's safer than staying here. We'll make it."

"Yes, because I'll take you." Gerrit didn't want to leave again so soon, but the paratroopers needed to be taken to safety. The men in this attic, and the others hiding a few houses down. Cornelis had been gathering them for days. Gerrit looked at Ingrid. "But you'll move on, won't you? To a home where he can't find you?"

Ingrid nodded. "Yes, as soon as we can find someplace."

"I'll explain the problem to Pap." Anita folded her arms, and sadness touched her lips. "He's attending a woman in labor, but I imagine the baby will be born before morning. He knows enough people, even in Velp, that he can probably find us a new place by morning."

Ingrid glanced at the men in hiding. "I'll go to the kitchen to see if they can spare anything for your journey." She climbed down the stairs, and Gerrit followed her, but not before he saw Lieutenant Bridger take Anita's hand.

"You just came back," Anita whispered.

Bridger looked at their intertwined hands. "I know. But what if I come back again, when the war is over? I don't want this to be our last goodbye."

Gerrit stepped down from the attic to give them their privacy, or as much privacy as they could have in an attic full of British soldiers. That was another reason for Gerrit to leave with Lieutenant Bridger and the paratroopers tonight. With Gerrit as guide, they would have a better chance of reaching the safety of American lines. And maybe if that happened, Lieutenant Bridger could keep his promise to Anita.

CHAPTER 23

Gerrit clung to Ingrid for a long time when he embraced her goodbye late that night.

"Are you coming back?" she asked.

"It depends on orders. The queen's son-in-law is in charge of all resistance forces now. Prince Bernhard might organize us into regular units. Or he might want a steady supply of information on the Germans from behind the lines. Or he might not care about what someone like me does."

"I care what someone like you does. Whatever your orders, be careful."

"You too." He relaxed his arms and gave her a brief kiss goodbye. "Stick to the plan. Leave in the morning, before Altbauer can visit you again."

Ingrid nodded. "Opa said the woman who just had a baby will take in a few refugees if we help with her other children."

Gerrit reached into his pocket. "I almost forgot." He handed Ingrid the toy dog he'd made by cutting pieces of a tin can and melting them together, then turning the edges so they weren't sharp. "There's a little boy upstairs with a sick baby sister and a missing dog. I made him this. But I imagine he went to bed a long time ago. Will you see that he gets it?"

Ingrid held the toy gently. "I love your soft spot for children."

"It's not as big as my soft spot for you." He kissed her again but not for very long because one of the paratroopers cleared his throat.

Gerrit wished the men would have taken a little longer to make their way from the attic to the home's back door. Regardless, they had jumped out of an airplane to help liberate his country, and they'd fought a hard battle. He would forgive them for interrupting his kiss with Ingrid, and he would do his best to see them to safety.

Ingrid put the tin dog on a nearby table. "I'll go outside to see if everything looks clear. If it is, I'll bring the others here."

Ingrid slipped away, and Gerrit checked each of the men. They wore civilian clothing, other than three pairs of ammo boots. Gerrit planned to keep them out of sight completely, but he also wanted them aware of any liabilities, like those that came with distinctive footwear. If stopped, those in British boots with the laces threaded in a ladder pattern needed to stay in the back of the group. Ingrid could translate when she returned, but Lieutenant Bridger might be a better choice. He was an officer, and the paras hadn't caught him kissing anyone.

Where had Bridger gone?

Gerrit motioned for the men to stay where they were and went back down the home's now-quiet hallway. He peeked into the kitchen and found Bridger and Anita saying their goodbyes with their arms wrapped around each other and mouths pressed together. Gerrit backed away as silently as possible. A smile he couldn't help pulled at his mouth. Hopefully, the paras wouldn't write off both guides as unprofessional on account of their amorous goodbyes.

Gerrit waited with the British paratroopers for Ingrid to return and for Bridger and Anita to finish. He preferred not to rush either since Ingrid would use the time to gain useful information, and Lieutenant Bridger and Gerrit's aunt were unlikely to see each other again until after the war. And since September, the end of the war hadn't seemed nearly as close as it had all summer.

"Where are you from?" one of the British soldiers asked. His Dutch was off, but Gerrit could understand the words.

"All over. A farm in Gelderland. Rotterdam. Utrecht. Arnhem." He hadn't lived in Arnhem long. Just long enough to come to know it, then see it destroyed. He hoped those memories of his boyhood spent living with his paternal grandparents on a farm would help him lead the men to safety. Since the man spoke a little Dutch, Gerrit had him tell those with ammo boots to hide their feet if they were stopped.

Ingrid slipped back inside. "I couldn't see anything suspicious. The other men are waiting outside. Nine of them." She looked around. "Where is Luitenant Brug?"

"Saying goodbye to Anita. I thought it best not to interrupt."

The couple must have been listening for the door, because Bridger and Anita joined the group soon after that. After a few final goodbyes, Gerrit stepped into the night to lead sixteen men home.

Bicycles would have made the trip to Allied lines easier, but Gerrit didn't have any way of getting that many working bicycles, not even with Cornelis's help. The first night, he led the group to a burned-down farm. They hid the next day, half of the men in the cellar, half in the empty chicken coop. The Germans had burned the home to the ground after finding onderduikers hiding there, but that had been months ago. Gerrit didn't think they patrolled the ruins, and Cornelis had said it was safe when he'd met them with rations.

The next night, they made it to the Waal. Gerrit felt along a tree until his fingers brushed an iron spike that had been driven into the trunk as a signal for members of the resistance. Very little of it protruded, and that meant whoever had hammered the spike into the tree had seen German soldiers patrolling the nearest road.

"There's a patrol," he told Bridger.

Their group was large enough to fight off a normal-sized patrol, but most of the men weren't armed, Gerrit included. And if the German patrol were larger than expected, or if the Germans called for reinforcements, not everyone would make it across the river tonight. With only two canoes to work with, they needed enough time to make several crossings without being discovered.

Bridger gave soft orders, and two pairs of men headed in opposite directions, monitoring the road from farther away. The rest of them waited in the darkness. Three distinct taps of what Gerrit guessed were two sticks sounded from one direction, then from the other. Bridger motioned everyone forward, and one by one, everyone crossed the road. The men who had been sent on reconnaissance returned, and Gerrit led them through the sparse brush to the river.

The bank ended in a steep decline into the water. "Have everyone stay down," Gerrit said. If the men all crouched or lay in the grass and bushes, they would be invisible to German patrolmen. Gerrit slid to the water's edge and searched for the canoes as water seeped into his shoes. Cornelis had told him where to look, but it still took ten minutes to find them both. Each could carry four men at a time. Gerrit went back to the group and motioned for them to follow.

The bank rose steeply behind them, which would help shield them from view. Gerrit was glad they would cross the Waal at night, not in daylight, like the 82nd Airborne had.

Lieutenant Bridger organized the passengers. In one boat, he put two wounded men, then motioned Gerrit over. "Can you go over with them and row it back?"

Gerrit nodded and climbed inside. Bridger had apparently questioned the British paras to see which of them had rowing experience, and the fourth man in Gerrit's canoe handled the oars well. Gerrit was glad for that because he had the feeling he would be rowing back and forth across the Waal River more than once that night.

As they rowed, he figured out how many crossings it would take with four men going over, and one man coming back each time. Three trips should do it, but given the number of men with injuries, Gerrit would probably need to row across the river five times.

The canoe hit shore, the men disembarked, and the one without a wound helped turn the canoe around for Gerrit to take it back. The other canoe reached shore before Gerrit had taken more than three strokes.

Across the river he went again, and again, and again. His arms were sore by the time he made it back to pick up the last of the men. The other canoe had fallen behind, and he couldn't see it, but based on when he'd passed them last, he guessed they were near the other shore.

Bridger had his pistol out when one of the paras helped Gerrit angle the canoe along the shore. He met Gerrit's eyes and put a finger to his mouth. Gerrit listened. Dogs. Several of them, and their barking was growing closer.

Gerrit sprang from the canoe and motioned for the remaining three paratroopers to climb inside.

He stepped next to Bridger. "How long ago did you hear them?"

"Maybe five minutes."

Gerrit quickly formed a plan. "You go. I'll distract them. Have the other canoe turn around mid-river."

Bridger stared at him. "I'm not leaving you behind for the Nazis."

"Yes, you are, because my arms are too tired to row that canoe out of range before they get here, but you'll manage. And the para rowing back this way will understand you when you tell him to turn around. I'm worried about Ingrid. It's better for me to draw them away and go back to my family. Once you cross the river, you'll run into an American sentry soon enough."

Bridger still hesitated, so Gerrit added one final phrase. "We don't have time to argue."

Bridger handed Gerrit his pistol and went for the canoe.

Gerrit ran downriver. He might not be able to outrun the dogs, but he could outrun the men handling them, even with wet shoes. And if they released the dogs, Bridger's pistol would take care of that problem. He didn't bother trying to be quiet. The whole point was for the patrol to notice and chase him instead of the other men. Strands of grass whipped his legs, and his lungs burned. The dogs were getting closer. When he glanced over his shoulder, one was in view. He paused, turned, and fired.

Poor dog. Gerrit hadn't wanted to hurt it, but the alternative was even more unpalatable. The other hounds weren't far behind. He might have enough bullets if he didn't miss and if he were quick enough, but he spotted a log and thought of a better escape. He put his pistol in his jacket pocket. Then he pushed the log into the Waal and followed it into the water, where the current would pull the log—and Gerrit—away from the enemy. The dogs continued barking, but in the dark, the patrol wouldn't be able to see Gerrit's head hovering at the waterline, with the log between him and the shore. Beams of light from the men's flashlights illuminated the river, but no one spotted the bedraggled man clinging to the log.

Gradually, the barking grew more and more distant. When everything from his toes to the tips of his ears was numb with cold, Gerrit swam to shore and headed back to the safe house.

He spent the night soaking wet and shivering. He hid the next day, and on the second night, he headed out, arriving at the village where Opa and the others had been when Gerrit had last seen them. He knocked on the back door, fervently hoping Ingrid was no longer there but also hoping she'd left a clue as to how to find her.

A woman he didn't recognize opened the door. "May I help you?"

"My opa stayed here a few days ago. Dr. van der Veen. Is he still here?"

She motioned for him to come inside. "No. He moved on, but you best get off the streets, or they'll round you up for work detail."

"Do you know where he went?"

The woman shook her head. "No, but the hospital will know."

"And my aunt and cousin? They came with him."

"All moved on, I'm afraid."

Gerrit resigned himself to another day of hiding.

The little boy Gerrit had made the tin dog for came into the kitchen holding his new toy. He smiled in recognition. "Thank you for making me a new dog!"

Gerrit doubted a tin dog could replace a pet. He just hoped the boy's real dog hadn't met the same fate as the hound that had almost caught Gerrit at the river. Regardless, Gerrit spent the next several hours fashioning a second tin dog to go with the first. In the afternoon, he held the boy's sick sister while the mother went to the hospital with a message for Opa.

When she came back, she handed Gerrit a small slip of paper. "I suppose it's a shopping list, but I'd be surprised if you could find even a quarter of the items, especially now that all the railroad workers are on strike." Some of her brunette hair had escaped her bun, and she tucked it behind her ear. "You shouldn't be going outside at all with the way the Germans have been acting. You'll end up in a truck heading to Germany, just like my husband."

"I'm sorry they took your husband. They took my father and my uncle too." Gerrit examined the list. Opa's handwriting. "It's just a challenge." Gerrit made something up. "Points if I can find any of the items."

The woman looked unconvinced. "Well, don't go looking for them when the Germans might get you."

Gerrit borrowed a pencil and went to the attic to work out the A and B forms of each letter. He hadn't thought Opa knew how they encoded messages for the resistance, but he recognized the variances. Subtle but clear. What else did Opa know and pretend not to notice? Gerrit turned each letter into dots and dashes, and a street and house number emerged. He could remember that well enough, so he slipped the paper into the fire when the lady of the home lit a burner to prepare supper.

Only when it was fully dark did Gerrit thank his hosts and venture outside. Thirty minutes later, he knocked on another door, and Anita pulled him inside.

"We hadn't any idea when we might see you again." She gave him a hug. "Did everything go all right with . . . well, with your assignment?"

"I took them as far as the Waal. It should have been easy from there, but I was too busy creating a distraction to see if they were pursued."

Ingrid came through the hallway and embraced him tightly. He held her in return, glad he'd sent Bridger on and had come back himself so he could know she was well.

"I'm glad you're safe," she said.

"And I'm glad you've moved to where German intelligence officers can't track you down."

Anita and Ingrid looked at him with sober faces, but neither spoke.

"You did get away from him, didn't you?" he asked.

Ingrid shook her head. "He called on me again this morning. I don't think he suspects we were running from him—I mentioned how crowded the previous home was. I said there was more room here, and that seemed to explain it, even if it's not true."

Gerrit's mouth went dry. Altbauer was persistent. "How did he find you?"

Ingrid shrugged. "He may have simply asked around. I haven't been strolling along the street for leisure, but Cornelis had a few things for me to do. It wouldn't have been hard for someone to spot me."

"What did he want?" Gerrit asked.

"He brought food again. And spoke with me in the garden for a while."

"What about?"

"The weather. His frustration with the rail strike. His mother and stepfather died in an air strike. His sister survived only because they sheltered her with their bodies. His uncle hired a nanny to tend her. He told me about that."

Gerrit hoped romance was the only thing Altbauer was interested in and that none of his visits had been tests to see if Ingrid knew something she shouldn't because of resistance work. Now that he was back, Gerrit would do his best to protect her. In the meantime, he had a question for his aunt. "How long has Opa known how to use your code?"

Anita's forehead furrowed in surprise. "He doesn't."

"He does. He's the one who gave me the address."

Anita frowned. "Well, I suppose he's had adequate time to see my reports. He must have figured it out on his own." A small laugh escaped her lips. "I haven't any idea how long he's known."

After a small meal—half of it courtesy of Leutnant Altbauer—they retired to a single room. Anita and Ingrid shared the bed, and a cot had been set up for Opa. As Gerrit lay on a blanket on the floor, trying to fall asleep, he focused on their largest problem: Rupert Altbauer was going to cause trouble for them. Even if the German wasn't suspicious, his presence was dangerous. If he was any good at his job, he would discover something amiss eventually, unless Gerrit found a way to stop him.

CHAPTER 24

Ingrid forced a smile when Rupert called on her the next day. She didn't want to anger him or make him suspicious, but nor did she want to encourage his attentions. If he sincerely wanted a relationship with her—friendship or courtship—he ought to recognize how unbalanced their positions were. He held all the power, so any agreement from her could easily be from coercion instead of genuine acceptance.

"How is the new home suiting you?" He wore his uniform and had several parcels tucked under his arm.

"Well, thank you." She didn't want him to stay long, so she kept her remarks brief.

He handed the parcels to her. "For you. More bread. And cheese and sausage."

Cheese, sausage, and more of the expensive bread. Ingrid swallowed to keep her mouth from watering. Food from the enemy. It might be ethically questionable, but everyone was hungry. "Thank you. This will make a big difference."

"May I escort you on a walk?"

Strolling with a German soldier along the main street of the village would make all her neighbors suspect she was a Nazi. She cringed to be thought a traitor. When Berend questioned her loyalty, it had not only hurt her pride but had also hinted at punishment and revenge. She didn't want to be an outcast among the Dutch who were loyal to their queen. But appearing to befriend the enemy could also lead to opportunities. Dutch Nazis might confide in her. Gerrit, Anita, Opa, and Cornelis would know where her loyalties really lay. For now, their opinions were the only ones that mattered. "Will you allow me to put this away first?"

Rupert nodded. "Of course."

Ingrid slipped inside. Gerrit waited just around the corner to the home's entry. She handed him the food. "He wants to take me on a walk."

Gerrit's face hardened. "And you think that's wise?"

"The more we know about how German intelligence works, the easier we can defeat it."

Gerrit didn't like the idea, she could tell. "Fine. I'll follow from a distance."

Alarm flared in Ingrid's chest. "No, you won't. He'll see you, maybe arrest you, and I want you right here waiting for me when I come back. I'm not bringing my coat, so I'll complain of the cold before we go too far, and then I'll be back." She stood on her toes and kissed Gerrit gently on the mouth. He didn't seem to mind. "I'll come back to you, and you'll be waiting. Agreed?"

His resistance seemed to have shattered with her kiss. He nodded. "Watch your words. He's trained to glean information. And be careful where you go. The law will be on his side, no matter what he does."

"I'll be careful." She squeezed Gerrit's hand and turned back to the door. When she was younger, she'd had a friend whose oldest sister was courted by two men at once. Way back then, it had seemed so dreamy to be pursued by two suitors instead of one. But it wasn't dreamy, not at all. When one of the men held her heart and the other held the power to throw her and everyone she cared about into prison, it was a nightmare.

She pasted a smile on her face and stepped outside.

Rupert offered her his arm. "Do you know the neighborhood well?"

"No. I've mostly been inside caring for children."

"I'll have to come by more often to ensure you make it outside regularly."

Ingrid tried to keep her expression unchanged. They'd spoken only a few lines, and he'd already turned her words against her.

Rupert looked her over. "Ingrid Lang, becoming a nanny. I wouldn't have expected that."

She wasn't sure if surprise or satisfaction was his dominant emotion. She considered her words to make sure they didn't reveal more than they ought to before speaking. "It's only temporary. But I like children, and I'm happy to help."

"I like children too." His face grew sober. "I miss my sister. She was like sunshine. And my time fighting in the east was like those short gray days in early January. I needed sunshine again. I worry about how she's doing now."

Ingrid patted his arm in sympathy. She wouldn't forget that he was the enemy. But he was also a man who missed his family, a man who had suffered losses. She understood. She had the hope of seeing Karl and Anna again, but the four and a half years since she'd last seen her siblings had brought its share of longing and grief. Its share of gray, sunless stretches. "War is hard on families, isn't it?"

He nodded. "That's the one thing I sometimes regret."

"That you had to leave your family?"

"That too, I suppose. My mother was finally happy for the first time that I could remember. My stepfather was a good man. Like your papa. Or . . ." Rupert trailed off, perhaps remembering that her father was dead. Or remembering that her father had refused to serve the Reich. "Anyway, he treated her well. I was happy to fight to protect them. Protect the entire Fatherland, of course, but I wouldn't love the Fatherland half so much if I didn't love the people inside it."

Ingrid glanced at the canal. "So you don't regret leaving?"

"No."

"Then before, what did you mean about regret?"

Rupert joined her study of the canal water. "Sometimes I see that same dynamic with my work—couples who are devoted to each other, like my mama and stepfather. Misguided, too, if I've been assigned to question them. But that doesn't mean they love each other any less."

"What do you do when that happens?" Ingrid wasn't sure she wanted to know the answer, but she wanted to keep him talking about his work.

Rupert straightened his shoulders. "My duty, of course. I convince them to cooperate with me, and when they do, I can keep the consequences reasonable."

"And when they don't?"

Rupert shrugged. "Then, it's regrettable. But the good of the Reich must come first."

Ingrid didn't reply. The silence felt heavy and awkward, but she kept her mouth shut rather than filling it. She didn't want to merely react to each phrase he said. She wanted to plan.

"You could return to the Reich, you know. My uncle has been away, doing his duty for the Fatherland, but he has ensured your family's estate is taken care of."

Curiosity about what had become of her home mingled with anger at Wilhelm Sauermann: Rupert's uncle and her father's killer. "Have you been to Falcon Point since the war started?"

"No. I've had few opportunities for leave, other than my convalescence after Stalingrad. It wouldn't have felt right to visit with your family gone and my uncle away with pressing military matters."

Rupert's beloved uncle would have an unpleasant surprise when the war ended: justice. Ingrid intended that he face it. "What type of work is your uncle doing?"

"He hasn't told me details. Intelligence work, I believe."

She almost replied, "Like you," but she wasn't supposed to know that much about Rupert's work. "And you?" she said instead.

"Whatever is needed. Mostly putting puzzles together."

"What type of puzzles?"

He seemed pleased with her interest but wary about saying too much. "Human actions. Trying to figure out why and how and who. All in defense of the Fatherland."

The Fatherland hadn't had any reason to defend itself from the Dutch. Until the Nazis had started a war, the Netherlands had been neutral. The injustice rankled, but she suppressed it. "Tell me about a typical day."

"It varies. I won't bore you with details. But you look cold. Let me get you something." He gestured toward one of the town's main roads. Several restaurants lined the street. None of the locals could eat there anymore. Only the occupiers and those collaborating with them.

Ingrid wasn't a collaborator, but Rupert was a source. One giving her only crumbs of information, but maybe if he relaxed over a meal, he would share more. She smiled. "Something warm to drink would be wonderful, thank you."

He took her to a small café and ordered coffee and rolls. Ingrid doubted it would be real coffee, but she was accustomed to the local substitutes. As long as it was warm, the ersatz version—this one, when it arrived, made from acorns—was palatable. Rupert remained courteous, but whenever Ingrid tried to steer the conversation to his work, he moved it a different direction. Did he suspect that her interest wasn't casual? She was halfway through her coffee substitute when another German soldier entered the café, approached their table, and saluted.

Rupert gave her an apologetic smile before turning to the man. "What it is, Jung?"

Jung leaned next to Rupert's ear and whispered, but not so softly that Ingrid couldn't hear. "We found someone at that suspected safe house south of Arnhem. The one with the broken-down chicken coop. He left a package for a contact to retrieve tonight."

Rupert nodded. "You know what to do. I'll meet you back at headquarters within the hour."

Ingrid stared at her coffee, pretending she hadn't heard. Inside, a chill that a warm drink couldn't cure twisted around her stomach. There were a lot of farmhouses with broken-down chicken coops to the south of Arnhem, but she suspected they spoke of the one she'd often traveled to while leading onderduikers around or passing on intelligence. If someone had been arrested there, it was probably one of her associates, one of her friends. Someone who knew who she was and what she did.

Gerrit had spent nearly all of Ingrid's absence in a nervous bout of pacing, much to the consternation of Mevrouw Bakker, the home's owner. Either she didn't approve of Ingrid's outing with a German soldier, or she didn't approve of Gerrit's clear attachment to Ingrid, or she simply craved stillness. Gerrit had tried to hold still. He had lasted only a minute or two before the worry had eaten at him again. When the front door opened and Ingrid came inside, her mask of calm fell away to reveal panic.

"What's wrong?" Gerrit asked.

Ingrid glanced at Mevrouw Bakker, then toward the stairs. "I need to speak with Anita."

Gerrit followed her up the stairs to their room. Anita sat on the bed, reading a storybook to one of the Bakker children. She looked up when they entered and seemed to sense something was wrong. She began summarizing the final pages of the story rather than reading them, then took the little girl into her own room for a nap.

Ingrid had seemed reluctant to speak in front of the child, but Gerrit's curiosity burned. "Did Altbauer hurt you?"

"No. But he's setting a trap for someone. I know where but not who or exactly when." Something about her posture made her seem fragile. Gerrit put a hand on her arm, and she stepped toward him, letting him pull her into an embrace. He wanted to offer her more than comfort, wanted to promise that they could foil the trap, promise that the war would be over soon and then they'd be free. Reality meant he could offer nothing but his presence.

Anita opened the door quietly and slid inside. "What's wrong?"

"Rupert took me to a café. While we were there, one of his men came in. Said they caught someone at the safe house south of Arnhem with the broken-down chicken coop and that their prisoner left a package for someone to pick up. They're setting a trap."

Anita pulled her coat on. "Cornelis might know who's involved. He can warn them. I'll call him from the hospital telephone."

Ingrid relaxed for a moment, then tensed again. "Whoever they caught might be a friend."

Anita nodded. "Maybe Cornelis will know who is missing. I hope it's not him."

Gerrit hoped so too. Cornelis knew the names of every resistance fighter in multiple cells. If he were caught, it would be a disaster. But there was another problem neither of the women had yet mentioned. "If we warn whoever was meant to pick up the dead drop, and they don't show, Altbauer might suspect that Ingrid was the leak."

Ingrid pulled back from Gerrit's chest. "They whispered, so they don't know I heard them. And anyway, danger or not, we have to try warning them."

"I'm not saying we shouldn't, but nor should we forget that sounding the alarm increases your risk."

Ingrid nodded. "We need to be ready to dive under, even though it's so much harder now. Opa might not agree to it."

"Not for himself," Anita said. "He'll keep working as long as he has patients and is free. But he'll understand if we need to."

Gerrit looked around the room. With four of them sharing the small space, it was far from tidy. But none of them had many items. They could pack in minutes. Or they could pull on an extra layer of clothes, tuck the most important things in their pockets, and walk away.

Anita buttoned her coat. "I have a phone call to make."

Disappointment was stalking Rupert. Yesterday's arrest should have yielded better results. Jung had quickly extracted key information, including a list of addresses, from the prisoner, yet no one had come to retrieve the explosives left at the dead drop. Rupert and Jung followed up on the addresses, but all of the homes had been destroyed or evacuated. No one lived in any of them anymore.

But the man had been arrested at a home owned by Christiaan van der Veen, a name that caught Rupert's attention because it was the same man Ingrid had taken refuge with. Did the van der Veens have a connection with the resistance? Unless the family had moved from the modest home where Rupert had last visited Ingrid, he could arrest them all.

Did he want to arrest Ingrid?

No. He wanted her as a romantic conquest, not as a suspected member of the resistance, sitting in the cells of one of the local prisons.

Ingrid might have heard Jung reporting on the safe house. But Jung had said so little. Not enough for anyone to know which home they'd been talking about. Any number of factors might have scared off whoever was supposed to pick up the explosives. Someone might have noticed the arrest or been scared away by the men Jung had hidden around the grounds. The prisoner might have lied. Maybe the items weren't to be picked up until today or tomorrow.

Which was more likely? That a prisoner had lied during the initial hours of his interrogation or that the woman Rupert was courting had understood far more than was spoken in a café and had somehow figured out who to warn? Rupert shook his head. Ingrid was intelligent—he liked that about her, had liked it about the rest of the family, too, until her father and brother had proved themselves traitors—but she couldn't pull information from thin air, and the two of them were destined to be together, so she wouldn't work against him. He gathered his greatcoat and hat. It was time to visit the prison.

When Rupert arrived, he requested that the prisoner be brought to a room for interrogation. While he waited, Rupert looked over Jung's notes. The man went by Willem, but his real name was Augustijn Hoekstra. His father had been a prominent businessman with a few forays into politics. Taken as a hostage. Executed as part of a reprisal. That execution had sent the son on a quest for revenge. War was, after all, hard on families.

Two guards brought Hoekstra into the room. He seemed a perfectly ordinary middle-aged man. No bruises marred his face. Surprising. Denhart had taught Rupert that the right questions were often more useful than physical barrages. Rupert had followed Denhart's advice, partially because it was effective, partially because he'd long ago sworn he would never batter people the way his father had battered him and his mother. Yet many of those he worked with disagreed with old Abwehr methods, especially when it came to captured members of the resistance.

"You were arrested at a safe house south of Arnhem?" Rupert began.

Hoekstra shook his head. "No. I was arrested in Arnhem, but I believe your man first saw me at the farmhouse and followed. He's to be commended. I didn't see him tailing me."

"And the home in Arnhem? What was it to you?"

Hoekstra shrugged. "Just another home destroyed in the battle."

"How long since you were last inside the home?"

Hoekstra hesitated. He looked away, and one of his feet vibrated. "I hadn't ever been inside before."

Had Hoekstra really never been inside before, there would have been no reason for him to think about the answer before giving it. The man was lying. "What of these other addresses?" He passed over the sheet of addresses Hoekstra had told Jung the day before.

Hoekstra nodded. "I've left information at those places before."

"When was the last time you were at each of them?"

Hoekstra gave dates, but they seemed to form a pattern. Real life wasn't so neat and tidy. He was making it up, naming abandoned homes and pulling precise dates to match, all of them from before the failed British attack.

"And the van der Veen home? When was the last time you were there?"

"I already told you, I hadn't been inside until yesterday. That's just where I happened to be arrested."

"But you knew the owner?" Rupert hadn't told Hoekstra that the van der Veens owned the home where he'd been arrested. Hoekstra had known that himself and forgotten to hide it.

The man's face went pale. "Most people know that house. A doctor used to live there. I have an old wound that's been acting up. I was seeking medical care."

Rupert turned that over in his mind. It seemed Dr. van der Veen had treated members of the resistance. Had he known who they were when he'd cleaned and stitched their wounds? The battle had already shown that the doctor was willing to treat British paratroopers along with Dutch civilians and German soldiers. It might be against the law to care for criminals, but Rupert had a hard time condemning a doctor for giving the best care he could to anyone who asked for it. Still, the doctor ought to report suspicious patients to the authorities. Rupert would remind the doctor of his duty, for Ingrid's sake, but he had better things to do than put a doctor in jail because some of his patients had done something wrong.

Rupert finished his questions and returned to headquarters to evaluate the items taken from the resistance safe house. Jung had mentioned explosives. He had failed to mention the jewelry left with the bombs. The resistance needed money, of course.

Jewelry could be used to buy food on the black market, bribe a guard, or purchase items for sabotage. It wasn't unusual to confiscate money and other valuables when a member of the resistance was arrested. What was unusual was the fact that this set of pearls looked familiar. A triple strand with a golden clasp engraved with the initials *L. L.*, for Liselotte Lang. He'd been with Ingrid when she'd tried to sell it in a Berlin jewelry store.

What was Ingrid's mother's necklace doing in a resistance safe house?

CHAPTER 25

Ingrid wasn't surprised when Rupert called on her again. Gerrit had given her numerous tips on how to show Rupert that she wasn't interested in his attentions. It was good advice, but much of it would depend on the situation, and she felt less and less able to guide their conversations or activities with each of Rupert's visits.

"Good afternoon, Ingrid." Rupert bowed politely. He hadn't brought food today. Maybe that was a good sign, but everyone in the Bakker home would be a little hungrier as a result.

"Good afternoon. How are you today, Rupert?"

"Well enough. Perhaps I could speak with you in private for a few moments?"

Ingrid didn't want to invite him in, so she motioned to the side of the house. "The garden, perhaps?"

Gerrit had fixed Mevrouw Bakker's garden bench the day before. He had fixed all sorts of things in the Bakker house. Loose baseboards, wobbly cupboards, a broken dumbwaiter. Ingrid admired his way of making every place he stayed a little better, and she envied the way he could bury his nerves in work, even when they might be arrested at any moment.

Rupert followed her to the garden bench. Ingrid peeked at a window. Cracked, despite the chilly temperature. She suspected Gerrit's ear was behind the curtain, listening to everything she and Rupert said.

Gerrit didn't need to be jealous. If she hadn't been so frightened of Rupert, she would have found the situation amusing. But there was nothing amusing about the possibility of arrest and execution.

"Ingrid," Rupert began. "The doctor who took you in. How well do you know him?"

What did she know about Dr. van der Veen, her surrogate opa? He worked harder when he was worried, when he was grieving, or when there was a need. His kindness was deep, his heart was large, and his grief over the war and all the suffering it had caused was strong enough that she didn't think he would fully recover, even when the war ended. She wouldn't tell Rupert any of those things. "I told you, he and his daughter have become like family to me."

"Do you think he might be mixed up with the resistance?"

Icy tendrils of fear crept across Ingrid's neck. Something had prompted Rupert to ask that question. What did he know? Ingrid forced a smile. "Dr. van der Veen, running around blowing up railway junctions? Nonsense. He is completely absorbed in his medical practice. And as for assassinations—he's a doctor. It's against his oath to hurt anyone. He'd never do that."

"Not everyone in the resistance is a saboteur or an assassin. Has he had strangers come visit him at odd hours, needing treatment?"

Ingrid forced her face to relax. "Medical emergencies don't always happen during normal office hours. Even before the war, he would get telephone calls at all times of the day and night. That only changed when our telephone was destroyed."

"What of people coming to the house after curfew?"

If she denied it completely, it would backfire. No one would believe that in four and a half years of Nazi occupation, not one person had broken curfew to see a doctor. "Rupert, please don't be angry at him. There was a time, but it was only a little after curfew. And you can't blame the mother—her little boy was bleeding so much. Of course she ran over so Dr. van der Veen could stitch up the tear in his arm. You would do the same thing for a child, wouldn't you?"

"What about bullet holes? Men attacked by dogs? Have you seen any of those after curfew?" Rupert was relentless.

Ingrid shook her head. "Anything that serious he would see at the hospital, not at his home." Her statement wasn't entirely true, but it matched Opa's preference. That made the statement not completely untrue either.

"Will you pass on a message for me?"

Ingrid nodded. She couldn't really refuse.

"Remind him that it is his duty to report any suspicious patients."

"I'll remind him." Ingrid forced a smile. Opa had overlooked so many resistance meetings and plans, welcomed so many onderduikers into his home. He wouldn't turn a patient over to the enemy. She knew that. Yet she would warn him that German intelligence had their suspicions. She doubted it would change his actions. Some men, like Opa, followed their own moral compass regardless of what an occupying power decreed.

Rupert nodded. "I was also wondering what you could tell me about this." From his pocket, he pulled the pearl necklace that had been sewn into her coat when she'd fled Falcon Point.

Surprise was so strong that she gasped aloud. She immediately wished she hadn't because now any denial would be pointless. She had given the necklace to Cornelis so he could buy supplies for hidden airborne troops. Had Cornelis been captured? She kept her eyes on the jewelry rather than on Rupert. "My mother had one very much like it. You remember. I tried to sell it at a jewelry store in Berlin, but the owner wouldn't give me a fair price because my parents weren't there."

"Is this the same necklace?"

Ingrid tried the clasp. "I suppose it could be."

"I had a jeweler examine it. He confirmed that the quality is of the highest order. And I recognized the initials on the clasp. Do you want to explain how your jewelry came to be in the possession of a known resistance member?"

Ingrid fingered the pearls. "I don't know. I thought they were lost in all the recent moves, or stolen."

"You think the necklace may have been stolen?"

Ingrid nodded. "We've been moving from place to place. So many people everywhere. I had my jewelry tucked away in a knapsack, but I suppose someone could have dug around and found it. They're bulky enough to be felt even through the sweater I wrapped them in."

"When was the last time you saw them?"

She pretended to be thinking and let her mind play over the words before she spoke. Rupert seemed to have latched on to the possibility of theft, so she continued with that explanation. "Not since I packed them when Arnhem was evacuated. It was foolish not to check, but I felt checking would make theft more likely because we were with strangers so often."

Rupert nodded. "Well, they're evidence now. I'll see if I can get them returned to you when the investigation is over."

"Thank you, Rupert." She handed them back but didn't hide her reluctance. Her mother's jewelry in the hands of the Nazis. That in and of itself was a tragedy, made worse because someone in the resistance had probably been arrested when the jewels had been seized. "I would be ever so grateful if you could find a way to return them to me. I have so little left of home now."

Rupert stiffened. "I can arrange for your return to Falcon Point tomorrow, if you like."

"I can't leave the van der Veens. They're like family now and—"

"Yes, you've mentioned that. But now all of you are refugees. You've no home. Not enough food. And your jewelry is being stolen. Isn't it time for you to go home? My uncle is also like family. He's known you since your birth. Go to him, and he'll ensure you have a home to live in and food to eat and a place to keep all your jewelry safe. And my sister's there. She needs someone, and you could help her in her grief."

Ingrid shifted on the bench. "I'd be glad to meet your sister, but my father and your uncle had a bit of a falling out." That was an understatement, but she doubted Rupert would appreciate it if she accused his uncle of murder.

"I heard." Rupert's hand fisted briefly before he relaxed it. "They disagreed because your father's loyalty to the Reich was questionable."

"Then, you understand why I can't seek protection from your uncle or anyone else who thinks ill of my father."

"Come, Ingrid. No one is going to hold you responsible for something your father did. It's been a long time. Onkel Wilhelm will welcome you back."

Ingrid doubted that. Sauermann had tried to kill her brother so Karl couldn't accuse him of murder. He might do the same to her.

"The Netherlands is dying," Rupert continued. "Nothing is moving by rail. The homes are all without power. Food is growing scarce, and winter is coming. As much as I enjoy visiting you here, I worry about you. You'd be better off in the Reich. We can stay in touch through letters, and I can visit you again when I next have leave." He took her hand. "Please, go somewhere safe."

She looked at his hand folded over hers. Maybe he really did care about her. But she didn't feel the same for him, and should she confess that her sentiments were in line with her father's, she suspected Rupert Altbauer would haul her to the local prison. "I'll think about it."

He gripped her hand tighter. It wasn't hard enough to hurt, but it caught her attention. "Tell me you haven't become like your father. Tell me you're still loyal, that you would never betray the Reich."

"I am still loyal to the country of my birth." That was Austria, not the Reich. She wondered if he would catch the distinction.

Rupert studied her for a long time, as if deciding whether he could really trust her. Eventually, he released her hand and stood. "Be careful, Ingrid. I'll try to track down the thief."

It took her a moment to understand what he was talking about. Her pearls. "Thank you."

He took a small notebook from his pocket. "Where have you stayed since Arnhem was evacuated?"

"Just the two homes you've visited."

"And the names of the other refugees staying there?"

The last thing she wanted was for Rupert to question everyone she'd come into contact with in the last few weeks. What if one of the children mentioned men hiding in the attic? Or what if his questions tricked someone into revealing more than they should? She swallowed. "Well, there are the van der Veens, of course. But they wouldn't have stolen anything. And Mevrouw Bakker and her children. But they wouldn't have stolen anything either. She has a newborn and hardly leaves the house."

"And at the other home?"

Most of the people in the De Groot home had been involved in the resistance or turned a blind eye to resistance activities. "Let me see . . . there was a Smit. Pieter? And a Jan . . . Jan Visser. And so many people who only stayed a night or two. Honestly, it was probably one of the people passing through." She'd pulled two names from the air and hoped it would be enough to protect the others. She would have to warn the De Groots that a German intelligence officer might question them. She hadn't meant to put those who had sheltered her and the van der Veens at risk. Why did Rupert have to have such a keen eye for details?

A cry came from the house. Not the mewling of a newborn. One of the older children, and she was grateful for the interruption. "I should go help."

Rupert glanced at the house. "I'll let you know if I find the thief. And think about going home, Ingrid. It would be for the best."

Ingrid agreed to think about it, then she slipped through the back door, into the Bakker home. The child's cry stopped. Footsteps came down the stairs, and she met Gerrit at the bottom of the staircase.

"You heard?" she asked.

He nodded, and lifted one arm so she could lean into him. Tension and fear seemed to melt away while he held her, but in the back of her mind, she knew the risk remained.

"He knows my father chose treason over following the Nazis," she said. "And he knows my necklace was being used to fund the resistance. I think I'm going to have to work extra hard to convince him not to arrest me."

Gerrit ran his hands along her arms and looked into her eyes. "I know how to fix this."

"You do?" Relief calmed her wildly beating heart.

He nodded.

"How?"

"That's what I do. I fix things. Bicycles, lamps. A few minutes ago, I fixed your interrogation by promising a three-year-old a piece of gum and making her cry when the wrapper was empty."

"The poor girl." The crying child had been exactly what Ingrid had needed, but she'd never seen Gerrit be cruel, especially not to a little girl.

"I gave her the gum when Altbauer left. She's fine now. And you needed an escape."

She nodded, grateful the girl's disappointment had been remedied and that Gerrit's unkindness had not only served a purpose but had also been brief. "So what do we do?"

Gerrit looked toward the back door. "I need to figure out a few details. And I think you need to warn our former hosts that a German intelligence officer is going to be asking them a lot of questions. Just make sure he doesn't see you leaving."

Ingrid nodded. "I'll go now, and I'll take back roads and hope they don't have another batch of paratroopers hiding in the attic." She still wore her coat from sitting outside with Rupert, so nothing kept her in the Bakker house, except perhaps the look on Gerrit's face—sober, adoring, and capable of tugging on her heart in a way she hadn't known was possible. She lifted a hand to his jaw. "The world has felt broken for a long time, but I'm glad people like you haven't given up on trying to repair this little bit of it." She let her hand fall to his chest. "I should go."

His eyes fell to her lips. "Kiss me goodbye?"

She didn't plan on staying away long, but they had privacy now that they might not have again for a long time. She leaned closer. Gerrit's hand rested on her back, and his mouth met hers for a lingering kiss. It was warm and sweet, thrilling and comforting. His lips alternated between playful and passionate, and she enjoyed every moment of it. Kissing Gerrit felt like coming home.

When she pulled away, the expression on his face surprised her. "You seem sad," she said.

He shook his head and planted another light kiss on her lips. "How can I be sad when I'm kissing you? But you better get going so they have time to plan their story."

Anita put her hands on her hips when Gerrit explained his plan. "That's the worst idea I have ever heard."

He hadn't thought she would love his plan, but he'd hoped she would see the wisdom in it. "Ingrid is in danger. Opa is in danger. This will get them both out of danger, and it might yield intelligence we can use. It's the best option for Ingrid. It's the best option for Opa. It's the best option for you and Cornelis."

"But it's too risky for you!"

Gerrit studied the aunt who had always been different from all his other aunts in so many ways but who was still just as protective. "I'm not a boy anymore. I've seen executions in the street, I almost killed a man, and I've watched soldiers not much older than me come from halfway around the world to fall from the sky and die trying to save my country. I'm old enough to lose my heart to a woman and see the threat to her swell to overwhelming, and I'm old enough to try to stop it. Anita, you have to start treating me like a man."

Anita brushed her hand along the top of his head, the way she'd done that first summer his mother had brought him and his siblings to visit Arnhem. He'd been a great deal shorter than her back then. Now he was taller. "You may have grown up, but that doesn't make your scheme any less reckless."

"Do you have a better idea of how I can save Ingrid and Opa?"

Anita's arm fell to her side. "You haven't given me a lot of time to come up with anything better, have you?"

Gerrit shook his head. "You won't come up with anything better because there isn't anything better. All our options are bad, but this one is the least likely to end in our collective deaths. Trust me, I've been trying to figure out what to do since I came back, and it all came to me when Altbauer had Ingrid in the garden. I'm the perfect choice. Any of the locations I knew from the old network are different now, so if things go wrong, I can't give anyone away."

"Except your family."

Gerrit had to give her that. "Yes. But we don't have much time, and my family is already in danger."

Anita didn't exactly smile, but her frown softened. "Ingrid isn't really your family. Just as well since you aren't supposed to kiss your cousins."

That was another point Gerrit would have to concede. "I would do anything to protect her. This is the best I can do."

Anita folded her arms. "Altbauer will have all the advantages. Staying a few steps ahead of him won't be easy. Your plan may very well mean dying for her."

"I know." Gerrit had realized the risks the moment the idea had come to him, but Ingrid was worth the danger.

Rupert put Ingrid's jewelry back into the box with the other items seized at the safe house. Had it been stolen, as Ingrid had claimed? Or had Ingrid been funding the resistance? He desperately wanted to trust her. But she had lied to him before, when she hadn't told him that her father was dead. And her father, whom she still looked up to, had turned from the Reich. Had Ingrid done the same?

"Did you learn anything?" Denhart asked.

"The necklace was reported stolen. Could have been taken by any number of refugees in the chaos."

"And the person it was stolen from?"

"I'll keep an eye on her." That was the prudent thing to do, as much as Rupert didn't want to.

"I had hoped the latest arrest would give us more." Denhart looked at the necklace and at the explosives. "Augustijn Hoekstra hasn't been very talkative, has he?"

"No. We could let our associates in the Gestapo have a turn with him."

Denhart frowned. "They might take over anyway. If we can't tie him to a foreign contact or country, then it's not counterintelligence work, and it's no longer our jurisdiction. Perhaps I'll explain that fact to him and see if it loosens his tongue."

After Denhart left, Rupert's eyes wandered back to the necklace. He wanted to trust Ingrid. They'd been friends as children. But had anyone else acted as nervous as Ingrid had that day in the garden, he would have assumed them guilty. When it came to Ingrid, was his heart hijacking his head? He ought to bring her in for questioning. Someone like Denhart would be reasonable, wouldn't use physical pain as a lever, and would give Rupert a more neutral opinion. As soon as Denhart returned, Rupert would explain what had happened and do what he should have done earlier that day: interrogate Ingrid Lang.

Jung had been writing something at his desk, but he stood and stretched, then looked at the box. "How much do you think that necklace is worth?"

"More than you and I earn in a year, combined."

Jung whistled. "Do you suppose the local resistance networks have any other stockpiles like that lying around?"

"Doubtful. And unless Denhart gets Hoekstra to sing—or the Gestapo does—it sounds like we've run into a dead end." Unless Ingrid was guilty.

"We just have to outthink them." Jung clasped his hands behind his back. "Predict their next move before it happens."

Predicting moves, like in a game of chess. Maybe they needed to create a situation that would have a limited number of reactions. Force the resistance to take one of several likely options. Rupert couldn't predict what they would sabotage. Nor did he have the manpower to search every home in the area for hidden paratroopers. Paratroopers . . . that might be the key. "Jung, do you know anyone who speaks English well enough to pass as an Englishman?"

"Daalmans." Daalmans, with his scarred face that showed recent injury . . . He might be perfect. "Why?" Jung asked.

"We can't find every paratrooper hiding in attics and cellars. But if we have a paratrooper who needs help getting to his own lines . . . then the resistance will come to him."

Jung smiled. "And we'll be waiting."

"Please ask Mynheer Daalmans to join us at his earliest convenience."

Jung nodded and headed out. Rupert began to plan. He wouldn't need a uniform for Daalmans because most of the refugees from the battle would have changed into civilian clothing. But something like a pair of British boots, maybe one of those red berets. That might offer just enough authenticity. They could wrap part of Daalmans's face, if needed, to explain any imperfections in his English.

"Leutnant Altbauer?"

Rupert looked up at one of the guards. "Yes."

"There's a Dutchman here to see you. Says he has information you might be able to use."

An informant. So many of them ended up being greedy, petty people with scores to settle against neighbors, but if the neighbors really were guilty, it could yield another opportunity. "Show him in."

Rupert studied the newcomer when the guard brought him to Rupert's desk. Average height, sandy hair, blue eyes. Nervous, but most people were when they came to see him. The guard handed the man's papers over. Gerrit Hendriks. Nineteen. From

Utrecht. Rupert placed a finger under the city name and showed it to the guard. He would know what to do: call the Utrecht office and ask if they had anything useful on the man. Given his age, he should have been working in Germany.

"You have something for me?" Rupert asked.

Hendriks nodded. "I want to help, but I'm not sure how this works." He spoke accented German. That made things easier.

"You can start by telling me why you're in Gelderland when you're registered in Utrecht." Plenty of Dutchmen left the city of their registry, but usually because they wanted to avoid the Germans, not so they could seek them out.

"I ran into a little trouble in Utrecht, so I came to visit family until things died down."

"What kind of trouble?"

The man stared at a spot on the desk. "I wanted to infiltrate the resistance, help you catch part of the network. They grew suspicious."

"What did you learn of the Utrecht Resistance?"

"Just an alias for one member: Smit. He's probably changed it now."

"And you are hoping to infiltrate the Arnhem networks now?"

"Yes. I've made a little progress. I wanted to speak to you at once, but in Utrecht, I think meeting with my handler was what tipped my resistance contact off. So this time, I waited until I had earned their trust. Bought it actually. Stole a necklace and donated it to the cause."

A stolen necklace. "Can you describe the jewelry?"

"Pearls. A little old-fashioned but good quality. They were eager enough to have it."

Ingrid's necklace. Relief washed through Rupert's chest. She hadn't been lying. It really had been stolen. Indignation quickly followed the relief. Hendriks had stolen something precious from Ingrid. Hendriks ought to be punished, but Rupert kept his expression calm. "Did they tell you how they planned to use it?"

Hendriks shook his head. "They're cautious. Another reason to see you now. If you can tell me what you need, then I can focus on what's most important rather than risking my cover for something you can't use anyway."

Rupert considered the offer. The man seemed to know what he was getting himself into, because he'd run from resistance justice in Utrecht. Any help, even from a thief, could be useful. "For now, maintain your cover. Learn the names of as many resisters as you can, and where they can be found."

"Yes, sir."

Rupert wasn't ready to dismiss Hendriks, not without getting a better feel for the man. "Other than your donation, how did you earn their trust?"

"Most of it's saying the right things. I had an uncle who was a Communist. I just repeat what I've heard him say over the years. And one of my relatives is a doctor.

I arranged treatment for two of them. The doctor had no idea what they'd been involved in, but he had his doctor's oath to follow, and after a long day, he didn't bother with questions about politics."

"What is the connection between the doctor and the woman you stole the necklace from?"

Hendriks frowned. "I found the necklace in a bag. I'm not sure who it belonged to."

Some of Rupert's resentment softened. Hendriks had stolen from Ingrid, but not intentionally. "I see. And your relative's name?"

"He won't be in trouble, will he? He didn't know he was helping the resistance."

"I'm not interested in punishing doctors for treating patients. Nor am I heartless. There's a shortage of doctors already without me arresting one who accidentally treated an enemy."

Hendriks nodded.

"And the name?" Rupert asked again.

"He was tricked, you realize? Not guilty? I hear he also served a great many German soldiers during the battle of Arnhem."

"Yes, I understand. He's your relative, so you don't want him punished for accidentally treating the wrong people. You have nothing to worry about on that account. His name?"

"Van der Veen."

It all fit together. One of the doctor's relatives would have had access to Ingrid's bag. And if the relative were manipulating him, that explained the doctor's occasional lapses in caution when it came to caring for the injured. "His relation to you?"

"He's my grandfather."

"So you know the woman staying with him, Fräulein Lang?"

"I've met her."

"What is your sense of where she stands, politically?"

Hendriks looked away. "She's just trying to survive. Like most civilians. Finding food and fuel for a fire takes up most of her day."

Rupert almost pointed out that stealing jewelry from Ingrid would only make it harder for that particular civilian to find food and fuel. But Hendriks had stolen for the Reich. He could forgive the man for that. "What drew you to the cause?"

"My teachers explained the benefits of economic cooperation with the Reich. And I had a friend in the NSB. Someone in the resistance assassinated him. I want revenge."

Revenge. That was a strong enough motive. Rupert clasped his hands together. "And will you be seeking compensation for your services?"

Hendriks looked uncomfortable. "I would gladly tell you what I know out of hope for a better future. But if you are willing to provide compensation, I won't turn it down. Food is, after all, getting harder to find."

"Meet me again tomorrow. There's a café in Velp, one block south of the Park Hotel. Two o'clock in the afternoon. I'll have something for you then, assuming you have something more for me."

"Yes, sir."

Rupert called one of the guards over. "See our guest safely to the civilian area."

As soon as they were out of sight, Rupert called over another guard, this one in civilian clothing. "Follow him. See where he goes. Keep your distance because we don't want to scare off any of his contacts."

"Yes, sir."

Rupert returned to his desk to write down notes about the meeting. Satisfactory, even if nothing else came of it. Ingrid hadn't lied to him. And the doctor who had taken her in hadn't knowingly disobeyed the law.

"Leutnant Altbauer?"

Rupert looked up to see Jung standing next to his desk with Daalmans by his side. He'd nearly forgotten their plan to entrap part of the local resistance. "Thank you for coming, Mynheer Daalmans." He stood and gestured to a seat.

Daalmans sat. "We saw a young man in civilian clothing on our way in."

Rupert only shared information about his limited sources when he had reason. Compartmentalization kept things safer. "Yes, it's been a full afternoon."

"I've seen him before. He was tailing me in September, just before I was almost killed in a kitchen explosion. I pointed him out to one of the Green Police, and he ran."

Rupert placed the pencil he was still holding back on his desk. Why had Hendriks been tailing Daalmans?

CHAPTER 26

When Ingrid made it back to the Bakker home, Anita waited for her.

"How are the De Groots?" Anita asked.

"Well enough." Their home was still full of refugees, but for the moment, they assured her they had no hidden onderduikers or airborne troops in their attic. "They're prepared for a search, and they plan to tell anyone who shows up asking the wrong questions that they let a rather questionable middle-aged man sleep there one night, and after he left, someone noticed a missing watch and someone else noticed a missing pair of earrings. I hope it will be enough."

Anita's expression grew wistful. "Maybe it could have been that simple."

"It will be. As long as Rupert believes them, and as long as he doesn't suspect me."

Anita led Ingrid to a sofa, where they could sit. "Gerrit didn't think it would be enough. He wrote a letter to Pap saying we should leave, stay with relatives elsewhere."

They'd already been forced from Arnhem, but to be forced even farther away, when they would lose contact with Cornelis and Berend? That was too much. "But what about your work here?"

"All my work was to help the Allies when they came to liberate us. They already came, and the Germans were too strong." Anita's face fell in defeat. "Cornelis has contacts. We can start work again somewhere else. We just have to convince Pap that the people in Haarlem or Amsterdam need him as much as the people here."

Ingrid didn't want to run away. "I might be able to get useful information from Rupert."

"And he might suspect you now that he's recognized your jewelry in a resistance dead drop."

Would the suspicion return? "The De Groots will report other robberies, and that will make my story more believable. And Gerrit promised he was working on an idea."

Anita frowned and handed her a piece of paper. "Yes, he left you a letter."

Ingrid unfolded the paper and began reading.

And David said to Saul, Let no man's heart fail because of him; thy servant will go and fight with the Philistine.

Gerrit was quoting the Bible to her? She skimmed the rest of the page, the story of David slaying Goliath. She recognized the A and B versions of the letters and stood to grab a pencil from a drawer in a little desk. The letters became dots and dashes, and soon Gerrit's intended message took shape.

Dearest Ingrid,

I don't think you'll like my plan, but I hope you'll trust me. Sometimes an idea strikes with so much force that it can't be put off, no matter how dangerous or difficult it is. I need to plant information with Altbauer so he doesn't turn his suspicions on you. One person in the right place can explain why the resistance had your necklace and why they came to Opa for treatment. Me. I'm going to pretend to be a double agent. And maybe I can learn something useful from the enemy in the process.

If all goes well, we'll meet again soon in a location far away from Altbauer. He'll look for you because he's in love with you. But if he doesn't suspect you, maybe he won't chase you. He wants to believe in your innocence, so I'll give him a reason he can trust you instead of suspect you.

Everyone knows that sometimes Goliath wins. But I'm going to pick up my sling anyway and hope for the best. Hope that I can make things better for you and for my family and for my country. I know the risks, but I willingly face them.

When it comes down to it, I don't have a choice because you're in danger, and you aren't almost everything to me, Ingrid. You are absolutely everything.

Love,
Gerrit

Ingrid lowered the letter and swallowed back a swirl of emotions. Awe of Gerrit's courage. Gratitude for his love. Terror at the danger he was walking into. "Did he tell you?"

Anita nodded. "I tried to talk him out of it . . . but you're under suspicion, and Pap is under suspicion too. Maybe this will get both of you out of danger."

Ingrid swallowed back the taste of bile. "Only because Gerrit's now in danger of the worse kind. Those summers when Rupert came to visit, he gave my father a challenge at chess, and my father was brilliant. Rupert thinks ahead and plans, and . . . and what if he ends up being more clever than Gerrit?" She loved Gerrit, but that didn't mean he could outsmart Rupert.

Anita took her hand. "His plan is simply to plant the information and then get away. He won't come back here because it's the first place Altbauer will look. Gerrit will meet us at one of my brothers' homes. It will be hard to get to Cas's house in Amsterdam or Aart's house in Haarlem, but we'll manage somehow. And once we get there, we'll do what we can to speed the war's end. The Nazis are going to lose, and then all the fear and all the worry will end. We just have to hold on a while longer."

"Is that what he told you?"

"Not in those words but the same ideas. He's been chased by the enemy before and escaped. This time, if he plays it right, they won't be chasing him."

Gerrit had noticed the tail almost at once, but he wasn't sure if that meant Altbauer suspected him or if it simply meant Altbauer didn't trust him yet. Gerrit had planned to sleep somewhere other than the Bakker home tonight anyway. The tail simply confirmed his decision. Eventually, he would lose the man, and then he would find a bicycle and head to one of his uncles' homes. Or maybe he'd go back to Utrecht. The Gestapo search would have long ago ended, and he missed Johan and Nellie. Though he might miss Ingrid more if she went with Opa to Amsterdam or Haarlem.

He took an easy-to-follow route and hoped that would make the man tailing him sloppy. In Velp, he knocked on a door and asked the woman who answered if he could work for a meal and a place to sleep, just for the night. She declined, and looking past her, Gerrit could see that the home was already crowded. She suggested he try the church, so Gerrit spent the night there.

In the morning, he slipped from the church before dawn. Shadows still shrouded the streets, making it hard to tell if anyone followed him. He took a series of four left turns, and no one on the street continued with him for more than two of them. He took a few more random turns, stopping in front of windows on occasion to check the reflection for anyone behind him.

When he was confident no one tailed him, he headed for Velp hospital. He'd asked Opa to leave a chalk letter on the southwest corner of the building: an *A* if he planned to take Anita and Ingrid to Amsterdam or an *H* if he planned to take them to Haarlem. Opa might insist on staying. Refugees from Arnhem and Oosterbeek crowded little Velp. Crowds brought disease, and Gerrit had never seen or heard of a time when Opa had turned his back on anyone. Except perhaps his own daughter when she'd come to him seeking his blessing in marriage to Georg Hendriks.

The hospital came into view, and Gerrit picked up his pace.

"You there!"

Gerrit turned as two Green Policemen approached him. Both were armed, and they were close enough that Gerrit didn't think they would miss if he tried to run for it. Beyond them was a group of men in civilian clothing, guarded by two additional Green Police. "Yes?"

"All men without exemptions are to report for work duty in five minutes. You're walking the wrong direction. Do you have an exemption?"

Gerrit patted his jacket, as if feeling for papers. "Local work duty?" Spending a day digging graves or pulling down unstable buildings was unpleasant but endurable. Being shipped to Germany was an entirely different matter.

"In Oosterbeek. You'd better hurry. Or were you trying to shirk your duty?"

Gerrit looked at his wrist, but he didn't have a watch. "I didn't realize it was so late. I was going to check on a friend in the hospital."

"Visits to friends will have to wait."

Gerrit hadn't intended to see Altbauer ever again, but perhaps the current situation called for a change of strategy. "I'm supposed to meet with someone important this afternoon. Can you take him a message, telling him I've been conscripted into a work party?" Gerrit had planned to disappear before his meeting with Altbauer. Now he suspected German intelligence would be looking for him by the time he was dismissed. Maybe he shouldn't have worked so hard to lose his tail.

"We're not a postal service."

"No, but SD officers don't like being kept waiting."

One guard looked to the other, who appeared much less relaxed than he'd been only moments before. The guard took a small notebook and pen from his pocket. "I won't promise anything, but I'll look into it."

Gerrit took the offered pen and paper and scrawled a short note. *Delayed by compulsory work detail. Suggest postponement of 24 hours. Hendriks.* Then he addressed it to Leutnant Altbauer at SD headquarters. Maybe Altbauer wouldn't start looking for Gerrit until tomorrow.

Rupert, in civilian clothing, watched the work crew clear away rubble from the battle between the British paratroopers and the German Army. Hendriks and another man moved a slab of rubble and pulled back in disgust. The other man turned away and vomited. Hendriks spoke with one of the crew supervisors and was handed an old sheet. He went back to the body he'd found and transferred it to the cloth and away from the rubble.

They were far enough distant that Rupert couldn't smell it beyond the stench that already permeated all of Oosterbeek. Couldn't even tell if the corpse was soldier or civilian. Maybe the work crew's efforts would help improve the smell. That, or the coming of winter would.

Yesterday, Rupert had thought he understood Hendriks: a man out for revenge against the resistance, someone who enjoyed the thrill of undercover work. He'd believed him, but perhaps that had only been because he'd wanted to believe the resistance had Ingrid's necklace for a reason other than that she'd given it to them.

Then Daalmans had recognized Hendriks. Word from Utrecht had come that Hendriks was wanted for questioning after being named as an associate during the interrogation of a resistance member. And Hendriks had somehow managed to lose his tail. Three reasons for suspicion.

The overseer called the end of the day, and the men returned their tools. Hendriks met Rupert's eyes and walked over to meet him.

"I'm afraid I haven't anything useful for you. I've spent the entire day clearing rubble." Hendriks had wrapped strips of cloth around his hands, and he pulled them off now, revealing large blisters. He stared at the damage. "I don't suppose you could have shown up before my hands turned raw?"

"You should have worn gloves."

"My work gloves are in a pile of rubble somewhere in Arnhem."

"Then, you should have stolen replacements."

Hendriks grunted. "There wasn't any warning that I'd be pulled into a work crew today."

"All able-bodied male civilians are expected to help with work duty. Why should you be an exception?"

Hendriks glanced around to make sure no one was close enough to overhear them. "Because any able-bodied man can use a shovel. But not everyone can infiltrate the local resistance networks and bring you information."

Rupert motioned to the street. "Walk with me."

Hendriks complied.

"When you tried to infiltrate the Utrecht Resistance, who was your contact?"

"I don't think he ever told me his real name. Went by Smit."

"And his first name?"

"Can't remember. Doubt I ever heard it."

"The Utrecht authorities said you were associated with two brothers, both members of a resistance network. They were arrested this past summer. Niels and Klaas Dijkstra."

"Klaas was arrested too?" Hendriks's mouth twisted with surprise.

Ah, so Hendriks did know the first names of the contacts. "Yes. And when questioned, both brothers gave the authorities your name."

Hendriks focused on the uneven sidewalk, though Rupert suspected the man could have navigated the rubble-strewn pavement perfectly fine if he hadn't needed time to think.

Hendriks swallowed. "Of course they did. It would have been a perfect way for them to get rid of me. If they were arrested, that means I didn't really have to leave Utrecht."

"So there were two men from the resistance after you?"

"I only had contact with one of them, but he mentioned a brother."

Rupert suppressed a smile. Hendriks might not realize it, but he was tying himself in knots. What was Hendriks's game? Payment for information? That wasn't likely now that Rupert couldn't trust anything he said. "Do you know a Dirk Daalmans?"

Hendriks's arm twitched slightly. "Daalmans? From around here?"

"Yes."

"Do you have a picture? The name doesn't mean anything, but maybe I would recognize him."

"I expect you would because he recognized you."

Hendriks's step faltered, though he tried to hide it by kicking away a small piece of rubble. "Did he say how?"

"He arrived at my office yesterday, just after you left. Said you tailed him sometime before the failed British invasion."

"How long before?"

Rupert was nearly done with the questions. He would arrest Hendriks and let the Gestapo figure out if he knew anything useful or if he was simply a thief full of stories. If he proved uninteresting to the Gestapo, he could go work in Germany. The Reich always needed more laborers. "Late August, early September."

"I was asked to tail someone about then. The resistance had it out for him. Don't know the man's name."

"What did the resistance want with him?"

"He was a threat. I think . . . well, I'd have to see a picture to be sure, but that's about the time I heard my contact say they blew up the man's kitchen."

Rupert hoped he hid his shock better than Hendriks had hidden his. The fact that the kitchen explosion hadn't been an accident was insider knowledge. Maybe Hendriks really did have useful information. "What else did they tell you about him?"

"Mostly just that he worked for you. Rounded up onderduikers, Jews, resistance men. That you trusted him. I followed him because they asked me to, and I thought it would help me earn their trust. I didn't realize they wanted to kill him until it was too late."

Maybe Rupert didn't want to turn Hendriks over to the Gestapo just yet after all. Rupert still didn't trust him, but maybe he would prove useful. "Do you speak English?"

Hendriks shook his head. "A few words. No more."

"Pity. I'm looking for men who can impersonate British paratroopers. You're about the right age, and finding a few pieces of a uniform wouldn't be difficult. But without the language skills, I doubt it would work."

"That depends on if I would need to talk."

If Daalmans did all the speaking and Hendriks stayed silent, it might work. Daalmans, as the older man, would be a believable superior. Not that Daalmans's face showed age now. Instead, it was a mass of angry scars. Regardless, Daalmans was reliable, and Hendriks was questionable.

"It's likely you would need to speak. Perhaps if this proves effective, we'll try again and see how a silent soldier plays out with any resisters who come to help our sham paratroopers."

Something in Hendriks's expression shifted. The lines around his mouth firmed, showing determination, where before, Rupert had seen curiosity. "You're having your agents pretend to be British airborne troops, and when the resistance offers to help them, you'll arrest them?"

"Arrest or follow."

"Clever." Hendriks looked around. "Since we didn't meet at the café today, should we try tomorrow instead? I'll come as planned, unless I've been rounded up for another work crew. Or perhaps you can arrange a pass so my hands have a day or two to recover?"

Now that Hendriks knew of the scheme to entrap members of the resistance, Rupert wasn't about to let him walk away. Hendriks might prove useful, or he might have more loyalty to his resistance contacts than he claimed, and Rupert didn't want the man warning them. He raised his hand, signaling his driver forward. "Actually, I think it best that I take you into protective custody. I recognize one of the other men on the crew. He knows who I am. If he's a member of the resistance, you could be in danger."

Hendriks frowned. "Then, why don't you arrest him instead of me?"

"You aren't under arrest. We'll investigate the other man in good time."

Hendriks stiffened when the car pulled up. "But it's my grandfather's birthday tonight. He already lost his home, and we haven't had a decent meal in weeks. His one request was that we all join him for a modest supper."

It was a rather pathetic excuse for someone who had referred to the man as *Dr. van der Veen* rather than *Grandfather* the day before.

Rupert understood reluctance to be detained, even if it wasn't a formal arrest. "Write him a note. I'll have my driver drop it off at the hospital on our way through Velp."

CHAPTER 27

INGRID RODE THE FINAL FEW meters to the Bakker home as the sun slipped below the horizon. Physical exhaustion clung to her because she hadn't been on a bicycle since her crash before the failed invasion. Her ankle had healed, but she was grateful that of the two assignments from Cornelis that day, Anita had given her the shorter one: documents to be passed to an associate in the resistance. Anita and Cornelis were taking the longer assignment: leading a British paratrooper to a safer hiding place.

More than that, Ingrid's emotions were ragged. Gerrit loved her. Gerrit was trying to outsmart a snake, and if anything went wrong, the viper's venom might prove deadly. Maybe everything had gone according to plan, and Gerrit was halfway to Haarlem by now. Anita, Opa, and Ingrid would leave in the morning. Gerrit had wanted them to leave earlier, but Opa had needed a day to finish at the hospital, and Anita had wanted to speak with Cornelis one last time so he could adjust his shrinking network. Cornelis couldn't have done everything by himself today, so despite the sore muscles in her legs, Ingrid was glad they'd stayed.

She pulled the bicycle into the garden and went into the home through the back door. Opa met her within moments. "Do you know where Anita went?"

"Yes." Anita had planned to meet Cornelis and the paratrooper at a safe house in Driel, then lead him to a farmhouse near Ede. Ingrid hadn't been to Driel since the Polish parachute brigade had landed there and the village had become embroiled in a battle, but she thought she could still find the safe house, as long as it hadn't been destroyed.

"Can you take me there?"

"I can, but why?" Opa had never asked to be included in their resistance activities before.

He pulled a note from his pocket. "I was in surgery when this came. I left as soon as I deciphered it, but we may already be too late."

While Opa grabbed his coat and bag, Ingrid read the note. Gerrit's handwriting, so he must have survived his initial encounter with Rupert. The message was an innocent-looking apology that he wouldn't be able to return for Opa's birthday supper. Someone, Opa she assumed, had already marked the letters as dots and dashes. She read the hidden message: *Detained. Warn Anita. Phony para a trap.*

How long ago had Gerrit written this? Anita and Cornelis were supposed to meet in Driel in an hour.

"We better hurry," Ingrid said when Opa returned. "I hope the ferry is still running."

Driel had been a quiet, sleepy village as recently as several days after the British had dropped into Arnhem. That had changed when Polish airborne troops had arrived on the fifth day of the battle. Ingrid saw evidence of the hard-fought war between the Poles and the Germans in every damaged and destroyed Dutch home she passed. So much destruction.

All that determination. All that courage. All that sacrifice. Yet she and the other civilians were worse off than they'd been before. Regardless, the brave men who had jumped from airplanes to liberate the Netherlands had fought their best against massive odds, and so the resistance was doing their best to hide them. That Rupert would take that loyalty and gratitude and twist it into a trap . . . It was unforgiveable.

As the safe house came into sight, a pair of shots sounded so close together that they almost sounded like one. Icy fear made it hard for Ingrid to breathe, and another shot rang out.

Ingrid and Opa both froze for a moment. Someone emerged from the bushes by the house, and when a shadow left the back door, the two figures clashed. Both were men, or women in pants—darkness and distance made it hard to see details. In any case, neither figure was Anita, because she'd been wearing a dress.

One of the shadows subdued the other. A car pulled up, and one man forced the other inside. As the car pulled away, Opa rushed toward the home.

"Wait!" Ingrid whispered once she caught up to him. "Let me make sure it's safe."

Opa ignored her. She was certain he had heard her. He simply chose not to heed her advice, which wasn't so surprising when both of them suspected Anita was still inside. Ingrid stepped through the doorway. The beam of Opa's flashlight had already found Anita lying on the floor in a pool of blood.

Horror filled Ingrid's chest. No! Not Anita. As Opa knelt beside her, Anita's eyes fluttered open, and relief made it so Ingrid could breathe again. She could barely understand Anita's soft, strained words, but Ingrid knew the injury was serious, and Opa would need better light to fix it. Ingrid stepped to Opa's bag and pulled out another flashlight.

"Check the other body," he said.

Ingrid hadn't noticed another body, but she switched the flashlight on and soon found it. She stepped closer but didn't bother taking the pulse. The man was dead. One shot in the shoulder and another in the center of his forehead. His lifeless eyes stared across the room. The face was changed, but something about those eyes . . . that hair. Daalmans was the phony paratrooper, wearing British ammo boots for a disguise.

Ingrid's hands shook. That wouldn't help anyone. She had to focus on Anita. She turned back to the van der Veens. "He's dead," she reported.

Opa nodded. "I'll need clean linens and hot water."

"You can't operate here," Ingrid said. "The Germans might come back any moment."

"We can't move her all the way back to Velp in this condition."

Anita's hand brushed her father's. "Leave."

"I'm not leaving you."

"We . . . can't . . . stay."

Opa turned to Ingrid. "Are there any other safe houses nearby?"

Ingrid didn't know of any, but they only had to find someone who wouldn't mind their barn or parlor turning into a temporary operating room. "I'll find a place."

Ingrid ran out the door and headed for the nearest home, then thought better of it. That would be the first home the Germans searched when they returned. She knocked on the fourth door she passed.

"There's a medical emergency," she said when a middle-aged woman opened the door. "Please, it's vital that we operate at once."

The woman nodded, though the confused look on her face suggested she didn't really understand.

"We'll need hot water."

"But there's hardly enough wood to last the week as it is."

Ingrid unbuttoned her jacket and unpinned the broach she'd fastened to the inside, the one her mother had once fastened on her coat for Christmas. "We'll pay."

The woman accepted the broach when Ingrid handed it to her.

Ingrid didn't give the woman time to protest any further. She ran back to Opa, who had already wrapped Anita in a blanket and was carrying her in his arms. Ingrid took the black medical case from his hands, led the way to the home, and pushed open the door for the van der Veens. The woman had sprung into action, and she and two teens, a boy and a girl, had cleared their dining room table and brought in candles and an oil lamp.

Opa laid Anita on the table. The lighting was dim, but it was brighter than flashlights in the safe house, and it was enough to show the sickly, pale color of Anita's complexion.

"Stay with her while I wash," Opa said.

Ingrid took one of Anita's hands and clasped it in hers. "You'll be all right," she said. "The best surgeon in Gelderland is going to take care of you."

Anita's mouth twitched in acknowledgment, and she gave Ingrid's hand a feeble squeeze.

Gerrit knew the cell he'd been locked in for protective custody was better than most cells the Germans locked prisoners in. It contained a real bed with sheets and a blanket, a chest of drawers, and a writing desk. Had it not been for the lock on the door, it would have been a pleasant guest room. But it did have a lock on the door, and that made it a prison.

Ingrid was still in danger because even though Altbauer seemed to believe Gerrit had stolen her necklace, that wasn't going to make Altbauer leave her alone. Opa was in danger because he'd treated members of the resistance. And the entire network might be in jeopardy because Altbauer and Daalmans were setting a trap.

Keys jingled outside the room, and Gerrit sat on the bed, trying to look relaxed rather than as if he'd been pacing and worrying. Altbauer himself stood at the door beside the guard with the keys. "Our plan worked, and we caught one of the resisters. I was wondering if you might like to join me for the interrogation."

Gerrit most certainly did not want to watch a loyal member of the Dutch Resistance be questioned or tortured. Nor did he want one of his colleagues to think he was a traitor. "I'll have a hard time infiltrating the resistance if one of them sees me in your company."

"Oh, we won't be letting this one free again. I guarantee it."

Cold dread formed in Gerrit's stomach. It sounded as though one of his friends had earned a death sentence. If not one of his friends, then one of his Allies in another network. Yet Altbauer's statement carried more insistence than invitation. Gerrit didn't have a choice, not if he wanted to stay on Altbauer's good side. "Then, I'll join you."

The knot of worry didn't ease as Gerrit followed Altbauer through the corridors into a room with a single worktable and a few chairs. The room was empty other than Altbauer and Gerrit. Footsteps, one of them slow and scuffling, sounded in the hallway. The door opened to reveal two guards and, standing in between them, Cornelis.

His eyes met Gerrit's, then looked away. Bruises clustered along Cornelis's forehead and temple, and when the guards pushed him into the room, he limped.

Gerrit remembered his training. He would pretend he didn't know Cornelis, and he expected Cornelis to do the same. Yet Cornelis's arrest was a mortal blow. He knew every member of Anita's cell and Berend's cell, and he was the link between several other networks. Even if he said nothing, his arrest would cost the resistance dearly.

"Thank you," Altbauer said to the guards. "You are free to leave now." Altbauer turned to Gerrit. "Do you know him?"

"No," Gerrit lied.

Altbauer nodded. "I see. And you"—he walked up to Cornelis—"have you ever seen this man before?"

Cornelis shook his head.

"He's not working with you?"

"No." Cornelis's voice sounded wrong, and Gerrit suspected his face and his leg weren't the only things the Nazis had injured.

Altbauer clasped his hands behind his back for a moment, then released one to gesture at Cornelis. "Caught trying to lead what he believed to be a British soldier away from us. Won't reveal the names of his contacts. Won't reveal how he heard there was a paratrooper in need of a guide, though that isn't necessary since we already know how the information was passed on. I could turn him over to the Gestapo, but a few of the guards already tried those techniques, as you can see, and they weren't very effective."

Gerrit watched Altbauer and Cornelis in turn. Altbauer triumphant, and Cornelis silent. Had Anita told Cornelis Gerrit's plan, or did he think Gerrit was a traitor? It was worth it, to be thought a traitor, if it would save Ingrid, but it still stung.

"In short," Altbauer continued, "he's guilty, but he refuses to make himself useful. So it's time to execute him."

Gerrit's lungs seized for a moment. Cornelis was his friend, so he tried to play for time. "Do you want me to talk to him?"

"No." Altbauer pulled out his pistol and handed it to Gerrit. "I want you to do the honors."

Gerrit gripped the Luger in his right hand. "You want me to shoot him? Here?"

"Yes. Whenever you're ready."

Gerrit swallowed. "But I've never killed anyone before."

"Well, this is war. It's time for you to start."

Cornelis caught Gerrit's eye and gave a slight nod, as if to tell him to go ahead and shoot. Logically, he understood the reasons. Cornelis would be executed one way or another, and if Gerrit was the one to do it, he could maintain his cover. What was more, a quick death would save Cornelis from further torture and prevent him from confessing under duress.

Gerrit felt the heft of the pistol. A Luger held eight bullets in its magazine. One for Altbauer. Seven to get Gerrit and Cornelis out the door, down the corridor, and through the building's main entrance. Maybe more than seven because Cornelis could grab a rifle from the guards outside. The odds were against them, but they would have the element of surprise.

"Anytime, Hendriks," Altbauer said.

Gerrit held the pistol with both hands and aimed at Cornelis, who looked at his feet. Gerrit pivoted, bringing the weapon around to aim at Altbauer and pulled the trigger.

It didn't fire.

Gerrit pulled the trigger again, but again, it failed to fire. Gerrit ejected the magazine and confirmed what he'd begun to fear. The weapon wasn't loaded.

Altbauer's face showed far too much pleasure for a man who'd just had a pistol aimed at his chest. "Ah, Hendriks. I wasn't sure about you, so that was a test of your loyalty. And you failed. Guards!"

The two guards entered immediately, before Gerrit could reposition the pistol to use it as a club.

Altbauer motioned to Gerrit and Cornelis. "I'm finished with both these men. You can turn them over to the Gestapo."

Gerrit and Cornelis were handcuffed, marched down a hall, and shoved into the back of a car. Gerrit knew the most likely destination: the Gestapo interrogation rooms in the basement of number 85 Utrechtseweg, Arnhem.

Gerrit leaned next to Cornelis's ear as the car began its journey. "I'm sorry. I tried to send a warning about the trap."

Cornelis nodded. "Your cell leader told me your scheme. I hope it worked."

"I think I just blew it." Altbauer knew Gerrit had lied about which side of the war he was on. He might question the stolen necklace now too.

"No. Stick with part of it. You stole for the resistance. Wanted to get information from the Germans."

Gerrit nodded. A slight change in his story. He would try it and hope Ingrid made it safely to one of his uncles' homes in Haarlem or Amsterdam. Gerrit had never made it to the hospital to see which location they had chosen. Just as well. Now he couldn't reveal their destination under torture. "Daalmans pretended to be a paratrooper?"

"Yes. Your cell leader recognized him. He shot her. I shot him. He's dead."

"Is Anita all right?" Gerrit shouldn't have used her name, but it slipped out with a wave of fear.

"Gut wound. I'd say her chances are slim. She told me to run, but I ran right into one of the Nazis."

Gerrit squeezed his eyes shut. Not Anita. She was too thorough, too meticulous in her work to fall into a trap. And she was too full of goodness and hope for her life to end now.

Cornelis leaned in again. "They know about me and Willem. If the questioning gets too hot, you can use our names."

Gerrit swallowed. His aunt might be dying. His sweetheart and his grandfather were under suspicion. And he was about to be tortured.

"I wish you had shot me," Cornelis said. "This is going to be much more painful."

Ingrid held Anita's hand as dawn cast its murky light through the windows of the Driel home where they'd stayed that night. With no power, Ingrid had opened the curtains as soon as the sky had lightened because there wasn't any internal light to black out.

Opa had spent an hour removing the bullet and stitching together the damaged portions of Anita's intestines. He'd used a hefty dose of brandy in an attempt to prevent infection, but Ingrid had longed for the sulfa packs the wounded paratroopers had used in Arnhem.

Anita hadn't woken since the surgery, and her face still seemed pale and shadowed. Anita was like a sister, and Ingrid didn't want to lose another sibling. Ingrid hadn't slept all night. She'd prayed and felt Anita's ever-warmer forehead and fussed and prayed some more. Opa, too, had hovered all night, checking the wound for redness or other signs of infection, feeling Anita's pulse, pacing across the small parlor.

Ingrid took a rag from Anita's forehead, dipped it in cool water, then wrung it out and replaced it. Opa brought the thermometer over and placed it in Anita's mouth. They watched the temperature climb to forty degrees Celsius. Too hot.

"What can I do?" Ingrid asked. "If I find someone with a car and we drive her to the hospital, will that help?"

Opa shook his head. "Moving her in this condition would be too risky, too hard on her body. And once there, she'd be arrested." He placed the back of his hand on her temple, then her cheek. He did not weep, but the pain was visible in his expression. She'd never seen him look so sad, not even when the Nazis had invaded his country or when the telegram had come telling him Judith was dead. "These types of infections are difficult to overcome, and the hospital . . . It has no miracle drugs, no equipment that would increase her chances. For now, we can do our best to make her comfortable and pray that her body overcomes the infection."

Making her comfortable . . . waiting to see . . . "Does that mean you're giving up?"

Opa squeezed his eyes shut. "It means that she needs a miracle. In triage, I would have . . . I would have assumed nothing could be done. But I tried anyway. How could I not? I've done my best, and I'm still hoping for a miracle." His voice fell. "But sometimes, even our best efforts aren't enough."

A warm tear rolled down Ingrid's cheek. She knew that already. She'd seen the best efforts of the British paratroopers at the bridge, the men trying to hold on even when the ground forces were delayed, even when the opposition was much stronger than expected. They had fought so hard only to lose the bridge and lose the battle.

Anita had survived four years of war. She'd gathered intelligence, couriered information, and organized a network that had saved a hundred people, maybe more. She'd been a friend and a mentor, someone to cry with and laugh with, someone to share a wardrobe and lean rations and hope with. And now her life hung in the balance.

Anita's face pulled with pain, and a little moan escaped her lips. Minutes passed, and Ingrid caught a few more sounds, none of them coherent. Then Anita's eyes opened, showing confusion.

Opa said something in Indonesian, and Anita's expression calmed. "Pap." Her voice was soft, but in the quiet of the home, Ingrid could hear.

"You gave us a fright." Opa's voice shook. "How bad is the pain?"

"Constant. Where I was shot. And my head."

"I'll see if I can find anything to help." Opa went to his bag.

Anita turned her head toward Ingrid. "You look discouraged. News of Gerrit?"

Ingrid tried to smile. Failed. "He sent a warning about the trap, but we didn't get it soon enough to reach you."

Anita shivered, and Ingrid adjusted the blanket. Anita was burning up. She shouldn't be cold, but fevers did strange things. "Is he all right?"

"I don't know." Ingrid tried to sound brave, but uncertainty gnawed at her. About Anita, who seemed lucid but wasn't out of danger. And about Gerrit. She wasn't sure what *detained* meant. If he'd been arrested, he couldn't have sent a note. But if he'd been able, he would have warned Anita himself.

"He's so good. But he's so lost. You'll look after him, won't you?"

Ingrid nodded, not sure if she really could. Regardless, she wanted to, and Ingrid thought intentions were more important than anything else just then.

"Tell Henry that I'm grateful he loved me and that I wish things could have ended differently. He was . . . he was everything I wanted."

"You can tell Henry that yourself when the war ends and you've recovered."

Anita's hands pulled at the blankets. "What was my last temperature?"

"Forty."

"Too high."

Opa brought a glass of water and a pill. "Aspirin will help with the temperature and the pain."

Anita's mouth twisted into a partial smile. "Gut wounds always lead to infections."

"Not every infection kills." Opa helped Anita raise her head enough to sip at the water.

Anita swallowed her pill and rested a moment. "Most do."

"Anita," Opa's voice shook just a little. "You've had my heart since the day you were born. I'm proud of what you've done and who you've become."

She grabbed her father's hand and held it. In just the few minutes she'd been alert, Anita seemed to have grown weary, and her eyes soon closed, and her face relaxed in sleep.

"Does this mean she'll get better?" Ingrid asked.

Opa felt his daughter's forehead again. "All night, I was begging God to heal her, to let her survive. Then I changed my prayer and asked for a chance to say goodbye." Opa's lips drew together, and he seemed to struggle against his emotions. "That's when she woke up."

Had that brief conversation been a promise of recovery or only a small moment of mercy for a father about to lose his youngest child?

"You didn't sleep at all, did you?" Opa asked.

Ingrid shook her head.

"Go rest. I'll sit with her."

The woman who owned the home led Ingrid to a clean bed, and it wasn't until midafternoon that Ingrid woke on her own accord. She walked down the hall to the parlor, where Anita still rested, tended by Opa.

"How is she?" Ingrid asked.

Opa stood and stretched his back. "No better. She woke up an hour ago, but she was delirious."

"Do you want to rest now?"

Opa shook his head. "No. I want to be with her when it's time."

They took turns replacing the cloths on Anita's forehead, and they took her temperature every hour. The blankets and all but one layer of clothing had been removed in an attempt to lower her temperature, but it didn't help.

The woman who owned the home brought them soup. Ingrid ate two bites before worry banished her appetite. She didn't even know the woman's name. Maybe that was for the best. If they didn't know each other, they couldn't give that information to anyone who questioned them.

The convulsions started as the sun slipped near the horizon. They were horrifying, but they were brief. Anita's last breath disappeared with the day's final sunlight.

Ingrid had wept off and on throughout the last several days, but now it was as though something burst inside her, and she could barely breathe through the sobs. She had loved Anita. The world wouldn't be the same without her—Ingrid wouldn't be the same without her. Anita was supposed to survive the war to enjoy the freedom she'd worked so hard to win back. She was supposed to study medicine, like her father, and race a bicycle, a good one with rubber wheels. Henry was to have come back to sweep her off her feet. And she and Ingrid were to have been the best friends until they were both old. Anita was too young, too good to be gone.

Guilt settled in too.

"I was supposed to kill the man who shot her. If I had done it, she'd still be alive." Ingrid wiped at her eyes. Berend had been right. Unstopped, Daalmans had created more betrayal, more pain, more death.

Opa put a hand on Ingrid's back. She hadn't heard him crying, but a new pain lined his face, and he looked a decade older than he'd seemed the night before. "They might have used another man to play the role of paratrooper, and then you would still have lost Anita and damaged your soul in the process."

Ingrid shook her head and fisted her hands. "She should still be alive."

"Yes." Opa paused and pressed his lips together. "She should have lived a full life. She would have made a good one." Opa shook his head. "The Nazis took that from her. And they took both my daughters from me. Maybe some of my sons as well. And possibly a grandson. I would very much appreciate it if you would go back to the Bakker home to see if Gerrit left word for us. I'll see to the body."

Ingrid wasn't done grieving yet, but the war wouldn't pause just because one woman had lost the best friend she'd ever had. Grief over Anita hadn't wiped away worry for Gerrit, so Ingrid obeyed.

CHAPTER 28

When Ingrid returned to the Bakker house, no news of Gerrit awaited her. Had he left for Haarlem? That had been the plan, but he'd sent a warning to Opa after he was supposed to have left, so something must have changed, and Ingrid wasn't ready to leave Velp until she knew what had happened.

Neither Rupert nor any other members of the German occupation forces had visited the home since Ingrid and Opa had left the previous day. To Ingrid, it felt as though far more than a day had passed. Opa returned, briefly, the following morning, then left for the hospital. He, too, had heard nothing new from Gerrit.

"Will the other Mejuffrouw van der Veen be returning?" Mevrouw Bakker asked after breakfast.

Ingrid swallowed in an attempt to keep herself from crying. Mevrouw Bakker had proved a gracious host, but she didn't know about their resistance work, and that was for the best because she had three small children who wouldn't have anywhere to go if their mother were arrested for sheltering enemies of the Nazis. "No. She needed to move elsewhere."

"And Mynheer Hendriks?"

"I'm not sure. He spoke of traveling to visit family. Maybe he sent a message, and it got lost."

"If that's the case, it was lost before it came to me. I haven't misplaced any letters."

Ingrid hadn't meant to question the woman's dependability, but maybe it was safer for Mevrouw Bakker to fret over that instead of suspecting the truth.

A familiar knock sounded from the front of the home, and Ingrid went to the nearest window to confirm what she'd suspected with the second rap of knuckles. Rupert Altbauer, not in uniform today, stood on the porch. It looked as though he'd brought bread again, and she hoped that meant he no longer suspected her of giving her necklace to the resistance. But the relief soon tumbled into fear because the most likely reason he would think that was if Gerrit's lie had worked.

"I assume he's calling for me." Ingrid checked her reflection in a nearby mirror. Her hair needed a good wash, and her eyes were red and shadowed from crying and sleep deprivation.

"You seem like such a nice girl to have a German beau."

"I don't want a German beau—but I can't really tell him no without being arrested."

Mevrouw Bakker's expression didn't show condemnation, but nor did it show trust. "I don't wish to be accused of collaboration when the war is over."

"My opa and I plan to move on soon, and then Leutnant Altbauer won't be a problem." Ingrid hurried to the front door. She didn't want to be accused of collaboration with the Nazis either. Berend had already doubted her because of her birthplace. What would he think if he saw her chatting with Rupert multiple times a week?

It was hard to think of a reason to smile, but she imagined her mother pinning the Christmas broach on her coat all those years ago. Mama still alive. That was a memory worth smiling over.

She and Rupert said their greetings, and then Rupert handed her the package of bread, cheese, and sausage. Ingrid could understand why so many women did things they normally wouldn't when war or hunger came. Ingrid had no romantic interest in Rupert, but it was tempting to let things last a little longer anyway just because she was sick of being hungry, and the food he brought would feed not only her but also Opa and the Bakkers.

"Can I take you out for coffee?"

Ingrid nodded. "Let me grab my coat and put your package somewhere safe."

Ingrid returned shortly, and Rupert led her to the street.

"I found the thief who stole your necklace," he said.

Ingrid did her best to appear surprised and pleased. A smile was difficult to manage, but she left her mouth open slightly as if the news was unexpected. "You did? Who took it?"

"Dr. van der Veen's grandson, Gerrit Hendriks."

"Gerrit took it?"

"He claims he didn't know it was yours at the time."

Ingrid stayed silent for what she hoped was the right amount of time. "He shouldn't have taken it, but I'll talk to him to make sure it doesn't happen again. I don't wish to press charges. Dr. van der Veen has had enough losses without his grandson getting into trouble."

Rupert huffed. "I would think the theft of a necklace as valuable as that would require more than a few minutes to forgive."

"I didn't say he was forgiven." If she ever saw Gerrit again, she intended to give him quite a tongue-lashing for putting himself at so much risk without consulting her. "But after everything that's happened since September . . . Rupert, I've seen entire neighborhoods destroyed. So many people dead or wounded. What is a lost necklace against all that pain?"

Rupert cut through an alley, and she followed. He looked around, making sure they were alone. "It's not a simple theft. The necklace was being used to finance the resistance. You may not wish to press charges, but I'll not be releasing him. I can't trust him. He tried telling me that he was buying his way into the resistance so he could gather information for us. But he's not very clever when it comes to lies."

"You're sure it was a lie?"

Rupert stopped walking and met her eyes, and Ingrid regretted her question. "Certain. Did you know he was working with the resistance?"

"No." Ingrid hoped she was better at lying than Gerrit was. "Are you sure?"

Rupert nodded. "Yes. You never suspected?"

"No." She hadn't suspected because she'd known. But what could she say to help Gerrit? "He hasn't been living with the van der Veens as long as I have, so maybe before he came to Arnhem . . . but I haven't heard or seen anything to make me suspicious since I met him."

Rupert grunted.

Ingrid took a few steps toward the road. She didn't think Rupert would kill her, but this was the type of out-of-the-way alley where someone suspected of disloyalty could meet a quick end. It made her nervous for herself, and she already felt terror for Gerrit. "What will happen to him?"

Rupert didn't move to follow her, so Ingrid stopped. Rupert seemed to be studying her every move and scrutinizing her every word. "The Gestapo is questioning him. After that, I assume he'll be treated as other members of the resistance are treated."

The Gestapo? Ingrid put a hand on a nearby wall for support. She'd walked by Gestapo headquarters more than once and heard the cries of the tortured. A chill clutched at her chest. Gerrit was in the hands of the Gestapo. Hope for him seemed to fade in the same way hope for Anita had grown smaller and smaller with each increase in temperature. Helplessness weighed her down. Yet Rupert had offered to help her before, and he had the power to change Gerrit's future. "Please, Rupert, isn't there something you can do?"

"He's a member of the resistance. He's broken the law."

"What has he done? Other than stealing a necklace and giving it to the wrong people?" Ingrid knew some of Gerrit's activities, but not all of them, and she hadn't any idea which ones Rupert was aware of.

"I told him to execute another resistance man. When I handed him my pistol, he pointed it at me and pulled the trigger. Would have killed me if I'd left it loaded. The penalty for that is death."

Ingrid knew Gerrit's life was at risk, but to have Rupert pronounce a sentence like that made her heart beat harder and her palms itch and desperation squeeze the air from her lungs. The incident with the pistol would make it harder to talk Rupert into mercy. "But you're unharmed, and the war's almost over. Haven't enough people died?"

"His work has led to death for some of our men. The cell he's part of has sabotaged rails, and that led to blocked supplies or delayed reinforcements. And the intelligence they've passed on has made our work harder, and told the enemy where to strike us. He may have cost the Reich a great deal indeed. We can't show mercy to saboteurs. And I can't pardon him when he's clearly shown he's willing to kill me."

Gerrit wouldn't have wanted to kill Rupert, but if the choice had been killing Rupert and escaping with another prisoner or shooting a resistance comrade . . . Ingrid would have made the same choice. "Can you at least delay the execution?"

Rupert shook his head. "It's out of my hands."

"But you arrested him, didn't you? Surely you have some say."

"Some."

"Then, won't you try? Please? As a favor to me?" Rupert was Gerrit's best hope. The resistance had arranged rescues from prisons before, but those were extremely difficult to plan, and Ingrid didn't have the connections Anita and Cornelis did.

Rupert studied her for a long moment. "Who is this man to you?"

Ingrid swallowed. "I told you. He's the grandson of the man who gave me a home when I had nowhere else to go. He's part of my adopted family."

Rupert stepped closer. "Is that all?"

No, that wasn't all, but revealing her relationship with Gerrit might result in more danger for her or more danger for Gerrit. "He's a friend. He's a good man. He loves his country and wants it to be free again. I don't know what trouble he's been getting into with the resistance, but when the war is over, the Netherlands—the world—will need people like him to rebuild."

Rupert shook his head. "Rebuild? I'm still fighting for the Reich's survival. And I will be ruthless when needed!"

He turned as if to leave, and Ingrid took his arm. "Please, Rupert. I'll do anything if you'll just have mercy and spare his life."

He paused. Looked her over carefully. "Anything?"

Something in his tone made her worried, but she nodded anyway.

"Does that include joining me in my quarters?"

Ingrid swallowed. She hadn't set out to sell herself, but could she refuse when it would mean Gerrit's death? She's just lost Anita. She couldn't lose Gerrit too. "If that's what it takes for you to spare him."

Rupert stepped closer. All her instincts told her to step away, to put more space between them, but she knew she couldn't flinch. He put a hand on her waist, and the distance between them shrunk to inches. He was half a head taller than her. He held her gaze for what she guessed was a full minute, but she didn't look away. Then he brought his mouth to hers. There wasn't anything inherently wrong with his kiss. He wasn't rough, his breath wasn't foul, and his mouth wasn't unduly moist. But she had more fear than fondness for him, and she knew he couldn't love the person she truly was because she'd carefully hidden away all her real feelings. She wanted to shove him away, but she stayed where she was, letting his lips explore hers and his hands caress her neck.

There was no magic in a forced kiss. Maybe Rupert realized that, too, because he stopped and pulled away with a frown. "I thought I wanted you. But not like this. I want you to want me back."

Ingrid closed her eyes for a moment, gathering her courage. "Let me try again. I'll make it right this time." She put a hand on his shoulder. She would kiss him, and she'd pretend she was kissing Gerrit, and maybe that would be more convincing.

He shrugged her hand away. "If you wanted to *pretend* you cared for me, you should have done it earlier. It's too late now. I may have wanted you, but I can't even trust you anymore." He shook his head. "To think I almost compromised my duty for you."

No, no, he couldn't order Gerrit's execution. She had to change his mind. "Please, Rupert. Give me more time. I'll prove you can trust me. I'll come to love you. I'll do anything you want!"

Rupert's face tilted in thought. "You love him, don't you?"

Ingrid doubted she could lie about that, so she looked away.

"Unbelievable. Did you work with him?"

She shook her head, denying it, hoping Rupert wouldn't detect the lie, hoping he wasn't about to arrest her too.

He stepped closer, looming over her. "Then, if you love him, I won't release him, not for all the wealth of Falcon Point."

Horror made her throat dry, but his last words echoed in her mind. Falcon Point. All the wealth of Falcon Point. "But don't you realize what money like that could do for you? A nice home, a spot at university, a new start anywhere in the world you like. I can offer the jewels of Falcon Point. Money for mercy. I have jewelry now, and I can get more after the war. They'll go far toward whatever you want out of life."

"I wanted *you* out of life!" The expression on his face hardened. "And now I find you love someone else—a poor Dutch criminal, of all men." He shook his head. "Go away, Ingrid. Those pearls you tried to sell in Berlin are already in my custody."

Tears streamed down Ingrid's cheeks. She was going to fail, and Gerrit was going to die. Just like Mama and Papa and Anita. Rupert had adopted his uncle's loyalty to Hitler. Why couldn't he also have more of his uncle's greed so a bribe would sway him?

"I'm not talking about the pearl necklace," she said, desperate for one last try. "You can have these now." She took the pearl earrings from her ears and pressed them into his hand. "And I have a pair of sapphire-and-diamond earrings—the ones my father commissioned for my mother as a wedding present. They're worth more than you've earned since the start of the war. I'll give them to you in exchange for his freedom. But if you kill him, I'll never forgive you."

Rupert was quiet for a moment, staring at her mouth, then at the pearl studs. "I'll think about it."

Rupert went directly to the jail after his visit with Ingrid. He had the guard unlock the cell holding Gerrit Hendriks, who sat on a flea-infested mattress. Hendriks looked up to see who was there, then looked at the floor. He had two black eyes, a scab along his mouth, and bruises visible on every portion of his skin not covered with clothing. Probably on the other parts too. Even after his most violent bursts of temper, Rupert's father had never left Rupert or his mother so battered, but Rupert felt no sympathy for the criminal before him.

"Are you in love with Ingrid Lang?" Rupert asked.

Hendriks's eyes shot up, then away. He said nothing, but the muscles of his jaw hardened.

Jealousy and resentment made Rupert want to rush into the cell and pound his fists into the man, wanted to make him feel pain the way Ingrid's rejection and total devotion to Hendriks had caused Rupert pain. But physical pain wouldn't be enough revenge, not when Rupert had been drawn to Ingrid since he was a boy of sixteen.

"I saw her less than an hour ago. She kissed me."

Hendriks's hand fisted, then slowly spread out again.

Rupert let his mind dwell on that kiss. He'd wanted to kiss Ingrid for years, ever since he'd seen her in that Berlin jewelry store. He'd always imagined her reciprocating his feelings rather than standing there limply. But even though the kiss hadn't lived up to his fantasies, it hadn't been without its pleasures. "Her lips are the perfect blend of supple and firm, aren't they?"

Hendriks folded his arms and looked at one of the walls.

"Her waist is slimmer than I'd imagined. Probably not getting enough to eat, though I have tried to help with that."

Red grew along Hendriks' cheeks. Frustration? Rage? Jealousy?

Rupert pushed on. "And those legs. Maybe next time I'll be able to devote more attention to them."

A slight growl escaped Hendriks's mouth.

Rupert chuckled. "Maybe I will keep you alive a while longer. Ingrid's willing to pay for your prolonged existence, as miserable as it might be, with favors."

"Favors won with fear rather than affection?" Hendriks gave Rupert a look of such contempt that it robbed him of the pleasure he'd taken in gloating.

Did Rupert want his rival dead so he was no longer an obstacle? Or did he prefer to use Hendriks as a way to get whatever he wanted from Ingrid? Only it wouldn't be whatever he wanted. He might be able to kiss her or seduce her, but if Ingrid was willing to trade away the earrings her mother had worn on her wedding day in order to save Hendriks, Rupert's chances of winning her heart seemed minuscule. He fingered the pearl earrings in his pocket. They were worth something, and the earrings custom-made for Liselotte Lang's wedding gift would be worth even more.

Could he be satisfied with using Ingrid when he knew she didn't love him? He'd never forced himself on a woman before, even when war had provided ample opportunity. He wanted Ingrid's affections, not just her body. And was taunting Hendriks more or less satisfying than seeing him dead? Which was better? Physical satisfaction from a woman who didn't love him? Mental satisfaction from tormenting a resistance man he'd already outsmarted and arrested? Or a Lang heirloom and all the opportunities it could give him as he moved past the nightmare of Stalingrad and the heartache of Arnhem?

Gerrit could hardly sleep the night after Altbauer's visit. Sleep was difficult in the prison anyway, with throbbing bruises and nothing but a thin, rancid mattress with no blanket. Even with an uninjured body and a clean, comfortable bed, the cries of the other prisoners, the slam of doors, and the slap of the guards' boots on the floor would have kept him awake. But he doubted he would have slept even if the prison had been silent and his body free of pain, not when he knew Altbauer had kissed Ingrid's mouth and held her waist.

She didn't love Altbauer. That wasn't the worry. But if Altbauer was holding something over her, it was probably Ingrid's safety or Gerrit's safety, and what would it lead to? Gerrit had gone to Altbauer as a double agent so he could save Ingrid, not so he could become leverage for Altbauer to use against her.

When Altbauer had handed Gerrit his pistol and told him to shoot Cornelis, Gerrit had been sure the resistance leader had really wanted Gerrit to shoot him. So Gerrit's cover could remain intact? So Cornelis couldn't be broken and forced to reveal information about the resistance? Gerrit understood now, even more than he'd understood as two Gestapo thugs had beaten him until he could no longer stand, then beaten him until he'd fallen unconscious. He would rather die than be a prisoner in this situation. He didn't know enough to let something slip that would harm Berend or Petrus, assuming they were still free, but knowing the price Ingrid might be paying for his life . . . it was more than he would have asked of her.

The guards had taken away his shoelaces and suspenders after fingerprinting him and taking his photograph. He couldn't hang or strangle himself, couldn't take himself out of play so Altbauer would stop using him to hurt the woman they both loved.

Gloom clutched at Gerrit's heart, and failure pummeled his mind. The Germans were going to lose the war, eventually, but Gerrit doubted he would live to see it, doubted he had done much to change the overall outcome. And when it came to the most important people in his life, he had let them all down. He'd tried to save Ingrid, and instead, he'd put her in greater risk. He'd tried to warn Anita about Altbauer and Daalmans's trap, but the message hadn't gotten to Anita or Cornelis in time. If Gerrit had been with Anita, maybe Daalmans would have shot him instead, and Anita would have walked away unharmed. He still didn't know if she was dead or alive, and that uncertainty hurt, especially when he might have prevented it.

Flashes of memory brought to mind the ration coupons he'd smuggled around Utrecht and the airmen and paratroopers he'd led to safety. None of those things by themselves would affect the war's outcome, but each had made a difference for the people he'd helped. He just wished that when the cost of the war was finally balanced, he would have brought more good than ill to the world in general and to Ingrid in particular.

Gerrit hadn't prayed in years. His mother had taught him, then reminded him most nights, and somewhat less consistently in the mornings. After she died, there hadn't been any reminders to keep praying, and Gerrit's faith, never large anyway, had shriveled away to nothing. Not even being surrounded by people like Opa, Anita, Ingrid, and Henry had pushed him to his knees for prayer. But now, in Koepel Prison, he had already been brought to his knees, figuratively and literally, time after time when the guards had tried to beat information out of him. Praying might not help. But nor would it hurt.

"Please," he whispered. "Please protect Ingrid." He wouldn't ask for mercy for himself—he didn't deserve it. But Ingrid had been through so much. Surely God could spare a little mercy for her.

CHAPTER 29

The door to Gerrit's prison cell slammed open, waking him. Moving hurt, but he obeyed when the guard ordered him to stand.

The guard cuffed Gerrit's hands in front of him, then gave him a little shove. "Out."

With his shackled hands angled so he could hold his pants up, Gerrit followed the guard into the hallway and shuffled along a corridor lined with doors on both sides. Another guard followed him. Both were armed. Hunger gnawed at Gerrit's stomach, and fear made his throat tight. They might be taking him to another interrogation. Or transferring him. But he knew so little, and there was no question of his guilt. Executions happened every single day. In his gut, Gerrit suspected that his turn had come.

The guard led him into an enclosed courtyard, where a military truck waited. Six battered men sat on the canvas-covered truck bed while armed guards watched. Gerrit's guards ordered him up. As he stepped on a crate, then into the truck, it felt as if he were walking into a coffin.

One of the other prisoners lifted his head. Cornelis. Gerrit sat beside him. They didn't speak until twelve more prisoners had been shoved into the back of the truck and the engine rumbled to life, making it unlikely that anyone would overhear them.

"I'm sorry," Gerrit said. "I thought I could outsmart him."

In the dim light, Gerrit spotted the white of Cornelis's teeth. Maybe he'd grimaced. Maybe he'd forced a smile. "As far as I know, it worked. They got you, but your arrest didn't lead to any others. He outsmarted me, too, and that's why I'm here, and your aunt is either dead and buried or lying in a hospital."

Maybe Cornelis was right, and Gerrit had protected Ingrid from suspicion. That was small comfort when, instead, Altbauer was blackmailing her, but maybe that would change when Gerrit was shot.

"Do you think this will be a public execution or one they do in secret, in the woods somewhere?" Either way, Gerrit would be dead, but if it were public, word might reach Ingrid, and Altbauer could no longer use Gerrit as leverage against her. She could slip away to Haarlem or Amsterdam and find safety there.

"I don't know," Cornelis said.

The truck rumbled forward. A cold wind slipped through the canvas, making Gerrit shiver, though he might have shivered anyway. Occasionally, he would catch sight of a star out of the truck's back opening. A car followed them, but its headlights had been blacked out to narrow slits. Might that small bit of light be enough to attract a strafing by an Allied airplane? That would probably kill most of the men in the truck, but the guards were likely to kill all, not just most, so Gerrit preferred the airplane.

No Allied planes came. The horizon turned from charcoal to iron. The road beneath the truck's wheels grew bumpier and more jarring, so Gerrit assumed the execution would be secret. But then the roads smoothed again, and undamaged buildings came into view.

The vehicle pulled to a stop, and someone said the name of the village. Gerrit had ridden through it on bicycle at night a few times, but he'd never seen it in daylight. It seemed he wouldn't live long enough for that to change, though the sky had lightened to ash.

Two guards positioned themselves at the back of the truck, where they could haul down the prisoners. Another German stood behind them, and Gerrit's eyes narrowed. Altbauer. He hadn't thought German intelligence officers stooped to attending executions themselves, but it seemed Altbauer had made an exception.

Gerrit struggled to stand. His limbs were sore and bruised, and the hard, cold floor had left parts of his battered legs numb. The cuffs on his hands further hindered movement. Cornelis stood first and helped Gerrit up.

"Thank you," Gerrit told him. "I'm sorry it's come to this. It's been a privilege to serve with someone as brave as you."

"Same to you. See you on the other side."

The other side? Gerrit wasn't sure he believed in an afterlife. In that moment, he wished he did, but it still seemed like a fairy tale. Something people told themselves because life was hard, and they needed hope. In a world controlled by Hitler, hope itself seemed like an illusion.

As guards pulled the other prisoners from the truck, Gerrit could see the wall the prisoners were lined against as well as the gathering crowd of civilians. They'd probably been stopped and forced to watch. Or maybe they were Dutch Nazis and were glad to see their opponents punished.

"There's a canal two blocks south," one of the prisoners whispered.

Gerrit passed on the rumor, hoping it was true and that someone could escape. But the rattle of the shackles about his wrists confirmed the inevitable: he would die in the square. If he ran, he would be shot. Even if by some miracle he made it to the canal, he couldn't swim without his hands free. Float, perhaps, but that would make it easy for the guards to finish him off.

A glance at Altbauer told Gerrit that he wouldn't get that far anyway. The man watched him with hawklike eyes. Had he come for a final taunt? Or to ensure Gerrit really died? Gerrit wanted to spit at the man, drive pain into his heart with the truth that Ingrid loved Gerrit Hendriks, not Rupert Altbauer, but provocation might backfire. Gerrit was as good as dead, and the execution ought to be blessedly brief. Ingrid still had to navigate the rest of the war, and angering Altbauer might make it harder for her. Gerrit would hold his tongue as a final gift to Ingrid, though she would never know.

Altbauer climbed into the truck and stepped in front of Gerrit as Gerrit approached the exit. Gerrit had planned to ignore him, but that no longer seemed possible. Altbauer stared at him for a long time. Gerrit straightened his shoulders and refused to duck his chin. Altbauer had won when it came to life and death and the resistance, but when it came to the war, Germany was going to lose. And when it came to love, Ingrid would never choose Altbauer.

Something moved in Altbauer's hand. A truncheon. Altbauer frowned, brought the truncheon back, and then smashed it into Gerrit's face. Hot, sharp pain stabbed across Gerrit's cheek and jaw. White flashed in his eyes.

He didn't remember falling, just remembered opening his eyes again, and he was lying in the empty bed of the truck with the taste of blood filling his mouth.

He blinked, tried to move, felt the pain again, so strong that it made him dizzy. Outside, someone called out the order to aim. A voice began singing the Wilhelmus, but Gerrit couldn't tell whether it was one of the prisoners or someone in the crowd singing the national anthem of the Netherlands. The order to fire sounded, and rifle shots pierced the air in a burst of noise. Then everything was silent.

Gerrit was supposed to be in the square with the other prisoners. Why on earth would Altbauer spare Gerrit? Maybe Gerrit would be hauled out now, shown the other dead prisoners, and then be given an alternate method of execution, undoubtedly one worse than a carefully aimed gunshot.

Altbauer climbed back into the truck. Gerrit tried to sit but only succeeded in sliding back, away from the German intelligence officer.

Altbauer crouched over Gerrit and used his truncheon to force Gerrit's head from side to side. He clicked his tongue in distaste. "That's a face no woman would want to kiss."

Was that why Altbauer had given Gerrit a reprieve? So he could taunt him?

Gerrit didn't ask why he'd been spared, but Altbauer explained anyway. "I don't expect you'll live through the winter, but I'm keeping you alive for two reasons: Officially, so that I can call you back for further interrogations. Unofficially, because letting you die a slow death in prison instead of an immediate death here is going to be profitable for me. I'll collect Ingrid's heirlooms later today. If she goes back on her offer, I'll see you shot before sunset."

Ingrid had offered her jewelry to save Gerrit's life? Of course she had. He would have done the same had their roles been reversed, except he had no assets large enough to use as a bribe. Poor Ingrid. Didn't she realize that she would lose her jewelry, and it would merely delay Gerrit's death, not stop it? "And after you take her jewelry, will you leave her alone?"

Altbauer tilted his head to one side. "I suspect that if I investigated, I'd find a reason to arrest her."

Gerrit's throat went dry. "She was never involved." He'd said the lie so many times since being arrested that Altbauer had to believe it.

Altbauer shrugged. "I doubt that. But if she pays up and doesn't do anything to hurt the Reich, I'll leave her be. Not for your sake, of course. For hers, because her family was good to me when very few people were."

Gerrit wished he could see Ingrid one more time to warn her that Altbauer suspected her, to insist she keep her jewelry and run, because Gerrit was lost, and she would need whatever she was using as a bribe to stay alive until the end of the war. But Gerrit was never going to see Ingrid again. That seemed certain. Gerrit remained quiet, and Altbauer stood, then motioned for the guards to load the bodies of the other prisoners back into the truck.

"That German officer is here again." Mevrouw Bakker stood in the doorway to the room Ingrid had so recently shared with Anita, Gerrit, and Opa. Now she shared it only with Opa.

Worry made her hands tremble. Was Rupert here to tell her that Gerrit was dead? "Is he alone?"

Mevrouw Bakker nodded.

Ingrid hoped that meant Rupert wasn't here to arrest her. "If he takes me away, will you tell my opa?" She hated to think of Opa losing her, too, so soon after Anita and Gerrit.

Mevrouw Bakker bit at her lip. "I'll tell your opa. Or I could tell the German that you stepped out. You could run."

Ingrid shook her head. Her chance of escape was slim, and if there were any possibility that talking to Rupert might somehow save Gerrit, she had to see him. "He might have information I need." But she wouldn't risk everything on Rupert's continuing mercy. She begged for a moment to freshen up, then shut the door and fetched the handgun hidden under the mattress, slipping it into her jacket pocket.

Rupert waited in the garden. In contrast to his previous visits, there was no warmth in his face when he saw her. She should have been glad that he no longer seemed interested in romantic pursuit, but his sternness added to her dread.

"I've come for my payment," he said.

Ingrid held her breath for a moment. Rupert had said he'd consider releasing Gerrit in exchange for a bribe, but the more she'd thought it through, the more she'd doubted he would. Too many people would be involved, and though the war looked bad for the Germans, signs of impending defeat hadn't seemed to make them any less cruel. "You'll let Gerrit go?"

"No. But I'll spare his life."

"I offered to trade my earrings for his freedom."

Rupert kept his face even. "I'm offering this instead: You can take the deal, and the note on Hendriks's file will say to hold him in case I need to question him further. Or you can reject the deal, and I'll send a note to Westerbork ordering his execution."

"Westerbork?" Ingrid almost choked as the name of the camp rolled off her tongue. "You're sending him to Westerbork? That's as good as a death sentence."

Rupert shrugged. "I can't release him. Hendriks can go to Westerbork, or I can issue a real death sentence. Your choice."

A small chance of life or the certainty of death? Ingrid decided quickly. "I'll be right back."

Rupert was a Nazi, and he'd modified the original offer. She could return and shoot him. Maybe she could hide the body, and his existing orders to hold Gerrit for questioning would stand. But that wouldn't increase Gerrit's chances of survival. It would be murder, and the only benefit would be that Ingrid could keep her earrings. She valued the jewelry from her mother, but she wouldn't tarnish her soul with murder in order to keep it.

Her few belongings all fit into one knapsack. She pulled the small, stained jewelry box from beneath her spare dress. Inside were her mother's favorite earrings. Even in the window's dim glow, the gems seemed to capture the light and release it again with a bit of magic.

Ingrid pulled the earrings from their black cushion. She hadn't promised Rupert the box, so she would keep it along with the key sewn into the back of the velvet pad. After today, she wouldn't have much left of her family: the box with the key, passports for her father and brother, and a pair of Karl's mittens. But Gerrit would have the possibility of life. And after the war, she would find her siblings again, and then hanging on to mittens and a half-burned passport that didn't belong to her would no longer be necessary. She almost put the earrings on her ears for a final time, but delaying would only make it harder, and she didn't want Rupert to change his mind. He held all the power in their negotiations. It wasn't fair, but it was reality.

Rupert was pacing in the garden when she returned, his eyes darting here and there as if expecting an attack. Perhaps he'd read her mind or noticed the way her coat hung unevenly because something heavy was concealed in one of the pockets. Or perhaps caution had become habit while he lived in a country that didn't want him.

Ingrid handed over the earrings. Rupert wrapped them in a handkerchief and slipped them into his pocket. He didn't examine them, but he would know their value when it came to a chance to change his future.

"May I see him again, before you send him to Westerbork?" Ingrid asked.

Rupert raised one eyebrow. "I would advise caution from you, Fräulein Lang. I might not have proof that you are involved in the resistance, but in my position, I don't need proof. Suspicion is enough, and your association with Gerrit Hendriks provides that."

Ingrid looked away. "I don't want to join him at Westerbork. I just want to see him one last time, in case I never have another chance."

Rupert put his hand in the pocket where he'd stored the jewelry. He gave a reluctant nod. "Come with me."

She thought he would lead her to the prison, and as much as she didn't want to enter it, she would risk it for a chance to say goodbye. She grabbed the old bicycle with wooden blocks rather than rubber wheels, one Gerrit had repaired so many times.

But instead of leading her to the prison, Rupert led her to an overlook and pointed to a truck driving north. "He's inside."

There wasn't any way she could catch the truck. It was already far ahead of her, and though the road was pitted with divots and gaps, the truck's engine would far outpace a bicycle.

That didn't stop her from mounting her bicycle and riding as hard as she could, chasing the prison truck. What she would do if she caught it she didn't know, but she had to try. She'd lost her parents, then her sister, then her brother. Her dreams of liberation had been raised to the heavens by an army falling from the sky, only to be shattered in a heartbreaking, soul-crushing defeat. She'd lost the woman who had become like a sister. And now, the first man she'd ever fallen in love with was being wrenched away, and this might be her last chance to ever see him.

Her legs burned. So did her lungs. And the truck drew farther and farther ahead of her. Then one of the wooden blocks on the wheels began to wobble, and the bicycle's speed was cut in half. At the foot of a hill, she left the bicycle behind and ran to the crest, lungs heaving, in time to see the truck fading in the distance. She'd done all she could, and it wasn't enough. Gerrit was going to a concentration camp, and he might never return.

No one in the truck would be able to see the gesture, but she raised her fingers in a *V* for victory and held it until the truck disappeared from view.

CHAPTER 30

January 1945

For four and a half years, Gerrit had kept track of how many days his country had been under Nazi occupation. Each day had been a new wrong, a new reason to fight for justice and freedom. But sometime over the winter in Westerbork's punishment barracks, he'd lost count. Days were now a strange muddle of pain and fear and suffering. The winter solstice had passed weeks ago. At least, he thought it had been weeks ago. The weather wouldn't warm, not anytime soon, but the days weren't quite so short.

His breath came out in a cold, opaque cloud as he removed part of the panel of a crashed airplane. He wished he had a scarf or a hat or an extra pair of socks. Even more newspaper to use as insulation inside his clothing would have helped. More wood or coal to burn in the stove. But he and the others working nearby were essentially slaves. They received no pay for their work, scarcely enough food to stay alive, and nothing but the clothes they had come with and a single, threadbare blanket at night to stave off the frigid winter temperatures.

There were worse assignments than taking apart pieces of aircraft to scavenge useful parts or materials. Some days, he even found it interesting to remove the dials and strip the wires to save copper, as long as he could avoid thinking too much of how the metals saved were going directly to the German war machine. He hated that his work would help the enemy, but he'd rather recycle bits and pieces of aircraft than dig graves or do the manual labor his body had grown too weak for.

"Bring it here," one of the other prisoners said.

Gerrit met the eyes of a nearby man. He looked to be about Opa's age, someone new to Westerbork, and together they lifted the panel and brought it to a table.

The not-so-distant sound of a shot rang out. It repeated again and again.

The man who'd been helping Gerrit looked in the direction of the sound, and his bushy, gray eyebrows pulled with concern. "What was that?"

"Executions," Gerrit said. "Performed behind the crematorium." Having a work assignment, no matter what the task, was far better than having one's name called out and being led to a corner of Westerbork, blindfolded, and having everything extinguished.

The man crossed himself. "What did they do?"

Gerrit shrugged. He didn't know, but he could guess. Their supposed crimes were probably not so different from his own. Sabotage. Working with the resistance. Hiding someone the Germans wanted. Aiding enemy paratroopers.

The man came around to stand beside Gerrit. "How long have you been here?"

Gerrit motioned toward one of the dials. "You'd better get to work if you want to eat."

The man took the hint and started taking apart the pieces of the panel.

Gerrit watched for a moment. "What was your occupation before coming here?"

"Mechanic."

"Then, I imagine you can teach us all a thing or two."

The man shrugged. "If the goal is to do the work well."

Gerrit had once thought like that. Why do the work well if it would benefit the enemy? But Westerbork had taught him hard lessons. "The goal is survival. You came yesterday, right?"

The man nodded.

"Any news from the front?"

"My news is old now. I was processed in Amsterdam. Spent weeks in a prison there. Before I was arrested, the Germans launched a big offensive, pushed the Americans back into Belgium."

Gerrit focused on a screw that needed more than his usual effort before it could be pried off. Another setback for the Allies. Another change that made his chances of survival smaller, because the longer the war went on, the more likely death seemed. He'd already lost significant weight, a cough plagued him at night, and Rupert Altbauer had only to give the word, and Gerrit would be led behind the crematorium and shot through the head.

"How long have you been here?" the man asked again.

"Since October."

The man kept working. "I've heard rumors about the Nazi camps. Not that I want things to be worse . . . but I expected . . . well, how frequent are the executions?"

"Not every day. They used to send people east, and no one ever came back. But the trains don't run anymore." Those had stopped when the British and American airborne troops had dropped into the Netherlands in a failed attempt to open a corridor into the Ruhr. Westerbork had been constructed before the war. During the occupation, the Nazis had taken it over, changing it from a place meant to house Jewish refugees on their journey to freedom into a place meant to gather those who had offended the Nazis by their beliefs or merely by their birth. For years, Jews and other undesirables had been collected in Westerbork, then shipped to places like Auschwitz and Sobibor. Places, rumor said, where people were executed wholesale. Death still visited the inmates of Westerbork, in disease and in executions, but now that the trains no longer left, Westerbork's purpose was economic benefit for the enemy rather than extermination. "Westerbork was a transit camp, not a death camp."

That didn't mean the food rations were sufficient. Nor did it fully stock the hospital with supplies or staff. Slaves, in the eyes of the enemy, didn't need to be warm or healthy. They worked long hours, though not quite as long as they had when Gerrit had first arrived. Downed airplanes were getting harder to come by as the Germans lost the war. Though if the latest rumors were true, they weren't losing it nearly fast enough. Time was Gerrit's enemy, a Nazi accomplice. He felt it every day in hunger pangs that were never fully satiated and in less vigor as he walked and worked. Hope, too, seemed to be growing more and more elusive. When he'd left Gelderland, he'd assumed he wouldn't return, wouldn't live to see his family again. Yet as his bruises had healed at Westerbork, the neglect had seemed to make survival possible, at least for a while. Until that pain had sneaked into his lungs and taken up permanent residence.

When the group finished processing the airplane scraps, Gerrit followed the others to the food line. He shuffled along in a pair of wooden clogs that were a little too small for him. No one other than the guards had shoes anymore. He turned up the collar of his shirt to block a few inches of wind. The group standing in line for watery soup was a ragged bunch, resembling corpses more than they resembled living men. The sky was gray, with only a small amount of light, and the light was fading, much like the health and hope of every inmate of Westerbork.

Weeks passed. The days grew longer, but the temperatures didn't moderate. Spring, warmth, the possibility of freedom—all remained out of reach. Gerrit moved more slowly. His body hurt in new places. The cough that had crept in at night no longer retreated during the day. Sometimes it hurt to breathe.

He didn't know how Ingrid, Opa, or his siblings were faring. Didn't know if Anita was dead or alive. Didn't know how the battle lines might be moving. He just knew that here, now, life was ebbing away, and any change could shift the ebb into a sudden end.

He had taken to working with Adriaan, the man from Amsterdam, learning about his family and more efficient ways of dismantling the ruined airplanes. Some days, efficiency was their goal. Some days, it was not. All the inmates were gradually growing slower and weaker. For Adriaan, the change to Westerbork rations had been an abrupt one, and his health had melted away with astonishing speed.

One day, Adriaan didn't leave his bunk when it came time to report for work duty. Gerrit helped him to the hospital. Gerrit visited the day after and the day after that, but Adriaan made no improvement. Pneumonia, a nurse said.

Gerrit spooned watery soup with a few pieces of potato into Adriaan's mouth.

"I miss Astrid. And her cooking," Adriaan mumbled.

Working side by side for so long, Gerrit had heard Adriaan describe in detail each of his favorite meals his wife had made. Some days, it was hard to focus on anything other than food. "Was she arrested?"

"Yes, but I told her to say she didn't know anything about my work with the resistance. She kept to the plan, and they released her."

"They believed her?"

Adriaan nodded. "I took the blame."

"Well then, you'll have to get better. So you can see Astrid again. Seems only fair, after taking the blame for her."

"And you? Have you a woman to go home to?"

Ingrid's image came to Gerrit's mind. He thought of her every day, fell asleep most nights remembering the past and imagining a future. "Not a wife. But if I make it out of this, I intend to find her again. To say thank you, if nothing else."

"Thank you?"

"I was supposed to be executed. She bribed someone, so I was sent here instead. The end result might be the same." He broke off to cough. "But she sacrificed for me."

"Then, don't let her get away."

Gerrit shook his head. "We're from different worlds. If not for the war, we never would have met, let alone fallen in love."

"But there was a war. And you did meet. And you did fall in love."

A cough prevented Gerrit from replying, and when it finally passed, he switched subjects. "Do you want me to read to you?" Dwelling on all the reasons he and Ingrid might never be together hurt, and there was enough pain in Westerbork without adding more. For now, he needed the hope of seeing her again. Gerrit gestured to the small New Testament half hidden under the jacket Adriaan was using as a pillow. A smile formed, unintended, because Gerrit could almost imagine the look Ingrid would give him if she could see him now, volunteering to read the Bible.

Adriaan nodded, and Gerrit read, stopping often to cough. He came back the next day and the next. The day after, Adriaan was too weak to stay awake and listen, so Gerrit kept his visit short. The day after that, Adriaan was gone. The medical orderly handed Gerrit Adriaan's book. "He wanted you to have this."

Maybe someday, if he survived the war, Gerrit could take the Bible to Astrid and tell her that the book had helped her husband keep hope when everything else offered only despair. And maybe, in the meantime, Astrid wouldn't mind if Gerrit read the book himself, because he needed hope almost as much as he needed food and warmth.

CHAPTER 31

INGRID RAN A FINGER THROUGH the tulip bulb she'd just ground into powder. It looked and felt a lot like flour, the expensive kind she had seen whenever she'd gone to the kitchen at Falcon Point to help bake. Tulip bulbs were the only food she'd been able to purchase the last time she'd gone to the store. They weren't the grocer's normal produce, but as tulip farmers hadn't been able to plant the bulbs that fall during the battles, they had been persuaded to sell their stored stocks for food. Tulip bulbs, turnips, and a few odds and ends were the only items staving off starvation.

Opa came into the kitchen. They lived with one of his associates, Dr. Kley, in Velp, where it would be harder for Rupert to find her, either to arrest her or to court her. Safer, too, for Mevrouw Bakker and her children. In the small home, Ingrid slept on a couch. Opa slept on a small mattress they stored against the wall during the day. In the autumn, they had talked of going to stay with one of Opa's sons in Haarlem or Amsterdam, but there were no trains to take them, no cars, no working bicycles. Any journey would be by foot, as winter approached, likely with harassment by German soldiers or policemen at every crossroad and every village they passed through. Nor had Opa wanted to leave his patients. So they had stayed in Gelderland.

Opa glanced at the ground bulbs. "Did it work?"

"It feels fine enough to turn into a pie crust or streusel, if the other ingredients for things like that could be found. I'll see how it bakes up after I let it rise."

Opa nodded. "I'll eat at the hospital, so have my share for me. Tell me how it turns out."

Ingrid nodded. With the limited items she had to work with, she imagined the loaf would be hard, unappetizing, and too small to be filling. She was thankful that Opa could eat the occasional meal at the hospital, because even though he frequently told her to eat his share—and she did—her clothing dwarfed her diminished frame, and hunger constantly gnawed at her stomach. The past few months, since Anita had been gunned down and Gerrit sent to a concentration camp, were being referred to as the Hunger Winter. No one had enough to eat. The trains still didn't run, so no food could be brought from outside. Even if the trains had been working, the occupied parts of the Netherlands were cut off from the rest of Europe by the front line. They were isolated and starving.

During the early part of winter, Ingrid had tried to resurrect Anita's resistance cell, but deaths, disappearances, and displacement had scattered the few living survivors, and trusting strangers felt like too large a risk. When that had failed, she'd approached Opa about working at the hospital, but by then, there simply hadn't been time. Every day, she had to travel farther and farther to find food and fuel. And each day, it was harder and harder to get out of bed and begin her search. The sun was shining longer now as spring approached, but she was going to bed earlier and earlier and often had to stop for long rests after walking mere blocks. Running would have been out of the question—she now wheezed when she overexerted herself. She suspected bicycling would also be too much of a strain, but she no longer had a working bicycle, so she hadn't been able to test her theory. It was as though her body had grown ancient in the course of one season. If she was still in Velp, and starving, and barely able to go through the motions of survival, what must it be like for someone in Westerbork?

"Do you suppose they'd tell us if anything happened to Gerrit?" she asked.

Opa frowned. "The Germans can be meticulous when it comes to records, but sending notices to their victims' next of kin won't help them stave off defeat."

Ingrid nodded, unsure if Opa would pass on ill news even if he did receive it. Too many lost: Papa, Anita, Cornelis. Too many others missing, with an uncertain fate: Gerrit, Karl, Anna. Ingrid added the powdered bulbs to yesterday's dough, hoping the leavening would spread and that it would work on flour made of bulbs rather than grain. She'd give it time to rise while she went to harvest more bulbs and look for something to burn in the small emergency stove. It used wood as fuel, and she controlled the temperature by opening a small door in the bottom and blowing. An oven would be better, but civilians in Velp hadn't had electricity since September, and it was now March.

"How are your ankles?" Opa asked.

Ingrid looked down, though she could have answered without looking. Most of her body was shrinking, but her ankles were swelling. The pain had disturbed her sleep the night before, but Opa had enough to worry about without her complaining about a little pain from swollen ankles. "They don't hurt so much in the morning."

Opa nodded, said his goodbye, and went to the hospital. Ingrid set her dough aside and hoped for a miracle. She left the home and walked along the sad little lane. Trees had been chopped down and fences disassembled for fuel. Windows had been shattered or broken out. If she stopped to look inside the homes she walked past, she suspected the rooms would be missing pieces of furniture, also sacrificed as fuel.

Ingrid followed directions to a home Opa had made arrangements with and dug in the abandoned gardens for tulip bulbs. The task sobered her, not only because it marked how desperate she was for food, but also because once eaten, the bulbs would no longer produce flowers. The needs of the present would rob the future of some of its beauty. The small trowel she used wasn't heavy, and the bulbs weren't deep. Still, she was out of breath in minutes.

When she had gathered as many bulbs as she could find, she paused to rest. Walking was easy. Why did it take so much effort to begin the journey? She wished Anita were here. She could laugh at how slow and clumsy Ingrid had become, almost like when they'd first met and Ingrid had had two broken legs.

Ingrid's throat, already tight with the efforts of digging out the bulbs, constricted further as memories of Anita surfaced. If only Anita were still alive. She would have made the slow winter of starvation seem not quite as bleak. Maybe if she hadn't died, Opa would smile when he recounted a successful surgery or when they heard good news of the war. As it was, Ingrid hadn't seen him smile since autumn.

As she journeyed back, she had to stop to rest from time to time, and it was difficult to pick up her feet. She couldn't take any shortcuts because she had to avoid minefields. She finally stumbled into the house and sat on the first chair she came to, breathing as hard as if she'd just followed Karl up the side of one of the mountains around Falcon Point.

She'd forgotten to look for fuel.

The temptation to use the wooden handle of the trowel or part of a kitchen cupboard was strong, but she knew that if she wanted to eat, she had to go out again. And she very much wanted to eat, even if the dough she'd made looked only marginally edible.

A glance at the clock told her time was moving far more quickly than she was. She forced herself to stand and took three steps toward the door. But on the fourth, she collapsed. Her legs wouldn't hold her, and it was hard to breathe. She gasped, trying to fill her lungs, until her heart rate returned to normal and the swell of nausea passed. Despite an overwhelming sense of weakness, she gingerly tested her feet. They seemed no stronger than before. Maybe sleeping would help, just for a while. She couldn't make it to the couch a dozen steps away, so she lay on the floor, planning to rest for only a short time until she had the strength to gather something to burn so she could bake her dough.

She was still lying on the kitchen floor when Opa returned from the hospital and woke her that evening.

Rupert would be on the losing side of the war, that was certain. What would Germany be like when the Communists overran it? Looking into the future was like staring into a black abyss. Horror was all Rupert could see. The mighty Reich was being invaded from all sides, and they were unlikely to receive any mercy. In his heart, he knew the Reich had also given little mercy. He imagined Berlin turning into a Stalingrad or an Arnhem. Maybe it was just as well that his mother and stepfather wouldn't have to see the destruction that was to come. Would Heidi be sheltered from it at Falcon Point? Or would she experience the full terror of war the same way so many other children had?

"There's someone to see you, Altbauer." Denhart's voice.

Rupert looked up to see his hauptmann standing beside Dr. van der Veen. Rupert stood at attention for Denhart's sake, then motioned for the doctor to sit.

"I remember you," Rupert said when he and the doctor were both seated.

The doctor looked weary, but his posture was impeccable. "I have come to ask for your help."

Rupert scoffed. "My help? I doubt there is anything I can do, and even if there were, why would I help the grandfather of a known resistance member? According to Daalmans, there is reason to believe you yourself have been involved in illegal activities."

The accusation didn't ruffle the doctor's calm. "I have always been a doctor. Before the war. During the war. And while Mynheer Daalmans was a patient in the St. Elisabeth Hospital."

"Most of us have more than one role in this life." Rupert didn't have a strong inclination to arrest the doctor, but nor would he hesitate if the doctor gave him reason. "You wouldn't be the first doctor to treat patients *and* cooperate with the resistance."

"It's possible that some of my patients were members of the resistance. Some of them were members of the German Army. I treat all my patients as well as circumstances allow, regardless of their beliefs or status in this war."

"And your purpose in coming here?"

The man looked away for a moment, as if hesitating. But he had sought Rupert out, and he must have known it was too late to change his mind. "Ingrid has famine edema."

Rupert had seen edema, knew what it could do. Denhart had explained it succinctly: It began in the feet. When it reached the heart, the patient died. "How far has the swelling spread?"

"Above the hem of her skirt. She also has severe anemia. She needs more to eat. Red meat would be best."

Disease caused by nutritional deficiency couldn't be cured with one hearty meal. The doctor would know that, which meant he was asking Rupert for continuing help. That was something Rupert wasn't willing to do, not for a traitorous woman who had scorned him. Nor was he sure he could. His rations had been cut repeatedly over the winter. Most nights, he went to bed accompanied by hunger. "Times are hard for everyone. She'll have to muddle through the best she can." Rupert hoped the doctor would leave then, but he remained seated.

"You gave her food before," Dr. van der Veen said.

"That was before I found out she was in love with a criminal."

"You were friends as children. Her family was kind to you."

Rupert hesitated. What the man said was true. But the Langs had also proved traitors, and he didn't think Ingrid was an exception. He hadn't investigated her, even when he probably should have, because of their past. But he owed her nothing more. "Ingrid Lang and her health are not my responsibility."

The doctor looked down. "No. Her health is my responsibility. But I've done all I can. There's no extra food to be bought, even when I receive a paycheck, which isn't often. I've already passed my portions on to her, but it's not enough."

"If she's eating your portions and still falling ill, perhaps it serves her right. She's a glutton."

The doctor's jaw clenched. "Six hundred calories a day is not the diet of a glutton. She'd be dead already if she weren't eating my share. I told her I was eating at the hospital. She assumes I'm getting as much or more than she is."

"Are you?"

Dr. van der Veen shook his head. "Maybe once a week. Most days, we barely have enough food for the patients."

Rupert could almost feel sorry for the old man. He was sacrificing to save someone, but despite all his efforts, it wasn't enough. But the Dutch had brought this upon themselves. The Germans had been magnanimous to the Netherlands. In return, the Germans had met resentment and resistance. "Ingrid's father once told me that we can pick our choices but not our consequences. The Dutch chose the railway strike. The Hunger Winter is the consequence."

"Ingrid is not a railway worker."

"Maybe not," Rupert said. "But she chose to throw in her lot with the Dutch. Now she will have to suffer the consequences."

"Those consequences might include death. Already, I fear her health will be affected for the rest of her life. If she ever wants to have children—"

"Why should I care?" If Ingrid didn't want to have Rupert's children, he hardly felt the need to preserve her health for some other man's progeny, especially if that other man were the one he'd sent to Westerbork.

"You should care because war may have placed us in circumstances where we are not allies, but I think that underneath your uniform, you're a good man. Someone to step in when an old friend's life is at risk and you can save her."

Rupert huffed. "You can leave now."

"Please." Dr. van der Veen leaned forward. "Please help her. If I had money, I would offer it, but my home was destroyed and all my assets along with it. I've lost two daughters already in this war, and I've not heard from some of my sons in years. I don't want to lose Ingrid too."

"Go away, old man. Or I'll have you arrested."

The doctor stood. "You're right. I'm just an old man who's lost his home, his town, and most of his family. And you're just a young man who has lost his soul."

Rupert swallowed back anger that quickly turned to grief. He might not want to admit it, but he had changed, grown harder. That was part of surviving a world at war. "No one made it out of Stalingrad with an intact soul."

Dr. van der Veen put his hat on his head. "I've seen a lot of things heal over the course of my life. There is no cure for death, whether the cause is edema or something else. But there are cures for souls damaged by war, and they usually start with goodness instead of indifference."

Rupert sat at his desk for a long time after the doctor left. *Goodness instead of indifference.* What nonsense. Rupert wasn't indifferent to the war: he was dying a little inside knowing that all his work, all the Reich's efforts, all their victories and sacrifices would end in defeat. Nor was he indifferent when it came to Ingrid—he had cared so much that her rejection had broken his heart. She had made her choice. And Rupert was making his choice to move on. He owed her nothing.

Ingrid hadn't left Dr. Kley's home for two weeks. Walking as far as the toilet winded her. The kitchen was empty, so there was rarely a reason to go there. Most of the time, she lay on the couch because her body was so wasted from hunger that sitting upright was no longer comfortable. Opa found little bits of food—a slice of bread, a single piece of dried fruit, a shriveled tulip bulb—but never in quantities sufficient to fill her stomach.

"Would she be better off in a hospital?" Dr. Kley asked Opa. They were around the corner, but Ingrid still heard their words.

"We don't have food there either. So many are dying. So many who would recover with proper nutrition."

"I hear it's even worse in Amsterdam. Five hundred, six hundred people starving to death every week."

"And to think that liberation was so close last September." Sadness coated Opa's voice. "When it failed, I should have told both girls to guide paratroopers away from Gelderland. Then maybe Anita would still be alive and Ingrid wouldn't be dying."

Was she *dying*? Opa hadn't told her as much, but the prognosis felt true. Energy and flesh were both disappearing. She didn't know if the home contained any paper that hadn't been used to fuel the stove, but she would ask for paper and pen and leave letters for her siblings. Wherever Karl and Anna were, she hoped they had enough to eat. And Gerrit. She knew where he was. Or where he had been, but she doubted the inmates of Westerbork ate well.

A knock sounded on the door. Firmer than she would have expected from a member of the resistance. Not urgent enough to be threatening, so probably not the Gestapo. Most likely, it was someone looking for a doctor.

Ingrid forced herself to sit, but Dr. Kley reached the knob before Ingrid could stand. He opened the door to reveal Rupert Altbauer. Ingrid swallowed. If he arrested her, she would be dead within days.

He looked beyond Dr. Kley and met her eyes. His expression held no contempt for her suspicious loyalty to a Dutch family, no disgust at her sickly appearance. Just surprise. "You really are dying, aren't you?" His words were a whisper.

Was her condition so obvious? She hadn't looked in a mirror recently, but it had been five months since she'd last seen Rupert. Much had changed since then. "How did you know I was ill?"

Rupert looked to Opa, and understanding dawned. Opa was trying to save Ingrid from starvation, and he was desperate enough to ask an enemy for help.

Rupert still stood in the doorway. He bent to the side, then rose again holding a crate. "May I come in?"

Dr. Kley glanced at Opa, who nodded. Ingrid wasn't sure if Dr. Kley was involved in the resistance in any way, but most people thought twice before inviting a German soldier into their home, especially now, when radio reports and rumors promised a German defeat.

When Dr. Kley stepped aside and motioned Rupert in, Rupert hesitated. He couldn't feel threatened, not by two men who looked older than their six decades, not by a woman of twenty who was too weak to even stand. But maybe fear of hostility was what made him pause. Ingrid had, after all, rejected his romantic overtures. And Rupert had, after all, exiled Opa's grandson and Ingrid's sweetheart to Westerbork. Finally, Rupert stepped forward and set the crate beside Ingrid on the couch. He remained standing. "Go ahead, look through it."

Ingrid held his gaze for a long moment, then reached for something wrapped in brown paper. Liverwurst, perhaps half a kilo of it, and it had left smears of grease on the wrapping. Smears of grease meant fat, and that was something Ingrid hadn't eaten in a very long time. Next came dark bread, the standard fare for German soldiers. Two loaves of it. Then flour, three cabbages, and seven potatoes.

"It won't provide a feast worthy of Falcon Point." Rupert shoved his hands into his pockets. "But food isn't easy to get, not even for German leutnants."

Ingrid's eyes had stung as she'd unwrapped the gifted food, and now the moisture threatened to overflow. She blinked and wiped away a stray tear. "Thank you, Rupert. This feels an awful lot like a miracle. After everything that's happened, I didn't expect something like this from you."

Rupert piled the cabbages and potatoes back into the crate so he could sit. "It was your jewelry. I put it by a pendant from my mother, and . . . she would have chosen mercy. Your mother's earrings are from another time, another place, and I don't see how we can ever get back to those years when we were friends and I was welcomed into your family home. That past is gone, but I didn't want that pretty girl I once danced with to never dance again. Even if you'll never again dance with me. I can't save the Reich or stop the hunger spreading throughout the Netherlands. But maybe this will help you. And maybe the next time I look at your earrings, my conscience won't tell me I abandoned you."

Ingrid wiped at another tear. No, they could never go back. She could never truly trust him, not while he served the Reich. Nor could she ever forget what he had done to Gerrit. But Rupert wasn't just a ruthless intelligence officer. He was also the abused boy who had escaped to Falcon Point for a handful of summer vacations. He was the old friend who had given her money for a train ticket when she'd been stuck in Berlin and the jeweler hadn't bought her necklace. And his gift of food might just save her life. She grasped his hand and repeated her earlier words. "Thank you."

He smiled, and in that smile, she saw more of the old friend and less of the enemy. "Hopefully, it will tide you over until the food from the Swedes is distributed."

"They sent more?" In January, several ships from Sweden had brought flour, margarine, and cod-liver oil. She imagined it had saved countless lives, but the need was still so great.

"Yes. A second shipment arrived at Delfzijl." Rupert stood and took a small envelope from his pocket. He handed it to Opa. "Iron supplements. I couldn't get many from the medical officers, but I trust you'll know how to best ration and dose it."

Opa took the envelope with a motion that was almost reverent. "Thank you for changing your mind." It had to be hard for Opa, but he offered his hand to the man who had sent his grandson to a concentration camp and set the trap that had led to his youngest daughter's death. Rupert grasped and shook it.

Rupert nodded at Opa, then at Ingrid, then left the home.

CHAPTER 32

Gerrit scratched at the back of his neck as he read. Like everyone else in the barracks, he had lice. Or maybe they were fleas. Regardless, they left welts that itched and throbbed. When daylight disappeared and he could no longer see the words, he slid Adriaan's Bible under the blanket of his narrow bunk and stared at the ceiling, thinking about Peter the disciple. Trying to walk on water. Getting scared. Starting to sink. How often had Gerrit felt like that? Trying to liberate his country had proved as improbable as walking on water. He'd faced fear time after time, been unable to save friends or change the tide of battle or match wits with the enemy. Gerrit was drowning: in war, in failure, in sin, in despair.

When the world has gone dark, don't turn away from the light. The words Ingrid had written that first time they'd coded together came to mind. The world had gone dark when the war had started. Darker when he'd been sent to Westerbork. There didn't seem to be much light to hold on to in a camp like this, but maybe Gerrit, like Peter, needed to reach for his Savior. He didn't need to be pulled from a sea. He needed to be pulled from the wrongs that surrounded him—those his own misguided actions had created and those the war had created.

Something about the story . . . It matched the desperation that had been growing in Gerrit's heart for years. He needed a Savior. Now. He'd needed one before, too, but all the excuses, all the doubt, none of it held up anymore, not when everything was dark except Christ.

As Gerrit had read Adriaan's New Testament over the past few months, he had recognized in the Savior someone who had seen all the worst the world could offer: hunger, hatred, betrayal, prison, torture, oppression, and loneliness. He had suffered it all, but He hadn't turned bitter, hadn't lashed out, hadn't loved any less.

Regardless of whether Gerrit ever left Westerbork, he would be different. Instead of clinging to rage, he would help others and trust God because that was what the Savior had done. Over the course of the night, Gerrit prayed and pleaded and promised to be better, if he could just be given another chance. When dawn came, the hope he had been clinging to felt more and more tangible. He didn't want to live in darkness anymore. He wanted the Lord's light, now, in Westerbork, and later, when the war ended, because Gerrit needed more than a ceasefire. He needed the peace that came only with true redemption.

Guards entered the barracks as they had so many times before. One read names from a sheet of paper. "Gerrit Hendriks," he called out along with the names of two others.

For months, Gerrit had dreaded the possibility that his name would be among those called. Men on those lists never returned. Always, before an hour had passed, shots equal to the number of men led away would echo behind the crematorium. Gerrit's body, already chilled, now felt like ice. Spring had come, rumors spoke of German losses on all sides, and Gerrit had finally found peace with God. Now he would be executed?

He climbed from his bunk and held the bed frame for a moment as a wave of dizziness made his legs and head sway. Months and months of hunger made even standing difficult. The only reason he or any of the other prisoners were still alive was because of Red Cross packages that arrived from time to time, but Gerrit suspected he had seen his last Red Cross parcel and the last of the watery soup that was the camp's standard fare. He slipped on his clogs and eased in a lungful of air. Men in nearby bunks wouldn't meet his eyes. They, too, knew what the summons meant.

Gerrit had little choice other than to obey. He supposed he could have refused to move, but that would likely earn him a beating prior to his execution, and it wouldn't save his life. He and two other men followed the German guards outside. Gerrit wondered if somewhere in his file, Rupert Altbauer had instructed his captors that Gerrit wasn't to survive the war.

Evidence of battle—the rumble of artillery, clouds of dust on the horizon, and fear in the eyes of their captors—had reached the camp in recent days, growing ever closer. Liberation was near, and maybe this time, the Allies wouldn't be surrounded and forced to fight until the last bullet while they waited for a woefully tardy armored column to rescue them.

Early-morning light revealed a line of prisoners marching through the camp gate, about one hundred of them. All women. Guards surrounded them, making it clear they weren't being released. Were they being transferred or marched off to a mass execution?

Other guards with prisoners from other barracks joined Gerrit's group as it shuffled toward the crematorium. Gerrit listened to the distant boom of artillery, wishing it were a little less distant. How many times in this war would he be surrounded by Nazis, with help mere kilometers away—so close but not close enough?

Another group left the camp through the main gate. This one was smaller, they rode in cars, and they had luggage—the camp commandant, his mistress, and other top officers.

"Are you sure you want to execute us?" one of the prisoners asked the highest-ranking guard.

The unteroffizier didn't answer, but one of the other soldiers did. "We have our orders."

The prisoner tried again. "The man who issued those orders just fled because soon, the Allies will control this camp, and Kommandant Gemmeker doesn't want to be arrested and charged with war crimes. What do you think you'll be charged with if you carry out executions after Gemmeker has left?"

The unteroffizier hesitated. "All militaries understand orders and the need to follow them."

"Do you know who's coming?" Gerrit asked.

"Does it matter?" One of the guards pushed Gerrit up against the wall, then did the same to the other prisoner who'd been trying to convince them to disobey orders.

"Yes," Gerrit said, clutching at straws. "I was at Nijmegen. I remember the German prisoners there. They were terrified because they'd heard rumors that the American paratroopers would show no mercy to them in revenge for what happened when the 82nd landed in Sainte-Mère-Église."

"If there were prisoners, the Americans must not have massacred them," one of the guards said.

Gerrit shrugged as if he weren't pleading for his life. "There were some. More surrendered than made it to the prison cages."

One of the guards shoved another prisoner against the wall. "The advancing troops aren't American."

"You think the British will be any more merciful after what happened in Arnhem?" Gerrit's words made several of the guards pause. He doubted they had been at Arnhem, but they would know how hard that battle had been fought.

A third prisoner spoke up. "Your kommandant just left. If he comes back, you can execute us then. But he wouldn't have run if he didn't think this camp would soon be in Allied hands. They're the ones you want to think about, not the coward fleeing with his treasures."

The final prisoners were lined against the wall. The guards pointed their weapons at those sentenced to die. No last letters, no last meals. Just grim-faced guards threatening them while the sound of the Allied advance remained painfully out of sight but not out of hearing.

The guards spoke in quiet tones. Kept their weapons aimed. Peered into the distance, as if to see who was closer, their former kommandant or whatever Allied army lay beyond the horizon. The discussion took a long time, each moment fraught with the chance of death and the chance of life. All it would take was one order, one firm decision, and Gerrit and the others would be gunned down. Or the discussion might turn the other way and offer salvation.

Gerrit silently prayed, leaning against the wall because his body was too weak to stand without support. He prayed for mercy, and if not for life, then for the courage to meet death without cowering. He prayed for Opa, for Ingrid, for Johan and Nellie, for Anita if she was still alive, for Pap, and for his aunts and uncles. And he prayed for the army coming toward Westerbork. His hunger to see the future didn't diminish, but his fear began to vanish. Whether he lived or whether he died, his soul, surrounded by his frail body, was finally starting to heal.

The guards seemed to end their debate. The unteroffizier stuck out his chin and straightened his back. "Prisoners are to return to their barracks."

Relief made goose bumps stand out on Gerrit's arms. The unteroffizier might at any moment change his mind, or a setback at the front might make the kommandant return and see the end of all dangerous prisoners. But for now, Gerrit's prayers had been answered. He and the others had been given deliverance.

The temporary pardon grew into minutes, then into hours, then into a day. The camp was strafed by Allied aircraft, artillery shells exploded in the distance, and the battle lines drew closer. Eventually, one of the prisoners was put in temporary command, and more of the guards slipped away, hoping to avoid capture. Hope of survival no longer seemed like a dormant seed but, instead, like a living plant sprouting and reaching for the sun.

Then a Canadian tank smashed through the barbed wire fence, bringing with it freedom and an ecstasy of celebration that swept through the camp. Gerrit fell to his knees in awe and gratitude. The enemy had been defeated at Westerbork. He asked someone the date: 12 April 1945. For Gerrit, liberty was finally restored after four years, ten months, and twenty-eight days. When newly freed prisoners hoisted the Dutch flag up the flagpole, Gerrit sang the anthem with a crowd of other newly liberated Dutchmen. He wiped tears from his eyes and hugged the first Canadian infantryman he saw, a tall man handing out cigarettes to the prisoners between accepting embraces from men who had just been granted an escape from the grave.

Food followed. Bully beef and sardines, tea and evaporated milk, hardtack and chocolate bars. The soldiers told the prisoners to take it slowly. Gerrit's stomach had shrunk enough that he was forced to follow their advice. Previous deliveries of Red Cross parcels had taught him that a stomach was like a fire. Once gone out, it needed kindling before it could consume more bulky fuel. He started with hardtack dipped in tea rich with evaporated milk.

"When can we go home?" Gerrit asked a Canadian officer.

The officer frowned. The front line had passed through the camp, and the war continued outside its breached gates. "There's still a battle waging out there. So not yet."

CHAPTER 33

GELDERLAND BECAME A WAR ZONE again. The rumbles of artillery sounded in the distance as Ingrid fried slices of tulip bulb. There wasn't any fat in the pan—or in the home, for that matter—so perhaps frying wasn't the proper term. Regardless, the heat would change the texture.

If the Allied armies were coming by land instead of by air, did that mean they wouldn't be surrounded in the same way they had been at Arnhem? Maybe this time, the promise of liberation would prove real.

She prayed that it would, because Opa's health had taken a turn for the worse. All those times he had told her to eat his share—she hadn't realized until too late that most of the time, he hadn't been supplementing her food by eating elsewhere; he'd been supplementing her food by not eating. Her own health still felt fragile. Her ankles were still swollen. Her lungs still struggled to function even under mild exertion. But food and medicine from Rupert had helped and so had food sent from Sweden.

It was strange to owe her life to someone who had first been a friend, then an enemy. Someone who hadn't executed Gerrit but might have sent him to die. Rupert had looked too thin the last time she'd seen him. The Germans, too, had suffered during the Hunger Winter. Now winter had passed, but the hunger remained.

Ingrid took the cooked bulb slices to Opa, who slept on his thin, narrow mattress. She had offered him the couch, but it wasn't long enough for his tall frame. She knelt and laid a hand on his arm to wake him. It took him a while, but eventually, he sat and accepted the food.

"What will you do when the war ends?" she asked.

He finished chewing his tulip and swallowed. "I'll return to Arnhem. It might be a ghost town, but more than anything, I want to find my family again. That's where my sons will send letters or telegrams. Where they'll look, if they come back. And that's where Gerrit will look."

Ingrid nodded. She wanted to find her family again, too, but maybe even more than that, she wanted to find out what had happened to Gerrit.

Fire, from rifles and from artillery, sounded off and on for days. Sometimes Ingrid peeked through the windows, but she rarely saw other civilians. Neither Opa nor Dr. Kley left for the hospital. Most civilians stayed in basements, out of sight, and as the firing increased, Ingrid only ventured outside when they needed water.

One morning, Dr. Kley sniffed the air. "That smells like real tobacco."

With the exception of the Allied paratroopers, no one in Gelderland had smoked real tobacco for years. Dr. Kley crept from the cellar, and Ingrid followed. An empty window pane showed a changed world. German tiger tanks had guarded the street the last time Ingrid had fetched water. Now a different type of tank rolled past.

When they opened the door and stepped outside, they found a soldier leaning against the wall of Dr. Kley's house, rifle in one hand, cigarette in the other. On his shoulder was a patch with a white polar bear.

"*Goedemorgen*," Dr. Kley said.

The soldier looked the two of them up and down and spoke in English. "I assume that means 'good morning'?"

An English-speaking soldier. Ingrid inhaled with joy. "Yes, hallo. You are English?"

"Canadian."

Before Ingrid could say anything else, emotion choked her throat, and tears came to her eyes. The war was over. At least she hoped it was. But they'd been liberated before, and it hadn't lasted. "You'll stay in Velp?"

He shook his head. "Not for long. We're gonna chase the krauts until they surrender. All the way to Berlin, if needed."

"The Germans . . . they won't come back, will they?"

He shook his head. "Not the way they're retreating."

She translated for Dr. Kley, who grinned and thumped the man on the back. While he and the Canadian soldier shared cigarettes, Ingrid ran to the cellar to tell Opa.

Opa's eyes were closed in sleep. Normally, she wouldn't wake him, but liberation wasn't something she wanted him to miss.

She placed a hand on his shoulder. "The Canadians are here! The war is over!"

She helped Opa from the cellar. Strange how strongly hunger could hobble them until hope replaced it, and then it became imperative that they venture out to be part of their new freedom. Neighbors emerged from broken homes and dark basements. Then onderduikers appeared, most of them with pale faces because they hadn't seen the sun in months or years. People cried. They sang. They cheered. Banners and armbands appeared, orange for the house of Oranje or red, white, and blue to match the flag of the Netherlands.

Ingrid cried and cheered and hugged the Canadian soldier who had stopped to smoke outside Dr. Kley's home.

Despite his recent illnesses, Opa joined the neighbors in celebrating. He took in all the joy, all the hope, all the promise. The holiday atmosphere continued, but gradually, pockets of anger punctuated the cheer. Part of the crowd dragged collaborators away. Others held women who had been too friendly with the enemy, and amid jeers and anger, their hair was shorn.

Opa whispered into Ingrid's ear. "A German soldier brought you food, and you were born in Austria. It's probably best that you go inside until cooler heads return."

Ingrid had been a member of the resistance, but she'd not seen any of the people she'd once worked with in months. Anita and Cornelis were dead. Gerrit and most of the others were still missing. She longed to be part of the celebrations. She'd endured almost five years of Nazi occupation in the Netherlands, and Austria had been taken over two years before that. Just like the other people in Velp, she had suffered fear and hunger and loss. But she would heed Opa's warning. She wasn't a collaborator, but while emotions were high, one of Rupert's visits might be enough to endanger her.

Waiting inside through liberation wasn't much of a hardship, not compared to the rest of the war. It was easier than waiting inside through duels between German tanks and British paratroopers. Even with the enclosed space and the limited food, knowledge that she was free made everything better. And in the coming weeks, as Canadian troops moved through Gelderland, food returned. Three weeks after Velp was liberated, Opa's application to return to Arnhem was approved, so he and Ingrid packed their meager belongings and bid Dr. Kley farewell.

Arnhem still bore signs of the struggle that had enveloped it that past September. On the stretch of the Utrechtseweg, where the ruins of the van der Veen home stood, few houses had more than half their walls, and those were pitted with bullet holes and stained with smoke. Windows lacked glass, shutters hung crooked, and tiles cluttered the ground instead of lining the rooftops.

Opa stood before his home a long time before speaking. "Well, you said it was destroyed. A most accurate statement."

Ingrid eyed the home that held so many memories. Further fighting and a long, cold winter had made the damage even worse. "I'm sorry, Opa . . ." She paused. She'd started calling him Opa as part of her cover, but the war was over now, and so was their need to pretend they were relatives. She was glad to leave behind most of the lies she'd lived during the war, but this one was different. A fib she'd like to keep, but he valued honesty. "Should I call you Dr. van der Veen now?"

He put a hand on her shoulder. "I've lost enough family without losing you too. Unless you object, I'd still like to be your opa."

Ingrid squeezed his hand and blinked back tears. She wanted to keep him as her opa forever. They both had other family they hoped to find, but they also had each other, and regardless of what happened, that bond would endure. Kindness, tragedy, and sacrifice had forged it into something unbreakable.

They got to work, slowly, because the Hunger Winter had ravaged their bodies. They pulled down what was dangerous, salvaged what was usable, and cleaned away the blood and soot from the basement, where so many wounded paratroopers had sheltered. During the battle, artillery had stripped the trees of leaves and branches until they looked more like telephone poles than living plants, but new growth had started to emerge. Within days, freedom, food, and springtime made the hovel feel almost like a home.

Opa soon returned to St. Elisabeth Hospital, and within a week, he found a wireless set. Now that possession of a radio was no longer a crime, they listened almost nonstop. To the east, the Red Army took Berlin, and to the south, the British, American, Canadian, and French troops forced retreats and surrenders of the once mighty enemy.

In parts of the Netherlands not yet liberated, hunger remained. Allied bombing crews, who all through the war had dropped explosives from high altitudes, instead flew low over the countryside of Holland and dropped crates of food to the starving civilians below. Ingrid and Opa were already liberated, but they cried tears of joy when they heard reports of the food drops. The British, Canadian, New Zealand, and Australian pilots called their deliveries Operation Manna. The Americans called theirs Operation Chowhound.

The war in Europe finally ended, and all around Arnhem, people tried to rebuild. Opa and Ingrid did, too, and every time the Red Cross published a list of those confirmed dead, they searched the names, fearful of who they might find there. May passed, and so did most of June. Opa heard from his son in Amsterdam and his son in Haarlem but not from the sailor or from the sons in Indonesia. Gerrit's name didn't appear on any Red Cross lists, but nor did he return to Arnhem. Gerrit's aunt in Utrecht wrote to Opa, confirming that Gerrit's siblings had both survived the war, but Gerrit hadn't returned to them either. Like so many others, Gerrit Hendriks had disappeared.

The warmth of July kissed Ingrid's skin as she returned to the van der Veen home after a trip to the green grocer. Food wasn't as plentiful or as high quality as it had been before the war, but she could always find something to eat now, even if it wasn't exactly what she wanted. The results of war would take a long time to fade. She was certain that some things—the memories, the pain—would never go away.

Most of the van der Veen home still needed to be rebuilt, but the basement and part of the ground level were usable. Ingrid cooked in the kitchen, albeit without most of the home's prior equipment, and curtains divided the basement into two bedrooms: one for Opa, one for her.

Opa came up from the basement while she put the purchases in the kitchen, startling her. His shift at the hospital wasn't supposed to end until evening. "You're home early," she said.

A smile grew on his face. A genuine, joyful smile that seemed to come from deep inside his soul. Despite the happiness on his face, his voice trembled when he spoke. "Come."

Intrigued, Ingrid left the bread, milk, and vegetables on a counter and followed Opa down the stairs into the dim basement. He pulled back a curtain to reveal a man sleeping on Opa's mattress. She didn't recognize him.

"I'll need to send a telegram to his aunt and siblings, but I didn't want to leave him alone when he's been ill. When he came to the hospital looking for me, I almost didn't recognize him."

Ingrid studied the sleeping man more carefully. The lighting in the room was poor, and the mattress lay on the floor rather than on a bed frame, so the shadows were deeper there. The man was little more than a skeleton with skin. She walked closer. The face shape wasn't quite right because there wasn't enough flesh on his cheeks, but other things—the shape of his eyebrows and his ears, the color of his hair—revealed that the sleeping skeleton was Gerrit. Gladness bubbled up inside her, but it was tempered with soberness because he looked so fragile.

"Where was he?" she asked.

Opa shrugged. "He didn't say. He was exhausted by the time he made it from the train station to the hospital. I thought about keeping him there, but he wanted to come home."

Ingrid kept her voice a whisper in case Gerrit could hear in his sleep. "Will he be all right?"

Opa's smile faltered. "I'll be his personal physician, and he'll receive the best care possible. I pray it will be enough."

Opa needed to finish a few things at the hospital and send a telegram to Utrecht, so after Ingrid put away the groceries, she brought a stool downstairs and sat with Gerrit, just staring at him, letting it sink in that he was alive, and he was here. Hours passed before he finally stirred. He shifted and blinked and met her eyes. His face had changed, but his eyes were the same. And the smile that grew on his face was familiar.

"I hoped I would see you again," he said.

Ingrid moved to the mattress and sat so she would be closer to his level. She reached for his hand and held it tightly. "I was afraid you were dead, and it terrified me." Even now, holding his hand, emotion threatened to choke her words.

His smile wavered. "It was close—a few times."

"Where have you been? We've been worried sick."

"Westerbork. Canadian troops liberated us in April, but the front lines were still so close, and they didn't want us to leave and get killed. Then the authorities were suspicious of any survivors. Most of the people who passed through Westerbork were sent east, but not us. By the time I had the chance to explain that I was arrested after the deportations stopped, I was sick, all the time. So I was stranded in the hospital."

"Did they say what was wrong?"

"Typhus. General malnutrition. But I'm ready to forget about that place." He looked away, then squeezed her hand and met her eyes again. "How long were you watching me sleep?"

Nearly three hours had passed, but Ingrid shrugged. "Doctor's orders. Opa didn't want you left alone when you've been so ill."

His smile returned. "We've been through a nightmare, but I've never woken up to a better sight."

CHAPTER 34

For Gerrit, recovery felt like a river rather than a canal. It didn't follow a straight path toward restored health but, instead, twisted and curved and wove from days when he could hardly get out of bed to days when he felt almost normal, at least for a few blissful hours.

Upon finally being released from Westerbork, he had faced a choice: Arnhem or Utrecht. But until he was stronger, he could contribute little to a thriving household. He'd known that if he went back to Utrecht, he would be a burden to his aunt and siblings and cousin. And he had left important unknowns in Arnhem: Anita's fate and Ingrid's danger from Altbauer when the German held suspicion of her resistance work and leverage to make her bend to his will. So Gerrit had decided on Arnhem. But the city had changed so much. He'd passed through after the battle, but night had masked most of the destruction. Now, months later, the city remained scarred, parts of it in ruin.

Like the city, Opa and Ingrid had changed since he'd last seen them. Both looked older, thinner. But Opa spoke with him now like he never had before, man to man, about medicine and religion and philosophy. Anything, really, other than the war. And Ingrid . . . War was the helpless frustration of occupation, the agony of battle, and the hell of Westerbork. And Ingrid was peace.

She had changed, grown frail, and she no longer burst with barely restrained energy as she went about tasks in the damaged home. But there was something steady and purposeful about her now. War had hurt them all, but Ingrid was rebuilding, and whenever Gerrit or Opa seemed to stumble and let the past wear them down, she somehow pulled them back into the new beginning they were creating.

Not a day passed that he didn't wonder what would happen between Ingrid and him. He still loved her. She cared for him with a kindness that made her more and more endearing each day, but he could see the disappointment when she asked questions about their time apart, and he gave her only partial answers or changed the subject. The past was painful. The future was uncertain. And the present . . . It felt transitory, as if they were all waiting for something to happen before anything would really be permanent.

"You've a letter from Utrecht," Ingrid said one day when he came into the kitchen after a nap. His body still couldn't manage a normal day without a break.

Gerrit thanked her when she handed the envelope to him. He had exchanged several letters with Tante Petronella, Johan, and Nellie since his return. Their letters usually came all in the same envelope, though this one felt thinner. When he opened it, he saw why. This envelope contained only a single letter, from his aunt.

> *Dear Gerrit,*
>
> *Johan and Nellie send their greetings. They miss you. We would all like to see you again, when your health permits. I would invite you to come, but your opa can do more for your recovery than I can, so perhaps Arnhem is the best place for you at present. Our flat is very full because Nicolaas has returned. He was never able to send a single letter, but three days ago, we received a Red Cross postcard telling us he would arrive at the train station, and yesterday, he returned to our family after so many years of forced work in Germany. The conditions were harsh, but I know you have also had your share of miserable conditions and time away from family. I am overjoyed that my husband has returned, but he brought tragic news. He and your father worked together for a time, but Georg fell ill last winter. Nicolaas says Georg was hardly ever sick when they were boys, but in those conditions, it was hard to stay healthy. Harder to recover when anything went wrong. I'm sorry, Gerrit. Your father won't be coming back.*

Gerrit set the letter down. He couldn't claim surprise, not after everything he'd seen, but despite their close meaning, *confirmed dead* felt vastly different from *likely dead*. Logic and precedent didn't make the loss any less devastating.

"Is everything all right?" Ingrid asked.

He didn't trust himself to speak, so he simply handed her the letter.

She read, with one hand over her mouth, and when she spoke, her voice sounded as though she were fighting emotion. "I'm so sorry, Gerrit." She blinked, then wiped a tear from her eye.

Processing the news took time, as memories of his father flooded through Gerrit's mind, and as realization sank in that they would never have a chance to make any more memories. Pap, so passionate in his beliefs, so firm in his love for family. Willing to stand up against injustice, even when the Nazis had wielded complete control. Gone. Ingrid's single tear seemed to give Gerrit permission to grieve, too, and soon tears streamed down his face and sobs racked his lungs.

Ingrid pulled him into an embrace. "I know how you feel, because I lost a father to the Nazis too."

Gerrit clung to Ingrid as sorrow threatened to overwhelm him. So many gone. So much degradation and injustice since the Nazis had stormed across the border all those years ago. So much that remained unfair and wrong in the world.

His breathing gradually slowed and the tears stopped. He wasn't done grieving for his father, grieving for the hardships the war had brought. Yet something about holding Ingrid—that was right, despite everything else. For the moment, he was calm, and when Ingrid kissed his cheek, it was like a balm easing all the pain. Then he shifted and brushed his lips against hers, and she kissed him back, and it was hard to think of anything except her. Everything else might be dark and uncertain, but Ingrid was hope.

A few days later, Ingrid looked in on Gerrit and found him sleeping. Sometimes, he seemed as hearty as he had before Westerbork, for a while, fixing one of the numerous items in the home that needed repair or taking her hand and looking at her as if he were in love with her. But he still grew fatigued so easily. Opa said Gerrit would improve with time and that he ought to eat and sleep as much as he could, but everyone longed for the recovery to speed up, even if those wishes were unrealistic. Whenever Ingrid's stamina waned far before evening, whenever she decided to read rather than work in the garden, she wondered how long the effects of the Hunger Winter would last. Gerrit's deprivation had been longer, and so, she suspected, would be his recovery.

A knock pulled Ingrid from her thoughts. She left the basement and opened the front door to reveal Luitenant Brug. He wore his uniform rather than civilian clothing, he seemed in the peak of health, and as she looked closer, she saw that he was now Kapitein rather than Luitenant Brug.

"I wasn't sure how hard it would be to track you down, but I thought I'd start here." He grinned. "It's a pleasure to see you again, Mejuffrouw van der Veen."

Ingrid didn't take the time to correct him when it came to her surname. She threw her arms around him in an embrace that he instantly returned. For a moment, joy at seeing him again, seeing him whole and healthy and not worn down by the Hunger Winter or Westerbork, made her want to celebrate. But then, with a sudden, painful lurch, she remembered that he hadn't had any contact with the family for almost ten months. Not since before Anita had walked into the trap Rupert Altbauer and Dirk Daalmans had set.

Gerrit came up behind her, and Kapitein Brug's face changed to worry. "I'm glad to see you again, Gerrit, but you look . . . like you've been through something hard."

Gerrit and Ingrid met each other's eyes. Then Ingrid turned back to the American. "You'd better come in."

Gerrit looked out the window into the garden, where Bridger had excused himself to after hearing about Anita's death.

"How long should we give him?" Ingrid asked.

Bridger had been outside for an hour. He hadn't cried in front of them, but his face had turned pale, and breathing had suddenly looked like it was a struggle.

"I don't know. He cared about her enough to come back. So, to find out she was shot . . . ."

Ingrid made tea and poured it in the single piece of crockery that wasn't marred with a crack or a chip. "Maybe you should check on him."

Gerrit took the suggestion and the tea and made his way out to Bridger. Ingrid and Opa had done a reasonable job with the garden. All the debris of the war had been cleared away, and the rows of vegetables were tidy and thriving. Already, they'd harvested peas and spinach.

Bridger sat with his back against the wall of the house, probably getting dirt on his uniform, but Gerrit doubted that mattered at the moment. Gerrit remembered the pain when Opa had told him Anita was dead. It had gutted him, even knowing for months that her injury had most likely been fatal. Bridger, in contrast, hadn't had any warning.

Bridger straightened and accepted the tea when Gerrit handed it over. "Thanks," he whispered.

Gerrit sat beside him.

"I never asked what happened to you after that night at the river." Bridger sipped his drink.

"It seems so long ago." Gerrit thought back. "It was wet and cold, and I had to shoot one of the dogs, but I got away. Did everyone on your end get to safety?"

Bridger nodded. "You look like one wet night isn't the worst thing that's happened to you."

Gerrit grunted. "No. I ended up in Westerbork."

"I've heard about the camps. I'm glad you survived." Bridger looked him over more thoroughly in the fading light. "After my leave ends, I'm headed to Nuremberg. They're holding trials for top Nazi officials, and I'm helping with the preparations. Would you mind if I took notes on your experiences?"

Gerrit didn't want to relive his time at Westerbork. How many times had he changed the subject when Opa or Ingrid had asked about it? "I don't think my experience was very different from most other prisoners."

Bridger didn't speak right away, but after a while, he explained. "We're trying to document as much as we can for prosecution. It's important to record it, to remember it. Not just for justice. For recovery too."

Dwelling on a nightmare seemed unlikely to help Gerrit move past it. But maybe he wasn't the only one who needed to recover. Everyone, in some way, had been hurt by the war. If his testimony could help bring the kommandant and others who had mistreated so many to justice, maybe it could aid someone else's healing. "I'll help."

Bridger finished his tea. "Should we go inside? It will be easier to take notes at a table."

"You want to do it now?"

Bridger nodded. "I need to do something. There are so many things I can't fix. So many hopes that have fallen apart. It hurts to focus on Anita." He inhaled sharply, like he was in sudden pain again. "Let me focus on justice for a while."

Gerrit nodded. Were their positions reversed, and he'd come home to find Ingrid dead, Gerrit would have wanted a distraction, too, though he would have picked a broken appliance to repair over a piece of paper and dredging up someone else's horrors.

Gerrit took the teacup while Bridger went to the US Army jeep he'd parked along the Utrechtseweg and pulled out a duffle bag. They went into the kitchen because the dining room hadn't been rebuilt yet, but the small kitchen table could act as a desk.

Bridger pulled a notepad and a fountain pen from his bag and placed it on the table, then laid aside a smaller bag and some clothing. He handed the rest of the bag to Ingrid, who had joined them. "I heard food is still a little scarce, so I loaded up on as many rations as I could for your family."

The first things Ingrid pulled out were a handful of Hershey's chocolate bars, then a can of Spam, and the bag still looked mostly full. A smile lit her face. "Thank you."

Bridger nodded. "Your family fed me for a long time."

While Ingrid unpacked the bounty of American rations, Bridger asked Gerrit about his time in Westerbork. Gerrit could tell Ingrid was listening. He hoped she wouldn't be hurt that he was answering Bridger's questions when he'd so often avoided hers. They covered the lack of food, the unsanitary living conditions, the forced labor, the degradation. The memories were strong, painful, even as he tried to state only the facts.

He was starting to regret the interview when Ingrid gasped.

She turned around holding a small, open box. Inside was a diamond ring. "For Anita?" she asked.

Bridger's face was pale. He nodded. "I didn't realize it was with the food."

Ingrid handed the box back to him. "She would have said yes."

Bridger bit his lip and nodded. All were silent for several long moments, each grieving in their own way.

"Ingrid?" Opa's voice came from behind Gerrit, and Gerrit turned, wondering how long his opa had been there, how much he had seen, and how much he had simply figured out by looking around the kitchen at the American guest, the American food, the ring, and the tragic faces. "Why don't you make up some of that coffee? Sometimes our memories and our griefs, like a piece of shrapnel or a tumor, have to be removed. It can be agony, but it's a necessary step if you want to heal."

Following Opa's advice and knowing Bridger needed a distraction, Gerrit answered the questions about torture and his two near-executions.

"Do you know the names of any of the men responsible?"

"Leutnant Rupert Altbauer ordered the beating, and he taunted me about Ingrid, but he also kept me from being executed." Gerrit felt his nose. He hadn't spent much time examining it with a mirror, but it seemed to have healed straight. "Punched me hard enough to make me black out, broke my nose, but he also saved my life."

"Do you know why?" Bridger asked.

Opa and Gerrit both looked at Ingrid.

She looked down. "I bribed him. He was supposed to let Gerrit go in exchange for jewelry. He didn't release him, but in the end, Gerrit came home, so I don't regret it, even if it involved working with the enemy."

Bridger took down some notes. "I can see if there's enough evidence to try him for war crimes."

Ingrid shifted in her seat, as if it were no longer comfortable. "He was a loyal German soldier, and he hurt the resistance, there's no question of that. But he also brought me food and medicine when I was ill this spring. I think he saved my life. Part of me hates him for what he was and what he did to Gerrit and Anita, but . . . he wasn't completely evil."

Bridger put his pen down. "Would you prefer that I don't start a case against him?"

Ingrid hesitated, but then she nodded.

Bridger turned to Gerrit next. Gerrit studied Ingrid, remembering Altbauer's taunts about her mouth and her body. He took her hand in his. "Did he ever use me as leverage to make you do something you didn't want to do?"

Ingrid looked down at their entwined hands. "Once, I let him kiss me. I had hoped it would earn you mercy, but when he figured out that I love you . . . he accepted jewelry after that, nothing more."

How many nights had Gerrit worried about Ingrid and what Altbauer might do to her? He should have asked earlier because a huge weight of guilt and worry lifted from his shoulders. "I think we had best respect Ingrid's wishes. If he saved her life, then I owe him more than I want to admit."

Gerrit slept late the next day, which wasn't so unusual. When he did wake, he washed up and entered the kitchen in time to hear Ingrid telling Bridger about the day Anita had died. Both were emotional. Ingrid seemed to welcome the interruption and told Gerrit to sit while she fixed him breakfast. Bridger sat lost in thought until Gerrit had nearly finished his meal, and Ingrid had gone out to the garden.

Bridger tapped a piece of paper. "I heard that sometimes it's helpful to have a letter from an Allied officer about your work during the war. Before I came, I wrote out recommendations for you, Anita, Ingrid, and Cornelis. Cornelis didn't make it, did he?"

Gerrit shook his head. "He was executed. I was supposed to die, too, that day. I would have, if not for Ingrid's jewelry."

Bridger nodded. "He was a good man."

"Yes. I wish . . . I wish things would have played out differently. A lot of good men—and women—are gone now." Gerrit thought of the failed airborne invasion, the Hunger Winter, the arrests that had broken his resistance cell. "What will you do now?"

Bridger shook his head. "I don't know. My country's still at war. I'll follow my orders until Japan is defeated. Maybe until all the trials are over. My father is a diplomat, so I've lived abroad most of my life. In Europe, in Asia. I think maybe now I'm ready to go home, when my assignment with the army is over." He swallowed. "I don't suppose I'll ever stop missing Anita. I would have died for her, if I'd been given the chance."

"I don't think I'll ever stop missing her either." Gerrit crossed his arms, hoping the motion would help him hide the grief threatening to spill.

"What will you do?" Bridger asked.

Gerrit had a country freed from Nazi occupation, and he had his life. But when it came to the future, he'd never made plans beyond surviving until liberation. "I don't know. I didn't finish my schooling at the lyceum. All the good instructors were replaced with Nazis. It wasn't an education. It was propaganda. But going back now . . . I'm not a schoolboy anymore. I can't be one again, not after Westerbork and Nijmegen and almost becoming an assassin. I suppose I'll try to get a job at a factory as soon as my health improves. But so far, my recovery has been slow."

"You can be a student without being a schoolboy. It's never too late to learn something new."

Gerrit didn't argue. He wanted to learn more, but he also wanted to support himself. He couldn't depend on Opa and Ingrid forever.

Bridger placed the box with the engagement ring in front of Gerrit. "I wanted to marry her. But I also wanted to repay your family for saving my life and helping me save so many others. Take this. Sell it. Use it for tuition or training or the tools to start your own business."

Gerrit was stunned. "You don't owe anything to my family. You were risking your life to free our country. We owe you." Gerrit swallowed. "And that ring was supposed to be Anita's future. How can I take it?"

Bridger blinked rapidly a few times. "I think Anita would have approved." Neither of them said anything for a long time. Then Bridger shifted the conversation. "What are you going to do about Ingrid?"

Gerrit looked toward the garden. "I'm not sure." He wanted to be with her for the rest of his life. But how could he ask that of her when he had no way to support himself, let alone a wife and family?

"She talked to me for a long time this morning," Bridger said. "About Anita. About you and what happened. It sounds like you were willing to risk death in order to keep her safe after Altbauer found her jewelry. Yesterday, she said she loved you. Seems to me that nothing short of death should come between a love like that. Unless you've changed your mind."

Gerrit shook his head. "I haven't changed my mind. But I don't have anything to offer a woman right now. And she's . . . her family had money and land and a lot more than I could ever give her. I promised I'd help her find her family when the war ended, but I haven't even done that yet. I'm not sure where to start. And she hasn't been able to start either. I think she was waiting to see if I came back. And now she's staying to take care of me."

Bridger frowned. "What happened to her family?"

"Her mother died before the war. Her father was killed by the Nazis. She was separated from her brother and sister, but they were all supposed to meet in London. I guess that's the place to start looking for them, but everything's a mess. It's hard to book a train to the coast and a ship to England when the war has destroyed so much. And money . . . I don't have any. I don't think she does either, not anymore."

"I can arrange for a telegram," Bridger offered.

Gerrit shook his head. "She doesn't have an address. Just a name and the church where the woman worshipped. It's not much to go on."

"So Ingrid needs a trip to London." Bridger picked up the jewelry box. "I might be able to help with that. If you think Anita would have approved."

CHAPTER 35

"I HOPE YOU FIND YOUR brother and sister," Opa said as he embraced Ingrid goodbye. "But either way, you'll always have a home with me. You're family now."

Ingrid smiled. Regardless of what happened, she had no plans to give up her opa. She turned to Gerrit next, and he folded her into his arms. She pulled him close. She'd waited so long for Gerrit to come back, and now he was here . . . and she was suddenly unsure if she really wanted to leave him, even if it were temporary.

"Ingrid, I . . ." His words were a whisper. Then a sigh. "You'll write to me, let me know how it goes?"

Ingrid put a hand to his cheek. "This isn't goodbye, Gerrit. We'll see each other again." She wanted to find Karl and Anna, but she was determined not to lose Gerrit. She didn't know how it would all work out or what paperwork they would need if she were to live in the Netherlands or if he were to come to England or Austria. Those were mere details. No matter what she did or didn't find in London, she wanted Gerrit to be part of her life.

Gerrit forced a smile and gave her a chaste kiss on the cheek. "Good luck, Ingrid."

"You keep getting better."

She wasn't sure that was a fair request, but he nodded. "I'll do my best."

"Ready?" Kapitein Brug—Captain Bridger—asked.

She nodded. It was time to finish the trip she'd begun five and half years ago.

Captain Bridger took her small suitcase. Inside was everything she owned, which wasn't much. She had both her papers—the expired Reich passport hidden away in the lining in case she needed to prove her real identity, and the forged Dutch passport that said her name was Ingrid van der Veen. When she needed to return, the Dutch papers ought to allow her back into the Netherlands.

Captain Bridger drove the military jeep, and she rode beside him. She'd been in a car so infrequently since the war had begun. She'd forgotten how much she loved the way the wind swirled around the dashboard and played with her hair.

"Now, if anyone asks, you're an important witness to war crimes in the Netherlands. That's how I've justified getting you on a flight to England. But my commanding officer has a few daughters, so when I told him your story, he was willing to cooperate. And the navigator on the airplane was a friend when we were kids."

"What will I do when I get there?" She spoke English, albeit with an accent. She'd even been to London before, but that had been years ago.

"I've arranged for someone to meet you at the airfield. He'll help you look for your family. You'll also have to meet with one of my associates. He'll ask you about the battle, about anything else that might help sort out who should be brought to justice." He paused and glanced her way. "But you don't have to tell him anything you'd rather keep secret."

"Will it be like the interview you gave Gerrit?"

"Yes. And I could do it here . . . but then there wouldn't be a reason for you to go to England."

"What if . . . I mean . . . I didn't actually see all those Jews murdered. I only saw them rounded up and forced onto trucks and into trains. I saw British paratroopers die, but it was during the battle, not while they were prisoners. And I've seen people shot on the street, but if your officer wants to speak to everyone who saw things like that, he'll have to talk to nearly everyone in the Netherlands. Maybe all of Europe. Won't they see through it?"

Captain Bridger kept his eyes on the road. "We can't talk to everyone, but it's still important to record what happened. Why not you instead of one of your neighbors, who isn't looking for family in London?"

They neared Deelen airfield. Ingrid had traveled there before in search of information, but she'd never driven though the main entrance.

Captain Bridger spoke with the Dutch guards at the gate. Dutch, not German, and that made Ingrid smile.

An American B-17 stood on one runway. Ingrid had watched them fly over Gelderland on their bombing missions often enough, and she knew they were big, but she hadn't realized just how enormous they were until Captain Bridger parked beside the plane, and she looked up at it.

Captain Bridger pulled an envelope from his uniform and handed it to her. "In case you want to come back."

She lifted the flap to find a generous supply of British pounds. "How did you arrange all of this?"

He glanced at the plane. "I've got an old boss with a lot of pull. And a new boss with a lot of pull. But, uh, don't tell anyone what I was doing in the Netherlands during the war. I'm not supposed to talk about it."

Ingrid clutched the gift with gratitude. "Why are you doing all this for me?"

Captain Bridger thought for a moment before answering. "I've seen a lot of things during this war. Felt a lot of things. So much pain. So many lives ruined. So many people who didn't get a chance to see the peace. I can't fix it. I can't bring Anita back or rescue any of the people killed in bombings or gas chambers or sunken ships. But if I can do something good for your family, fix one person's grief, then maybe it will help everything else feel not quite so hopeless."

A man in a flight suit walked around the nose of the plane and waved at Captain Bridger, who waved back. "I guess it's time to go," Captain Bridger said. "But will you do me a favor?"

Captain Bridger had just restocked the van der Veen kitchen, he had found a way for her to search for Karl and Anna, and he had loved Anita and then lost her. There were few requests Ingrid wouldn't agree to for him. "Yes," she said.

"Don't forget about Gerrit."

She smiled. "I could never forget about Gerrit."

Major Stevens, the bomber's navigator, chuckled at Ingrid's awe as they took off from Deelen. The crew didn't need a bombardier now that peace had been declared, so she was in the nose of the aircraft with Captain Bridger's childhood friend.

"It's a great view, huh?"

Ingrid had never flown before, and even if her stomach seemed to lack enthusiasm for it, her eyes told her why so many of the airmen she'd hidden or led to safety over the course of the war had been so passionate about it. "It's incredible!" The flat fields of the Netherlands flew past below, cut into lines by roads and canals. "Everything seems so peaceful from up here."

Major Stevens nodded. "Now that there aren't any flak batteries firing at us, I'm happy to help Henry's office whenever they need something or someone flown from one point to another. Especially if it's in England because that's where my wife lives."

Beyond the view, there was something extraordinary about soaring over everything. Away from a city still scarred by war, away from hunger and fear and grief. She wasn't sure she could put the feeling into words, but she hoped she would have a chance to try explaining it to Karl and Anna later that day.

She didn't know the name of the base where she landed that afternoon, but she recognized the airman waiting for her when the plane stopped and Major Stevens helped her from the bomber and handed her the small suitcase she'd salvaged from the van der Veen home.

"Welcome, Miss Bergman." Sergeant Cervantes grinned at her. "I received a telegram from a mutual friend asking me to escort you wherever you need to go." He reached for her suitcase. "I don't have a car, I'm afraid, but there's a train station ten minutes away. Where do you want to start?"

"You're going to show me around England?"

He nodded. "You showed me around Holland, remember? I wanted to repay you somehow. My crew dropped food in the Netherlands this spring, but that was near Amsterdam, not Arnhem. I don't suppose it helped you at all, but I sure thought of you and your family with every crate of food we shoved from the plane."

Ingrid put a hand on his arm in thanks. "We were liberated before Operation Chowhound, but we knew what it was like to be hungry. Thank you. We cried tears of joy when we heard about it."

Sergeant Cervantes kept his grin. "Where to, Miss Bergman?"

Ingrid had repeated the instructions her brother had given her five years ago so often in her head that they came easily to her tongue. "St. Michael's Church in London, by the Stockwell tube station."

Ingrid, still accompanied by Sergeant Cervantes, was welcomed into the warden's office at St. Michael's Church later that day.

"Were you here in 1940?" Ingrid asked.

The man nodded. "Since long before that."

"I'm looking for my siblings," Ingrid explained. "We were separated when the war started, and we were to meet at the flat where our nanny's sister lived. Do you know a Helen Davies? That was our nanny's name, but I don't remember whether her sister had a different surname."

The man was quiet for a moment. "You're from Austria, aren't you?"

Ingrid nodded. Surely if he knew that, he had talked to at least one of her siblings.

Sergeant Cervantes seemed surprised, but he kept quiet. He'd likely assumed she was Dutch.

"Would you like some tea?" the warden asked.

Tea had been scarce for so many years. She wouldn't turn it down. "Yes, please."

When the warden left, Sergeant Cervantes turned to her. "You're not Dutch?"

Ingrid shook her head. She'd filled in Sergeant Cervantes on what had happened to her, Anita, Gerrit, and Opa after he'd left, but she hadn't delved into times before he'd been shot down over the Netherlands. "The Nazis killed my father, so Karl and Anna and I left, but we were separated. I ended up in Arnhem with a pair of broken legs. I wasn't a relation of the van der Veens. Just the first of many they took in during the war, and I ended up staying longer than anyone else."

The warden returned and served them both tea. "I met your brother first. He came looking for two sisters and a former nanny. Spring 1940. But he sounded German, and

I . . . well, Mrs. Davies hadn't returned from abroad yet, so I couldn't verify his story. I let him leave a letter for them, should they arrive. And they did. Mrs. Davies and a pretty little girl with blonde ringlets and bright-blue eyes. Like yours."

Ingrid smiled as a few tears leaked from her eyes. She'd left her brother at the train station in Vienna, and for five years, she'd been terrified that she had left him to his death. Yet somehow, he had escaped and found Anna. "Where are they now?"

The warden stared at his tea for a long time. "There was an air raid. I'm sorry, miss, but your sister and Mrs. Davies both died."

In an instant, Ingrid's burgeoning joy turned to crushing grief. She'd already lost Anita. She couldn't lose Anna too. Anna had been so young, so innocent. Ingrid swallowed, but that didn't fix the ache in her throat or the growing agony in her chest. Sergeant Cervantes offered her his hand, and she took it and held it tightly. But what she really wanted was Anna back. Barring that, she wanted Gerrit or Karl to console her. "Does Karl know?"

The warden nodded. "He came by again, not long after it happened. Left a letter for you." The warden stood and began looking through his shelves and drawers.

Ingrid quietly wept. All this time, she'd been praying for her little sister . . . and her little sister had died years ago.

Despite his search, the warden couldn't find Karl's letter. "He was a sailor. Told me the name of his ship the first time he came. What was it . . . ?"

The next morning, Ingrid woke to a gentle knock on her hotel room door. She remembered little of the evening before. Sergeant Cervantes trying to convince her to eat, finding a place for her to stay. Her crying for Anna. Wishing Karl's letter hadn't been misplaced.

She went to the door. "Who is it?"

"It's Sergeant Cervantes. And I think I've put together a plan."

"I'll be right out."

"There's a restaurant downstairs. I'll meet you there."

Ingrid washed and dressed, then went to find the American. Her stomach rumbled. She hadn't felt like eating the night before, but her appetite now shouted to be appeased.

Sergeant Cervantes stood and helped her into her chair, then motioned for her to help herself to the eggs, toast, and beans laid out on the table. It was more food than she'd seen at a breakfast table in years.

She gathered some of everything. "If this is what you're used to eating, I fear we didn't feed you nearly enough while you were our guest in Arnhem."

He smiled. "You fed me, even when there was little to go round. I thank you for that. This"—he gestured to the food—"is the least I can do to pay you back."

"We were happy to help. If not for men like you, the Nazis would still rule the Netherlands."

"And if not for people like you, I may have ended up in a POW camp and starved to death. I didn't talk about my family much when we were in the Netherlands, but I have a wife and a baby girl waiting for me, only Maria's not a baby anymore." He slid the food closer to Ingrid's plate. "I went back to the church this morning. Mr. Roberts, the warden, still can't find your brother's letters, but he remembered the name of his ship. The *Gracechurch*. So we find out who owns the ship, and then we find your brother. Even if he's not part of the crew anymore, the company ought to have records of him somewhere."

Over the next two days, Ingrid and Sergeant Cervantes searched shipping ledgers, newspapers, and government archives. When they learned that the *Gracechurch* had been sunk in October 1940, Ingrid feared that her brother, too, had disappeared into the Atlantic, but Sergeant Cervantes said he must have survived, because Mr. Roberts remembered a letter from him later in the war. Their last trip before the end of Sergeant Cervantes's leave was to the offices of the Torlin Line, owners of the *Gracechurch*. The clerk referred Ingrid to the Liverpool office for records of sailors.

"How long is a train ride to Liverpool?" she asked Sergeant Cervantes. Each day, the physical strain and emotional exhaustion of the trip felt closer and closer to overwhelming her, but finding Karl—or at least a way to contact him—finally seemed within her reach.

"I've never been, but I imagine you can do it in a morning or in an afternoon."

Ingrid nodded. "I'll leave in the morning." She had an appointment with Captain Bridger's commanding officer later that day, and she couldn't miss it.

Sergeant Cervantes nodded. "Good luck. I hope you find the name of his new ship. But even if you find it tomorrow and write him a letter, it might not reach him for weeks, maybe months. What will you do in the meantime?"

Ingrid didn't have to think long. "I'll go back to Arnhem. I miss Gerrit and Opa."

CHAPTER 36

GERRIT STARED AT HIS HALF-FINISHED letter to Johan and Nellie. They had asked about his health in their most recent letters. He didn't want to confess how tired and weak he still was, but he wanted them to understand why, physically, he couldn't yet make the trip to Utrecht to visit them. Would they feel he'd abandoned them? Tante Petronella had written that both were doing well in school and had appetites that were making up for the deprivations of the war years. They were happy and safe, and Tante Petronella said Utrecht was now their home, but Gerrit still missed them.

He missed Ingrid too. He wanted her to find her family, but he was also terrified that if she found them, she would join them for a comfortable life in England or Austria, a life that he would have no part of. Already, she'd been gone ten days, and his ache for her was overwhelming. If she didn't come back, could he be happy for her, even if she moved on and left him behind in Arnhem? And if she did come back . . . Frustration pulled at him, as did that familiar yearning for a body that was once again healthy and capable of building a future rather than relying so much on others.

Opa didn't seem to mind that Gerrit could do so little, but Opa had always cared for and healed others. After losing Judith and Anita, after not hearing from his sons in the Netherlands East Indies, Opa was simply glad to have a grandson return, even if the Gerrit who had come back was sickly and slept more hours than he was awake.

Gerrit's stomach rumbled, so he ate bread, cheese, and a pear. Did Ingrid like pears? Rationing had been so severe in the time they'd known each other that he hadn't ever seen one in her presence.

He answered the door when a knock came, wondering if Ingrid had sent a telegram. Instead, a nun stood on the porch. "Are you Dr. van der Veen's grandson?"

"Yes."

"You'd better come. We think he's had a stroke."

"What?"

The nurse repeated herself, but the problem wasn't that Gerrit hadn't understood her words; the problem was that he understood what that might mean all too well. He hurried to keep up with the nurse as they walked the route to St. Elisabeth Hospital.

"Have you noticed any symptoms?" the nun asked. "Has he had more headaches or felt fatigued?"

Gerrit shook his head. "I'm still recovering from . . ." Gerrit didn't want to mention Westerbork to the nun, so he trailed off. "My health has been slow to return after the war. I've slept longer than anyone else in the house, so if he felt exhaustion or had headaches, it was probably after I went to bed."

The nun nodded.

"How bad is it?" Gerrit asked.

The expression on her face, with her lips pursed tight and her eyes blinking rapidly as if to ward off tears, was answer enough. "He hasn't woken yet."

Dread surrounded Gerrit as he arrived at the hospital. Opa had always been so healthy. But surely he had suffered during the Hunger Winter. An ordeal like that took a toll. Add in his long work hours and worry over missing children and grief over dead ones . . . maybe a collapse wasn't such a shock.

Gerrit followed the nurse into a room where Opa lay on a hospital bed. His breathing seemed deep and regular, as if he were simply indulging in a nap—a rarity for him. Yet his face was gray, and his left eyelid and lips seemed to droop.

Opa couldn't have been in a better place for an attack like this. Other doctors and nurses tended him with the thoroughness of concerned colleagues and devoted friends. But they all gave Gerrit apologetic glances as they came and left.

Sorrow and frustration swarmed Gerrit's chest. He'd already lost so much. Was he going to lose Opa too? Or would Gerrit need to somehow care for and support Opa in a partially recovered state? It seemed only right. Opa had taken Gerrit in when he'd had to flee the Nazis, then again when he'd been released from one of their camps. But was Gerrit, as feeble as he was, capable of caring for his grandfather?

Gerrit held Opa's hand when the others left. And he prayed, begging God that Opa would recover fully or that Gerrit would be strong enough to give him the help he would need if his recovery were only partial. But it seemed that God had different plans, and as evening shrouded the sky, Opa breathed his last.

Nurses and doctors tried to revive him but without success. Opa was gone. One of his colleagues suggested Opa would be happier this way rather than having his brilliant mind trapped in a body that no longer functioned properly, but the thought offered Gerrit no comfort. He hadn't even had a chance to say goodbye, a chance to thank him. Gerrit had slept in that morning, so the last words the men had spoken had been a casual good night the evening before. Comfortable and friendly, perhaps, but not very significant.

Gerrit cried, leaning forward and sobbing into the blankets covering his dead grandfather. He'd lost his mother, his father, his favorite aunt. He might not ever see Ingrid again, and now Opa, too, was dead. He had faith now that his family wasn't gone forever, that they continued somewhere beyond the mortal realm, but the comfort of faith wasn't strong enough to wipe out the overwhelming sense of loss and grief.

When he felt a hand on his shoulder, he assumed it was one of the nuns, there to console him, or to send him away so they could take care of Opa's remains. He inhaled and tried to quiet his grief. Then he looked up, and met the tear-filled eyes of Ingrid Lang.

No words were needed. Gerrit stood and embraced her, holding her like a lifeline. She held him tightly in return. They didn't speak, but they wept together. The grief was still bitter, but having Ingrid there with him—that was a balm.

Eventually, a nurse asked if they had finished their goodbyes. Ingrid grasped Opa's hand a final time and kissed him on the forehead, and then they left the hospital.

Ingrid took Gerrit's hand when they reached the street. "When?"

"One of the nuns came to find me this afternoon. He died maybe an hour before you came."

She sniffed. "I wish I could have said goodbye."

Gerrit put an arm around her waist. "He loved you like you were his." Gerrit didn't know whether Opa had thought of her more as a daughter or a granddaughter, but Opa had loved Ingrid. They had been family, though not Ingrid's only family. "Did you find your siblings?"

Ingrid shook her head. "My little sister was killed in an air raid. And my brother somehow made it to England, but I don't know where he is now."

Gerrit pulled her closer. "So you've lost a sister and a grandfather all at once. With a brother still missing."

She nodded and blinked away more tears.

"I'm sorry, Ingrid."

"At least I still have you."

Gerrit thought of Ingrid's words the rest of the way home. She still had him. He still had her. But was that enough? He could no more care for a wife than he could have cared for Opa, not while his health was so poor and his prospects so bleak. Worry wormed its way into his stomach. He loved Ingrid. If he'd had any doubts, the ache over her absence the last ten days had confirmed the fact that he wasn't whole without her. But he still couldn't see a future together.

When they arrived home, he voiced the question growing in his mind, shaking him to the core. "What are we going to do now?"

"I don't know." Ingrid's beautiful lips curved into a frown. "We'll just have to keep moving forward, one step at a time."

"But where? And how? No one in their right mind would hire me. My aunt in Utrecht barely has room for my siblings. She might try to help, but I would be a burden to them."

"Then, I'll find work. It might not make us rich, but it will keep us from starving." Ingrid put a hand on his arm.

She was offering to help him, but that wasn't her responsibility. "I don't want to be a burden to you either." He was supposed to take care of her, not the other way around.

The quiver in her lips told him he'd somehow hurt her. "Then, do you want me to leave?"

"No!" His answer came out immediately. "The whole time you were gone, I ached for you to come back. But we can hardly keep living here together, unmarried, without ruining our reputations. Even if we could, now that Opa is gone, the house will go to someone else. I don't want to send you away, but . . ." Could he go to Utrecht and hope that his health would someday recover enough to have a future with Ingrid? He sighed. "I don't know what to do, Ingrid. If Opa were still alive, we could wait to see if I got stronger. Or if I were healthy, we could get married. But he's gone, and I'm still weak, . . . and . . . and you would probably be better off without me."

Her breath hitched, and her eyes filled with sorrow. "My parents are gone. My little sister is gone, and my older brother is lost. Anita is gone, and so is Opa. Don't make me lose you, too, Gerrit. I don't want to be all alone."

He understood her sense of loss because his was so similar. He took her in his arms and held her for a long while. She clung to him in return, as if afraid of losing him. "You'll never be alone, Ingrid. Your Savior will be with you."

She pulled back to look at him. "That's not something I would have expected to hear from you."

"You once told me that when the world is dark, I shouldn't turn away from the light. There wasn't much light at Westerbork. No one to turn to except Him."

Her hand moved along his arm in a caress. "Then, be with me, and help me remember that, because right now, the grief is so crushing that I'm having a hard time feeling any hope."

"Ingrid . . . if you're already being crushed by grief, I don't want to weigh you down with a husband who can't work and has nothing in this world to give you."

She shook her head. "I know what it's like to go hungry, Gerrit. I won't lie and say that I'm not scared of starving again. But do you know what scares me more? Waking up and not knowing where you are. Losing what little faith I have left because I have no one to remind me of God's goodness. More than I need food, I need someone to love me by *staying* with me. I don't need another person to show their love by sacrificing for me. Papa already did that, when he tried to keep my family free and was murdered for it. Karl already did that, when he made sure I got on the train and he didn't. Opa did it, when he gave up his food and ruined his health for me during the Hunger Winter. And you did it, when you went to Rupert and ended up being sent to Westerbork. Don't do it again, Gerrit. *Stay, please.*"

Gerrit swallowed. "Ingrid . . . it's not that simple."

She went to the suitcase in the hallway—her suitcase—and dug through it until she pulled out a folded sheet of paper and handed it to Gerrit. The letter he'd written before trying to become a double agent. On the surface, the story of David and Goliath. Transformed from its code, a profession of love. "Did you mean it?" she asked. "When you said I meant absolutely everything to you?"

Gerrit nodded.

Ingrid blinked away fresh tears. "And is it still true?"

"Yes."

"Then, if you feel that for me, and if I feel that for you—and I do—we need to face whatever comes next together. Even if my faith is almost broken and your health is frail and we've lost more than we can ever hope to have again. We need each other."

Gerrit couldn't answer. He couldn't deny that he loved her, would still face death if it would help her. Marrying her, on the other hand, seemed selfish. Yet not marrying her seemed like torture. "Maybe we do need each other. But would it be better to wait? See if I get better? See if you locate your brother and that somehow changes things?"

Ingrid shook her head. "Staying here together, unmarried . . . rumors will get around. Temptation might get the better of us. Even if it didn't, we'll probably need to move, and a place with a single room would be easier to afford."

Gerrit took her hand. "Ingrid, I won't ever be rich. I promised God that if He would let me live, I would always say yes when anyone needed help. If I had food, I would share with anyone who didn't. If I had the skills to help someone move apartments or paint or repair a broken piece of furniture, I would do it. If we were married, you'd be tied to that too."

"I would be honored to be married to a man so good."

A man so *good.* He wasn't worthy of that title, not yet, but he would do his best to someday earn it. He might not ever be a man so *strong* or a man so *wise*, but he would strive to be a man so *good.* "You really want to marry me?"

"Yes."

"Now?"

"Yes, Gerrit."

"While I'm still sick and your brother is still missing and we don't know where we'll sleep beyond tonight?"

"Yes, that's what I want. That's what I need." Ingrid stepped closer and tugged him toward her for a kiss. He followed her lead with no resistance. He ran a hand along her hair, then her back, mumbled that he loved her. Kissed her with added heat when she said she loved him too. He had longed for her return, feared that she might disappear forever, but now she was back, and she wanted to be with him. Everything else seemed to be a storm, but that kiss with Ingrid was a moment of calm.

The next morning, Ingrid woke in the kitchen, where she'd spent the night, and tiptoed down to the basement to check on Gerrit. He still slept, and she wouldn't wake him. Yesterday had been a roller coaster for her, coming back to an empty home, going to the hospital, looking for Opa, expecting to see him between surgeries, and instead finding him dead. Then had come all the emotions as she and Gerrit had worked out their plans. He, too, would have felt that. She would let him sleep as long as he liked.

She looked through the cupboards to see what she could fix for a wedding meal. A few American rations remained, along with plenty of flour, a few eggs, and milk. All the ingredients for her to bake her own wedding cake.

As she slid the batter into the oven, she heard a creak and turned around to see Gerrit watching her with a contented smile on his face.

She dusted a bit of flour from her apron. "How long have you been there?"

"Maybe three seconds."

"You're still going to marry me today, aren't you? Because I don't think I can find enough sugar to make another cake. I didn't have real sugar anyway, just sweetened milk from Captain Bridger's rations."

Gerrit's smile shifted, but the contentment didn't fade. "I think most people would tell you that you can do better than marrying an uneducated skeleton like me, so I think we should talk to very few people today, other than perhaps the judge or pastor and whoever we're going to ask to be witnesses. I don't want anyone talking you out of it."

Ingrid reached for his hand, and he stepped closer to take hers. "They can say whatever they like. I've successfully ignored Nazi propaganda for years. I'm sure I can ignore any slights against my future husband, for today and for a lifetime. Are you hungry?"

Gerrit chuckled. "More often than not nowadays." She sliced pieces of bread while Gerrit boiled water for tea. "How was your trip, other than the news about Anna?" he asked.

She tried to smile, but it fell flat. Parts of her trip still hurt too much. "It's hard to get over that—the thought of Anna dying in an air raid. It doesn't seem fair, but a lot of things about war haven't been fair. My brother became a sailor, and we found a name for his ship, and then we found out who owned the ship, and I went all the way to Liverpool to find records about Karl, but they claimed they've never had anyone named Karl Lang on any of their crews." She blinked away threatening tears, and Gerrit put an arm around her and pulled her close. As they ate, she told him about her grief, about the kindness she'd been given by Captain Bridger and Sergeant Cervantes, about her trip back to Arnhem via train, ship, and then more trains, and about her fears. "The warden at the church where we were to meet said Karl sent another letter for me, but he couldn't find it. He doesn't remember exactly when he received it, but it was years ago. What if Karl is dead too?"

"Do you think he might have gone home?" Gerrit asked.

"To Austria?" Ingrid could almost picture Karl returning home. What would he look like five years after she had last seen him? "Maybe. Herr Sauermann killed Papa, and he might still be there, but the Nazis aren't in charge anymore. Maybe it's safe now."

"I need to send telegrams to Oom Cas and Oom Aart about Opa, and I have a letter to mail for Johan and Nellie. Do you want to send something to your family home? Or could that backfire if it gets to Sauermann instead of your brother?"

Ingrid thought for a while. "I don't want Sauermann to have my address, but his nephew already knows I'm in Gelderland. I expect Rupert to cooperate with him because he doesn't have any family other than his uncle and his little sister. But I doubt the Dutch border agents are letting holders of Reich passports through without very good reason. I could only get back into the Netherlands with the papers Opa got for me as Ingrid van der Veen."

Gerrit had a mug halfway to his mouth, but he paused and put it back down. "Ingrid, what papers did your brother have?"

"What do you mean?"

"You had four passports that day you jumped from the train and broke your legs. Two for you, one for your father, and one—"

"One was Karl's." Ingrid gasped as her mistake in Liverpool became blatantly apparent. "I had his real passport. He just had his fake one, so when he signed on as a sailor, he would have used Eckerstorfer as his surname, not Lang. Of course the shipping company couldn't find him. I gave them the wrong name." She shook her head in frustration. "I don't know why I didn't think of that then."

Gerrit put his hand on hers. "You were mourning your sister, and it's been years since you've used the Eckerstorfer name."

She nodded. She'd also slept poorly most nights in England, and the plentiful food, so wonderful the first day, had strained her body, which was still a little frail from the Hunger Winter.

"Do you still have the address?" he asked.

"Yes. I kept them all, just in case. Gerrit, you're brilliant."

He smiled. "Not brilliant. Just overly suspicious the first time we met. And eager to keep my promise to help you find your family again."

She leaned across the table and pressed a kiss to his cheek. "Brilliant. And after today, *you* will be my family."

Ingrid wrote a letter to the Torlin Line's office in Liverpool as soon as the cake finished, but she didn't write to Falcon Point. Not yet. Sauermann still made her uneasy. She wanted to find Karl. She knew he'd been a sailor, because she'd heard so from Mr. Roberts, so writing to his shipping company made perfect sense. But she had no evidence that he'd returned to Falcon Point. She would pursue that clue only if the Torlin Line became a dead end.

On their way to the church, she and Gerrit mailed their letters and sent telegrams to Gerrit's uncles in Haarlem and in Amsterdam. It seemed strange to send notices of a death on the way to a wedding, but the world had been a very strange place since war had turned everything upside down.

The pastor at Opa's church took some convincing, but when they explained that their chaperone, a long-standing member of his congregation, had died and that by marrying them that day, he would help prevent them from falling into sin, he agreed. Gerrit made a phone call to the hospital, and twenty minutes later, two witnesses arrived.

Ingrid had only three dresses. She had worn her favorite. It wasn't the wedding she had pictured when she was a girl, but Gerrit was the groom, and that was what mattered. Where else would she find someone who brought out the best in her, had very nearly died for her, and who drove away all her feelings of being lost?

At the pastor's direction, Gerrit cleared his throat and repeated his vows. "In the name of God, I, Gerrit Hendriks, take you, Ingrid Lang, to be my wife, to have and to hold from this day forward, for better, for worse, for richer, for poorer, in sickness and in health, to love and to cherish, until we are parted by death. This is my solemn vow."

As she gave her own vows, she felt tears prick at her eyes. But this time, the tears weren't tears of sorrow. These were tears of joy.

Ingrid noticed the slower pace of Gerrit's steps on the way home from the wedding, saw the weariness in his face, caught the yawn he tried to hide.

"Why don't you rest for a while," she said.

Wedding day or not, yesterday's events had wearied them both. With Opa gone, it was up to Ingrid to help Gerrit regain his strength. He kissed her softly on the mouth when they reached their home but didn't argue about his need to lie down.

While he slept, Ingrid looked through the help-wanted ads from an abandoned newspaper she'd found on a park bench. Her trip to and from England had taken most of the money Captain Bridger had given her, but she'd brought a few pounds back to the Netherlands and converted them into guilders. Enough remained to buy food for a few weeks. She needed to find work before the money ran out.

The garden would help the money stretch, so she went out to tend it after looking through the ads. Weeds had grown up in force during her absence. Opa hadn't had the time to pull weeds, and Gerrit hadn't had the strength. She didn't mind. Nurturing the garden felt like nurturing her own soul. So much had happened around that garden, but now it produced life-giving food. If it could endure an occupation, a battle, and abandonment and still survive and flourish, maybe she could do the same.

When she finished the rows of greens, peas, and carrots, Gerrit joined her at the tomatoes.

"I'm sorry it's a mess," he said. "I tried to take care of it while you were gone, but I kept getting dizzy."

"Are you dizzy now?" she asked.

"No." He plucked out a weed. "Just thinking about our vows. We're starting with poorer, in sickness, and we've seen a lot of the worst life has to offer. If we can love and cherish each other through that, then I suppose we can love and cherish each other through the for-better and richer and healthier parts. If they come."

Ingrid met his smile with one of her own. "Do you suppose that's marriage advice we should pass on?" Ingrid pulled the last weed she could see and started gathering the uprooted discards into a pile. "Marry when you, and the whole world around you, are at rock bottom. Then there's nowhere to go but up."

"I hope the world won't hit rock bottom again anytime soon. So maybe that's something that applies just to us. A one-of-a-kind marriage to a one-of-a-kind woman." Gerrit put away the tools and helped Ingrid to her feet.

Ingrid followed Gerrit in and washed with him at the kitchen sink. It was the only working sink in the home. She supposed what remained of the van der Veen house would be someone else's soon, and maybe that was just as well. She had long ago scrubbed the blood stains from the stairs to the cellar, but she couldn't banish the wounded who had stained them from her memory. Debris from the burned upper floors had been cleared away, too, but sometimes, she dreamed of the fires.

"What are you thinking about?" Gerrit asked.

"About all this house has seen."

Gerrit looked around at the patched-up walls of the kitchen, the window covered with a screen but no glass, the chipped dishes in the cupboards with no fronts. "This house and its inhabitants."

Ingrid stood before him and leaned against his chest. He wrapped his arms around her. They were both a little like the house: almost destroyed by war. But things that were almost destroyed could be rebuilt, and now she knew Gerrit would be with her in the process, and that made the coming restoration feel like it would really succeed.

She stayed in his arms for a long time, inhaling the scents of soap and tomato vines. "Shall I prepare our first meal as husband and wife?"

Gerrit's arm moved, and his hand caressed her jaw, gently encouraging her to look up. "First, I'd like to kiss my wife."

Ingrid smiled her consent, and Gerrit's mouth met her lips a moment later. To have and to hold . . . to love and to cherish. If this was what her wedding vows meant, their thrown-together wedding, so simple but so needed, was going to be the best thing she had ever done. Gerrit pulled her against him, and his kiss left her giddy. They repeated the process a few times, each kiss growing more and more passionate.

She wanted to continue, to explore every element of what husband and wife meant, but she couldn't forget Gerrit's fragile health. "Do you still need to ration your energy?"

His forehead leaned against hers, and warmth from each breath he took glided across her upper lip. "I want to spend it all now. On this."

That was all the encouragement she needed to kiss him again.

Gerrit whistled as he worked on the same broken radio he'd been trying to fix for a neighbor since the day before Opa's stroke. He'd cannibalized another broken radio, using the workable parts from the second to replace the broken parts in the first. He used tools that had somehow turned up the day Captain Bridger left, and Gerrit had no doubts about who had purchased them. He plugged the radio in and waited for the tubes to warm up.

Life seemed simpler this morning. He had experienced times of narrow aims before: drive the Nazis from the Netherlands, survive Westerbork. But the new focus of his life—be a good husband to Ingrid—offered far more joy than any of the other goals he had strived for. The future was uncertain, but knowing they would face it together took away the worry that might otherwise accompany a frank look at their situation. They had nothing, other than each other.

He tuned the radio, and the signal came through with a news broadcast. He'd fixed it. Maybe he could fix other things, too, and earn something for it. The announcer spoke of a city in Japan being destroyed by an American bomb, and dark memories of Rotterdam flooded Gerrit's mind. The past, it seemed, would not be forgotten, no matter how much he wanted to focus on the future.

Regardless, the man on the radio had it wrong. He kept talking about a single bomb. Hadn't the man ever seen an air raid before? The bombers flew in swarms. The image of the bombers above Rotterdam, the fear that had gripped him when the bombs had been released—that was permanently imprinted in Gerrit's mind.

The front door opened.

"Did you have any luck?" Gerrit called out. Ingrid had planned to make arrangements for the funeral, then visit several of the places she'd seen in the help-wanted section. To be back already, she must have received a job offer at the first place she'd inquired. "Will they do the funeral tomorrow?"

The voice that answered wasn't Ingrid's. Not even close. "I didn't know I was expected to plan my father's funeral from Amsterdam."

Gerrit's head jerked around. A tall man stood in the doorway between the kitchen and the corridor. He held a suitcase in one hand and had a newspaper tucked under his arm. Gerrit might not have recognized the man if his portrait hadn't hung on the wall of that very home for years, until paratroopers had broken all the glass in the house and flames had destroyed most of what remained. "Oom Cas?"

The man nodded and extended his hand. "I assume you're Gerrit?"

Gerrit nodded.

Oom Cas smiled. "I haven't seen you since . . . well, it's been years. I wouldn't have recognized you, but since you sent the telegram, I expected you'd be here." He looked around the kitchen. "Can I assume you were expecting someone else?"

"My wife. She was going to make arrangements for the funeral."

"Pap wrote to me every week after liberation. He never mentioned you were married."

"It's a recent development." Gerrit didn't say how recent. Oom Cas might not understand a wedding the day after Opa's death. But Opa's absence had made it so Gerrit and Ingrid needed each other more than ever.

"Turn that up." Oom Cas motioned to the radio.

Gerrit complied. More about the bombing of a city called Hiroshima.

Oom Cas nodded. "I think the war is finally going to end."

"Cities have been destroyed before, and the war continued."

"Mm, but in 1940, the Dutch General Staff surrendered so that Utrecht and Amsterdam wouldn't receive the same treatment Rotterdam did."

Gerrit swallowed. Rotterdam again.

"And that took many bombs," Oom Cas continued. "This was just one bomb."

"What?"

Oom Cas handed Gerrit the newspaper from under his arm. "An atomic bomb. It's new."

Gerrit skimmed the headline and first few lines of the article. The broadcaster had been right. Just one bomb and an entire city was leveled. Horror at the destruction mingled with something its direct opposite—hope, because maybe the war really would be over soon.

Ingrid held Gerrit's hand during Opa's funeral. Their wedding had been small. Just her and Gerrit, the pastor, and a doctor and nurse from St. Elisabeth's who had agreed to be witnesses. Opa's funeral, in contrast, was large. Even with much of the city still in exile and so many dead from the war, the church was filled with people he had treated or worked with. Ingrid and Gerrit wouldn't be the only ones who missed him.

Ingrid cried. If not for Dr. Christiaan van der Veen, what would have become of her? With no money and three breaks in her legs, would she have been crippled for the rest of her life? Without a family to take her in and arrange Dutch papers for her, would she have been sent back to the Reich, into the custody of the man who had murdered her father? Without Opa's care, would she and Gerrit both be dead, her from hunger, him from the ravages of Westerbork?

Gerrit held her hand tightly. He kept his eyes dry throughout the service, but she knew his grief mirrored her own.

When Opa was buried, she, Gerrit, and Cas van der Veen returned to the family home. Aart van der Veen, Opa's second son, had also come for the funeral, but his wife had relatives in Oosterbeek, so his family went there.

"What will the two of you do?" Oom Cas asked as they sat in the kitchen.

"I've been looking for work," Ingrid said. "I inquired yesterday about a few positions that included lodging, but I'm not the only person looking for a job and a place to live."

Gerrit looked at the radio. "I'm hoping I can find more of those to repair. I want to work, but I'm afraid it will have to be on my own schedule for a while longer. Maybe in a few months, I'll be strong enough for a shift at a factory."

Cas nodded his approval. "There are a lot of broken radios in the Netherlands. Few new ones, even for those who can afford them. That ought to keep you fed. Where will you live?"

"We aren't sure yet," Gerrit said. "I assume Opa's house belongs to one of you now. And Arnhem has a lot of memories. Some of them are good, but . . . a lot of them still hurt."

Ingrid nodded her agreement. She had fallen in love with Arnhem and the van der Veen family only to see the city destroyed in battle and Anita and Opa buried.

"How would you feel about Amsterdam?" Cas asked.

Gerrit glanced at Ingrid. "I've never been there before."

"Nor have I," Ingrid said.

"Then, it holds no bad memories for you." Oom Cas leaned forward. "In my home in Amsterdam, my eyeglass shop is on the street level, with the family homes on the two levels above. Below the shop is another level, bordering the canal. It might be just the thing for a newlywed couple who don't want to be reminded of the war every time they walk down the street."

"You'd let us live under your shop?" Gerrit asked.

"Yes." Cas gestured to the home around them. "I want to rebuild this. I saw things in Amsterdam . . . My clients being beaten just because they were Jewish. People shot. Friends who disappeared and never came back. I know it doesn't make sense to move. I have a profession, a business. But Amsterdam . . . wartime Amsterdam haunts me. I think a new place would be good for me and my family. Maybe a new place would be good for you too."

Gerrit took Ingrid's hand and met her eyes for a moment. Cas was suggesting they swap living quarters, and that would offer both families a chance to escape cities that had been the source of so many wartime nightmares.

"We'll talk it over," Gerrit said.

CHAPTER 37

A new start in Amsterdam seemed to be exactly what Ingrid and Gerrit both needed. They had two rooms of their own in a home that hadn't been knocked to pieces in a battle. For now, Oom Cas's family continued to live in the floors above while Cas worked on repairing the Arnhem home. His wife, Tante Maude, helped Ingrid find a job at a high-end dress shop and lent her appropriate clothing to wear until she could purchase items of her own.

Gerrit's Tante Petronella brought Johan and Nellie to visit for a few days so Gerrit could see his siblings again and Ingrid could meet them. Ingrid still missed her own brother and sister, but having a new sister-in-law and brother-in-law brought her joy, and so did seeing Gerrit's delight over their reunion, with promises to see each other again at Christmas. Soon, envelopes from Utrecht contained letters not only for Gerrit but also for Ingrid.

Gerrit repaired Oom Cas's radio and then radios, lamps, and hot plates for a dozen other people along the street, until the kitchen was more of a workshop than a place for food preparation. Yet each meal served on a table only half-cleared of tools and spare parts was a celebration because Ingrid and Gerrit both remembered times when finding food had been a herculean task. Each night spent in each other's arms held a beauty they didn't take for granted because they remembered how easily one or both of them might have died before they'd had the chance to marry.

When Ingrid returned from work one day in late September, Gerrit waited for her to remove her hat, then gave her a thorough kiss.

She hoped that meant he was having a good day when it came to his health, but she asked anyway. "How do you feel today?"

"All right. Cas sent a letter for you."

"He did?"

"Forwarded from the Torlin Line in Liverpool." Gerrit reached for an envelope beside the radio he'd been working on and handed it to her. He'd opened the outer envelope from Cas, but he'd left the inner envelope from England for her to open.

Inside might be her brother's address. Or news of his death. She almost asked Gerrit to read it for her, but he knew very little English. She inhaled deeply and flexed one hand, hoping to stop the tremble that had begun there.

> *Dear Miss Lang,*
>
> *Our records show that your brother, Karl Eckerstorfer, was a member of crews for two of our line's ships. He signed on as an ordinary seaman on the SS* Gracechurch *and remained with her from February 1940 until the* Gracechurch *was sunk by enemy U-boat in October 1940. He then was a member of the crew of the SS* Hillingdon *from November 1940 until the* Hillingdon *was sunk in July 1942. Karl Eckerstorfer was one of the few survivors of the* Hillingdon, *but we have no records of him serving on our ships after that time. Sailors are at liberty to sign on to different crews whenever they fulfill a contract. We can assume his next ship was owned by a different company. Regrettably, he listed no permanent address on his paperwork with our company and no next of kin. We wish you luck in your efforts but can offer you no additional information to help you in your search.*

Ingrid translated it for Gerrit.

"Sunk twice?" Gerrit folded his arms. "Maybe he decided to find a different career after the *Hillingdon* went down."

"Maybe. I'm still surprised that he became a sailor. He never mentioned an interest in sailing when we were young."

Gerrit seemed to understand what she needed. He pulled her close and wrapped her in his arms. "So, the Torlin Line filled in a few of the missing years, but ultimately, he's still lost."

Ingrid nodded. Hope that using the right name would yield contact with her brother had been a comfort for weeks, and now it was stripped away.

"Is there anyone in Austria you can write to? A neighbor? Someone who worked for the family?"

Ingrid shook her head. "Most of the servants lived at Falcon Point. I remember where some of them came from but not an address, and when the war started, our staff grew smaller and smaller." Ingrid weighed the risks of sending correspondence to Falcon Point itself. According to Rupert, Herr Sauermann had been entrusted with the estate in the absence of the Lang family. But if her brother had returned, that would have changed. "I'll have to write to Karl at Falcon Point."

If Karl was at Falcon Point, he didn't write back. Ingrid kept hoping that he might simply be serving out a contract on a ship, but he'd return, and justice would be on his side, and he would find her letter and respond to her as soon as he read it. But fall turned to winter, and winter turned to spring, and she received no letters from Austria.

Gerrit waited outside the dress shop on her lunch break one warm day in March. He still napped most days, and the draft board seeking soldiers to fight the insurrection in the Dutch East Indies had rejected him as unfit for service, but his face was fuller now, and his limbs were once again lined with muscle. She sometimes walked home for her lunch break, and he never seemed to mind the interruption to whatever appliance or furniture he was fixing, but he rarely came to her during lunch because the timing depended on how many customers were shopping on a given afternoon, so she was never sure exactly when her break would come.

"Have you been waiting for me long?" She'd been bursting to talk to him. Had he somehow known?

He accepted her kiss on the cheek and smiled. "I would have waited longer, if needed." He pulled an envelope from his jacket pocket. "Oom Cas is visiting from Arnhem. He brought this. I didn't think you'd want to wait until tonight to read it."

The postmark revealed England as the origin, not Austria, so that tempered her hope. But the first missive was promising.

27 February 1946

Dear Miss Lang,

I recently came across these letters. I believe they were moved to below-ground storage for safety when the Nazis began firing rockets at London. I apologize that they were overlooked for so long.

Regards,
Kent Roberts, Warden, Church of St. Michael, Stockwell Park Road

Ingrid examined the other two envelopes folded into the letter from Mr. Roberts. *Ingrid Lang* was written across both of them in her brother's handwriting.

"These are from Karl!" She fingered the dried ink in awe. Six years had passed since she and her siblings had been separated, but here was something more.

Gerrit motioned her toward a nearby bench, where she sat and opened both, then checked the dates. October 1940 and August 1942. Neither of them very recent, but any word seemed like a miracle.

She began with the oldest.

24 October 1940

Dear Ingrid,

I'm sorry we lost each other at the station in Vienna. Not a day goes by that I don't wish things had been different and we could have stayed together. I miss you so much. I pray for your safety, and I pray for a reunion, but I don't know where to search for you. I don't even know where your train was heading back in February. Given the schedules, it might have been Venice, Belgrade, or Berlin. I didn't have the money to search in all those places, and I needed to get away from Sauermann, so I couldn't stay.

If you make it to the church, Mr. Roberts will give you this letter, and you can contact me via the Torlin Line. They have a small office in London and a larger one in Liverpool, where they can send a letter to my ship. I would tell you the name of my ship, but it was sunk by a U-boat last week. I've yet to find another, but the company promised us all positions elsewhere, and I plan to continue on with some of the crew I've been working with since February.

I'm afraid I have dreadful news to leave you. Anna and Frau Davies escaped and made it to safety. I tried to find them in March, but they hadn't arrived yet. It was months until I made it to London again. In the meantime, Frau Davies's flat was destroyed in an air raid while she and Anna were inside. Our little sister is gone. I would do anything to change that fact. I can imagine the pain you will feel upon reading these words because I'm feeling it now. I'm so sorry that I couldn't keep you both safe the way Papa wanted me to. Please forgive me, Ingrid. I'll understand if you're disappointed in me or angry with me, but please write to me anyway when you get this letter so I'll know that at least one of my sisters is safe.

Love,
Karl

She cradled the letter in her lap. She already knew Anna was dead, had already grieved, but feeling Karl's raw anguish brought all the sadness back. The guilt he felt wasn't fair. A Nazi colonel had killed their father and scattered the three Lang children. A Nazi bomb had killed Anna. Neither of those things was Karl's fault.

"What does it say?" Gerrit asked.

Ingrid swallowed. "He wrote it right after learning that Anna was dead. He was devastated."

Gerrit nodded. "And the other letter?"
Ingrid unfolded the pages.

31 August 1942

Dear Ingrid,

I'm writing you another letter to be left in care of Mr. Roberts. I haven't stopped looking for you in every port I visit, in every pub I walk into. I know it's foolish to think that one of these days we'll just happen to see each other again without any planning. A letter feels like a more practical way to find you again, assuming you remember the church near Stockwell Station.

I've been serving in the merchant navy since shortly after we were separated. I've grown to love the sea, and it's important work. The war can't be fought without all the materials we've been bringing across the Atlantic. I've sailed other places, too, but most of my voyages have been from Canada or the United States to Britain. I know how important merchant ships are. That's why the U-boats target them. I've been torpedoed thrice, but I've grown weary of being a target. I want to be the one to hunt the U-boats down and drop depth charges on them. Or have any other job on a warship rather than on a merchant vessel. As an Austrian, I've been ineligible for most branches of the British military, but their policies have changed recently, and I'll soon be joining the Royal Navy. I'll have training before I'm assigned a ship, but I will include the address for the Admiralty in a post script. You can send a letter there, and they'll forward it to me. Mail can get lost or diverted, so please don't give up. If you can manage it, send more than one letter.

The last letter I wrote to you included the worst kind of news. I'm happy that with this letter, I have something far more cheerful to tell you. I got married last week. I wish you could have been there. Millie is the most incredible woman I've ever known. She's beautiful, and her intelligence rivals Papa's. She's helped me find my way and given me hope so many times over these last few years. I look forward to introducing you to each other one day.

Love,
Karl

"Did that one have better news?" Gerrit asked.

Ingrid nodded, then did her best to translate the letters. Both were in English. Perhaps because the warden wouldn't have trusted something written in German?

When she was finished, Gerrit smiled. "It sounds as if your brother has a driving hatred of the Nazis. And that he's completely besotted with his wife. I can relate to him on both counts." Gerrit leaned in for a soft kiss.

"This letter is three and half years old." She put the letters back in chronological order. "I wonder if he's still in the navy."

Gerrit looked at the dates. "He could have a child by now. Or two."

With their parents and their sister gone, thoughts of a new generation of Langs warmed Ingrid more thoroughly than a summer sun. "Cousins for our baby."

Gerrit's gaze snapped from the letters to Ingrid. "Our baby?"

Ingrid took her husband's hand. "You know how I left for work a little early today?"

He nodded.

"I went to visit the doctor. I didn't want to say anything unless I knew because I didn't want to get your hopes up. I've gained a little weight, and I was queasy most of the winter, but I thought that it was just lingering effects from the Hunger Winter. My womanly cycle has been terribly unpredictable since the last year of the war, so I couldn't judge by its absence. I wasn't sure if we would ever have children after everything we've been through, but I want a baby, and it seems that we're going to have one."

Gerrit stared at her for several long moments. "We're going to have a baby? And you've suspected all winter? When were you planning to tell me?"

"As soon as I got home tonight. And I didn't really suspect all winter. I assumed it was something else. You know how it is. You think your body is finally getting over the war, and then you have a bad week or a hard month and . . . You aren't upset, are you?"

Gerrit laughed, put an arm around her, and gave her a kiss more thorough than was proper for a public bench. "No," he whispered when he'd left her well and truly breathless. "I'm not upset. I'm delighted. Did the doctor say when?"

She nodded. "He couldn't be completely sure, but he predicts July."

Gerrit's fingers moved as he counted out the remaining four months. "That's soon." He kissed her again. "And it's wonderful." He glanced at his watch. "We've been talking a long time. You had better eat your lunch, especially if you're eating for two."

She ate her lunch, kissed her husband goodbye, and returned to work. That evening, she returned home to find new stationery and several planks of wood. The stationery, she assumed, was for her letter to the British admiralty. They'd used the last of the paper the week before when writing to Gerrit's siblings. She gestured to the wood. "New project?"

Gerrit nodded.

"What are you making?"

"A cradle."

Ingrid fingered the golden-colored wood. Gerrit had made several pieces of furniture, but he'd never before made a cradle. "For us?"

He nodded. "For us."

She drew closer and ran a hand along the small of his back. He'd known about the baby for mere hours, and already, he'd gathered material for a bed. "You're going to be a wonderful father."

Gerrit met her forehead with his. "It takes more than a little carpentry to make a good father."

Ingrid placed her palm on his cheek. "Then, it's a good thing there is so much more to you than a little carpentry."

Gerrit knew what was coming when the foreman at the boiler factory pulled him aside toward the end of the shift.

"Hendriks, I don't think this is going to work out. I'm sorry, but we can't keep you on if you can't keep up."

"What about half shifts?" Maybe in a month or two, Gerrit's body would gain enough endurance that he could work his full hours. But for now, he needed something consistent . . . and half a wage was better than no wage at all.

The foreman shook his head. "I'm sorry. I have a brother who got rounded up and sent to Germany. He's still recovering too. But it wouldn't be fair to all the other workers or to their families. You can come back next Friday for a partial paycheck."

Gerrit wanted to protest more, but the foreman was right. The first day, Gerrit had been able to keep up with most of the others until the last few hours of the day. But for the past four days, his endurance had grown shorter and shorter. It was only lunchtime, and exhaustion, compounded over a week, left his limbs trembling and his lungs aching, as if he were coming down with influenza.

He retrieved his bicycle and pedaled home. Oom Cas was making progress on rebuilding Opa's home. By year's end, he'd move the rest of his family to Arnhem, and then he'd sell the home in Amsterdam, and the new owners might not wish to rent out their basement. If they did, they would certainly charge for it. Maybe by the time Gerrit and Ingrid had to move or pay a hefty rent, Gerrit would be able to work a full shift. It would have to be at a different factory, though, because he didn't think the boiler manufacturer would give him another chance. Far sooner than a move, a baby was coming. He'd made a cradle, and they'd gathered clothing, diapers, and a few blankets, but that didn't seem like enough, especially if Ingrid worked fewer hours when their baby came.

He arrived home well before his wife. He meant to sit on the couch for only a minute or two, but when he woke, the angle of the sun had shifted significantly, Ingrid's legs were draped across his lap, and Ingrid's fingers were playing with the hair behind his left ear.

He blinked a few times. "I didn't mean to sleep that long."

"When did you get home?" she asked.

"They let me go at lunchtime." He'd told her yesterday that he was having trouble keeping up, so her expression held acceptance rather than surprise. "I'm sorry. I tried, but . . ."

"You have nothing to apologize for."

He undid the straps of her shoes and started rubbing her feet. Her job meant she stood on a hard floor for most of the day, and she'd mentioned sore feet more and more as the pregnancy had progressed. "I'm afraid you married a failure."

"Hardly."

"A baby is coming, and I am physically incapable of working long enough to support even a small family. It's hard to imagine a failure worse than that."

She rested a hand on his shoulder. "We'll figure it out. I can keep longer hours for a while yet."

"You shouldn't have to."

Ingrid was quiet for a moment, one hand resting on him, the other resting on her swollen abdomen. "Gerrit, during the war, when you went to Leutnant Altbauer, did you realize it might cost you your life?"

"Yes."

"Then, why did you do it?"

He met her eyes and gave her a halfhearted smile. "Because I was in love with you, and I thought it might save your life. And because I wanted my country free of the Nazis, and I thought I might be able to outsmart them."

"If you could go back, and if someone told you that it wouldn't cost you your life, just your stamina, would you act differently?"

Memory of Cornelis and the others executed in that small village square flashed through Gerrit's mind. If Gerrit hadn't gone to Altbauer, that might have been Ingrid's fate. His throat felt parched, and panic made his heart beat a little faster. "I would have done whatever I could to save you. No matter the cost."

"*This* is the cost." Ingrid took his hand. "You're not a failure, Gerrit. You're a brave man who sacrificed for love and liberty. We don't know how long the cost of that sacrifice will last, but I'll never stop being grateful that you made it."

"Gratitude shouldn't obligate you to marriage with someone like me."

Ingrid smiled. "It's not just about gratitude. I'm certain I'll never grow tired of your foot rubs. Or of your kisses."

"Hmm. Is that a hint?"

Her smile turned sly. "Why don't you come closer and find out?"

He leaned over and met her lips. That mouth of hers still drove him wild, and today, it held an unexplainable ability to drive away his frustration and sorrow.

"Feeling any better?" she asked.

"Much. But we still don't know how we're going to get by when the baby comes."

"We've figured out how to do a lot of things together, Gerrit Hendriks. We'll figure out how to do this too. Maybe over dinner? I won't say I'm starving, because I know what starvation is, but I do have an appetite."

Gerrit kissed her again softly. "So, something that I can make quickly, like fried eggs or a grilled-cheese sandwich?"

"Would I sound greedy if I asked for both?"

Gerrit smiled. "Both it is."

When the meal was ready, they said a prayer over it, then ate.

"You're good at repairs," Ingrid said. "And you still enjoy it, don't you? You could keep doing that from home."

"I think I've already repaired every broken appliance on the block. Unless people start breaking things with reckless abandon, there's not enough demand left to make ends meet."

"What about the rest of Amsterdam? Surely our neighbors aren't the only ones with things that need fixing."

"Yes, but without a shop, how would strangers know how to find me?"

Ingrid speared the last of her fried egg with a fork. "We could advertise."

"That sounds expensive." And if it didn't work, they'd be out of money all the sooner. Failure had been his companion for so long now that lackluster advertising results sounded almost inevitable.

Ingrid thought for a moment. "It won't be free, but if it brings in enough business, it will be worth it. Let's try it once or twice and see what happens."

"I'll ask a few papers about prices tomorrow."

When he said it, Gerrit had every intention of following through the next day, but when Ingrid woke him in the early hours of the morning complaining of excruciating pain, everything seemed to change.

"Is it the baby?" he asked.

Ingrid rubbed her side, and a sliver of fear touched her voice. "I think so. But it's only June."

The doctor had predicted a July birth, but he hadn't been sure. "I guess we aren't going to have to wait quite so long before we meet our son or daughter."

Ingrid grabbed his hand when he offered it. "But that's a month less of work at the dress shop."

"Then, I'll pray that someone needs me to repair something for them soon." Gerrit feigned confidence he didn't feel. Ingrid didn't need to worry about money right now.

She squeezed his hand and whimpered slightly. Then her breathing grew ragged.

"Keep breathing, Ingrid. In through your nose, out through your mouth." Gerrit had picked the advice up from Opa. It hadn't helped much when Gerrit had been beaten in a Gestapo prison, but maybe it would help with childbirth.

When the pain passed, he felt her forehead. "What do you need? Are you hot? Cold?"

She shook her head. "I'm not hot or cold." Her voice dropped to a whisper. "But I'm terrified."

Gerrit held his wife and kissed her softly on the forehead. "You're going to be all right, Ingrid." He hoped he was telling her the truth. Would those months of famine haunt her body during childbirth? Gerrit felt his own fear because life without Ingrid would be like life without sunshine. He wished Opa were still here, but grieving his dead grandfather wouldn't help his wife at that moment. He and Ingrid had discussed childbirth several times with Tante Maude. Labor was likely to last at least a few hours, maybe closer to a day. Gerrit reached over and switched on a lamp. "Did you wake me when the first contraction came?"

Ingrid's breath changed again, so he walked her through the pain, rubbing her back and holding her hand, coaching her as she breathed.

When the contraction ended, she inhaled again and squeezed her eyes shut. "They started as soon as we went to bed. I woke you when they got worse."

They might be farther along than he thought. He grabbed the watch he'd inherited from Opa. "Do you think it's time for me to call the doctor?" Gerrit and Ingrid didn't have a telephone, but the doctor did, and there was a phone in Oom Cas's shop.

"I don't want you to leave me alone."

Gerrit nodded. "After the next one, I'll fetch Tante Maude. I'll only be gone a minute." Tante Maude had given birth to four children. He hoped she would know what to do.

CHAPTER 38

The warm light of sunset bathed the basement apartment in an orange glow when the sound of a baby's cry met Ingrid's ears. She didn't think she had ever lived through a longer day. The pain and physical labor had shocked her, frightened her, and worn her down, but in a moment, a new feeling engulfed her: Joy. Her baby was here.

"You have a son," the doctor said.

She leaned into Gerrit, who'd sat behind her to hold her in a better position for the birth. Tears of relief followed the tears of pain that had accompanied her that day.

Gerrit shifted, and the doctor shook his head. "Stay there. Another push for the afterbirth."

One more push and it would be done. The now-familiar pattern of pain formed across her abdomen, and as she had done so many times before, Ingrid pushed as hard as she could.

"There. Well done," the doctor said.

Gerrit helped Ingrid into a more comfortable position, and then Tante Maude brought Ingrid's son to her and placed him in her arms. Little white spots dotted his nose, and soft lengths of fair, fuzzy hair covered the top of his head. Ingrid held his tiny fingers and examined each perfect length.

Gerrit made a sound that was part awe, part delight, and she met his gaze and smiled. He ran a soft finger over the baby's hair and gently touched the small ears. Then Gerrit turned to her, pressed a kiss to her temple, and whispered, "You were amazing today."

Ingrid felt the warmth of her husband's love and the miracle of new life. With the small baby in her arms, she felt complete in a way she never had before. Love for the little boy came quickly, and it overwhelmed her.

The doctor suggested Gerrit bring the baby over for an examination while Maude helped Ingrid change. Gerrit cradled his new son in his arms as gently as if he were holding a priceless vase and brought the baby to the doctor.

Maude brought Ingrid a fresh nightgown, then gathered up linens in need of cleaning.

"Thank you for your help," Ingrid said. "I don't know what we would have done without you."

Maude smiled. "I don't know what Cas will do when I tell him I no longer want to move to Arnhem when I've such a precious grand-nephew living in the basement. I'll do the wash, and I'll bring something for you to eat. I daresay you and your husband need some rest."

Ingrid looked for Gerrit, but he and the doctor were huddled over the baby with a stethoscope. He would be exhausted after such a long day. But the look of delight on his face . . . Being a father might wear him out, but she was certain he would love it.

Maude took the baby from Gerrit as he approached. "Such a small little bundle. How much does he weigh?"

"Two and a half kilograms."

Maude frowned slightly. "Ah, well, he'll grow."

Maude placed the baby back in Ingrid's arms and helped her feed him for the first time.

"How much did your children weigh?" Ingrid asked when the baby had latched on and begun nursing.

"The smallest was three and a half kilograms. But they were all born before the war."

He might be tiny, but as Ingrid watched her son, she was sure that she had never seen anything so perfect in her entire life.

Gerrit followed the doctor into the other room while Ingrid fed the baby. "When it comes to your fees," Gerrit began, "do you have any work I can do to help offset part of it? I'm good at fixing things."

The doctor nodded gravely. "I'll think of something. Come and sit." The doctor motioned to the kitchen table.

Gerrit was weary to the bone, so he sat and hoped the doctor wouldn't want any work from him today.

The doctor lowered his voice. "For now, enjoy your baby. I'm afraid he'll not be long on the earth."

The doctor's words felt like a physical blow. "What?"

"Your son has a congenital heart defect. I suspected as much at the last appointment when I listened to his heart. Today confirmed it. I'm afraid his heart won't survive any type of stress. Strenuous exertion, an illness, even a growth spurt might be too much for him."

Gerrit swallowed and tried to understand what the doctor was saying. "Are there surgeries?"

"Operating on a heart would mean death for the patient."

"What if he were in a hospital? Would that help?"

"I'm afraid nothing we could do in a hospital would make any difference."

Gerrit's throat felt tight, and his limbs trembled. "You're telling me that my baby is going to die?"

Tante Maude came in from the other room with a bundle of laundry and closed the door behind her. The pallor of her face indicated that she'd heard.

The doctor nodded.

Tante Maude put her hand on Gerrit's shoulder. "Oh, Gerrit. I wondered . . . when he was so small. Is it his heart?" she asked. She must not have heard that part of the doctor's diagnosis.

"Yes," the doctor said. "How did you guess?"

Tante Maude frowned. "I doubt you remember, Gerrit, but between your birth and Johan's, your mother had two babies. One girl. One boy. They both died within a month. Heart problems."

Gerrit's throat felt tight, but he still managed to get out a few words. "I have more than one brother and one sister?"

Tante Maude nodded. "I'm sure your parents would have told you eventually, but I think it hurt too much for them to talk about it."

Gerrit glanced at the closed door that separated him from Ingrid and the baby. "How am I going to tell my wife that our newborn son is dying?"

Tante Maude patted his shoulder again. "Give her today. Tell her tomorrow."

Gerrit nodded. "I'm going to check on her."

When Gerrit went into the bedroom, Ingrid gave him the biggest smile he'd ever seen light her face, but it dimmed quickly. "Are you all right, love?"

He tried to hide the heartache eating away at what should have been one of the happiest days of his life. "Don't worry about me. I missed a few naps this week. I'll be fine after a good night's sleep."

"From what I know about babies, a good night's sleep might be some distance in the future." Ingrid laughed. "Come and see his toenails. They're the sweetest things I've ever seen."

Gerrit sat on the bed and held the baby. He tried to push aside the grief and simply feel awe over what his and Ingrid's love had created. From the outside, everything about their son looked perfect, miraculous, and hale. If not for the doctor's prognosis, Gerrit would have thought the baby was just as he should be.

Ingrid rested her head on Gerrit's shoulder. "I think we should name him after Opa." The two of them had talked about names, but Ingrid had wanted to wait until she saw the baby before they made a final decision.

"I miss him." Gerrit meant his grandfather, but he knew that all too soon, the longing would include his son.

Ingrid smiled at their baby. "Christiaan Hendriks, welcome to the world. Your father and I did everything we could during the war to make it a safe place for you." She brought the sleeping baby up and kissed his forehead. "I already love you with my whole heart."

When Ingrid woke from a nap the next afternoon, the cradle in the room's corner was empty. Christiaan had woken up three times during the night, so when Gerrit had said he would take care of the baby so she could rest, she'd agreed, even though Gerrit had also been woken up the night before and seemed to be in the middle of another health setback.

She cracked the door to the other room, and it slid open silently. Months ago, Gerrit had adjusted and oiled the hinges so they were flawless. She smiled when she saw her husband holding a sleeping Christiaan near the window. But something was wrong because tears ran down Gerrit's cheeks.

"Those don't look like happy tears," she said softly.

Gerrit used a hand to wipe his face dry. "Don't you need to rest more?"

"Maybe you should rest. You've had several eventful days."

He shook his head. "I didn't just have a baby. Your rest gets priority for a while."

She had just given birth, and the last year of the war had ravaged both their bodies, but it seemed to have wounded Gerrit's health more than it had hers. "I didn't go to Westerbork." At the mere mention of the camp, a dread expression crossed Gerrit's face. "I'm sorry," Ingrid said. "I know you don't like to talk about it."

Gerrit reached for her hand and held it while she sat next to him. "I posted your letter for you."

"Thank you." She'd written to Karl earlier that morning to tell him of the birth. The Royal Navy still hadn't replied to her inquiry, so she had mailed it to the only address she had for him: Falcon Point.

"I think Christiaan has your eyes."

Ingrid looked, but the baby was sleeping. "That doesn't explain why you seem so sad. Are you disappointed?" Maybe he thought the baby was too small or Ingrid had shown too much fear and frailty the day before. Maybe he'd wanted the baby to have his eyes instead.

"I love our son. And I love you." He leaned in, and she met his mouth for a kiss.

"Then, what's wrong?" she asked. "I can tell it's more than just needing sleep."

Gerrit swallowed and spoke only after taking a few moments to gather his thoughts. "Yesterday, Tante Maude told me that I have two brothers and two sisters, not one of each."

"What?" Johan and Nellie wrote weekly, and they had come to visit Gerrit and Ingrid a second time the week after Christmas. If there were more siblings, why hadn't Gerrit known?

Gerrit shifted the baby. "The other brother and sister died when they were babies. Heart problems. It happened when I was too small to remember." Gerrit looked at Christiaan for a moment, then out the window. "The doctor said Christiaan has the same heart condition. He doesn't expect him to live more than a week or two."

Ingrid felt as if she'd just been blown across the room by a mortar. Christiaan was perfect. He wasn't going to die because of a weak heart. "How sure was the doctor?"

Gerrit shrugged. "He seemed certain."

Would God really take her baby after everything she had been through? Ingrid shook her head. "You weren't supposed to survive Westerbork, and I wasn't supposed to survive the Hunger Winter. Yet here we are. We're a family of survivors. And that includes Christiaan."

Gerrit didn't correct her, but the worry in his face didn't disappear either.

The wedge of fear wasn't easy to push aside, but Ingrid did her best. When a neighbor brought over dinner for the new family that night, she let the woman coo over how adorable and tiny Christiaan was. And when Ingrid and Gerrit bathed the baby the next morning, she assumed that there would be many more baths in a pot, until Christiaan grew bigger and they moved him to the kitchen sink and then the bathtub.

But Ingrid couldn't completely disregard the pain Gerrit was fighting, couldn't unsee the sorrowful looks from Tante Maude when she came to help. And then, when Christiaan was but four days old, her perfect infant suddenly seemed sickly, and dark panic welled up inside her. Gerrit went for the doctor, but his visit only confirmed his earlier diagnosis. Christiaan's heart had been damaged at birth, and it beat its last before the next dawn.

Ingrid had experienced loss before. Previous deaths had broken her, but this one shattered her. The war had ended. Their tragedies were supposed to be over. This . . . this was too much. Everything felt dark and hopeless, as if she had been consumed in something black and heavy, something she couldn't shake or ignore or overcome.

Gerrit picked out two planks of golden oak and shuffled to the register to pay the hardware store's owner.

"I suppose you're making something other than a cradle this time?" the proprietor asked.

Pain hit him so hard that Gerrit had to catch his breath before he replied. "A coffin."

The man looked at the boards and raised an eyebrow. They'd conversed fairly frequently since Gerrit's arrival in Amsterdam, every time Gerrit came looking for parts.

"A very small coffin," Gerrit clarified because he hadn't bought enough wood for anything close to what an adult would need. He gathered the boards and cradled them under one arm.

"Wait." The owner studied Gerrit for a moment, then slid Gerrit's money back to him.

"I'm not looking for charity." Gerrit and Ingrid didn't have much, but they weren't scared of hard work. Gerrit's father had never taken charity, except when it had come to medical care for Johan. Little wonder after losing two babies and being scared of losing a third.

The man glanced at the boards again. "It's not charity. It's a professional courtesy."

Gerrit hesitated. He didn't want to *need* help, but the man's eyes were kind. Maybe he wanted to *give* help, and Gerrit ought to let him. "Thank you."

In the yard by the canal, Gerrit sawed the boards into the correct size, fitted them together, and nailed them in place. Then he sanded the surface until it was soft enough to hold his son. Maybe he was a little like Opa, distracting himself from his grief by throwing himself into his work.

But after the coffin was made, after the baby was buried, pain still haunted him. And it ravaged Ingrid. She had sobbed when Christiaan died and cried when they had buried him, but as the weeks passed, her grief showed no signs of easing. She spoke and ate little. When Gerrit reached for her, she didn't reach back. And though she returned to work, she didn't return to church and never took a turn praying with Gerrit morning or night. It was as if a part of her had died, leaving behind a numb shell that moved and breathed and survived but no longer felt or planned or truly interacted.

"Ingrid?"

She'd walked past him and the broken radio he was repairing, but she stopped when he called her.

"I'm worried about you." He didn't know how to best phrase it, but it seemed that after she had shown extraordinary resilience time after time, this pain was too heavy, and nothing he said or did seemed to help.

She didn't turn to face him. "I just need some time."

"I love you."

She didn't reply. She simply walked into the room and closed the door softly behind her.

"I need you, Ingrid." But his voice was a whisper. She couldn't have heard. Gerrit put his tools down as a familiar ache gripped his chest. He had lost so much during the war. Peace had brought an end to the fighting. Eventually, it had brought an end to his incarceration. But it hadn't brought an end to the losses. Opa. Baby Christiaan. Now it seemed as if he were losing Ingrid too.

He'd felt hopeless before. In Westerbork, he'd learned to turn to God, and he'd tried to do the same in the weeks since his son's death. God had provided blessings: the hardware store owner, who had given Gerrit wood for free, friends of friends who had needed radios and lamps repaired and had paid generously for Gerrit's work. But all the prayers hadn't made the pain go away. And Ingrid . . . Gerrit was trying so hard to be strong for her, but nothing he said or did seemed to help.

Gerrit prayed at the table, begging for solace, for guidance on how to help his wife, because it felt like he was in danger of losing her love, and she was in danger of losing her faith. They needed each other now more than ever, but if she didn't see that, if she couldn't find whatever it was she needed, where would that leave them?

Praying should have helped Gerrit feel better, even if just for the length of his prayer. But it didn't. Pain at losing Christiaan, worry for Ingrid, frustration that his body was still weak and vulnerable . . . it all built, growing more and more overwhelming as he felt more and more broken and alone. Tears came. And sobs. His world crashed into darkness, and pain and despair left him raw.

Then he felt a hand on his shoulder. Startled, he looked up through eyes blurry with tears to see Ingrid. She was crying too. Without words, they seemed to understand each other. She sat on his lap, and they held each other and wept for their son and for all the pain they still felt from the war and its aftermath. They held each other until the sun went down, and then, when the tears were all gone, they held each other still.

Ingrid rested her head against his. "When Papa died, I never saw Karl cry. I sobbed so hard I could barely breathe, but I didn't see a single tear roll down his cheek. Opa never cried either. Not when the Nazis invaded his country, not when your mother died, not when Anita died. He just focused even more on his work. I know they grieved, and I know they hurt, but I couldn't feel it or hear it. It made me feel as though I were alone in my pain or weak because it was so heavy for me. But I heard you in the cellar in Arnhem, when you thought you'd killed Daalmans, and it made me realize that you felt the same anguish I did."

The cellar in Arnhem. Gerrit well remembered the episode with Daalmans, and his reaction, but he'd always thought he'd been alone. "But . . . you were in the cellar?"

"Yes."

"Why didn't you say anything?"

"I thought it would embarrass you." She wiped away one of his tears, and he tried to smile because she was right. He would have been embarrassed back then.

Her fingers lingered on his cheek. "When I hear you cry now, it reminds me that you loved our son just as much as I did. Losing him broke a part of me, and it broke a part of you, too, but maybe all those broken pieces help us fit together even more than we did before."

He tightened his hold around her.

"Grief for Christiaan has been so heavy. It felt like it would crush me. But he's gone." She swallowed back a sob. "I can't do anything for him anymore. But you're here. You stayed. I may have lost everyone else, but I still have you, and I don't want to leave you alone in your pain. You're the one person God returned to me after you'd been taken away. I want to take care of you, help you. And I need you to help me."

Gerrit used his cuff to dry his beloved wife's tears. "I'll do anything for you, Ingrid. You just have to tell me what to do."

She sniffed and nodded. "Maybe today, I just needed us to grieve together. And tomorrow . . . maybe tomorrow, we can find some hope."

Ingrid was lucky to still have a job after an earlier-than-planned interruption for childbirth and the depression that had gripped her so tightly after Christiaan's death. Gloomy shop girls didn't encourage purchases, and though she'd been adept at hiding her sorrow, much as she'd played a role whenever she'd gone into public during the war, she hadn't been able to muster up anything resembling happiness. Competence and being raised in a world where clothing was meant to be both serviceable and fashionable had helped her stay valuable enough that the owners hadn't let her go, but if Gerrit's heartrending sobs hadn't pulled her out of the hole she'd been spiraling into, she suspected her days as an employee would have been numbered.

Strange, how Gerrit had wanted to be strong for her, so he had tried to grieve in private. She hadn't known how to stop drowning in anguish until she'd realized how much her husband had needed her. But even when they hadn't known what to do, the Lord had known what they'd needed, and He'd somehow saved them from wretched despair and turned it into a sorrow that mingled comfort with loss, togetherness with the sundering pain of grief. Bittersweet rather than happy, but solid and real.

When the store closed, she straightened the displays, then left through the back door.

She smiled when she found Gerrit waiting for her. "It's a nice surprise to see you here."

He took her hand. "I was delivering a repaired radio about a block away."

"The one you were working on yesterday?"

He nodded.

"Did you fix it?"

"Yes. And they have a second that's hard to move, so I can walk you to work tomorrow when I go back to finish." He studied her face. "How are you today?"

"Getting by. Feeling grateful for you."

"Something came in the mail."

He wouldn't have mentioned a letter now unless it were important. "From Falcon Point?"

He shook his head. "From the British Admiralty."

"Did you open it?"

"No. I was tempted to because I suspect it's going to give you the best news you've had in years . . . or another loss. I hope I'm wrong, but the longer this has gone on, the more I'm afraid it's the latter."

Ingrid knew the chances of a reunion were growing slimmer, but a burning need to open the letter gripped her. Yet that need wasn't so strong that she couldn't recognize the concern on her husband's face. "And you're worried what another loss might do to me?"

Gerrit nodded.

She stood before him and met his lips with her own. "No matter what the letter says, I will still love you. And I will still need you, either to celebrate with me or to weep with me."

He brushed a finger along her jaw. "I hope it's a celebration. I think we're due for some good news."

They returned home, and Ingrid's fingers shook as Gerrit handed her the letter. Once she broke the seal and straightened the folded sheet, one sentence caught her eye.

> *It is my sad duty to inform you that your brother, Karl Eckerstorfer, perished in the line of duty on 2 June 1943.*

Other phrases swam before her eyes, such as *buried at sea* and *recipient of the George Cross*, but she put the letter down before reading it from beginning to end.

She met Gerrit's eyes. He seemed to know by her expression, or maybe he'd known before she'd even opened the letter. He took her in his arms and held her while she grieved.

News that her brother had died three years ago surrounded Ingrid in sorrow, but she clung to Gerrit, and somehow, he kept the pieces of her heart from undercutting the meager progress she'd made at recovery. Even so, she didn't read the entire letter from start to finish until the next day.

Gerrit rubbed her back after she translated the letter for him. "You can be proud of him. They don't hand out George Crosses to just anyone. He did something valiant to defeat the Nazis."

She nodded absently. Karl was gone. Like Papa, he had given his life in a fight against evil. There was no possibility of a reunion in this life. No grave to visit. Yet there was one lead she still wanted to follow. "Do you suppose Millie is his wife's real name, or is it short for something else?"

"Probably a nickname." Gerrit looked thoughtful. "Amelia, Millicent, Mildred, Emily, Camilla. If she's British. But if he sailed all over, she might be from anywhere. Speak any language."

She wished her brother had thought to leave contact information for his wife. "Can we track her down without a name?"

"The navy might be sending her some type of widow's benefits. Maybe they'd share her address or forward a letter."

It might be a stretch, and she didn't doubt that bureaucracy would make the process a slow one, but if Karl had a widow, maybe a child, she wanted to meet them. "I think I'll write a letter."

CHAPTER 39

Gerrit heard the knock on the apartment door, but Ingrid stood before he could and opened the door to reveal Tante Maude. "Someone is asking for you upstairs."

"If it's Mynheer or Mevrouw Beekhof for their lamp, I'm almost done." Gerrit tested the switch, and the light shone brightly. "I just need to put it back together. I thought I was supposed to deliver it to them."

Ingrid smiled. "If it's Mevrouw Beekhof, I can chat with her for a while. How long do you need?"

"Just a few minutes."

"It's a man, not a woman," Tante Maude said.

"Ah." Ingrid ran a hand over her dress to smooth out a wrinkle. "That explains the mix-up. Mevrouw Beekhof has told me a time or two about how well her husband doesn't listen to her."

Ingrid and Tante Maude went upstairs, and Gerrit screwed the base of the lamp back on. He liked repair work. Fixing something that was broken. Giving something new life when it might have otherwise been thrown away. Business over the last few months had been adequate to cover their expenses and put away funds for when they needed to find a new place to live. Word-of-mouth was spreading, and times were difficult enough that most people wanted to repair something old instead of buying something new, but if he ever wanted to support a family, his business had to grow, or his health had to improve enough that he could work a full day.

Ingrid now spoke of reclaiming her family's estate and held out hope that the financial change could assist him with school or training for a better career. She'd written to the Upper Austrian Land Authority to start the process, and maybe that would be for the best. Owning land in a foreign country wasn't so strange. Opa and several uncles had made their fortunes in the Indies. Part of Gerrit wanted to stay in the Netherlands, now that it was finally free of the Nazis. But more than that, he wanted to do what was best for Ingrid. Maybe if she didn't have to work so hard to keep food on the table, her health would improve, and so would the health of their next child. That grief still clutched at his heart more often than it didn't. At Ingrid's heart too.

Ingrid pulled the door open. "Gerrit, look who's here."

The man who followed her inside still had the ruthless gaze Gerrit had grown used to while the men worked together in the Arnhem Resistance. Gerrit stood and shook his hand. "Good to see you again, Berend. Or was that just an alias?"

"It's my real name."

"How have you been?"

"Busy."

Gerrit gestured to a chair. "Would you like to sit down?"

Berend stuck a hand in his pocket. "Actually, I've been working with the Political Investigation Service. I was hoping to ask you a few questions about the war."

Gerrit wasn't in the mood to talk about the war, but if Berend was hunting down former collaborators, Gerrit would cooperate. "We'll help in any way we can."

"Given the nature of the investigation, I've been instructed to speak with witnesses one at a time." Berend glanced at Ingrid. "Mrs. Hendriks already answered what questions I had for her. It's a pleasant evening, and I've seen little of Amsterdam. Why don't we go for a walk now that we don't have to worry about Gestapo patrols?"

Gerrit nodded his agreement. Too long of a walk would leave him weary in the morning, but benches lined the nearest canal. He'd suggest a stop if he needed one.

Ingrid gestured to the lamp. "Are you finished?"

Gerrit tested the switch again to make sure nothing had changed while he was putting it back together. "It's ready for delivery."

"I'll take it," Ingrid said.

Gerrit led Berend outside into a warm evening made pleasant with a soft breeze. Berend wore a coat that was heavier than Gerrit would have wanted, but maybe Berend was still recovering from the war. Gerrit still felt chilled more often than he had before Westerbork.

"I'm surprised you aren't in the East Indies," Berend said. "You mentioned a time or two how much you wanted to fight in the Dutch Army."

"I received a draft summons. Didn't pass the physical." The rejection had been a relief. Partially because he'd known that physically, he wouldn't be able to manage the life of a soldier, not anymore. Partially because he hadn't wanted to leave Ingrid. "I'm trying to build up my repair business instead. Do you enjoy your new work?"

"Yes, it's satisfying seeing justice win out, even years later. You know what they say, *God's mill grinds slowly but surely.* Not that either of us believes in God, but the idea's the same: Justice comes."

Gerrit shook his head at how much had changed since his last conversation with Berend. "Actually, I had a change of heart in Westerbork."

Berend raised an eyebrow. "Really?"

"I couldn't have faith in humankind remaking the world into a better place, not after experiencing a camp like that, not after all the things I saw during the war. But faith in a Savior . . . I resisted it for a long time, but then everything else was stripped away, and suddenly, it was the only thing to cling to."

"Well, you're not in a concentration camp anymore. You can cling to something else now."

"No, I can't, because I feel it's true." Gerrit smiled. "And finally admitting that made everything a lot easier."

"Easier because you believe in God instead of in Communism? Has your wife turned you into a petty bourgeoisie?"

Gerrit almost laughed. If Ingrid's claim on Falcon Point went through, Berend might not be too far off the mark, but they didn't plan to hoard the Lang family's wealth. They would use it to create good jobs for people who needed a way to feed their families. They'd use it to support worthy charities and rebuild a world still reeling from a devastating war. "I still want to help the lower classes rise. With legislation. With what my wife and I can do as good Christians. But I was more of a socialist than a Communist even before I found God. The war ended any support I might have had for violently overthrowing legitimate governments."

Berend lifted his chin. "My politics mellowed as well. A useful change for steady employment. And I've decided that maybe justice is as worthwhile a pursuit as equality."

"I suppose you're succeeding? In tracking down traitors and collaborators?" Gerrit had a hard time picturing Berend failing at anything.

Berend nodded as they approached a canal. "It's interesting work. Digging through old files from the enemy, trying to find people who don't want to be found. Some get away—leave Europe, change their names. Others are hiding in plain sight, if I can just connect a new alias to an old identity. And some are moving forward as if they have nothing to hide, hoping what they did will never come to light."

The way Berend said that last bit—the words hung with accusation.

"Berend?"

"I saw your name in German SD files. You offered them information."

Gerrit stiffened. "It wasn't like that. They were about to arrest Ingrid and my grandfather, so I came up with a plan to be a double agent. I wasn't going to give them anything useful, just gain their trust, plant some misinformation, and try to learn what I could from them. Not that it succeeded. They figured out my real allegiance soon enough, and I was sent to Westerbork."

"Sent to Westerbork . . . when you should have been executed? The Nazis killed millions of innocent men, women, and children. Why would they spare a known member of the resistance unless you'd made some type of deal?"

Gerrit's chest felt tight as memory of those awful days crowded his mind and Berend's accusations threatened the future he was so desperate to build with Ingrid. "I didn't make a deal for information or cooperation. Altbauer might have hoped to get information from me later, but the real reason he spared me is because he was bribed."

"Bribed with the names of your colleagues? Is that how Anita and Cornelis died?"

"No! I would have done anything I could to save Anita! And I tried to save Cornelis!" If Berend thought he was a traitor, Gerrit might end up back in Westerbork. The government had been sending collaborators there since before the wartime inmates had been released. Gerrit didn't want to mention Ingrid's role, but the truth seemed like the only thing that would exonerate him. "The bribe was jewelry."

Berend scoffed. "You had expensive enough jewelry to use as a bribe?" He gestured to the water. "The boy I pulled from one of Rotterdam's canals had lost everything. How did you find something valuable enough to tempt a German intelligence officer?"

"Ingrid had jewelry. She bought my reprieve with her last family heirlooms."

"Who can corroborate that?"

"Ingrid can verify the jewelry. Anita or Cornelis could have verified everything else."

Berend slipped a hand into his coat pocket. "As your wife, Ingrid is hardly an unbiased source. Anita and Cornelis are both dead, quite possibly because of your treason."

Gerrit shook his head. "I didn't turn on my own resistance cell."

"Then, why did everything fall apart? Why did so many of my friends die?" Berend kept the volume of his voice level, but each word seethed with rage.

Gerrit had asked the same questions, but they'd been involved in something dangerous, and they'd faced an enemy both powerful and intelligent. "Berend, are you here to arrest me?"

Berend took his hand from his pocket, revealing a pistol. Gerrit's blood turned to ice.

"I've seen a lot of trials for collaboration and treason," Berend said. "Men who I knew were guilty walked free. I have your name in an old German report, but anyone defending you will have a glowing write-up from an American officer about your assistance to him and his men. I've seen similar cases, and in each of them, the suspect was acquitted. But I saw that German intelligence report, and I remember everything that went wrong those few days."

"Berend, I never collaborated with the Germans. I went to them to gain information, not give it. I was stupid, and I underestimated the enemy, but I wasn't disloyal." Berend had to believe him because Ingrid had already lost too much. She couldn't lose her husband too. "If you don't believe me, give me a chance to defend myself."

"I already told you that the case against you isn't strong enough."

"Because I'm innocent!"

Berend shook his head. "I don't think so. Years ago, I pulled you from a canal. Now it's time to put you back in." Berend straightened his arm. He was going to shoot, and the only place Gerrit could run was into the water.

In a blur, Ingrid stepped from a nearby doorway and swung the end of the lamp Gerrit had just repaired into the back of Berend's head. Berend's pistol fell from his hand, and he collapsed to the ground.

Ingrid looked at Berend, then at Gerrit, and stumbled toward Gerrit for an embrace.

Gerrit could barely breathe as shock and fear and relief pulsed through him. "How did you know to follow?" he asked.

Ingrid squeezed him tighter. "His coat. It's too warm for a coat like that, but when he was training us, he said to wear layers because then you could hide a handgun or papers and the Gestapo were less likely to notice."

He placed his hand on her cheek and kissed her forehead. "You saved me. Again." He looked at Berend. "Is he dead?"

Ingrid bent to feel for a pulse. "No."

For a moment, Gerrit was tempted to drag the man into the canal. Alive, Berend was convinced Gerrit was a traitor, and if he'd tracked him down, intent on killing him once, he might do it again. But drowning Berend would be murder, and Gerrit had promised God he would never kill again. "We'll have to leave."

Ingrid met his eyes. In that one glance, he knew she was thinking the same thing he was. Any further news about her late brother's wife would be mailed to Amsterdam. So would any news of her family's estate. But if they wanted to stay together, if they wanted to live, they didn't have much of a choice.

Ingrid kicked Berend's handgun into the canal. Then she picked up the lamp and handed it to Gerrit. It appeared undamaged, save for a bit of blood that Gerrit quickly wiped away with his handkerchief. "Deliver this to Mevrouw Beekhof. Take any payment she'll give you, and then go directly to the train station." She spoke in a whisper. "I'll run home and pack what I can, and then I'll meet you there."

They left Berend where he was and hurried back to the main street. Gerrit prayed Berend would stay unconscious for a long time. "What destination?"

Ingrid squeezed his hand. "The first train leaving the station. Wherever that train is going."

Ingrid packed what would fit into the duffle bag Captain Bridger had once filled with American rations. She forced herself not to think about how far she'd be from her son's grave or how worried Tante Maude would be when she read Ingrid's short note saying she and Gerrit were going into hiding. She took the most important items, left the rest, and hoped she was still ahead of Berend.

Gerrit found her as she reached the station. "We can catch a train to Rotterdam in five minutes. I have an aunt and uncle there. Maybe they'll let us stay for a day or two. Make a plan. Then move on, if we need to. But Berend knows I lived in Rotterdam. He might look there."

Ingrid weighed the risk of returning to a place Gerrit had once lived against the risk of waiting for a later train. She also factored in the hardship of going to a place where no one could help them. "Let's buy the tickets and get out of here."

Gerrit took the bag from her, and she threaded her arm though his. Strain made his slim muscles tense. It did the same to her. Had she arrived even a few seconds later, Gerrit would be dead. She couldn't lose Gerrit, not after everyone else. If she hadn't remembered Berend's lessons, hadn't put the clues together, hadn't been holding a lamp with a heavy base . . .

They purchased their tickets, boarded the train, and took their third-class seats. Ingrid wasn't sure if Berend would have an easier time recognizing her or Gerrit, but she took the place by the window.

Gerrit leaned close so no one but Ingrid would hear his whisper. "What did he ask you when he first arrived?"

She smiled as if he were whispering sweet nothings into her ear instead of trying to figure out how much danger she was in from Berend. They already knew how much danger Gerrit was in. She put her head on his shoulder and whispered, "He seemed surprised to see me. I gather he still thought we were cousins of some sort. I told him our current status, but he didn't congratulate us. Asked after Opa, asked what we were doing now for work. What did he ask you?"

Gerrit told her the details of his walk with Berend as the train moved from the station. She finally felt like she could relax as it picked up speed. She held Gerrit's hand as he repeated all the threats, all the assumptions. Then, worn out, he drifted to sleep.

Captain Bridger's report would keep Gerrit from conviction, but it wouldn't prove his innocence to Berend, and Berend wouldn't give up. Nor would he believe Ingrid. Neither Anita nor Cornelis could corroborate. That left only one person alive who could prove Gerrit's innocence. But that option . . . that option involved danger and cooperation with an enemy.

She watched her husband sleeping. She hadn't been able to save Christiaan or Karl, Anna or Anita. This was different. She could save Gerrit, and was there anything she wouldn't do for him? He had been through so much, and Berend's threat felt very real, so it didn't take her long to plan her next step.

Gerrit shifted on his cousin's bed in Tante Francisca and Oom Antoon's apartment. His aunt and uncle still lived in the same rooms near the Willemsbrug in Rotterdam, though they had more furnishings now and two children: a boy of six and a girl of three. They'd welcomed Gerrit and Ingrid two days ago, but the scare with Berend and the trip from Amsterdam had left Gerrit more weary than he'd been in months, so he wasn't surprised to see Ingrid had already left the room, nor was he surprised to hear the noise of a child playing in another room.

He pulled on his clothes and rubbed his face, wondering how long the weakness would last this time. He hadn't felt strong since before Westerbork, but the trip from Amsterdam had taken more out of him than it should have. He followed the noise to the front room, where little Fenna played with a toy tea set.

"Did I miss Antoon leaving for work and Noud leaving for school?" he asked Tante Francisca.

She nodded. "Noud was sad not to see you. Antoon, too, but he understands."

"And Ingrid?"

"She walked Noud to school for me and said she had an errand to run after that. She left a note." Francisca gestured to the table.

Gerrit assumed Ingrid had gone to look for work. He picked up the envelope and broke the seal.

> *Dearest Gerrit,*
>
> *I'll be gone for a while. At least a few days. Possibly a few weeks. We've both lost so much. I can't lose you, too, not when I'm capable of finding a way for you to be safe. I know you'll worry, and I know you won't like my plan, but I hope you'll trust me. Please don't try to follow me. Just stay hidden and be patient and believe me when I promise that somehow I will fix this.*
>
> *When it comes down to it, I don't have a choice because you're in danger, and you aren't almost everything to me, Gerrit. You are absolutely everything.*
>
> *Love,*
> *Ingrid*

"Is anything wrong?" Tante Francisca asked.

Gerrit had almost stopped breathing. Ingrid was right—he didn't like whatever plan she'd come up with, even without knowing the details. "How long ago did she leave?"

Tante Francisca looked at the wall clock that Gerrit had repaired the day before. "Two hours ago."

Gerrit squeezed his eyes shut. Of all the days to sleep in so late. She'd probably already caught a train. For a moment, Gerrit considered checking the train station anyway, but train stations were the first places Berend would look, and Gerrit suspected Ingrid had planned her exit so he couldn't follow.

"Gerrit?" Tante Francisca walked over to him.

Gerrit swallowed. He and Ingrid had agreed to keep their problems with Berend a secret, even from extended family. "She's gone away for a few days."

"Without telling you?"

Gerrit folded the letter and put it back in the envelope. "That's what the letter was for."

"Did the two of you quarrel? She took a bag—larger than I'd expect for simple errands—but I didn't question her about it."

Gerrit shook his head.

"Is she coming back?"

Would Ingrid come back? He trusted her when she said she loved him. She would want to come back, intend to come back. But how was she planning to fix the problem? Would she eliminate Berend the way Berend had once ordered the two of them to eliminate Daalmans? What if, instead, he killed her? Or she killed him and was arrested? Even if she succeeded and escaped, what would that do to her soul? If there were another way to fix their problems, he'd yet to think of it. He answered his aunt honestly. "I'm not sure."

CHAPTER 40

INGRID LOOKED AROUND LINZ CENTRAL Station, where she had made a split-second, life-changing decision so many years ago. Here she had left Anna on the train with Frau Davies and gone to help Karl. If she hadn't left that train, she might have perished in the same air raid that had killed Anna. She never would have traveled through Arnhem, never would have met the van der Veens, never would have fallen in love with Gerrit or given birth to their doomed son. Karl might have been captured instead of living long enough to become a sailor and marry Millie.

Motivation to help Karl had been the reason she'd left the train, but she had also put in motion events that altered her life. This time, her trip through Linz had the potential to do the same. She prayed that once again, she would help someone she loved, hoped that this time the reprieve from an untimely death would last a lifetime.

War had damaged the Linz train station, yet she still recognized the platform where she'd driven a luggage cart into the men chasing her brother. She half expected to see her father's Mercedes-Benz 230 still parked where her brother had left it, but after six and a half years, it was no longer there. The familiar dialect of her childhood filled the air around her, and a pang of homesickness for Falcon Point tempted her to return to her family's manor. But she'd already taken too much of her and Gerrit's savings. Finding transportation to Gildenstatt or Falcon Point would be too expensive. Linz would have to do.

She found a hotel, sent a telegram, and then she waited.

Two days later, Ingrid slid into a chair across from Rupert Altbauer at a small coffee house.

"How did you know I'd be at Falcon Point?" he asked.

"It was a hunch." A guess Ingrid was glad to have gotten right, because as frightening as Rupert was, he made her considerably less nervous than his uncle did, and had Rupert not been there, her next telegram would have been to the man who'd killed her father. "I assumed you'd want to be near your sister, and Falcon Point is a good place for children. Beyond her, Wilhelm Sauermann is now your only family. Times are hard everywhere. Most families are sticking together."

Rupert nodded. "I was surprised to hear from you directly. I saw the letters written to your brother. Hendriks survived the war, and you married him?" Disapproval, or perhaps disappointment, colored Rupert's voice.

Those letters hadn't been meant for anyone other than Karl. Ingrid swallowed back the stabbing feeling of vulnerability that came with knowing her heartfelt letters to her brother had instead been read by an enemy. "Yes, I'm married. And that's why I'm here. You remember what happened with Gerrit after the failed airborne invasion?"

"Yes. He tried to get information from me and failed miserably. I spared his life at your insistence, but I would have been well within my rights to have him executed."

"Did he give you any useful information? Anything at all?"

Rupert studied her while a waiter placed cups of coffee in front of them both. "He tried to outsmart me, but he was far too stupid for that. He didn't know anything useful. We extracted no worthwhile intelligence from him. Neither did the Gestapo."

Ingrid ignored the insults to her husband and closed her eyes for a moment, trying not to imagine what methods of extraction Rupert and the Gestapo had used on Gerrit. "Will you swear to that in a written affidavit?"

Rupert sipped his coffee. "I can think of only one reason you would want something like that. Hendriks's loyalty has been called into question. If that's the case, I have no reason to help him. No reason to help you, either, because you married a man I loathe, and you turned your back on the Reich."

"Rupert, you're not a bad man. Surely you can recognize the crimes the Nazis committed for what they are. Mass murder. Destruction. Ruin."

Rupert looked away. "I may not approve of every action, but the Reich was still your home. It should have commanded your loyalty."

Ingrid had been hoping that Rupert, postwar, would be more like the young soldier who had bought her a train ticket or the man who had brought her food when she'd been starving. But she was prepared to deal with his more vengeful side. "I can prove that I am heir to Falcon Point. Your uncle will lose the estate. And if that's where you're living, you'll have to find a new home, as will your sister."

A frown creased Rupert's face, but he didn't deny the veracity of what she'd said.

"I'm willing to exchange Falcon Point for proof of my husband's innocence."

Rupert stared at her for a long moment. "You're willing to exchange your family's home, with all its lands, furnishings, artwork, and antiques—one of the richest estates in Upper Austria—for a sickly former resistance saboteur of, at best, average intelligence?"

Ingrid fingered her coffee cup. "Yes. And because you were once a friend, I can only hope that *someday*, you will love *someone* enough to understand why I would make a sacrifice like that."

"What about other claimants to the estate? Your siblings have just as much of a right to Falcon Point as you do."

Ingrid did her best to keep her voice steady. "Anna died in an air raid in 1940. Karl joined the Royal Navy and died at sea in 1943."

Rupert huffed. "So your brother was a traitor?"

"No. A hero."

"That's a matter of opinion. Do your parents have any siblings still alive or with living descendants?"

Ingrid shook her head "My mother was an only child. My father's brothers both died during the First World War. They never married."

"I don't suppose your uncles or your brother left any heirs or beneficiaries who could make a claim to the estate?"

Karl's wife, Millie, would have a stronger claim to the estate than the Sauermanns, but Ingrid wouldn't put a target on her back like that. Ingrid and Gerrit didn't know where she was, but Sauermann would have more resources. Karl's marriage was a secret she would keep from both Rupert and his uncle. "I've found none." Ingrid would keep looking, keep hoping, and if she ever did find her sister-in-law, she would tell her of both the promise and the risk of Falcon Point.

"And your son? Will you tell him how to claim it when he's older?"

Ingrid's breath caught. Grief for baby Christiaan was still raw. Maybe it was even more painful here because she couldn't lean on Gerrit. "My baby did not live to see his second week."

Rupert had the decency to look sympathetic. "I'm sorry. Can I assume that you hope for more children in the future?"

"The war took a toll on our health, so I'm not sure we'll ever have more children. If we're ever blessed that way, I can promise to keep Falcon Point a secret from them. My heirs and descendants will remain in ignorance about their rightful estate." It would be a hard secret to keep, but they needed a father more than they would need Falcon Point. Without proof of Gerrit's innocence, there would be no children.

Rupert sat back and studied her for a moment. "Then, we have a deal. I'll go before the occupying authority and issue a statement on your husband's absolute uselessness to the Third Reich and include my long-held conclusion that he was attempting to gather information from us rather than cooperate. You'll sign over your rights to Falcon Point, and then we'll trade documents."

If that was the best deal she could get, Ingrid would accept it, but she didn't just want to save Gerrit from Berend and the Political Investigation Service's wrath. She wanted both her and her husband to live their lives without looking over their shoulders in fear. "If I sign over my rights to the estate, I'll have no leverage. I need something I can hold over your uncle if needed."

"You have nothing to fear from me or from my uncle."

Ingrid crossed her arms. "Your uncle murdered my father, and I know what he did, so he will always see me as a threat. I will always need a way to protect myself."

"Your dead brother *alleged* that my uncle killed Leopold Lang. You've no proof."

"I have enough evidence to at the very least ruin his reputation." With time, she might be able to track down some of the servants who had been present that day, but she wouldn't bring up their names to Rupert. She didn't want Sauermann questioning or threatening them. "Once I'm safely away, you can inform your uncle that if I die a mysterious death, the land authority will receive further information about his crimes, and he will lose everything." She was bluffing now. She'd left no letter for anyone to mail to the land authority in the event of her disappearance. Gerrit might figure out where she'd gone, might try to see justice done, but if Berend killed him or saw him thrown in jail on false charges of collaboration, no one would ever interfere with Sauermann.

Rupert frowned. "My uncle has already had difficulty with the land authority because of your letters."

"I no longer live at the address I mailed those letters from. Any officials tasked with investigation will run into a dead end. Your uncle will continue as trustee as long as you prove my husband innocent and see that neither he nor I come to harm."

Rupert considered her offer. "I produce an affidavit confirming your husband's innocence, and you promise to walk away from Falcon Point and never claim it or give any future children the information they would need to claim it. Anything else?"

She didn't want to risk an agreement that offered legal absolution for Gerrit and protection for them both from the man who had murdered her father and threatened her and her siblings. Yet returning to the country of her birth, being so close to the mountains she'd grown up in, had left a gaping wound in her heart. It wasn't as severe as the pain that came from losing so many family members, but it still hurt. She swallowed. She could ask. He might refuse, but he wouldn't go back on what he'd already offered. Too much was at stake: Falcon Point manor and all its wealth. "I don't have a wedding ring. I want one of my mother's rings. One small piece of my heritage. One tangible connection to my family. That's all I ask. Jewelry from my old family. Proof of innocence for my new family."

Rupert didn't answer right away. "Most of the jewelry is missing, but I'll see what I can find."

Missing jewelry? Probably sold by Sauermann already, or maybe hidden by Karl and Papa that day before they left Falcon Point.

"I don't suppose you know where the missing items are?" Rupert asked.

That was an easy question to answer. "No. I don't know where they are." Even if she did, she wasn't going to tell Rupert Altbauer or Wilhelm Sauermann. She suspected the key in the bottom of the jewelry box her father had given her was a clue, but that was a mystery she had just promised not to solve.

"Very well, Ingrid Lang Hendriks. We have a deal. I'm not sure how long it will take for me to arrange an affidavit."

"Make it happen tomorrow, Rupert. I'll need two copies." Her money was rapidly running out, and Linz was too close to Sauermann for her to feel safe.

"That's easier said than done."

"You have an entire estate to work with, and your uncle may be a Nazi, but the local authorities seem to have forgiven him. You'll manage."

The next day, Rupert met Ingrid in the same café. Goodness, she was beautiful. The day before, when she'd spoken of her hope that someday he would love someone enough to understand a sacrifice that big . . . If only she realized how much he did. He knew the pain of unrequited love. It had pushed him to vengeance in his work for the Reich, and it had compromised his loyalty. If she only loved him back, he would be willing to make a sacrifice that large for her.

He slid over an envelope with his affidavit. He'd been nervous to approach the American authorities now occupying most of Upper Austria, but better the Americans than the Soviets, whose occupation zone nearly bordered Falcon Point. His rank had been low enough that no Allied investigators had come knocking at his door, accusing him of war crimes. Onkel Wilhelm hadn't been so lucky, but he'd managed to talk his way out of any serious consequences, arguing that he did nothing more than direct soldiers who abided by the Geneva Conventions. Wilhelm Sauermann had been detained for a year at the war's end, but he'd been released and returned to Falcon Point earlier that summer.

Ingrid opened the document and read through it.

"It's adequate, I assume?" he asked

Ingrid compared the second copy to the first, then nodded. "Yes. Thank you. And the ring?"

Rupert had looked for jewelry, but it was all locked away, he suspected in his new aunt's dressing room. Gisela and Onkel Wilhelm had married the last year of the war. She was closer to Rupert's age than to her husband's, and the way she relished in the home and its lavish furnishings made Rupert suspect that she'd been more interested in marrying the master of the manor than in marrying the man himself. She would notice if anything went missing. Rupert might have been able to talk to his uncle about his need, but taking something from Falcon Point manor without Onkel Wilhelm's permission had seemed like theft, even if he planned to take the item to the person who most had a right to it. Rupert had sold Ingrid's pearl earrings when he needed money to get home at war's end, so that had left him one option. "I couldn't find any rings, so I brought these instead." He reached into his pocket and drew out a handkerchief. He unwrapped the cloth to reveal the same sapphire-and-diamond earrings she had once given to him as a bribe to prevent an execution. "Will these do?"

Ingrid blinked rapidly and nodded. "Yes. My mother wore them on her wedding day. I think they were her favorites."

Rupert had expected as much because he'd seen them in family photos and in the large portrait of Leopold and Liselotte Lang that had been taken down immediately upon Onkel Wilhelm's return. "I couldn't take anything else when my uncle is the estate's trustee, not me. But, Ingrid, don't you want your whole home back instead of just one pair of earrings? Marry me, and let my uncle take care of all the business transactions, and you can enjoy your mother's jewelry and your father's library and everything else your family had."

"I'm already married. To a man I love more than I love Falcon Point."

Rupert knew that. She'd rubbed it in his face more than once over their last few meetings. "Leave him. I've gathered from your letters that his health is frail, and with someone accusing him of collaboration, you'll soon be a widow."

Ingrid took the affidavits and the jewelry. "We'll stick to our original deal."

Rupert gritted his teeth and nodded. "I had to ask. One last time."

"You'll explain the agreement to your uncle? No more threats to my family, or he'll lose control of the estate."

Rupert nodded. "Yes, I'll explain."

"Thank you. For the agreement. And for the earrings. And for the times you bought me a train ticket and brought me food. I won't forget that." Ingrid gathered her things and left the café, and as he watched her go, he had a painful feeling that he would never see her again.

He returned to Falcon Point that night, riding with a salesman from Gildenstatt.

"Rupert, where have you been all day?" Gisela met him at the foot of the wide floating staircase.

"Seeing to business in Linz. Is Heidi already asleep?"

"Yes, and I plan to follow her example." She patted her abdomen, which, despite her condition, still appeared fashionably slim. "Preparing for motherhood is exhausting work. Your uncle was looking for you. He's in the study."

Rupert escorted his aunt up the first flight of stairs. The motions made the ache in his leg worse. Maybe he didn't want to live at Falcon Point after all. Too many stairs.

When he entered the study, he found Onkel Wilhelm sitting before the large desk that had once belonged to Leopold Lang. "Do you have a minute?" Rupert asked.

His uncle finished writing something and put his pen down. "Yes."

Rupert hadn't told his uncle about Ingrid's telegram or her visit to Austria, but now he related all that had happened. Not the part about the jewelry. Nor the part about how Rupert had asked her to stay. But he explained that the other Lang children were dead and that Ingrid had promised not to claim Falcon Point so long as she and her husband were never threatened.

"You did this all without consulting me?"

"That was one of her requirements."

"I see." Onkel Wilhelm settled back into his chair. "Thank you. That's a long-time worry off my mind."

For all the times Onkel Wilhelm had written about his concern for the wellbeing of the Lang children, he seemed relieved, rather than saddened, to hear of Anna's and Karl's deaths. He seemed indifferent to Ingrid, so long as she didn't press her claims to Falcon Point. It struck Rupert then that he'd been complicit in helping his uncle take control of an estate that didn't belong to him.

Ingrid had given up Falcon Point, but she had her husband and the means of combating any charges of collaboration. Onkel Wilhelm, Gisela, and their unborn child had a home they loved. And Rupert . . . Rupert had a damaged heart to go along with his damaged leg. But he also had his uncle's gratitude, and his uncle had promised him a home and a livelihood as part of the estate, and his sister a home and tuition for the best schools in Austria when she was older.

But a question that had long ago wormed its way into Rupert's mind wouldn't go away. Had Karl Lang been speaking the truth when he'd told his sister that Wilhelm Sauermann had murdered their father? Rupert had learned how to most effectively question people during the war, and an outright request for the truth would likely backfire. He tried a circuitous route instead. "Now that Ingrid has pledged her silence and we know Anna and Karl are dead, is there anyone else who might accuse you of killing Leopold Lang?"

"No. One of the maids entered the room soon after Karl, but she couldn't have seen anything incriminating. During the war, she took a job in Leipzig. That's in the Soviet zone. I don't expect her to be a problem."

The way Onkel Wilhelm had phrased it . . . The maid wouldn't be a problem for several reasons, but none of those reasons included Onkel Wilhelm's innocence. Ingrid was right. Rupert's uncle was guilty of murder.

Gerrit put away the tools Captain Bridger had purchased. Ingrid had remembered to pack them even in their hurry to flee Amsterdam. A wife thoughtful enough to remember his tools would surely come back to him, wouldn't she? Two weeks had passed. Gerrit had purchased newspapers daily, and he'd listened to the news on Tante Francisca's radio every time it had broadcast. No news of deaths involving members of the Political Investigation Service. No letters from Ingrid, in code or otherwise. His wife had disappeared, and fear that she might never reappear kept him up at night and haunted his every waking moment.

He went to the kitchen for a glass of water. The apartment over the repair shop, where Oom Antoon had found work for Gerrit, still felt like a miracle. Work and lodging. A place to live, a chance to earn enough for everything else. The Lord had given Gerrit an enormous blessing. But had it been given so that he might support himself? Or so that he might support a family?

A knock on the door sounded. Probably his cousin Noud. He must have run from the schoolyard, or left early, because school had been out only five minutes, unless that clock Gerrit had repaired was off again.

He opened the door expecting a six-year-old boy. He instead found his wife. Neither of them spoke for a moment, and then he lifted one arm, and she rushed into an embrace. They held each other for a long, long time.

"I was afraid I'd never see you again." He pulled her inside so they were no longer standing in the doorway.

"I told you I'd come back."

"But I didn't know if you would."

"You aren't angry, are you?" Her smile wavered for a moment.

"Furious." Gerrit grinned, and then he kissed her long and hard. "How did you find me?"

"Your tante Francisca told me where to go."

"Please tell me you'll never leave again."

"There won't ever be a need again," Ingrid said. "Berend is no longer a threat."

Her words brought relief but not enough to still the worry and confusion. "What happened?"

"I visited him at the Political Investigation Service headquarters and explained that you were innocent."

"I already told him that, and he wouldn't listen."

"I had irrefutable evidence." Ingrid pulled away and dug through her bag. She pulled an envelope out and handed it to him.

Gerrit took the paper and read through it. An affidavit signed by Leutnant Rupert Altbauer saying that Gerrit had not betrayed the resistance, despite physical and emotional torture. Gerrit's blood chilled. "How did you get this?"

"It was a long journey, and I couldn't have taken you with me. I made it to Austria only because I had a Reich passport. And I made it back to the Netherlands only because I had a Dutch passport. And there were so many checkpoints. I saw American troops and British troops and Soviet troops, and I spent far more of our savings than I would have liked."

"You tracked down Altbauer?" He'd expected her to track down Berend, and that had been risky. But before she'd found Berend, she'd done something far more dangerous.

She nodded. "He's the only one still alive besides you and me who knows what happened. I had to find him."

Gerrit looked from the paper to his wife, recalling Altbauer's taunts. What had Ingrid sacrificed this time to save him? "He hates me. Why would he write something that exonerates me?"

"I made a trade. Falcon Point for this."

Astonishment kept Gerrit from replying right away. "You traded away your home?"

"Mostly. I made a promise that I wouldn't claim it, nor tell my children about it. His uncle doesn't own it, but he's the trustee, so he has full use of the estate and all its assets unless Karl's wife makes a claim. But if he threatens us, I'll pursue my inheritance. So now he'll have to leave us alone."

Gerrit swallowed, reeling with shock. "But, Ingrid, I don't want to be the reason you lose your home."

Ingrid took his hand in hers. "Don't you understand? *You* are my home. You are my everything, Gerrit. Without you, there is no place in this world where I won't feel lost."

He wrapped his arms around her again, awed that somehow, she loved him as much as he loved her. "And Berend? He'll let it go, even after we struck him on the head?"

"When I mentioned that vigilante executions are even more illegal than hitting people over the head, he backed down. I hope we never see him again, but he knows you weren't a collaborator, so we don't have to worry about him anymore."

He held her against him, his head leaning against hers. "It feels like all our wars are finally over."

"Our money worries, too, as soon as we sell these." She took a handkerchief from her pocket and pulled out a pair of sapphire-and-diamond earrings.

Gerrit had seen them before, after digging them from beneath pieces of a burnt plank in Opa's home in Arnhem. "The ones you used to bribe Altbauer?"

She nodded.

"The ones that belonged to your mother?"

"Yes."

He cradled her hands. "I never want you to sell them." He took the earrings from her palm, one by one, and clipped them onto her ears.

Her smile contained relief. "I'm glad you feel that way because I want to keep them. Even if I don't have anything to wear them with."

"You'll find the perfect dress for them one of these days." He gently kissed the skin beside her right ear. "For now, you can just wear the earrings and take off anything that doesn't match."

She chuckled. "Given how formal these earrings are, that would include everything."

He ran his hands along her back. "Well . . . you have been gone for a very long time, and our new apartment is very private. The owner hid onderduikers here during the war."

Ingrid looked around, and Gerrit relaxed his hug so she could explore the small apartment. She opened the door into the kitchen, then went into the bedroom and the water closet. "It will be perfect for us. How did you find it?"

"Oom Antoon has a friend who has a friend with a repair shop that has more work than he can keep up with. He knows my stamina isn't what it should be, but he doesn't mind if I break the work up or catch up on the weekends. If I work half hours—and I'm confident I can do that—I've earned the room. I'll be paid hourly for anything more than that. We aren't going to be rich, but we won't have to worry about starving anymore."

"That sounds wonderful." Ingrid took his hand and pulled him toward the bedroom. "I should unpack."

The apartment had a built-in set of drawers, and when Ingrid opened the top one, she immediately reached for the small ring with a blue bow tied around it. She gently pulled it out. "What's this?"

Gerrit swallowed, worried that it wouldn't be good enough. "We never had the time or money for wedding rings. I wasn't sure if you'd really come back, but I kept hoping, praying. I looked through the parts downstairs in the shop, scavenged, and melted the bits of alloys down . . . It's not very flashy. I'm not very flashy. But it's solid, Ingrid, solid like my love for you."

She studied the ring and blinked away a few tears. "You made this?"

"I did."

She untied the ribbon, and he slipped the ring over the knuckle of her left ring finger. She held out her hand, and the smooth metal band shimmered in the light from the window. "It's a perfect fit. Just like you." She beamed, then caressed his face and met his lips for a kiss.

EPILOGUE

Arnhem, September 1961

Ingrid gripped Gerrit's hand as they stood in the Arnhem Oosterbeek War Cemetery for the September memorial service. With the gathered group, they sang "O God, Our Help in Ages Past." Ingrid; Gerrit; their six-year-old son, Joost; and the other Dutch attendees sang in Dutch. The veterans who had returned to Arnhem sang in English, and the mix of languages seemed to make the ceremony all the more poignant.

O God, our Help in ages past, our Hope for years to come.

The mix of plea and gratitude in those words hit Ingrid with both memory and expectation. She couldn't count all the times God had been her help up to that point in her life, but it had been often enough to give her confidence that He would be there every time she needed Him in the future.

After the hymn, the school children took small bouquets of flowers to each of the white marble headstones that stretched across the calm, green grass of the graveyard. Joost was old enough to participate this year. Like the other children with flowers, he had been born to peace, yet the children all seemed to instinctively know what a solemn occasion they were taking part in. Joost stood at one of the graves a long time, the wind ruffling his blond hair as he sounded out the name of the fallen British paratrooper.

When the ceremony ended, Ingrid and Gerrit joined Joost before the grave of Major Q. E. Cavendish, DSO, one of over fifteen hundred soldiers and airmen buried there. Visiting the cemetery always brought back the sorrow of the war, but Ingrid found peace in remembrance and gratitude. She found solace, too, in the beautiful grounds that had become a final resting place for so many who had sacrificed so much.

Ingrid, Gerrit, and Joost walked past the rows of headstones and along the path to where they had left their bicycles. All had been purchased secondhand, but Gerrit kept them in such good condition that anyone who didn't know better would assume they'd been purchased in one of the finest bicycle shops in Holland.

Joost glanced back at the cemetery. "Oom Cas said there were paratroopers in the basement of his home during the battle. Are any of them buried here?"

Gerrit stooped to be level with Joost. "Some, maybe, but all the wounded paratroopers in that basement made it out because your mam was incredibly brave, and while the house was burning around her, she set up a truce with the enemy and had the injured men evacuated to a hospital."

Joost's blue eyes, so like her own, turned up to study her. "You did that, Mam?"

"I wasn't the only one, but I helped. So did your pap. We all did the best we could." And they had: The members of the resistance and foreign intelligence officers who had gathered information before the battle, the airborne troops who had dropped from the sky to liberate a country not their own, people like Anita and Opa, who had tended the wounded and done all they could to heal and hide and rescue those who were left behind during the withdrawal.

"But Oom Cas's home doesn't look like it burned." Joost had been on visits to the van der Veen home in Arnhem twice. It had been restored long before his birth.

"He rebuilt," Gerrit said. "We all rebuilt. But don't ever forget that your mam is brave and beautiful and strong." Gerrit winked at Ingrid. "Stubborn, too, so don't ever try to sneak your muddy shoes into the house. She won't back down about that."

Ingrid laughed. She might be an indulgent mother, but she'd been Dutch longer than she'd been Austrian, and the Dutch didn't compromise on the tidiness of their homes. Not in peacetime anyway. "Come on, Joost. We have one more cemetery to visit."

"More airborne troops?"

Ingrid shook her head. "No. Heroes of a different kind."

They rode to the Moscowa Cemetery next. Ingrid had prepared two more flower bouquets. One for Anita. One for Opa. Joost spotted a mushroom, and Ingrid let him explore while she and Gerrit made the last of their memorial visits.

Ingrid placed a bouquet before Anita's headstone, then placed her hand on the grave marker. "You asked me to look after Gerrit, and I've done my best. Most of the time, it's been easy because your nephew has become the good man you always knew he could be."

Some aspects of Ingrid's life were still hard. She mourned the lost pieces of her family. And several times, she and Gerrit had noticed a stranger tailing them, watching their apartment, going through their mail. They were never sure if Sauermann or Berend was trying to keep tabs on them. Regardless, they'd stopped their search for Karl's wife, afraid that an intercepted letter might make her a target. And each time they felt they were being stalked, they moved to a new place.

But each time she moved, it was easy to make a new home because she was with Gerrit. It wasn't just the fact that he always fixed everything in any home they moved to, and it wasn't just that his health had gradually improved. Gerrit had a gentleness about him now, an empathy and a generosity with others, a loyalty and a love so deep, so complete for her and for their son. After waiting so long for him, each year with Joost felt like a miracle, something to celebrate to the fullest. Joost's heart was strong, and he brought a joy to their lives that seemed to grow with every season.

Gerrit stood behind Ingrid and wrapped his arms around her. "Thank you for looking after me so well, Ingrid. For giving me peace when I was almost destroyed by war."

She leaned into him. "You've looked after me as much as I've looked after you, and I love you for it."

Gerrit kissed the back of her head. She enjoyed the gesture but turned around so he could kiss her mouth instead. They had been through so much together—war, grief, and sorrow. But also the beauty of peace, the comfort of faith, and the joy of love. No matter how many times they moved, no matter how many times disappointment reared its head or pain clutched at her heart, Gerrit was with her. And Gerrit was still her home.

INGRID'S FAMILY TREE

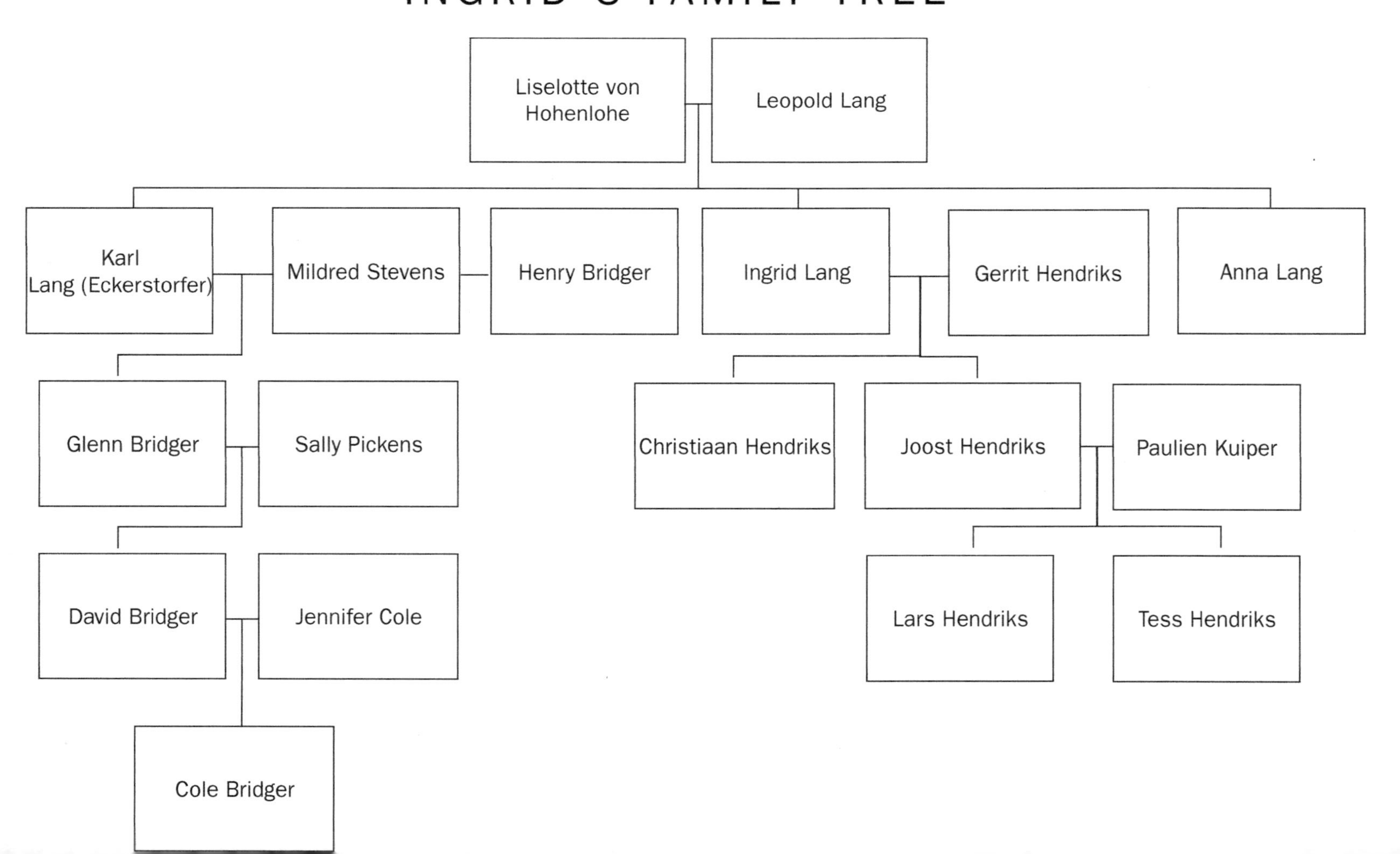

AUTHOR'S NOTES AND ACKNOWLEDGMENTS

Based on the events portrayed in *Heirs of Falcon Point*, I knew Ingrid's story would be set in the Netherlands, and when I began planning, I quickly settled on Arnhem. I briefly considered some of the other towns along the Market-Garden corridor, but paratroopers and a desperate battle were always something I wanted to be central to this story.

This book was a challenge to write. *Most* of that was my fault because I wanted to cover so many things: the varied nature of Dutch Resistance work during the war, the reasons Ingrid never returned to claim Falcon Point, and all the courage and heartbreak of Operation Market-Garden and its aftermath. However, if you are upset about Christiaan, that's Traci's fault, and if you're unhappy about Westerbork and its lingering health effects, that's Sian's fault. Having said that, I wish to thank Traci Hunter Abramson, Sian Ann Bessey, and Paige Edwards for taking me along for this multibook, multiauthor journey that began with *Heirs of Falcon Point*.

Accounts of wartime resistance to the Nazi occupation of the Netherlands vary widely, from people like Corrie ten Boom, who were motivated by a deep Christian faith to take risks and make sacrifices to protect onderduikers, to cells of committed Communists, whose fight against the Nazis included assassination of Dutch and German Nazis. In early September 1944, Prince Bernhard called for a unification of all Dutch Resistance groups, bringing together people who had a common opposition to Nazi rule but often with different ideas on how to best work against the invaders and varied goals for the postwar Netherlands.

Mention of the NSB, Reichskommissar Seyss-Inquart having a residence in Velp (though it was not his only commandeered Dutch property), and the common way Dutch schoolboys joked about his name and his limp are from the historical record. So is the situation around Dolle Dinsdag or Mad Tuesday in early September 1944, when a German retreat looked certain and Dutch celebrations began prematurely.

Opinions and analysis of Operation Market-Garden differ from historian to historian. Was it an intelligence failure because Dutch warnings of panzer divisions were ignored? Does the blame lie with General Gavin for failing to take the Nijmegen Bridge sooner? With General Urquhart for selecting drop zones too far from the Arnhem Bridge, then for venturing out on a fact-finding mission that led to him being trapped and cut off from his men for critical phases of the operation? Bad luck, when weather grounded planes and radios didn't work? Ultimately, I believe the fault lay in the plans conceived by Field Marshal Montgomery. They depended too much on every piece of the campaign going exactly right. Having said that, as I studied the 1940 German invasion of the Netherlands, I could see how four years later, Allied planners might have believed that Operation Market-Garden was possible.

Throughout the novel, I tried to remain true to historical accounts of the German invasion in 1940, their rules of occupation, the 1944 airborne operations, and their aftermath. Accounts of the Hunger Winter estimate that over 18,000 residents of the Netherlands starved to death. Tulip bulbs, Swedish food shipments, and Operations Manna and Chowhound kept that number from being higher.

After writing Millie's character in *Codes of Courage*, I decided to take a break from genius and semigenius characters because they are hard to write. So naturally, this book involved rocket science. But the V1 and V2 rockets gave Henry Bridger a perfect reason to be in the Netherlands. The original version of this manuscript had more of Henry and Anita, but length requirements meant that I had to cut something, even if I didn't want to. I did, however, save most of those cut scenes, and new and existing newsletter subscribers can read them. (To subscribe, visit https://alsowards.com/newsletter/)

I wish to thank the test readers who pulled off amazingly helpful reads on a very tight time frame: Kathi Oram Peterson, Mandy Biesinger, Ron Machado, Tina Peacock, and Bev Walkling. Also, thank you to the team at Covenant, especially to my editor, Samantha Millburn. Shout-outs also to Shara Meredith, Blair Leishman, Phil Reschke, Jason Tatom, Ashlyn LaOrange, Kami Hancock, Brookelyn Jones, and many others who do incredible work on my books.

If you enjoyed this book, I would be very grateful for your review on websites where books are sold or discussed or for your recommendation to other readers in person or via social media.

ABOUT THE AUTHOR

A. L. Sowards is the author of over a dozen historical fiction novels, with settings spanning the globe from the fourteenth to twentieth centuries. Her stories have earned multiple awards, including a Whitney Award, an LDSPMA Praiseworthy Award, and a Readers' Favorite gold medal. Sowards grew up in Washington state, spent a few decades in Utah, and now resides in Alaska with her husband, three children, and ever-growing library. She enjoys hiking and swimming, usually manages to keep up with the laundry, and loves it when someone else cooks dinner.

Sowards enjoys connecting with readers and can be found online at ALSowards.com or on Facebook, Goodreads, and Instagram. Readers can sign up for her newsletter at ALSowards.com/newsletter. Newsletter subscribers will have exclusive access to deleted scenes from *Roads of Resistance*.